THE
COMEBACK
GIRL

Also available by Katie Price

Fiction
Angel
Angel Uncovered
Paradise
Crystal
Sapphire

Non-Fiction
Being Jordan
Jordan: A Whole New World
Jordan: Pushed to the Limit
Standing Out
You Only Live Once

Praise for Katie Price's novels
'A page-turner . . . it is brilliant. Genuinely amusing and readable.
This summer, every beach in Spain will be polka-dotted with its neon
pink covers' *Evening Standard*

'The perfect post-modern fairy tale' *Glamour*

'*Angel* is the perfect sexy summer read' *New Woman*

'A perfect book for the beach' *Sun*

'Glam, glitz, gorgeous people . . . so Jordan!' *Woman*

'A real insight into the celebrity world' *OK!*

'Brilliantly bitchy' *New!*

'Celebrity fans, want the perfect night in? Flick back those hair
extensions, pull on the Juicy Couture trackie, then join Angel on her
rocky ride to WAG central' *Scottish Daily*

'Crystal is charming. Gloriously infectious' *Evening Standard*

'Passion-filled' *heat*

'Peppered with cutting asides and a directness you can only imagine
coming from Katie Price, it's a fun, blisteringly paced yet fluffy novel'
Cosmolitan

'An incredibly addictive read' *heat*

Katie Price x

THE
COMEBACK
GIRL

C

Century · London

Published by Century 2011

2 4 6 8 10 9 7 5 3 1

First published in Great Britain in 2011 by
Century

Random House, 20 Vauxhall Bridge Road,
London SW1V 2SA

www.rbooks.co.uk

Addresses for companies within The Random House Group Limited can be found at: www.randomhouse.co.uk

The Random House Group Limited Reg. No. 954009

A CIP catalogue record for this book
is available from the British Library

ISBN 978-1-846-05488-4

The Random House Group Limited supports the Forest Stewardship Council® (FSC®), the leading international forest certification organisation. All our titles that are printed on Greenpeace approved FSC® certified paper carry the FSC® logo. Our paper procurement policy can be found at: www.randomhouse.co.uk/environment

Then

Eden, Eden, Eden! We want Eden! The crowd were chanting out her name, so loudly that it almost felt to Eden as if the sound was a solid object she could reach out and touch. It was like a surging wave of wanting, of anticipation, and she was not going to disappoint them. She closed her eyes and shook back her long blonde hair, revelling in the chants and in the knowledge that every single person in the packed auditorium was there for her. She felt truly alive, more alive than at any other time. This was what she was born to do. This was what she couldn't live without. This love, this adulation, this validation. The assistant stage manager nodded at her. Eden stepped forward. It was time.

The stage was plunged into darkness and the crowd let out a roar of excitement as the beat of a drum took over from their chanting. And then, as the lights flashed on again in dazzling formations of pinks, oranges and mauves, mimicking a glorious sunrise, a giant gold scallop shell rose up from the depths of the stage. The shell slowly opened to reveal Eden. She was dressed in a gold sequined body stocking, cleverly designed so that it looked as if she was naked except for a smattering of shimmering sequins. And then her four male dancers, stripped to the waist and dressed in daringly tiny gold shorts, leapt on to the stage and lifted Eden out of the shell, holding her aloft like a queen as she surveyed the crowds in front of her. Let the show begin.

Two and a half hours and six costume changes later, Eden had finished her set. It had been one of the highlights of her career, a glittering performance which had entranced the audience. Her dancers and musicians were gathered in her dressing room to celebrate, drinking champagne and joyfully swapping stories about how the show had gone for them. It was the final night of Eden's European tour. Everyone was in a state of euphoria, on such a high, and no one more so than the beautiful blonde singer.

'Guys! Thank you so much,' Eden exclaimed, raising a bottle of champagne. 'That was the best ever!' She took a swig, not caring that it fizzed out of her mouth and cascaded down her dress. 'I love you all!' She danced round the room, hugging and kissing everyone.

'Eden, can I have a word?'

It was Ashley, her tour manager.

'Sure.'

'In private,' Ashley replied. Eden followed her out of the dressing room, certain that Ashley was simply going to complain about the dancers running up too big a bar bill. She kept a very tight rein on expenses and was the most ruthlessly efficient tour manager Eden had ever had.

'I've just had a phone call from your sister.'

Instantly Eden's stomach clenched in apprehension. 'Is it about Mum? Is she okay?'

Ashley seemed tense. She tentatively reached out one hand as if to comfort Eden, and then withdrew it; she wasn't known for her people skills. 'I'm afraid it's not good news. Savannah wants you to fly back to London straight away.' She hesitated. 'It seems like your mum doesn't have long.'

No, no, no! This couldn't be! When Eden's mum Terri was diagnosed with cancer six months earlier, she had insisted that Eden carry on as normal. She kept saying that she would get better and she didn't want Eden to put her career on hold. Eden had wanted to cancel the tour but her mum wouldn't hear of it. 'I'll be absolutely fine,' she had said, over and over, until Eden thought she would scream if she ever heard the word 'fine' again.

She leant back against the wall, fearing that her legs were about to give way.

'There's a car waiting outside to take you to the airport. I'll arrange to have your things sent on from the hotel.'

It was a nightmare flight back from Berlin. Eden sat rigidly in her seat, unable to do anything except pray to a God she wasn't even sure she believed in that she would reach her mum before it was too late. There were so many things she wanted to tell her.

Sadie Park, her manager, was there to meet her at Heathrow. The look on Sadie's face told Eden everything she needed to know. She was too late.

Sadie enfolded her in her arms. 'I'm so sorry, honey.'

Eden sobbed, great heart-wrenching sobs. 'I should have been with Mum! Why didn't anyone tell me sooner?'

'But we told Ashley before the concert. She was supposed to tell you . . . give you the chance to decide what to do.'

'She didn't tell me until afterwards! Oh my God, Sadie. If she had, could I have seen Mum?'

Sadie stroked her hair. 'I honestly don't know. But you were where Terri would have wanted you to be.'

She paused. 'And she was very out of it by the end – I don't think she was aware of who was there.'

'No! I should have been with her.'

It was so painful, walking into her mum's elegant house and knowing that, for the first time ever, Terri would not be there to greet her. Eden closed the front door, still half expecting her mum to appear, to hug her, ask how the tour had gone, and demand to know whether she was eating okay. Eden slipped off the high gold sandals that she was still wearing from the show. Terri had a strict shoes-off-in-the-house rule to protect her luxurious cream carpets.

Eden walked slowly up the stairs, hesitating at her mum's bedroom door before pushing it open. Someone had already cleared away all the bottles of medication that she remembered cluttering up her mum's pretty bedside table, along with the oxygen tank Terri had needed to help with her breathing. The bedroom was back to how it had been when she was well. Eden walked over to the dressing table and picked up the bottle of Chanel No. 5. She unscrewed the silver cap and breathed in the familiar, exquisite scent. Her eyes swam with tears. Her mum had worn Chanel No. 5 for as long as Eden could remember, and whenever she and her sister tried to get her to try something different, Terri would reply that if it was good enough for Marilyn Monroe then it was good enough for her.

Eden sat down on the bed and ran her hand over the thick rose-pink velvet cover. Terri always felt the cold and insisted on having the cover over the duvet, even though it drove Al, her fiancé, mad as he was permanently too hot.

'Oh, Mum,' she whispered, 'I'm so sorry I wasn't with you.' There was a vase of delicate blue and white freesias on the bedside table, her mum's favourite flowers. Eden leant over and inhaled their sweet fragrance. If only she hadn't given in to Terri over the tour, she could have been there for her mum. If only . . .

She looked up as the door swung open. It was her sister Savannah.

'So you've finally made an appearance, have you? Well, you're too late. Mum died at seven forty-five. How do I remember the time so exactly? Because I was there with her, holding her hand. Where were you?'

Savannah's usually perfectly groomed honey-blonde hair was untidy, her blue eyes bloodshot. Eden was shocked by the look of contempt on her sister's pretty face.

'I wasn't given your message until after the concert.'

'Oh, it's always someone else's fault, isn't it? Precious pop princess Eden couldn't possibly be to blame for not bothering to be at her mum's bedside when she died.'

Eden didn't think she had ever heard her elder sister sound so full of rage.

'Please, Sav, let's not argue. I'm sorry I wasn't here . . . sorrier than you'll ever know.' Eden felt a fresh rush of tears blurring her eyes as she got up and tried to hug her sister.

But Savannah pushed her away and said coldly, 'After the funeral, I *never* want to see you again. All Mum ever thought about was you and your career, and *you* couldn't even be here for her.'

'That's not true! She loved us equally.'

At that moment Al walked into the room. He was unusually pale and looked as if he had aged ten years since the last time Eden saw him. But he rallied to her defence.

'Eden's right. Terri loved both of you so much, you

were her life.' How like Al to be the peacekeeper, even in the midst of his own grief.

Savannah pointed at her sister. 'No, Eden was her life – and she sucked Mum dry. Even when Mum was so ill, she spent all her time worrying about *her*.'

Eden was about to protest once again that it wasn't true, but Savannah said bitterly, 'And now I'm going to arrange the funeral. And why? Because Mum asked *me* to. She knew Eden wouldn't be up to it!' And she stormed out of the room, slamming the door behind her.

Al and Eden looked at each other, then as Eden made to follow her sister, he said, 'Leave her for now. She's grieving, she didn't mean those things.'

But he was wrong. Savannah barely spoke to Eden in the week leading up to the funeral, nor on the day itself. By the time the mourners had left the wake, which was held at her mother's house, Eden was feeling desperate. She had tried so hard to hold it together but Savannah had blanked her for most of the day, looking at her coldly when she had broken down at the service as if to say, *Stop being such a drama queen.*

Al and Savannah's husband, Carl, were in the living room. Eden found Savannah in the kitchen, surrounded by stacks of washing up and plates of uneaten food.

'Leave that,' Eden said, as her sister threw a plate of mini quiches into the bin. They had wildly overestimated how much people would eat. 'We can do it in the morning. You must be knackered.'

She knew that her sister had barely sat down all day; had insisted on overseeing every last detail of the funeral. Savannah ignored her and continued to scrape food into the bin, the knife grating across the crockery in a way that set Eden's teeth on edge.

'Sav! You don't need to do all this now.'

'Terri liked her kitchen to be tidy.' Savannah paused for a second and finally looked at Eden. 'I'll go in the living room when you've gone.' There it was again, that look of contempt on her face.

Eden bit her lip. Why was Savannah being like this? 'I was going to stay the night, in my old bedroom.'

'Well, if you stay, I'm going.'

Eden couldn't bear it. 'Please, Savannah! I've said I'm sorry and I truly am! Stop blaming me!' Her voice was raised in distress, causing Al and Carl to come into the kitchen.

'What's going on?' Al asked.

'Nothing at all,' Savannah said in a falsely upbeat voice. 'Actually Eden was just about to leave. She has a busy schedule, as you know, and now that Mum's funeral is over, there really is no reason for her to stay.'

'Why won't you listen to me, Savannah? *Please*. I know you're upset. We're both upset.'

Savannah slammed the plate she was holding down on the table, shattering it. She looked aghast at the broken pieces. 'That was one of Mum's favourites.' She glared at Eden, her eyes blazing with fury. 'Why don't you get it? I hate you!'

Eden felt as if she had been struck.

'Come on, Sav, you didn't mean that,' Carl said reasonably. 'We're all upset about Terri.'

'I did mean it. She's selfish, self-obsessed, spoilt! She ruined Mum's life and I don't want her ruining mine.'

Savannah's cruel words were made all the worse by her calm, measured delivery. It didn't sound as if they were uttered in the heat of the moment and she would take them back once she'd calmed down. It sounded as if she meant them.

It was too much for Eden. She couldn't stay to hear any more. Ignoring Al, who called after her, pleading with her to stay, she grabbed her bag and fled.

Back at her own house she ignored all the phone and text messages from her friends and from Al. She took a bottle of wine from the fridge, poured herself a large glass, quickly drank it, poured another, drank that. But even as she drank to blot out the pain, she knew that she had lost her sister as well as her mother . . .

Now

Chapter One

Eden was not looking forward to the meeting with Sadie. She knew her manager was planning on delivering some home truths that Eden really didn't want to hear. So she did what she always did whenever she had anything unpleasant coming up: she pretended it wasn't happening. Which was why this Tuesday afternoon, when she should have been at Sadie's Wardour Street office hearing all the many reasons why her singing career had stalled and was going absolutely nowhere, she was instead sitting in the Fifth Floor Bar at Harvey Nichols in Knightsbridge.

She was halfway through a bottle of vintage champagne and deep into pretending that everything in her life was fabulous. She had spent the last two hours burning a hole in her credit card on clothes she didn't especially want and definitely didn't need; on an expensive exotic perfume, the overpowering scent of which was already giving her a headache; on presents for her boyfriend, Joel, to make up for the fact that they hadn't been getting on for the past month – she didn't know why; and on yet another peace offering for her sister Savannah, which would no doubt be returned to her along with all the other peace offerings Eden had sent.

God, this was all so depressing. She arched a perfectly shaped eyebrow at the bartender; he registered her expression and instantly walked over and topped up her champagne glass. If only all of her problems could be so easily dealt with. She looked down at the glossy designer bags strewn around her bar stool. Why had she blown all that money? She certainly didn't feel any better for it. There had been no surge of endorphins, no rush of pleasure at each purchase, only a kind of desperation instead, a vain hope that the next thing she bought might make her feel better, might fill the emptiness in her life. It did not. Especially as she had spent the day before having her ear chewed off by her accountant about her spending habits. He had issued her with the stark warning that unless she changed her ways, she was in serious danger of blowing the fortune she had made when she was a successful singer.

Fuck them all, she thought bitterly, draining her glass. No one told Eden Haywood what to do or how to live her life. The bartender once again walked over to her and Eden was about to tell him that she'd had enough when he said discreetly, 'Actually, Miss Haywood, there's a phone call for you. It's Sadie Park.'

Bollocks! How typical of Sadie to track her down. Eden had spent the day ignoring all her calls and texts. But her manager of over seven years knew her very well. She knew that when Eden was feeling blue she always went shopping and then hit the champagne. Eden hesitated, then reluctantly took the phone from the bartender.

'Get your arse in a taxi now, Eden. Jack Steele, the songwriter, has been waiting for you for the past two hours. This is his only window.'

Sadie didn't shout, rant or swear. Instead she stayed

icily calm, which made Eden realise that she really had pushed her manager too far this time. She had better turn on the charm.

'Oh my God, Sadie! I had no idea the meeting was today. I don't think Claude can have put it in my schedule. I'll be right with you, I promise.'

'It's been in your schedule for over a month. Please do not blame anyone else, especially not Claude who is the most efficient PA I have ever had,' came the terse reply.

And with that Sadie hung up.

'Shall I get you a car, Miss Haywood?' the bartender asked helpfully.

'Yes, and I'll have another glass of champagne before I go.'

Eden hated being told off. So what if she was a little late for some meeting with a songwriter she had never heard of? Things might be rocky at the moment but she was still the fucking star! Did Jack what's his name have two gold albums behind him, three MTV awards, two Brit awards, countless others . . . and even a waxwork in Madame fucking Tussauds?

However, in spite of her outrage at being summoned like a naughty schoolgirl, Eden made an effort to get her act together in the taxi ride from Knightsbridge to Soho. She checked her appearance: applied more black eyeliner to her already smoky eyes, put on a slick of raspberry-coloured lip gloss, and ran a brush through her long platinum blonde hair. She'd had the same signature look since she'd first found fame as a singer at the age of seventeen: a blonde bombshell/beach babe look. And her style of dress hadn't changed much in the last seven years – she'd always gone for a rock chick look, where she dared to bare.

Today was no exception and she was in one of her favourite outfits: Balmain skinny black leather trousers, wickedly high Jimmy Choo studded leather strappy sandals, a black Burberry quilted biker jacket and tight black vest embellished with a pair of black sequined lips on the front. It was an outfit that showed off Eden's enviable curves. Unfortunately, it also revealed that although she oozed sex appeal, she had recently put on weight and could do with losing a couple of pounds. Something else that Sadie was sure to comment on.

Eden had been devastated by her mother's death nearly two years ago and then by her sister's rejection. Since then her life had spiralled out of control. Grief-stricken, she had drunk too much, partied too hard and had a succession of disastrous relationships. The career that she and Terri had worked so hard to establish went into freefall as Eden outraged fans by cancelling a series of concerts at short notice, and being drunk when she was interviewed on a morning TV show as she'd arrived there straight from a night out clubbing. Two of the men she had gone out with had ended up selling stories about her out-of-control drinking which had further damaged her reputation as a pop princess. She had ended up in rehab.

For about six months afterwards she'd seemed to be back on track but then her record company started being extremely cagey about whether they would offer her another album deal. They were insisting on hearing the new material first before they would commit. It was a situation Eden could hardly bear to think about. Instead of coming up with ways to make the British public fall in love with her all over again, she reverted to her bad old ways of drinking too much and having yet another relationship which everyone else thought was doomed to fail.

She clicked her make-up mirror shut and popped a piece of gum in her mouth. The closer the taxi got to

Soho, the more nervous Eden felt. She would never admit it to anyone but actually she was shit scared of what Sadie was going to say to her, terrified that her manager might actually 'let her go', or in other words dump her. What the hell would she do then? Bad as things were, she simply could not imagine a life where she wasn't a singer.

'Hiya, Claude, love the suit. The PA wears Prada!' she exclaimed to Sadie's stunningly good-looking and well-groomed male assistant as she attempted to breeze into the office. Eden hoped that Claude might think it was her four-inch Jimmy Choos that caused her to stagger slightly and clutch his desk for support, and not that she was pissed. She dropped the designer bags on the floor.

'Good afternoon, Eden, they're expecting you. And FYI, the suit is Dior,' Claude replied. 'Shall I bring you in a black coffee?' He sounded perfectly polite and utterly professional as ever but had clearly seen straight through her. She was busted.

Claude knew she was drunk and that meant that Sadie would as well. Suddenly Eden regretted the champagne. It was such a stupid and reckless thing to do. But it had become such an ingrained pattern of behaviour that whenever she felt down, she would have a drink. And for a while she felt better . . . but only for a while, and then the paranoia and self-loathing kicked in.

Feeling incredibly nervous by now, Eden pushed open the door to Sadie's office. 'Boudoir' might have been a better description for it as it was a cosy intimate den. Red velvet curtains hung at the window, the walls were decorated with a rich maroon silk-effect paper, thick purple sheepskin rugs were scattered across the wooden floor, and flickering Diptyque candles filled the room with the musky scent of tuberose. Rather than sit behind her beautiful antique desk inlaid with mother-of-pearl, Sadie conducted most of her meetings lounging on an enormous zebra-print sofa. She was sitting cross-legged on it now, while a scruffy, bearded man sat before her desk. Both of them looked at Eden as she walked in, neither of them seeming especially impressed by her arrival.

Sadie had been a successful singer herself with a series of big hits in the eighties. Realising her singing career was coming to an end, she had cleverly re-invented herself as the manager of a very successful boy band, then she had taken on Eden and, later, Crystal. Now aged forty-nine, her image hadn't changed since her singing days. With her long honey-blonde hair, heavy black eye make-up, tight jeans, tee-shirts and leather jacket, she was verging on mutton, but it was impossible to imagine Sadie wearing anything else. She totally rocked that look. She could have been Eden's much older sister.

'Three hours late – a record even for you,' Sadie declared by way of greeting. Eden made to walk over and kiss her, but Sadie held up her hand. 'I might just want to slap you if you come any closer. Eden, this is Jack Steele.'

Jack stood up. At well over six foot, he towered over Eden, who even in heels was only just five foot six. She expected him to give her the typical media industry greeting of two kisses; instead Jack shook her hand. Nor did he give her any of the usual spiel about how *lovely* it was to meet her, and what a *huge* fan he was of hers, blah blah blah. He didn't even smile at her. Instead she was aware of a pair of intensely blue eyes coolly assessing her. They were set in a face which might possibly have been handsome had it not had a week's worth of stubble on it and been obscured by thick unruly dark brown hair which hid most of his features.

14

Eden liked her men ultra-groomed, had an eye for a pretty boy. Jack was far too manly for her. Too rough and ready. She didn't even bother to put on her best flirty, pouty smile for him. Instead, greetings over, she went and sat at the far end of the sofa.

Both Sadie and Jack continued to look at her without saying anything and Eden realised she was going to have to come out with one of her very rare apologies. She put on a fake smile and said, 'I am so sorry, guys. I genuinely didn't realise the meeting was today.'

It didn't go down well with Sadie.

'Spare us the bullshit, Eden! You knew exactly when the meeting was – you just didn't want to come! And so you went shopping and got drunk . . . same old, same old. Which would have been okay, except that Jack – who, by the way, is one of the hottest songwriters in the business right now – has come straight from Heathrow, as soon as he touched down from LA, to be here. So now that you have finally deigned to grace us with your presence, shall we get down to business?'

Eden opened her mouth, ready to protest her innocence yet again, caught sight of the fierce look in Sadie's usually warm brown eyes, and promptly closed it. And then her manager launched into a detailed and depressing analysis of exactly why Eden's singing career had stalled, concluding with, 'Your last album was too samey, too predictable . . . been there, heard that. There was no buzz about it. We need to generate that sense of excitement around you again. You need a more grown-up sound, to reflect the fact that you're a woman and no longer a teenager. I want depth. I want experience.'

Sadie spoke with passionate conviction, and part of Eden, the rational side of her, knew that her manager was only being so brutally honest because she cared about her and wanted her career to be a success again. After all, Sadie had been a close friend of Terri's. But the less rational side of Eden, the emotional side, felt stung by the criticism. And hurt. And defensive.

'And this is why I'm so thrilled that Jack has agreed to write some new material for you. He's just worked on Crystal's third album and it's fantastic . . .'

Eden's gaze strayed over to the huge new black-and-white photograph of Crystal that dominated one of the walls in Sadie's office. She couldn't help observing that the photograph of Eden herself, taken at the height of her fame, some three years ago, was considerably smaller. She was no longer Sadie's leading client. Crystal had certainly come a very long way since she had won *Band Ambition*, the TV reality show, with her group Lost Angels, and was now a hugely successful solo artist. She was married to the gorgeous and respected photographer Jake Fox, had an adorable three-year-old son, and by the look of her in the recent photo had never been more stunning. She was wearing a long white dress that clung to every curve, a dress that would have had Eden reaching for the Spanx and panicking about breathing in, but Crystal looked effortlessly looked slim and toned and ready for anything. Beautiful, graceful, she was every inch a star.

Eden couldn't stop herself from coming out with a bitchy remark. 'Yeah, but I think the public will always see her as just a reality-show singer, don't you?' She said 'reality-show singer' as if it was the lowest of the low.

It was an ill-advised comment. 'Just a reality-show singer who has sold over a million albums,' Sadie said quietly. 'Shall I remind you how many your last album sold, and why we're here? If we don't get this one right, you may very well not even have a record deal. And then you will be just another washed-up singer, whose moment has passed.'

There, Sadie had said it. Eden felt her guts churn with fear. 'Sorry, sorry, I didn't mean it,' she said lightly, trying to mask the terror that gripped her at the prospect of losing everything. Sadie shook her head. Eden was well and truly in the dog house.

Then Jack spoke. 'Shall I put on the tracks now? I think I might fall asleep if we don't do this soon. The jet lag is crippling me.' He yawned and stretched expansively.

'Darling, of course!' Sadie exclaimed. 'Go ahead. I can't wait for Eden to hear them.'

Eden frowned and folded her arms defensively. She never liked hearing new material when she was with other people; she needed to be on her own to con-centrate, almost to feel rather than to hear the music. As a result, when Jack pressed a key on his laptop and the music filled the room, Eden found herself completely unmoved by it. She was known for her pop anthems – uplifting, catchy numbers that worked their way right inside your head. She had sung some ballads in her time but pop had always been her first love. Jack's music was slower, the lyrics more complex, and she wasn't sure it was for her. It didn't help that he had recorded it with a male vocalist.

After three tracks he pressed pause. 'That's a flavour of it. I've still got two more tracks to write.'

Sadie turned to Eden. 'Well, I absolutely love it, and I think it is perfect for the new sound we want for you. What do you think?'

Eden felt completely underwhelmed. 'Um, it's hard for me to say right now. I need to listen to it some more. But I'm not so sure it's me . . .'

Sadie shot her a WTF look. 'I know what I'm doing, Eden. It is completely you. And this is what is going to happen – Jack is going to give you a CD and you are going to go away and listen to it, then we're going to meet up in the studio at the end of next week and record one of the tracks. The sooner we get moving on this the better.'

'Okay then, Sadie, you know best,' Eden said, unable to hide her reluctance. As far as she was concerned the meeting was over. She wanted to get the hell out of there, go back to her house and see Joel in the hope that he might somehow make her feel better. It was doing her head in, spending time with Sadie when she was being so bossy, never mind the skanky songwriter who wanted her to sing his miserable, depressing songs. Time to change the record and feel like she called the shots.

Eden got up from the sofa. The champagne had given her a pounding headache and her mouth felt horribly dry. If she didn't have something else to drink she would end up with a shocking hangover, and there was nothing more depressing than a hangover that kicked in late-afternoon.

'Nice to meet you, Jack,' she said half-heartedly.

'You too, Eden. See you in the studio. Call me, text me, email me if you want to go through anything. I'm completely at your disposal.' Jack leant across the table and handed her his business card.

'Cheers.' Eden stuffed the card into her jacket pocket. Like she would need to speak to him! Unless it was to advise him which hairdresser to go to.

'In fact, we'll all meet up at the party next week,' Sadie put in, finally getting up from the sofa and giving Eden a quick hug. 'And before you ask, it is in your schedule. And, yes, you are fucking going, whether you like it or not! Wear something fabulous, you need to do some serious schmoozing.' She lowered her voice. 'And get to the gym, Eden, you could do with toning up.'

Eden rolled her eyes. Sadie was always so straight talking and Eden couldn't deal with it at the moment. Could she do nothing right?

But Jack had overheard. 'Oh, I don't know, Sadie. I think Eden looks pretty damn fine in those leather trousers.'

Eden glanced over at him and he flashed her a wicked smile as he looked her up and down. He resembled the Big Bad Wolf and – ew! – Eden really didn't like the compliment coming from this furball. Who did he think he was to make a comment about *her* appearance?

She was still fuming about the meeting when she arrived back home in Notting Hill. Eden loved her three-storey Georgian town house, which was painted pale pink and situated on one of the most expensive roads in the area, or indeed London. Her accountant had warned her that she might need to think about selling up for something considerably smaller if record sales didn't pick up and she didn't cut back on her spending, but Eden chose to ignore the warning. She had bought this house with the proceeds of her first record deal and it was precious to her as a result. This was part of her history, it was her sanctuary; there was no way she was ever going to sell.

She closed the front door and instantly breathed a sigh of relief. The cleaners had obviously been in and the jumble of clothes, magazines, wine glasses and coffee cups Eden had left strewn across the hall and up the stairs had all been cleared away. Everything was in its place, everything looked clean and fresh.

She put her door keys down on the hall table, which was dominated by a beautiful arrangement of white flowers. Eden had to have fresh flowers in every room. She had overruled the accountant on that as well. So what if she spent several hundred pounds a week on them? They were essential for her well-being, soothed her soul and helped her to relax. How could you put a price restriction on that? Compared to him she was frugal! She dropped her shopping bags on the black-and-white marble tiled floor. Now she just had to find Joel.

'Babe, I'm back,' she called out. No reply. Where the hell was he? She ran upstairs, hoping to find him in the bedroom. He wasn't there or in any of the other upstairs rooms. She ran back downstairs. He was not in the kitchen, dining room or living room. She checked her phone. No messages. Finally she thought to look in the basement, where she'd recently had a sauna, swimming pool and steam room installed – against her accountant's advice, of course. And there, in the shimmering black marble-tiled pool with her initials picked out in mother-of-pearl on the bottom, she found Joel, performing a flashy front crawl. She took a few seconds to register his gorgeous physique: his broad shoulders, lean legs, tight bum, and smooth brown skin. Then he noticed her and swam over to the side.

He wiped the water from his face as he said, 'You've been ages. How did the meeting go? Are you going to get your record deal?'

Eden shrugged. 'I don't want to talk about it. How about we have a glass of champagne, a swim and a steam?' And then, she thought to herself, you fuck my brains out and I might be able to forget all the shit in my life right now.

'You never want to talk about anything serious with me,' Joel said, a petulant edge to his voice. 'I'm perfectly capable of understanding what goes on in the music business. Just because I'm a model, it doesn't mean I don't have a brain. Sometimes it would be nice if you'd acknowledge that.'

Joel's brain had never been the part of his anatomy that most attracted Eden. However, it seemed that to get what she wanted out of him, she had better play nice.

'Please, babe, there really is nothing to say about this afternoon. Sadie was a bitch and there was some soap-dodging songwriter hanging around. I just want to forget about it and have a good time with you.' She kicked off her heels.

The comparison between her sexy Joel and scruffy Jack was making her feel especially affectionate towards her boyfriend.

'Okay, I guess it could be an early celebration.'

Eden was so preoccupied that she didn't register the comment. She was already opening the mini-fridge and reaching for a bottle of champagne. Once she had drained a glass, she stripped naked and dived into the pool. She swam up to Joel and twined her body round his. She was already feeling turned on by the thought of having sex with him, but it didn't escape her that he didn't seem to share her enthusiasm. This had happened several times in the last few weeks. Joel only seemed to come alive in certain departments when Eden told him how fit he was. So she kissed him deeply and murmured, 'You looked so good when I saw you swimming. I want you so much, baby. You're so hot and sexy.'

'Tell me what you're going to do,' he murmured back.

Eden shook back her hair and put on the husky, sexy voice that she usually reserved for the bedroom. 'I'm going to kneel in front of you and suck your beautiful hard cock.' That seemed to be doing the trick. She could feel it stirring against her. This was more like it.

'Let's go upstairs. I want to look at you in the mirror while I fuck you.'

21

Or rather, Eden thought some time later, Joel had wanted to look at himself. Now he lay sprawled out on the bed. She snuggled up to him and waited for him to say something, anything, to make her feel good about herself. To her the sex had seemed mechanical rather than passionate. It had not made her feel any better, only more aware of the gulf that was opening between them.

Joel yawned widely and scratched his chest. 'God, I'm knackered!' he exclaimed.

'You are so gorgeous,' she murmured, kissing his neck. Again she waited in vain for him to say something tender in reply. She realised that it had been a long while since Joel had said anything complimentary to her at all. He just gave a small smile as if she had been acknowledging the obvious.

'I've bought you something wicked. I can't wait to see you in it.' She lay back on the bed and stretched her arms over her head. 'Why don't you go downstairs and get it?' Maybe once he had seen his gift he would tell her he loved her. She tried not to wonder if that meant she was buying his love.

Joel usually did pretty much whatever she wanted, so it was a surprise when he curled his lip and said, 'Christ! It's a bit much, even by your standards, that I have to go and get my own birthday present.'

'But it's not a birthday present, Joel, it's just a little gift.' Eden was still expecting him to get up and trot obediently downstairs, collect the shopping bags and then be sweetly grateful when he opened up the box meant for him and found the wildly expensive Theo Fennell diamond skull pendant inside.

He sat up in bed. 'You've forgotten, haven't you? I don't believe it! My birthday is on Friday!'

Fuck! She had completely forgotten. Eden tried to think on her feet, not easy after the half-bottle of champagne she had just consumed on top of the earlier one. 'I haven't forgotten, sweetie, this is just an early present.' She could give Pinocchio a run for his money.

'Really?' Joel turned to face her. Now she had his attention.

'Really. And, babe, I'll go and get your present myself.' Eden managed to pull herself out of bed, and slipped on a flowing black silk kimono. Her headache had returned with a vengeance. At the top of the stairs she caught sight of her reflection in the ornate Venetian glass mirror. Her eyes were bloodshot, her face looked puffy, her hair was all over the place. She looked rough. She *felt* rough. No wonder Joel hadn't been forthcoming with any compliments. It's okay, she told herself, I'll cut back on the drinking again. It'll be fine. It was only when she reached the hall and picked up the Theo Fennell bag that she realised Joel's birthday was bound to involve a heavy session. I'll get back on track at the weekend, I'm sure I can do it, she told herself.

Eden did not allow herself to reflect that it was always the day after or the weekend after with her, and somehow those days never seemed to come around.

Chapter Two

For the rest of the week Eden felt unsettled by her meeting with Sadie and Jack. She knew her career was on the line now, but found it almost impossible to sit down and listen to the music and give it her full attention. Partly it was the fear of failing that made her put it off, but she was also preoccupied with her relationship with Joel, which seemed to be going badly. She had been burying her head in the sand, pretending that everything was fine, but now she had to face the truth. He didn't seem interested in her in the way he had once been; it was almost as if he could take her or leave her.

She'd suggested they should go away to a luxury country hotel for his birthday, or she could whisk him off to Paris. Surely that romantic city would reignite the sparkle in their relationship? But Joel said he had arranged to go out with his friends. Nor did he suggest that they went away together another time instead. He claimed that he had modelling bookings every day that week, and in the evenings he was seeing his personal trainer as it was the only chance he had. And when Eden protested that surely he could have one night off from the gym, he insisted he had to keep in shape for work. It seemed to Eden that he was taking her for granted. They had barely been together for six months and already Joel was treating her as if they were six years into their relationship. The thought depressed her.

'But I've hardly seen you,' she told him on Thursday morning, after she had yet again asked him if he would go out with her that night, only to have him insist that he had to go to the gym.

'So why don't you come with me and have a session with my trainer? You said you wanted to get fit again but you've done fuck all about it.' Could he sound any more judgemental?

'Big wow, the gym?' Eden said sulkily. 'I think I'll see Tanya instead.'

And so while Joel hit the gym, Eden sat having cocktails with Tanya, her best friend, at the swanky Light Bar at St Martin's Lane Hotel. Eden was on the signature Raspassion Martinis. She'd had a couple of alcohol-free days and figured that she deserved a few drinks after Joel's recent off-hand treatment of her.

She had known her friend for over five years. They had met when Tanya was a dancer on one of Eden's music videos, and they had hit it off when both of them suffered wardrobe malfunctions in the outrageously tight PVC catsuits that the director had decreed they should wear. Tanya's had split at the crotch early on in the dance routine as she performed some smouldering hip-wiggling moves, and Eden's had split under one arm when she had waved it above her head a little too enthusiastically. It had taken all the stylist's ingenuity and black masking tape to repair both, given that they had to finish shooting that day. Eden and Tanya had found the whole situation hilarious, and whereas many people were wary of Eden because she was such a big star, Tanya had seen through the image and realised that Eden was just another girl.

Tanya had started out as a runway model when she was fifteen, before she had developed some serious curves. She had tried the extreme dieting route but it left her feeling miserable and ill. And then she became a plus-size model, which in reality meant she was an extremely toned size 14. She was absolutely knockout gorgeous with lustrous brown hair, huge hazel eyes, a very pretty face, and a figure that could only be described as hour-glass. It made any woman she was standing next to suddenly realise that there was more to life than dieting, and any man want to declare undying love to her. Tanya was warm, funny and very straight talking. In fact, she was the only person close to Eden, apart from Sadie, who dared to speak her mind to her. Eden had just spent the first ten minutes of their evening filling Tanya in on what had been going on in her life, especially with Joel. And as she talked about him she suddenly realised just how bad things sounded. She seemed to be describing a relationship on its last legs.

After hearing Eden's catalogue of woes, Tanya sighed, 'I have to tell you, babe, it doesn't look good. I thought you said it was fun being with him? It doesn't sound like fun from where I'm sitting. Has he been doing his big leaving number again?'

Several times in the last two months, after they had rowed, Joel had packed his bags, gone round to a mate's, drunk too much, calmed down, sobered up and then come back.

'He stormed out the other week,' Eden admitted. 'Maybe we've just hit a rough patch.' Though surely they should still be at the honeymoon, can't-keep-their-hands-off-each-other stage?

'Or maybe it's his true character coming out – that he is sulky and self-obsessed, cares more about himself than you? You don't need someone like that in your life, Eden, it's not good for you.'

But Eden hated being on her own, especially since her mum had died. And she had made a habit of going from one relationship to the next, with barely a break between. It was invariably her who did the dumping – but only when she had the next man lined up. And always she was hoping that the next one would be 'the one', and that he would make her feel good about herself, make her feel happy, complete. Would take away the darkness that threatened to take over at times . . .

She didn't tell Tanya any of this, close as she was to her, but instead tried to play it cool and keep it light. 'But he's great in bed, Tanya!' she joked, which wasn't strictly true, he was only okay in bed. But she couldn't imagine not having someone next to her, feared being alone. Cue eye roll from Tanya.

'Buy yourself a Rampant Rabbit. It won't break your heart or answer back, but it will go the distance and it will never be too pissed to perform, or need anything more in return than new batteries.'

Eden rolled her eyes back. 'I've got one. You bought it for me, remember? It's not the same.'

'No! It's way better! Tyler has hidden mine because he claims I was getting too obsessed with using it. I think it made him feel a bit inadequate!' Tanya laughed and then looked serious as she said, 'Face it, Eden, Joel is too high-maintenance. He's practically a girl. Last time we all went out together, I swear he spent most of the time looking at himself in the mirror.'

'He's a model, what do you expect?'

'Someone better for you, that's for sure.'

'No, everything will be fine, it's just a phase.' Eden couldn't allow herself to admit that Tanya was right. It would mean that she would have to do something about the situation, and she didn't know if she was strong enough. She had to keep up the pretence that everything would be okay. 'Maybe he's just touchy about getting older.'

27

This earned another eye roll from Tanya. 'He's going to be twenty-three!'

'Yeah, but it's tough being a model, isn't it?'

'It's tougher being a model's girlfriend,' Tanya muttered. 'You've got to ask yourself if he's really worth it.'

That did it for Eden; she had to change the subject after that.

But her concerns about Joel didn't go away. And even on his birthday Eden could not ignore the cracks that were developing in their relationship. He barely thanked her for his J12 Chanel watch that had set her back some four grand. When she took him to Zuma for lunch, which served divine Japanese cuisine and was usually Joel's favourite place, he spent most of the time checking messages on his iPhone. And when she asked him what was so important, he snapped back that he was expecting an email from his agent, and didn't she realise he had a career too?

Depressed by what was happening to them, Eden ended up drinking too much and eating too little. When she suggested they should go back to the house and spend the rest of the afternoon in bed, Joel replied that he had arranged to meet up with his mum to go shopping for his birthday present. FFS, he had chosen spending time with his mum over a hot shag!

And so by the time they went out clubbing with Joel and his friends, Eden was in a foul mood. She was bored and drunk as she sat in the VIP room – a lethal combination. What the hell was she doing here, surrounded by people she barely knew, with a boyfriend who hardly acknowledged her presence? All Joel's friends were models or worked in the fashion industry, and all of them were up themselves, in her opinion. And there was one particular friend, a stunning model called Bliss, who had seriously pissed Eden off by flirting with Joel. Well, that's what Eden had decided after the many, *many* cocktails she had consumed. She sat back on the sofa, drumming her fingernails against the leather arm rest, and glared moodily around. She'd decided that when Joel came back from one of the dance floors she would tell him they had to go. She deserved a bloody medal for putting up with all his friends for so long as it was.

'So, Joel told me that you're working on a new album with Jack Steele.' Bliss appeared and sat down uninvited next to Eden. She was extremely slim, with slender tanned legs that seemed to go on forever and long glossy black hair.

'Yeah, that's right. I'll have to see how it goes, I'm not sure Jack's material is going to be right for me. I was thinking of writing some songs of my own.' The latter part was a complete lie. Eden was a hugely talented singer but had zero talent for songwriting; but being next to someone as beautiful as Bliss was making her feel that she needed to big herself up.

'Wow, that's awesome. It must be wonderful working with such talented people as Jack Steele. Joel Googled him and said he's worked with *everyone*. And I've seen his picture and he's so good-looking, he could easily have been a star himself,' Bliss said enthusiastically. She sniffed several times and rubbed her nose. Eden recognised the tell-tale signs of someone who'd just taken coke. Thank God that was one route she had never gone down herself.

Eden gave a snort of laughter. 'Excuse me! If you like hairy scruff bags, then yeah. But, *perlease*, Jack Steele does nothing for me.'

'But Joel was saying that you needed to work with Jack to get your next record deal, because things haven't been going so well for you creatively.' Bliss must have been aware of how hurtful her words were, but she gave Eden a butter-wouldn't-melt-in-her-mouth smile and then sniffed again.

Eden really should have been able to rise above the barbed comment; it was hardly the first time that some-one had made a bitchy remark to her. But she felt hurt and insecure that Joel had been talking about her to this beautiful model with the stupid name but the body to die for. And, more to the point, *when* exactly had Joel been talking to beautiful Bliss? Jealousy, insecurity and paranoia got to work inside Eden.

'So when did Joel tell you all this?' She tried to sound casual.

'Oh, I don't remember. We were together all this week on an underwear shoot. Didn't he tell you?' Bliss giggled coyly.

She was such a bitch! And Joel hadn't said a word. 'Of course he told me. We don't have any secrets from each other.' Liar.

'So he told you how embarrassing it was when he got a hard on when we were being photographed together – well, embarrassing for him! Flattering for me, I guess. We blamed it on my black lace thong. It was very revealing! It took a while for the photographer to be able to get the shots.' Another giggle, and Bliss swished back her glossy hair.

If it had been nothing more than an embarrassing moment, surely Joel would have told Eden? The fact that he hadn't meant only one thing. He had a guilty conscience.

'Sounds hilarious,' Eden managed to say through gritted teeth. Now she *really* wanted to go home.

'It was! Anyway, good luck working with Jack Steele. He's got the Midas touch when it comes to songs, so hopefully he'll be able to write some hits for you.' Bliss paused momentarily before delivering the drop kick.

'When exactly was your last hit? Was it 2006 or 2005?'

Eden had underestimated her! She was a fucking super-bitch! She could give other bitches bitching lessons! It was time to retaliate.

'And you're an expert on the music industry, are you? Aren't you too busy trying not to eat and stuffing coke up your nose at every opportunity? I wouldn't have thought that left you much time for anything else . . . except for coming up with a pretentious name like Bliss.'

Eden should have been able to ignore the other girl but she couldn't. Maybe it was because Bliss was younger and thinner than she was, who knows? But Eden had the devil inside her now.

Once again she had underestimated her opponent. Bliss simply smiled and looked pointedly at Eden's cleavage that was threatening to burst out of her black sequined designer dress, and at her stomach which was being held in by a pair of control briefs that were killing her and which she was sure left a tell-tale roll of flab at her waist. 'Perhaps you should take a leaf out of my book sometime, Eden. And I could give you the name of my personal trainer. You'll need to work at it if you ever want to squeeze into one of your famous leather catsuits again. Joel said you were worried that you had put on weight. It was brave of you to wear that dress. I didn't know Hervé Leger made dresses in a size 14. Did you get it off your plus-size, aka lardy, friend Tanya?'

Maybe Eden might have been able to restrain herself if the comments had been directed solely against her, but Bliss slagging off her best friend was a dig too far. Eden saw red.

'Fuck you! You're nobody.'

And she stood up and threw her Mojito straight into Bliss's beautiful, smug face.

'Fat bitch!' she spluttered back and, launching herself at Eden, yanked at her hair and lashed out at her.

What followed next was a very undignified scrap in which Eden tried frantically to push Bliss off her, and had her face slapped and dress ripped in the process. For someone so skinny and calorie-deprived, the model sure packed a punch. And while Eden struggled to get away from Bliss's slaps and vicious nails a group formed around the warring girls. Instead of trying to pull them apart, Eden could hear cheers and exclamations of delight. 'Bitch-slapping fest!' 'Girl on girl action!' This was so not what she needed! And where the hell was Joel? Why wasn't he here to help her out? It took a good five minutes before the bouncers intervened and brought the spectacle to an end.

'She assaulted me!' Bliss shrieked, as she was pulled away from Eden. 'Call the police! I'm going to press charges against the bitch!'

'Give it a rest!' Eden panted. 'You attacked me, you fucking psycho twiglet! I'm sure the police would love to interview you about your little sniff-sniff habit.'

Bliss made no further attempt to lunge at Eden, but the bouncers still held her back. And then Greg, the suave club manager, appeared on the scene. Eden had known him for years and had always got on well with him.

'Why don't you come up to my office, Eden?' he said smoothly. 'I'm sure we can sort this out. And Joel, you had better come along too.'

Finally Joel had pitched up. He looked shocked by the state of Eden and Bliss. 'What the hell happened to you?' he asked.

'Isn't it obvious! Your fucking nutcase friend.' Eden pointed at Bliss, provoking her to screech out again, 'Call the police!'

But Greg was already swiftly leading Eden and Joel

away to the privacy of his upstairs office. Once there he poured out two generous measures of brandy and handed the glasses to Eden and Joel. He was clearly practised in the art of crisis management.

'I don't like brandy,' Joel commented, but Eden gratefully took a large gulp of hers. She was shocked by Bliss's attack. She winced as she gingerly felt her forehead where she was sure a large bruise was forming.

'God, Joel, why the hell are you friends with her? She completely overreacted to me accidentally spilling my drink over her.' Yes, this was her story, she would try and stick to it and just pray that no one else had seen what had actually happened.

'That doesn't sound like Bliss,' he replied. 'I've known her for years and she's never done anything like that before.' He didn't seem at all concerned that Eden had been hurt. She took a look at herself in the mirror and almost gasped in horror. Her hair looked as if she'd been dragged through a hedge backwards, her eye make-up was smudged, her lip was bleeding, a bruise was indeed blooming across her forehead, one of the straps to her dress had been ripped causing a major wardrobe malfunction. Eden's right boob, in all its La Perla black lace glory, was on display.

'Well, you're never going to see her again, are you?' Eden said, not at all appreciating Joel's lack of sympathy. She was bleeding and bruised for God's sake!

'What do you mean?' he demanded. 'I've just told you, she's one of my oldest friends.'

Eden was about to come out with all the many, many reasons why it was obvious that Joel couldn't possibly see Bliss again when Greg intervened.

'I'm going to arrange a car to take you both home. You can go out the back way, to avoid the paps. And I'll call Sadie. I'm sure she will want to put out a press statement about this, even if it's to say "No comment".'

Oh, that was just perfect! Sadie would be absolutely furious with Eden. Hadn't she told her to keep a low profile, to cut back on the partying and the drinking?

'Thanks,' Eden mumbled, 'I appreciate it, Greg.'

'You're one of our most important guests,' he replied, helping her into her jacket. 'Don't worry, this will all blow over.' Translation: I need you both out of here as soon as possible.

Joel didn't say a word to Eden on the journey home. She had dropped the tough-girl act; now all she longed for was for him to put his arms around her, tell her that he loved her, that everything was going to be all right. But Joel sat at one end of the back seat, arms folded, staring moodily out of the window, and Eden sat at the other. The distance between them seemed unbridgeable. Back home he kept up the silent treatment. Eden, who was always very good at doling out the moody behaviour herself, just hated it when it was directed back at her. When they got into bed together and he was still not talking to her but turned away instead of cuddling up to her as he usually did, she couldn't take it any more.

'Babe, I'm sorry if this ruined your birthday. It really wasn't my fault, but I'll make it up to you, I swear.'

'I want to know what happened to make Bliss react like that,' Joel muttered, still presenting her with a view of his tanned back.

Eden reached out and tentatively touched his shoulder. She was desperate for them to make up, but Joel gave no acknowledgement of this, only muttering, 'And I mean what *really* happened, not just the version according to Eden fucking Haywood.'

'She was vile to me, if you must know, said I was fat and needed a personal trainer. She made out that you had been talking to her about me, and then hinted that there was something going on between you. So, yes, I admit I lost it. And,' here Eden hesitated, 'I may have spilt my drink on her.'

Joel sat bolt upright. 'You threw your drink over her, didn't you? For fuck's sake, Eden, you can't expect to go around behaving like that and get away with it! Of course Bliss was going to be pissed off.'

'She said I was fat!' Eden repeated. 'And that you had both been spending a lot of time together.' She was shouting now. 'She was implying that there was something going on between you. So is there?'

'There's nothing going on between Bliss and me, we're just friends. And you've said yourself that you need to lose weight. It would help if you cut down on the booze.'

Wham! Joel's words were like a sucker punch. 'I forbid you from ever seeing Bliss again, or phoning her, or texting her. You can't have her as a friend and be my boyfriend,' Eden said coldly. She knew she was pushing Joel into a corner but she couldn't help it. She had to know that she was still his number one priority, that he would do anything for her. He always used to say he would.

Joel angrily threw off the covers and stood up. 'No, Eden, you don't get to tell me what to do any more. I've had it. It's a nightmare being with you. You always want everything your way . . . you're so selfish and fucked up.' He stood there glaring at her, male model beautiful in his black Armani boxers, and she knew it was make or break time.

She pulled the duvet around her like a protective shield. Part of her wanted to beg him to stay, to tell him that she would change, but she just couldn't show that level of vulnerability and need. 'Well, fuck off then, Joel. And I mean *now*. Pack your bags and piss off. I never want to see you again.' Even as the words were out of her mouth she regretted them, longed to take them back.

Joel shrugged. 'Sounds good to me. And here . . . give this to the next model.' He took off the Chanel watch and flung it on the bed. Then, without giving Eden another look, he marched into the dressing room and she heard him grabbing his clothes from the wardrobe. She allowed herself a bitter smile. *She* had bought most of those clothes.

Then she got out of bed, wrapped herself up in her kimono and went downstairs to the kitchen where she poured a large glass of white wine. She settled in the living room, curling up on one of her expensive designer sofas to wait. Although she had been the one to tell Joel to leave, she felt consumed by anxiety and insecurity. The prospect of him actually going terrified her. She tried to tell herself that this was just a blip that would soon be put right. Joel would pack up his clothes, storm off, and then come running back. He wouldn't take her seriously. He would surely know that her telling him to go was just something she had come out with in the heat of the moment.

However, some ten minutes later she heard Joel running downstairs. She waited for him to come into the living room; instead she heard the sound of the front door opening then slamming shut. But that was okay, Eden told herself. Joel would go round to one of his mates, bitch about her, crash out, and by lunchtime he'd be texting her to say that he was sorry. They had both had too much to drink. Once they'd calmed down and slept it off they would be fine. But still the anxiety wouldn't go away. And the sense that she was to blame, that she was a bad person.

It was four a.m. by now. She remembered reading somewhere that this was the time of day people were most likely to commit suicide. Maybe it was because it felt like the loneliest time, everyone else asleep, morning still hours away, everything hopeless. She got up and pulled open the thick silk curtains, wanting to feel connected to the world, but it was barely light. The street was deserted. Eden was all alone. She suddenly longed to speak to someone who was close to her. Savannah was the first person she thought of, but she knew that her sister would not talk to her, regardless of the hour.

She found herself saying out loud, 'Sav, I miss you so much.' Her words seemed to echo round the room. She shivered in the cool air and went back upstairs and got into bed. The pillow still carried the scent of Joel's Hugo Boss aftershave, another present from her, and she found herself pressing her face against it, and whispering, 'Please don't leave me, Joel. Don't leave me.' She must have fallen asleep some time after that.

The ringing of her mobile phone woke her the following morning. Joel! she thought, a spark of hope cutting through the dark depression that held her in its grip. But it was Sadie. Eden half thought about ignoring the call but knew that would infuriate her manager. She needed someone on her side right now, so she took it.

'Quite a night, I gather,' were Sadie's opening words. Eden could imagine her raising her eyebrows sardonically. 'I've spoken to three journalists and it isn't even ten o'clock. Care to tell me *exactly* what happened? And I mean *exactly*.'

Eden's worst-case scenario had just come true, and there was no talking her way out of it. 'I got drunk and ended up getting into a fight.' God, that sounded so bad! Eden tried to sound defiant, as if she didn't care. 'But before you lay into me, Sadie, it really wasn't my fault. And Joel's left me.' She couldn't keep up the don't-care act any longer. Her voice faltered.

'Eden, he's always leaving you . . . and you know what? If he did, it really wouldn't be such a bad thing. I don't want to sound brutal but here it is, honey: he's a star fucker. Major Tom, my Siamese cat, has got more personality in his tail than Joel has in his entire pretty-boy numbskull head! As for the fight, it's never your fault, is it, Eden?' There was a beat and then Sadie's tone softened. 'Honey, what are you doing with your life? You have to stop getting involved with these men who always end up hurting you. What would Terri have said?'

'She's not here, is she?'

Sadie sighed. 'I'll just say we've got no comment to make and pray the other girl doesn't take it further, though I have it on good authority that she's a massive coke head so I'm hoping she won't want to press charges or blab anything to the tabloids. In the mean-time, can you *please* do me a favour? Work on those tracks I gave you and keep a low profile. And I mean the profile of a *recluse*, a reclusive recluse! I don't want any more surprises before the party tomorrow night. I'll let you know how it goes with the press.' And with that she hung up.

Shit! Eden had completely forgotten about the record company party. The very last thing she felt like doing was being seen out in public after what had just happened. She would be a laughing stock. Why couldn't Sadie see that? And why hadn't Joel called her? Surely he should have by now. Against her better judgement she called him but there was no reply. She hung up, then thought better of it and called again. This time she left a message. 'It's me, Joel, please call me back.' A pause. 'I'm sorry.' Another pause. 'I love you.' But even as she said those words she realised they weren't true. It was more that she needed him.

*

But Joel didn't call her back. She texted him. No reply. And there was no way Joel wouldn't have seen the texts – he always had his phone with him and was forever checking it, even if he was in the middle of a shoot. She was powerless to do anything other than wait for him to contact her. Her phone rang plenty of times, and beeped with text messages from Tanya and other friends, but Eden couldn't face talking to anyone. By late-afternoon she was feeling desperate. She was still in her silk kimono, too stressed out even to face the task of getting dressed. She couldn't eat, but instead had drunk cup after cup of coffee. Joel *had* to call her back, he just had to, he couldn't have left her. She paced round the house, unable to sit still.

Outside on the pavement several paps were loitering about, all desperate to get a shot of her. News must have broken about the fight story. Her doorbell had been rung several times but she had ignored it, knowing it was bound to be one of the photographers chancing their luck. But at five when it rang again and she checked the entry screen, hoping against hope that it would be Joel, she saw Tanya instead. Feeling a stab of disappointment that it wasn't Joel, she buzzed her in.

'Why didn't you answer your phone!' Tanya exclaimed as she clattered into the hall and slammed the door firmly shut on the paps who had immediately started taking pictures as soon as it opened. 'I've been calling you all day. Sadie rang me to say what had happened. She's going to call in an hour to let you know what story the press are running tomorrow.'

Eden sat down on the stairs and put her head in her hands. 'It's been a shit day. I think Joel's left me.' There was an instant when her eyes glinted with tears, then she shook back her hair and said, 'But do you know what? Fuck him. He was only ever my pretty-boy accessory. I can get a new model, no problem.'

Anyone else would have taken Eden's harsh words at face value and instantly had her down as a number one bitch, but Tanya knew her too well and she wasn't fooled. She sat down next to her friend and put an arm round her. 'I don't especially like Joel, but you can be upset about it in front of me. I do understand what you're going through.'

But even to her closest friend, Eden couldn't let down her guard. 'Is it too early to have a drink?' she asked.

'Should you be drinking? I thought you wanted to cut down again.'

'Please, Tan, I'll just have a glass of wine . . . something to take the edge off.'

Tanya looked as if she would really rather not agree, but said, 'You can have one, but only on condition you have a shower and get dressed. And you've got to have something to eat.'

For a second it looked as if Eden might refuse, then she got up and dutifully hit the shower. Once out of it she again obsessively checked her mobile, but there was nothing from Joel. Maybe she would send him a text suggesting they meet up? She had never had to do this before when they'd rowed. He had always been the one to text her first. But maybe this time she needed to make the first move. She was on the verge of doing just that when Tanya shouted up, 'Don't even think about texting or calling him!'

Bollocks! That woman was bloody psychic; she was wasted as a model. Eden hastily got dressed, pulling on grey harem leggings and an off-the-shoulder black silk tee-shirt. Bliss's comment about her needing to lose weight made her want to cover herself up. She also applied some make-up: a flick of mascara, concealer for the dark shadows under her eyes, and some Eight Hour cream on her cut lip. The bruise on her forehead was already turning purple; God knows if she would be able to cover it up for the party tomorrow night.

Downstairs she found Tanya in the kitchen. Her friend had just opened a bottle of Sauvignon Blanc but instead of filling their glasses she seemed riveted by something on her iPhone.

'I did as I was told,' Eden declared. 'So now can I *please* have a drink? And then you can help me work out what to say to Joel. I really think I should meet him. The row just blew up out of nowhere. I know I shouldn't have said the things I did. I'm sure we can make it work again . . .'

Tanya frowned. 'I don't think so, Eden. I've just been on Facebook and Joel has updated his status to single.'

Eden felt sick. So it was official. It was over. 'Maybe he's just trying to get my attention.' Oh, God, why was she being so pathetically needy?

Tanya shook her head. 'He's not. He's also posted this comment.' She held up her phone and Eden read Joel's new post: 'Single and luvvin it.' The bastard had even put up a new profile picture that showed him looking very pleased with himself as he posed shirtless, flaunting his tanned, waxed chest.

Tanya reached out and gave Eden's shoulder a sympathetic rub. 'I'm really sorry, Eden.' She paused. 'He was very pretty but way shallow, wasn't he? He didn't have much to say on anything other than how Joel was feeling and what Joel was doing. Maybe you're better off without him.'

To hide the tears, Eden turned away from her friend, and busied herself with pouring the wine. 'It's fine. We broke up, end of story. I'll get over him.' She gave a bitter laugh. 'We'd been together nearly six months and that seems to be my limit with men.'

'Only because you never let them in. And you always pick the ones who are never going to be your equal.'

Eden was not up to any psychoanalysis – even if it was from her best friend. 'Can we change the subject? Maybe *I* should update my Facebook status.'

'Maybe you should just enjoy being single for a change and find out what you really want.'

Eden found that pretty rich, coming from Tanya who hadn't been without a boyfriend for as long as she had known her, and was engaged to Tyler and saving up to have the perfect wedding.

The two friends went into the living room with its huge floor-to-ceiling windows looking out on to a beautiful walled garden. Usually this was Eden's favourite room in the house and she loved the garden, which always seemed like an escape from the city with its beautifully kept lawn and flowerbeds and the cloudlike wisteria climbing the pale pink walls, giving off its delicate fragrance. It had also been her mum's favourite room in her house and so held special memories for Eden. But now she felt trapped in it. The paps were still staking out the front of the house and there was no other way out. This place had become her prison.

Tanya tried her best to cheer Eden up, telling her some of the latest gossip from 'Planet Model', as the two friends called it, but all the time Eden felt as if she was cut adrift from happiness. She was alone. No one wanted her. She was a bad person, a useless singer. Worthless. Behind the beautiful, *I've got it all* image that she tried to project on to the world, she was wracked with self-doubt. The wine tasted bitter in her mouth and, instead of making her feel better, only made her more depressed.

Sadie rang at seven. It wasn't good news. The story of the fight was going to run in all the red tops. And one of the clubbers had managed to take a series of pictures on their camera phone and those would be published, along with a video that would run on the newspapers' websites.

'And there's something else,' Sadie told her just when Eden thought things couldn't get any worse. 'Apparently Joel, or rather his manager, has been in talks with some of the papers about selling a story about his relationship with you. We could try and get an injunction but it will be expensive and there's no certainty that we will get it. You might have to ride this one out, Eden.'

'Oh, God, Sadie!' she burst out, appalled by the betrayal. 'Why's he doing this to me?'

'Why do you think? Money and fame. I did warn you about him. The best thing you can do is try and ignore it. Focus on your music and on looking fabulous for the party tomorrow night. I don't even think it's worth putting out a statement about him, it will only fuel the fire. Just choose more wisely next time, Eden. I'll see you tomorrow night. Please don't be late.'

After the phone call from Sadie, Eden drank even more wine. She badly wanted to forget everything that was wrong in her life, but every drink seemed to take her to a darker and darker place. After Tanya left around midnight, Eden carried on drinking alone until three. She couldn't stop herself from drunk-dialling Joel and leaving a message. In the morning she had no idea what she had said to him. Nothing to make him change his mind apparently because he hadn't called her back. He was probably too busy ripping her character to shreds with some journalist. Just another in the long line of men who had betrayed Eden and used her to make money and get a taste of fame. Maybe, she thought bitterly, that was the kind of man that she deserved.

Chapter Three

Star in bitch slap! . . . Has Eden lost the plot? . . . Pop Princess
in meltdown! . . . Is this the end of the road for Eden?

She felt sick as she took in the headlines. Sadie had
told her on no account to look at the stories, knowing
how upsetting Eden would find them. But of course she
couldn't stop herself. She had a horrible burning
compulsion to know what had been written about her,
and she would defy anyone to resist that.

She sat in her designer kitchen, at her expensive
designer glass dining table, on one of her expensive
violet leather designer chairs, her MacBook open,
scrolled through the stories and wept. She was being
portrayed as an 'out of control drunk', 'a fallen star'.
She was the 'troubled' singer, whose personal life was
threatening to 'spiral out of control' – and didn't the
press just love documenting every detail of her fall from
grace? They had even dragged up the stories about her
mother's death nearly two years earlier.

There were photographs of Eden at the height of her
career as the glittering star who seemed to have the
world at her feet, set against the pictures the clubber
had managed to snatch of her with their camera phone.
These showed her looking a total wreck with her cut lip,
bruised face and ruined dress. How could she face

anyone after this? It was humiliating beyond words. Everyone was going to think that she was a monster. She thought of her sister reading the stories and shaking her head in shame and disapproval, but all the time thinking that it was only what she expected of the selfish, spoilt Eden . . .

Tanya and some of her other friends had already left messages, sending her their support and love. But Eden didn't feel up to speaking to anyone. She wanted to hide away, be the recluse that Sadie had wanted her to be before the disastrous night at the club. There was no possible way that she could go to the party now. But she had reckoned without the iron will of her manager.

At midday Sadie arrived on Eden's doorstep with a young man in tow. At first Eden couldn't even bring herself to let them in and Sadie had to ring the bell several times. When Eden still didn't answer, Sadie resorted to phoning her up, telling her, 'If you don't open the door now, Eden, I swear I'm going to make the biggest scene ever out here. Do you really want to give the paps any more ammunition?'

Her manager had won that round. Reluctantly Eden buzzed them in.

She was expecting another earbashing from Sadie, and braced herself for the recriminations, but instead her manager marched in and hugged her, enveloping her in a cloud of her exotic Pomegranate Noir Jo Malone perfume. 'They're shits and they're bastards, and you will be letting them win if you carry on like this.'

'So what?' Eden mumbled, wondering who the hell the young blond man was who had OD'd on the Fake Bake. Another of Sadie's conquests? Her manager did have an eye for the younger guy.

'So nothing, it's time to get on with life. *Carpe diem* . . . seize the day and all that bollocks!' She turned to the young man. 'This is Jez, he's going to do your hair. I

45

phoned your hairdresser this morning and found out that you hadn't turned up for your appointment, and Jez is a very dear friend of mine who is going to be your saviour. He does Crystal's and Angel Summer's so you're in excellent hands.'

Jez beamed at Eden, showing off blindingly white teeth. 'I'm going to make you look fab-u-lous.'

'Right,' Eden muttered, glad he was so sure of himself; she didn't think fabulous, however you pronounced it, was going to be possible in the circumstances.

'Then at five Darcy is coming round to do your make-up. Your dress is sorted, isn't it?'

'Yeah.' Another mutter from Eden, who actually didn't have any idea what she was going to wear. She hadn't felt up to going shopping, but surely she must have something in her five wardrobes packed full of designer clothes?

'Great. Well, I'll leave you in Jez's capable hands and I'll see you at the party.' Sadie pulled out her notebook and checked through her list. She was old-fashioned that way. While her contemporaries were glued to their iPhone and Blackberry, Sadie liked to write everything down and then tick it off when it was done. 'I've arranged for Eddie to pick you up at seven. Do have something to eat first; you know how much champagne they'll be pouring down our throats when we arrive. And please, please, *please*, try not to drink too much. I know what a tough day you've had but I really need you to be on your very best behaviour tonight. No pressure, but there is a shitload riding on it for both of us.'

'I do understand, Sadie,' Eden said, wishing her manager would just go. Finally Sadie smiled at her. 'I don't mean to sound like such an old nag, I only want you to be the star that I know you can be. And I realise it hasn't been an easy few years,' she said softly.

Eden was touched by her comments but terrified of crying again, so quickly said, 'I'm fine, Sadie, really I am. I'll see you later.'

And then it was just Eden and Jez. Eden couldn't help feeling wary around him at first. She was deeply mistrustful of strangers and of anyone new coming into her life. It hadn't just been ex-boyfriends who had sold stories on her; in the past couple of years, when she was at her most vulnerable, there had also been a succession of people she had thought were her friends who had ended up talking to the press for money. It seemed that the lure of making an easy bit of cash proved too enticing and they had happily dished the dirt on Eden, more often than not making things up for added drama. But Jez was clearly such a sweetheart that she couldn't help warming to him. Within half an hour she had found out his life story: that he was gay and married to Rufus, a gorgeous personal trainer; that Rufus really wanted to adopt or father a child, but that Jez wasn't sure and felt they should get a dog first, to see if they could handle the commitment.

Eden was about to burst out laughing at the comment when he caught her eye and exclaimed, 'I do know it's not quite the same as a child! But we'll still have to walk it and feed it . . . and you can get some adorable little outfits for dogs these days. Not that Rufus will let me get a little dog. He's too macho. He's more of the Old English Sheepdog or chocolate brown Labrador type, whereas I'm keener on a Westie. You can get such fabulous coats for them – I saw one the other day in a to die for red-and-black polka-dot number.' Jez was so camp and funny that Eden found herself smiling for the first time in ages.

And what she appreciated most of all was that he didn't mention the stories in the press or ask her any personal questions. Instead they sat in Eden's kitchen while Jez worked his magic on her hair and gossiped about other celebs, films that they had seen, film-star crushes that they had. Eden admitted to having a thing about Brad Pitt, provided he was without the skanky beard, and Jez adored Dominic Cooper. It was like having time out from the real world. It turned out to be just what Eden needed. Sadie, as always, was very clever at managing her.

Jez had just expertly folded the last of the foils in to Eden's hair when her phone buzzed with an incoming text message. For a fleeting second she hoped it would be Joel, saying it had all been a terrible mistake, that he loved her and was sorry. Some hope. The message was from Jack Steele.

Hope you're doing okay. Look forward to seeing you tonight and hearing what you think of the music. Remember, what doesn't kill you makes you stronger. And you seem pretty strong already to me. Jackx

'I didn't expect to hear from *him*,' Eden commented.

'Who's that then, the gorgeous Brad?'

'Hah! Hardly. It's from Jack Steele, do you know him?'

'I don't know him personally but I *love* his work. And he's a bit of a hottie and likes the ladies by all accounts. And the ladies like him.'

At this Eden burst out laughing. 'He's a hairie! Definitely not a hottie. When I saw him he looked as if he should have been living in a yurt and weaving his own furniture out of facial hair.'

'Really? Maybe you caught him on an off day,' Jez mused. 'I remember seeing him in some magazine and thinking he was delectable, and I don't as a rule go for the hairies. I like it all off, if you know what I mean.' He winked at Eden.

Eden winked back. 'I do know what you mean.' She stood up and stretched. 'Now will you do me a massive favour and help me decide what to wear tonight? I don't think I'm up to making any decisions at the moment.'

Jez clapped his hands in delight. 'You mean, I get to peek at Eden Haywood's wardrobe! Oh, yes, please!'

Upstairs, Eden sat on the edge of her bed and watched Jez happily going through her many clothes – the elegant designer evening dresses, embellished with sequins and crystals, the outrageous revealing numbers, including the silver leather dress that she'd never worn (which was probably for the best), the white dress made entirely of feathers, also never worn (also a good thing), the divine off-the-shoulder Roland Mouret dress in emerald green, the sexy gold sequined Roberto Cavalli mini-dress. But at every dress he held up, Eden shook her head; nothing seemed to fit her mood. She didn't want to wear something glittery and feminine. She wanted to feel confident and feisty, not like the victim the press seemed to want her to be. And there was the issue of her weight. She knew that every single dress that Jez had selected would be slightly too tight and that she would feel self-conscious all night.

'I'm too fat for all those,' she said quietly.

'Oh my God! Of course you're not,' Jez exclaimed, outraged at the suggestion. 'You're a beautiful, sensuous woman. I bet every time you walk in the room every man in it wants to go to bed with you.' He paused. 'Usually I'd have said something much ruder than that, but I don't know you well enough yet so we'll go with that.'

'Well,' Eden said dryly, 'they certainly like screwing me after we've broken up. Do you know where my ex is right now?'

Jez shook his head. 'You don't have to tell me.'

But suddenly Eden wanted to confide in him. 'He's selling a story about what a bitch I am, and everyone will read it and decide that's exactly what they thought all along.'

'They won't. People aren't stupid. They'll think what a little shit he is for doing that to his ex-girlfriend.'

'They'll think I deserved it. And maybe they'll be right.'

Jez let out a theatrical sigh. 'Oh, my, we do have some self-esteem issues here.' And then he looked serious again. 'I'm sorry, I didn't mean to offend you. I couldn't help it, I got carried away because we've been getting on so well.'

If anyone else said something like that, even though it was a joke, Eden would have been sorely tempted to snap back at them and quite likely never see them again, but there was no way she wanted to do that to someone as adorable as Jez, so she just smiled.

'There are *so* many issues for me to address, but for now can we concentrate on what the fuck I am going to wear tonight?'

'Okay, give me a minute to think about it.' Jez actually stood in front of her, considering, hand on hip. 'I've got it. Plain black boyfriend blazer – I see you've got at least three – nothing on underneath except a push-up bra so we get a hint of those fabulous torpedo bazookas, which are apparently real . . .' He stared at Eden's chest, as if it was a fascinating but utterly unsexy phenomenon. It wasn't how men usually stared at her breasts, that was for sure.

'They're real. For now. I may upgrade at a later date.'

'And an outrageously short black sequined skirt, so that the *Daily Mail* can come up with a headline about how you forgot to put your skirt on when you went out – they're always coming out with headlines like that about women in short skirts. But, hey, it's bound to get you in the press. Wear a fierce pair of black ankle boots – I see you've got about ten pairs of those. One piece of statement jewellery . . . a diamond choker perhaps . . . just-got-out-of-bed hair, smoky eyes and pouting glossy lips. And *voilà*! We have Eden Haywood, femme fatale and rock chick. What do you think?'

Eden liked the idea very much. She was certainly not in the mood for flouncing around in a body-con dress.

'So legs *and* tits on show? That breaks all the style rules, of course, but I've never followed them.'

'Rules are made to be broken. Now come on, I need to check on how those highlights are doing.'

Some three hours later, Eden was good to go. Jez had repaired her trailer-park roots and given her the promised bed-head look. Darcy had worked her make-up magic, leaving Eden with flawless skin and smouldering eye make-up, which made her green eyes glitter. Her nails had been painted a gothic shade of burgundy, courtesy of Chanel. The outfit was knockout, though Eden was still convinced she looked fat in it. She consoled herself by thinking that even if her abs did need work, at least her legs were still okay. Jez had been wonderful company and had ended up staying for the entire afternoon. He was with her now as she travelled to the party at the private members club in Soho. He was meeting friends in the same area.

'Don't look so nervous!' he exclaimed as he caught sight of her anxious expression. 'Haven't you been to these kinds of parties like a million times?'

'Yeah, but I've always gone with someone, and that was when my career was going well. I can't help feeling that Sadie wants me to put on this big act to prove that I've still got what it takes.' And she was so close to adding that she didn't know if she did have what it took . . . not any more. But Jez got in there first.

'You've got what it takes, and I think you always will.' He smiled at her. 'You know, when Sadie asked me to do your hair, I was nervous about meeting you. But you're lovely. You just need to believe that yourself, and trust that it will be okay.'

'Are you sure you're a hairdresser, not a therapist?' Eden joked back, trying to laugh off his truthful observation.

'It's a thin line. And I swear I have taken the Oath of Confidentially of all hairdressers: never to tell. Cross my heart, hope to die, stick a needle in my eye,' Jez replied. 'It's fine if you drop me off here,' he added as the car turned into Old Compton Street. 'My stomping ground.'

As the car slowed, Eden leant over and lightly kissed him on the cheek. 'Thank you for doing my hair so beautifully, and most of all for taking my mind off all the shit that's been going on. Might you have time in your schedule to do my hair again? I think I'm about to dump my hairdresser for a younger, prettier model. I'll totally understand if you can't, I know you've already got lots of clients, and Angel Summer and Crystal must keep you busy.'

'I'll always make time for you, sweetie. And anyway, Crystal's going to the States for six months,' Jez told her as he got out of the car. 'Now go, girl, and wow some music execs!'

But Eden was not feeling very wow once she walked into the club, a three-storey Victorian building which the record company had taken over for the night. She had always hated going to parties on her own. As Sadie had predicted, the first thing that greeted Eden was a waiter holding a tray of champagne glasses. She took a glass, promising herself she would just have one for courage and then switch to water. She sipped her drink and anxiously scanned the room, looking for Sadie. At first she couldn't see any sign of her manager, and spent a panicky few minutes when she didn't see anyone she recognised and was all set to go upstairs to see if she was there. And what a saddo Eden would feel then, wandering through the club while trying to find a friend. Then she caught sight of Sadie at the far side of the room, deep in conversation with Crystal.

Instantly Eden was awash with insecurity at the sight of Crystal in a beautiful midnight blue maxi-dress. Eden self-consciously tried to tug down her skirt with one hand, suddenly aware of how very short it was. Why had she let Jez talk her into the revealing outfit? She would feel anxious enough about people looking at her because of the press story, without the outrageous skirt attracting yet more attention.

'I don't think that's going to work, do you?' A vaguely familiar voice had just addressed her.

She turned round to see a very tall, extremely handsome man, with intensely blue eyes. She was sure she recognised him but . . .

The handsome man smiled just as realisation was dawning.

'Jack Steele,' he prompted her.

'But . . . you look so different.' Indeed he did! Goodbye Jack the hairy yeti. *Hello* sexy clean-shaven Jack! The unruly brown hair had been cut short. It was quite a transformation.

He gave a nod of acknowledgement. 'When I met you at Sadie's I'd been travelling for two days, and before that I'd been working practically day and night on an album for several weeks. So, yeah, I hadn't shaved in a while and most likely wasn't looking my best.' He cocked an eyebrow. 'But, hey, at least *I* was on time.'

Eden pouted. 'We're not going to go through that again, are we? I got enough of a telling off from Sadie, as you know.' She had another sip of champagne. Damn, it was going down a little too quickly.

Jack smiled again. 'Sadie is a force to be reckoned with. And I know you've had a rough couple of days.' He lowered his voice as he added, 'She told me about your boyfriend walking out on you and threatening to sell a story. That's a lot of shit to deal with.'

Such a personal comment instantly caused Eden to become defensive. 'Actually I dumped *him*, if you must know, and he can say what he fucking well likes, it will all be lies!' And before Jack could reply, she said, 'Excuse me, I'm going to get another drink.' She quickly walked away from him and from a conversation she did not want to have. Never mind Sadie telling her to take it easy on the alcohol, she needed more champagne if she was to get through the night.

She ended up talking to a group of people she vaguely knew from the record company – Fifi in publicity, Drew in marketing, Si in promotions, and God knows who else, she lost track of the names, but they were all hell-bent on drinking as much as possible, as quickly as possible. It wasn't the best situation for Eden to find herself in. Instead of cutting back on the drink as she had planned, she held up her glass to be refilled every time a waiter swung by, which was frequently. Every now and then she was aware of Jack looking over at her, from where he stood chatting to a group that included Crystal, but she ignored him.

'There you are.' Sadie came and sat next to her. 'I want you to come and talk to Marc White, he's just arrived.'

Marc was the chief executive of Vermillion Records. Eden had been with them from the start of her singing career and had always got on well with Marc, but that meant nothing in the ruthless music industry that was all about sales. She could be Marc's twin sister, suffering from a terminal illness, a single mother with small children to support . . . he would still drop her in a heartbeat if her album wasn't selling.

'Oh, so now you've finished talking to all your other clients you have a window for me, do you?' Nerves and anger that Sadie had told Jack about Joel made Eden spiky and sarcastic.

Sadie looked at her sharply. 'I'll ignore that comment. And I thought I said to lay off the drink.'

'Yeah, well, thanks a lot for telling Jack Steele about my private life. I don't want him knowing my business.'

A sigh from Sadie. 'He's one of the good guys, Eden, someone you want on your side. Come on, it's be nice to Marc time.'

Sadie linked arms with Eden and walked her over to where Marc was holding court. He was a fifty something, seen it all before man, with a ruthless commercial instinct. Indie bands forget it; Marc was mainstream all the way. When he saw Eden he took off his black baseball cap and gave her a mock bow. 'My favourite pop princess.'

What followed was ten minutes of Eden trying to be on her best behaviour, laughing at all Marc's jokes – which were not funny – gushing about the tracks Jack had written for her, and generally trying to be the irresistible pop starlet Marc simply had to sign up again.

She thought she was doing okay until, right at the end of the conversation, he said quietly, 'And I really hope there aren't going to be any more punch ups in night clubs, Eden. I don't care how much someone provokes you, you walk away. You're supposed to have star quality, and getting involved in some bitch-slapping contest doesn't exactly scream that, does it? Don't let it happen again.'

He didn't need to add 'Or else' but the implication was there. Eden nodded. It was Sadie who said smoothly, 'Eden fully understands the situation, Marc. It won't happen again.'

But Marc still hadn't finished. 'There aren't going to be any other surprises coming out in the press that I should know about, are there?'

Shit! What could Sadie say in reply to this? Eden shot her manager an anguished look; this was going to test her managerial skills to the max!

'Eden's ex-boyfriend is threatening to sell a story about his relationship with her, but I really don't think it will be significant. And I'm hoping to line up a feature in one of the women's glossies, where we'll do a fabulous shoot with Eden and an interview where she gets to put across her side of the story in a calm and dignified way.'

Marc looked less than impressed. 'Well, I guess she could always talk about her mum. It sounds brutal but the sympathy vote is definitely worth having. And Eden hasn't talked about her before, has she? So it would be an exclusive. Magazines love that. Anyway, I look forward to hearing the new tracks, Eden.' And with that she and Sadie were effectively dismissed.

As they walked away, Sadie put her arm round her and whispered, 'It's okay, darling, I don't expect you to talk about Terri. Everything will be okay.'

Eden could only nod, too stunned by Marc's comment to speak. All she wanted to do now was leave the party. Instead she found herself caught up in a conversation with Zain, a young fashion designer, with spiky red hair. He told her they had met before – it was news to Eden – but she let the guy talk at her some more as she drank another glass of champagne. At one point she looked round the room and again her gaze fell on Jack. He was chatting to a pretty young woman. He certainly was easy on the eye, Eden thought as she looked at him in profile. She shouldn't have been so quick to dismiss him. He had a strong, handsome face, one that she was drawn to look at. Jack turned and caught her eye. He smiled, said something to his companion and walked over to Eden. Zain went off to find someone else to talk at.

'We haven't talked about what you think of the tracks yet. You mentioned at the meeting that you were going to listen to them. So come on, put me out of my misery, what's your verdict?'

Oh, God, not this, not now. Eden decided to play the sympathy card. She bit her lip and put her hand up to her forehead, where in spite of Darcy's best efforts the purple bruise was still visible. 'I'm still getting into it. I'm sure it'll be fine once I'm in the studio.' She was bluffing now. So much had been going on in her life recently that she hadn't listened to the songs at all. 'I've had a lot on.' An understatement.

Jack looked at her consideringly. 'So which one is your favourite? If you like, we can go with that one first.' He hadn't fallen for the act at all.

The bastard knew that she was lying! 'Oh, I wouldn't like to pick a favourite! I really like them all.' And suddenly Eden realised that she had better turn on the charm or Jack would go straight back to Sadie and report on her lack of commitment and then she would get yet more grief from her manager. Taking a deep breath, she shook back her hair and stepped a little closer to him. 'In fact, I'm very impressed by your talent.' Shit, that sounded way too cheesy!

'Very good of you to say so, Miss Haywood.'

She wasn't sure if he was being sarcastic or not, but decided to reply as if he were not. She had started this, now she had better finish it. 'I feel as if we didn't really get off to the best start, what with me being late and everything. How about we have a drink together now?'

'Why not? I'm done with talking to everyone else here.' It wasn't exactly the most enthusiastic of responses but Eden decided to make the best of it.

And as they sat down on one of the leather sofas, she put Plan B into operation: make Jack Steele happy by flirting outrageously with him. She had always had a gift for seducing men and invariably got her own way with them. It was time to bring out Eden the Vamp.

'So . . . I don't know anything about you, Jack Steele, other than that you write like an angel and scrub up well when you want to.' God, the corny lines were coming thick and fast tonight.

'What do you want to know?'

Eden leant forward to pick up her champagne glass, knowing that she would also be giving him a glimpse of her breasts in the black satin Agent Provocateur bra. 'How about everything?'

Jack laughed. 'You don't want much, do you?' But Eden was aware of his gaze lingering on her long slim legs as she crossed and uncrossed them, and her slender neck as she once again shook back her blonde hair. Okay they were the oldest tricks in the book, but what was wrong with old tricks if they worked!

'I've always been a girl who wants everything,' she murmured back, looking at him from under her long lashes. He really was transformed from their first encounter.

'And I'll just bet you always get it, don't you?' Gone was his sarcastic tone. Jack Steele could not keep his eyes off her now. Eden allowed herself a brief moment of self-congratulation; this was going to be easier than she had expected. She had Jack hooked. All she had to do now was to reel him in.

'Not always.' She smiled. 'But most of the time. Is that very bad?'

'I don't know if it's good for anyone always to get their own way, even if they are as beautiful as you.'

Eden laughed. 'No way! Nice of you to say so but I know I look rough at the moment.' She moved closer to him on the sofa. 'Look at the shadows under my eyes.' She stared straight into his blue eyes with a challenging *'Come and get me if you dare'* look.

And Jack Steele stared right back, with a look that said, *I dare.* And the flirtation carried on. They talked about music, her career, how he got into songwriting via playing keyboard in a nineties band that failed to make it; their favourite artists, both of them sharing a love for Dionne Warwick, Stevie Wonder, Billie Holiday, Al Green, Alicia Keys; they talked favourite places – Eden's was Phuket in Thailand, where she loved the unspoilt beaches; while his was San Francisco as he enjoyed the laid-back vibe out there.

Eden had started out wanting Jack to want her, wanting to have him in her power, but the more they talked, the more she realised how attractive he was. Jack Steele was a very sexy, very charming man. He was also incredibly easy to talk to. In the past she had gone for men of her own age or else younger, all caught up in their own egos and with being with Eden because she was a star. Being with Jack even for this brief amount of time didn't make her feel like that. She felt for the first time that she had met a man who wanted to get to know her and who was more than a match for her. Or maybe it was the champagne giving everything a rose-tinted glow. All she knew was that she found him very, very attractive and it was giving her such a buzz, sensing that he was interested in her. Joel walking out on her hadn't exactly been an ego boost.

It was after midnight by now. The party was getting more raucous, the music had been turned up and people were dancing. Eden was just wondering how to ask Jack back to her house when he got in first.

'I'm flat-sitting for a friend who lives round the corner in Soho Square while my place is being decorated. D'you fancy a drink there? And I can play

59

you those tracks again as you clearly haven't listened to them at all.'

'I have too!' Eden insisted.

'Liar,' Jack replied. Then, as if to make up for the accusation, he took her hand and lightly kissed it, afterwards turning it over to kiss the inside of her wrist. A shiver of lust ran through Eden at the feel of his lips against her skin. She felt as if she was no longer entirely in control of the situation.

'So will you come back?'

She nodded.

With that Jack stood up, reached for her hand again and led her out of the party. They didn't bother with goodbyes to anyone. By chance they left the club at the same time as Crystal, and the paps were so busy photographing her that they failed to notice Eden and Jack slip away into the cool March night. As they drew closer to his flat, Eden questioned what she was doing; did she really want to go through with this? *This* being sleeping with Jack because that's what *this* was about. It wasn't about listening to his music. And, sure enough, once Jack had shut the front door he took her in his arms and kissed her deeply, a passionate sexy kiss that ignited the white heat of lust inside her.

She really didn't want it to stop, but she pulled away. 'I thought we were going to listen to your music,' she said playfully.

But Jack just smiled. 'Fuck that.' He unfastened the button on her jacket and slipped it off, revealing her satin bra. He lightly caressed her hard nipples, sending shivers of desire through her . . . God, he was making her want him so badly. Any doubts she'd had about what she was doing melted away as she revelled in his touch and pressed her body against his, as if to say, 'Take me, I'm yours.' By the feel of him against her she could tell that he was just as aroused as she was. This was going to be so good. She slipped her hands under his shirt, wanting to feel his smooth skin. As she caressed his back, her fingertips encountered the raised line of a long-healed scar.

All of a sudden Jack flinched. He pulled out of her arms and moved away. 'Christ, what am I thinking of?' he muttered, more to himself than Eden who stood riveted to the spot. He straightened his shirt then said, 'I'm sorry, Eden, that shouldn't have happened. You've had a shit week and I don't want to add to it. I'll call you a taxi.'

What the fuck! Why was he being like this? Eden had been sure from the moment of that kiss that this was leading one place only, and it certainly was not supposed to end here! She felt totally humiliated. She pulled her blazer together. 'Don't bother, Jack, I'll make my own way home. Sorry I'm not good enough for you!'

She felt her bottom lip tremble and all of a sudden the events of the past couple of weeks caught up with her – the fight, Joel leaving her, and now this! Scalding hot tears blurred her vision as she pushed open the front door and bolted down the stairs. She heard Jack calling after her, but she didn't stop.

The following morning, after Eden had spent a sleepless night replaying every second of her encounter with Jack and feeling more and more humiliated, she drove over to Tanya's. She had to confide in her friend. Her mind was all over the place as she struggled to understand what had happened. She had set out to have sex with Jack, she wasn't re-writing history on that score, and was expecting nothing more than a fling. But she had definitely got more than she had bargained for. How the hell was she going to face him in the studio?

'What happened to you, babe?' Tanya asked as she let her in to her cosy Victorian terraced house in Ealing.

Eden was a perfect study of the morning after the night before, with her tousled hair, pale complexion and a pair of black Dior shades obscuring half her face.

'I've been such a fool, Tanya.'

She smiled. 'I'm sure you haven't. Come in, you look as if you need a coffee.'

Thank God for Tanya, who made coffee and toast, and listened sympathetically while she poured out her story. But Eden knew that Tanya would be shocked that she had intended to sleep with Jack so soon after meeting him. Tanya had never had a one-night stand with anyone; she maintained that she would feel that a man wouldn't respect her if she slept with him straight away.

'So why did he pull away from me?' Eden said, coming to the end of her tale of the night before. 'He was giving out all the signals that he wanted to sleep with me.'

'Maybe he had too much respect for you?' Tanya replied.

Eden grimaced.

'No, it is possible. Don't dismiss the possibility just because you haven't had that from other men. Or perhaps because you don't respect yourself enough.'

'No way, Tan! I do respect myself,' Eden protested. But the sceptical expression on Tanya's face said that she wasn't convinced.

'And maybe don't put yourself in that situation again. I know you always make out that you're so independent. If you want to have sex with a man, you'll go ahead and have it and why shouldn't you? But it's always more complicated than that, isn't it? You always end up feeling something for them, don't you?'

Eden frowned, knowing there was something in

Tanya's comment. 'Yeah, I guess. I suppose I'm still hurting because of Joel, and wanted to know that someone wanted me. But it was a stupid thing to do.' And what she didn't add was that she felt rejected all over again, by Jack.

Back home Eden put on the CD of his songs and curled up on the sofa to listen. She soon discovered that her initial reaction had been entirely wrong. The songs were wonderful; they were powerful, strong melodies, with beautiful lyrics. True, they were very different from the material she usually performed. Jack's songs were more grown-up and really took a hold of you. A bit like Jack, she thought bitterly, as she replayed the scenes with him over and over in her head: their easy conversation and flirtation; the way he had kissed her, held her, caressed her. It was going to be mortifying ever seeing him again. She half considered phoning Sadie and telling her what had happened, but stopped herself. She couldn't bear the thought of her manager judging her all over again. No, this was one problem she was going to have to sort out herself. And she would start by trying to be as cool about what had happened as Jack had been.

Chapter Four

'So, darling, did you get back from the party okay?' It was Sadie on the phone the following morning. 'I didn't see you when I left.'

'Yeah, fine.' Eden was glad it was a phone call because she was sure she looked guilty. 'Do you think the meeting with Marc went okay?'

'You did good, Eden, you looked fantastic, very sexy. But – and please don't get the hump with me – I really do think that you need to tone up. These next few months are crucial for us. We've got to get the album in the bag and you've got to wow everyone. We could get some really positive coverage of you getting fit again – you know the press and celeb mags love that kind of thing.'

'You think I'm fat! I suppose you want me to be seen out wobbling in a bikini and then making a fucking fitness DVD, from flab to fab!' Eden exclaimed. This was all she needed. Maybe that's why Jack had been so quick to dismiss her. He didn't want to shag the fat girl!

'No, no, I just think you need to cut down on the drink, eat more healthily and tone up,' Sadie said patiently as if to a small child. 'When you perform live, I want the press to be reporting on your fantastic comeback and not on your muffin top. Come on, think of Gwen Stefani's abs of iron . . . and she's had two children. You can do it, Eden!'

'Okay, I'll start going to the gym again,' she said defensively. 'But I thought I was supposed to be learning these new tracks?'

'I'm sure you're perfectly capable of doing both if you put your mind to it, but actually I've got a far better idea than you going to the gym on your own. I've booked you in with a fantastic personal trainer. In fact, he's coming round to yours this afternoon to give you an assessment. His name's Rufus, and strictly no flirting, Eden, he's a married man.'

'Do you mean Jez's husband? Of course I'm not going to flirt with him! And I wouldn't get very far if I did anyway!' God, who did Sadie think she was? And this was without her knowing what had happened with Jack.

'By the way, I saw you chatting to Jack Steele. It's good to see you guys getting on together. I knew you would like him once you gave him a chance. He didn't try anything on, did he? I adore him but he's got a terrible reputation with women. I meant to warn you, then I figured you're a big girl and you can look after yourself. And anyway, he's not one of the pretty-boy types you go for, is he? Jack's all man . . . definitely not a boy.' Sadie gave a throaty laugh.

Once again, Eden was relieved that this was a phone conversation. She was actually blushing, for crissakes! ''Course not,' she mumbled. 'And yeah, we got on okay professionally. But you're right, he's definitely not my type.'

'Just as well, as we're all going to be spending a lot of time together in the next few months and I need you to be completely focused. We don't need any distractions right now.'

*

65

After that phone conversation Eden felt entirely unfocused. In a way it was a relief when Rufus arrived at the house, even though Eden knew she wasn't going to enjoy the training one little bit. But anything was better than beating herself up about what had happened with Jack. Rufus had black hair, dark brown eyes, was lightly tanned and completely focused and professional. He probably was far more Eden's type than Jack, but she found herself unmoved by his good looks.

Within an hour Rufus had completed an in-depth assessment of her diet and drinking habits and declared her to be drinking far too much and eating all the wrong things. Like that was news to her!

'I promise I'll cut back,' Eden told him, crossing her fingers behind her back.

'Yep, you'll certainly be doing that as I'm arranging for your low-fat meals to be delivered, and I am going to be seeing you every morning. Believe me, if you've had a heavy night drinking, I will know. You will only be cheating yourself if you carry on drinking too much. Do you know how many empty calories alcohol contains?'

'Even champagne?' Eden wailed theatrically.

Rufus didn't even crack a smile as he replied, 'Even champagne.'

'Vodka?' she asked hopefully.

'Calorie count okay, but I wouldn't like to assess the impact on your liver. And if you drink that every night you're never going to get fit.'

'Oh, God! You're not going to be on my case as well? Isn't it enough that I've got Sadie on at me? And I know what that woman is like once she sets her mind to something . . . she's like a dog with a bone; she'll never give up. You and Jez are like bad cop, good cop. I need good cop Jez to tell me everything is going to be all right and that I'm gorgeous and fab-u-lous just as I am.'

She expected Rufus to banter back, like Jez would have done, but he was far too professional, 'Think of me as the voice of your conscience,' he told her. 'And I promise that once you start seeing results you'll find it so much easier to stick to the plan. Now we're going to clear out your cupboards and fridge of anything unhealthy and then get to the gym.'

And Eden was forced to watch as Rufus emptied her fridge of cheese, butter, chocolate and champagne. He cleared out the stash of chocolate Hobnobs that she kept for PMT emergencies, and generously allowed her to keep wholemeal pasta, brown rice, a packet of oatcakes and a box of green tea bags.

'I'm looking forward to dinner tonight!' Eden said sarcastically. 'Brown rice and oatcake surprise.'

Rufus raised an eyebrow and opened a list of diet meals. 'Actually you're having Sesame Chicken with wilted Pak Choi and Chinese greens. There will even be a snack of vegetable sticks and spicy tomato dip.'

'What more could a girl possibly want?' Eden shot back.

Rufus smiled and said, 'Time for the gym.'

An hour and a half later Eden had discovered that Rufus was a tough taskmaster who would not take no for an answer or listen to her moaning that she had a stitch/was out of breath/that her legs ached/that she might be about to have a heart attack. He had her alternately walk then sprint on the treadmill and afterwards do an intensive workout on the vibrating power plates, while ignoring all her jokes that maybe she should just sit on it and cut out the middle man. And after he'd had her doing three punishing sets of forty tricep dips, sit ups, lunges, and holding the plank position – her least favourite position of all time – she didn't find it very amusing either. By the end of the session she was scarlet-faced, sweating and absolutely exhausted. The only good thing to come out of the gruelling workout was that she hadn't given another thought to Jack Steele.

But that state of mind didn't last. When she was back home on her own, with just the 500-calorie meal which had been delivered to the house for company, she wondered about him once more. She went on Facebook to see if he was on it. He wasn't. A Google of his name though yielded more results – at least about his professional life. He had worked with some really big names, had won several awards, and there were a few photographs of him taken at a recent awards ceremony, wearing a black tuxedo, which Eden found herself lingering over. He certainly did scrub up well. She was amazed that she hadn't realised how devastatingly handsome he was the first time they met, with those piercing blue eyes and strong features. He had a face with such character, very different from all the pretty boys she had always gone for previously. There was a wildness and rawness about Jack that intrigued her.

And then, though she knew she shouldn't do it, she went on Joel's Facebook page and saw that he had posted up more new pictures of himself from a recent shoot for a new aftershave. He always used his Facebook page for self-promotion; his page was never so much 'This is what I've been doing' as 'Look at how hot I am'.

Eden was idly clicking through the pictures when one stopped her in her tracks. It was a picture of Joel and Bliss, arms wrapped round each other, smiling their beautiful smiles for the camera. They looked like the perfect couple. She wondered if he had been seeing Bliss all along, and if he had only been waiting for the right moment to get out of his relationship with Eden. She tried to ignore the stab of hurt. The two models deserved each other, they were both as shallow as they were beautiful. But the pain was still there as she thought of Joel walking out, selling a story about her as callously as if she had never meant anything to him. Why had she wasted any of her time on him?

Again a familiar feeling of loneliness washed over her and she longed to have a conversation with someone close. Above all she wished she could speak to her sister but she knew Savannah wouldn't talk to her. A few months after their mother's death Savannah and her husband had moved to San Diego for his work. So many times Eden had been on the verge of booking a flight over to see her sister, and each time she would remember Savannah telling her she never wanted to see her again . . . But now, feeling vulnerable and alone, she felt she had to connect with her sister somehow.

She began writing an email to Savannah, telling her how much she missed her, asking again if they could meet up, saying that she was sorry if she had done anything to hurt her. But every word, which she had already written many times before, only made her realise the distance between them. And yet once they had been so close, more best friends than sisters, had told each other everything, always been there for each other. Eden had no other family. Her father had died from a heart attack when she was only six months old. It had only ever been Eden, Savannah and their mum. Eden had thought it always would be.

She sighed as she read back over the message that was all about how much she missed Savannah. Then she deleted it and found herself writing about how she had messed up yet another relationship; had met Jack and messed that one up too; that Sadie was trying to get her back on track with her career and how she would probably mess up again. Eden had been more honest in this email than she had been with anyone before. She hesitated then pressed send.

She imagined Savannah seeing her sister's name

come up in her inbox. Would she delete the message without even reading it? It was possible. Savannah was incredibly tough. But Eden had to keep trying. She could not just sit back and accept that she was never going to see her sister again. And somehow, writing the email had been a sort of release.

For the next week Eden kept her nose to the grindstone and worked out every morning with Rufus; in the afternoon she had singing lessons, and she made sure she was doing something every night. She attended the latest Jennifer Aniston rom-com premiere with Sadie one night and resisted the temptation to give the press the finger as she posed on the red carpet, smiling sweetly, like a good little celebrity. She went along to Tanya's yoga class, even though Eden was the least yoga-inclined person ever, and got the giggles when she was assuming the dog position at one point. And she met up with Jez for champagne cocktails another night as she wanted to thank him for doing her hair and being so lovely to her when she'd most needed it.

'You look gorgeous!' Jez told her as she joined him in the Courtyard Garden of The Sanderson. 'Have you been to a spa or something? You look absolutely radiant.' He was looking as well-groomed as ever and as tanned.

'Ah, I knew there was a reason why I liked you so much!' Eden said, smiling at the shameless flattery and sitting down on the sofa next to him. 'It's all down to your divine but strict husband.' Even though she had only had a week of Rufus's fitness regime she could see that she was already starting to tone up. Cutting out most carbs had helped, along with not drinking, but she figured she was allowed a glass of champagne as a treat. Whatever Rufus said, she was sure it had fewer calories. She and Jez chatted away about what they had both been up to and, after a few minutes, Eden commented, 'God, I wish I could find a man as easy to talk to as you!'

'I'm afraid you just don't get that with the straight ones, honey, but you can *always* talk to me.'

'I'll be one in a long line of all your lady friends, won't I?' Eden joked. 'There will always be Angel and Crystal ahead of me in your affections. You'll never be my own gay best friend and mine alone!'

'Hey! There's room for all three of you.' He clapped his hands together. 'So, on to the important stuff . . . have you heard anything from Joel?'

She shook her head. 'I saw on his Facebook page that he was seeing someone else, so either he's a fast mover or he was seeing her all along.'

'Eden, you have got to stop that! Facebook stalking is the road to ruin and damnation and frown lines! Now I demand that you unfriend the little shit as soon as!'

'I will do. To be honest, I'm not so bothered about him any more. It sounds bad as we've only just broken up, but I think I knew the writing was on the wall for some time before it happened. I just didn't want to admit it. And actually, I've met someone else.' She paused, wondering if she should carry on.

'Someone else? Now who's the fast worker! Come on then, tell me everything. I'm a happily married man, I need excitement and thrills and I *demand* to know all the juicy details.' He winked. 'And don't worry, I'm a big boy. You can tell me *all* about it.'

Eden took a deep breath. She was anxious to make sense of what had happened, and needed someone else's perspective.

'Remember I told you about how I am going to be working with Jack Steele?'

'Sure. You said you didn't like him and didn't find him attractive at all.'

Eden winced but ploughed on with her revelation. 'It turns out I do find him attractive . . . so attractive that I very nearly ended up in bed with him, except for one thing – we were kissing and then he pulled away as if he couldn't bear to carry on.'

Jez's blue eyes widened. 'How extraordinary! And the kiss was good?'

'The kiss was completely amazing.' Eden almost got goosebumps thinking about it again. 'It might possibly have been the best kiss of my life. So why did he stop?' Suddenly she put a hand up to her face as she was struck by a mortifying thought. 'Oh my God! Do you think it was a bad kiss for him?' The levels of embarrassment just kept on going up.

Jez shook his head. 'I can't believe that you had such a great time and he didn't. I've no freaking idea why he gave you the brush-off because, I tell you, if I'd just had the best kiss of my life, I wouldn't be running away from the person responsible. Best kiss equals best sex, in my book.'

'Then what's the reason?' Eden said in frustration.

A shrug from Jez, then he attempted to joke. 'Maybe he has a really teeny tiny penis and didn't want you to find out.'

'It didn't feel teeny tiny,' Eden muttered into her champagne, and actually blushed at the memory.

'The man must have issues. Maybe it's best to steer clear of him, keep him at a distance.'

It was all very well Jez saying that, but how could she? They were going to be working together.

When Friday, the day of the studio session, arrived, it didn't help Eden's fragile emotional state that it was also the day that Joel's kiss and tell came out in the press. An early-morning phone call from Sadie alerted her. With a sinking feeling that had become only too familiar in the past two years, Eden logged on to her laptop and prepared herself for the worst.

There it all was: 'My six months of hell with selfish Eden. She acts like a spoilt princess and only ever wants things on her terms'; 'It's the world according to Eden Haywood, and no one else matters'; 'Eden used me because she can't bear to be alone'; 'Eden only ever wanted me for sex and to make her look good'; 'She didn't care about me and my feelings'; 'She wasn't interested in my career, only hers'; 'She's messed up, drinking too much, throwing her talent and her looks away'; 'She's insanely jealous'.

Every word was like a vicious stab. Had she been so horrible to Joel that he felt justified in wanting to hurt her like this? Was he exacting some kind of revenge? She knew that she hadn't ever really let him in emotionally and that she had been drinking too much when they were together. But surely she had done nothing to deserve such outright betrayal and character assassination? And if she had truly been that terrible to live with, why hadn't he said something at the time? He had certainly enjoyed the fame that he'd attracted by being her boyfriend. All the premieres and A-list parties that he'd been invited to as her plus one; all the gifts she had lavished on him; all the designer freebies he'd managed to blag for himself. He had acquired everything that went with a celebrity lifestyle. It was quite possible that he owed his entire success as a model to the fact that he had been her boyfriend.

After all, when she'd first met Joel he had been living in a grotty shared house in Uxbridge and working in Carphone Warehouse to support himself because he wasn't yet earning enough money as a model. Within two weeks he had left his job and moved into her luxury townhouse in one of the most exclusive areas of London. He had done very well indeed out of his connection with Eden Haywood. There was no mention of that, of course, in his story, nor of how she had bankrolled him for the last six months, and paid for his parents and sister to go on holiday, and how Joel had promised to pay her back but never had.

For a while she was gripped with a feeling of power-less rage, knowing that there was nothing she could do about the article. There was a grain of truth in some of the things he'd said . . . she had been drinking too much; she had been a bitch to him at times. But he had failed to see her insecurity and vulnerability.

Sadie rang, checking up on her, wanting to know that she was about to leave for the studio. 'I know that little shit's story is upsetting, but you've got to rise above it, darling,' her manager told her, sounding sympathetic but still focused. Studio time equalled money, Eden knew that and she would have to perform even though she felt shell-shocked, undermined and battered by Joel's story.

'I'm on my way, Sadie,' she said wearily.

Still, she thought bitterly as she got dressed, at least Joel's kiss and tell had temporarily stopped her from worrying about how she would cope with seeing Jack again. It was a small comfort. Outside it was a glorious sunny spring day, and the sky was a perfect optimistic bright blue. Eden would have preferred grey clouds and rain to fit her mood. She dressed entirely in black – black skinny jeans, a long-sleeved black tee-shirt embellished with a crystal love heart, black heels, black leather jacket and her black Dior shades. Rufus's hard-core workouts were definitely having an impact on her abs. The jeans fitted perfectly, not a muffin top in sight. She took her time over her make-up, needing to feel that she looked her best, subconsciously wanting Jack to see what he was missing. She felt as if she was putting on her armour, about to do battle with the world.

74

Before she even encountered Jack, she had to confront the paps who were circling outside her house like a pack of hungry hyenas. Well, fuck them if they thought they were going to get any shots of her looking devastated by Joel's story. She had nothing to hide, nothing to be ashamed of. She marched out of her front door, head held high. Instantly cameras started clicking away, and the paps began the ritual of shouting out her name and shoving into each other to get a better shot of her. But instead of being upset by the scrum, Eden smiled and waved. 'Hi, guys. I thought you would be round at Joel's place, seeing as how you love him so much. Oops, I forgot, he doesn't have a place, does he? He just lived off me.' A low blow but Joel deserved it.

'Eden – have you got a message for Joel?' one of the paps called out.

Another smile. 'Yeah, I have actually. How about this?' And she posed, hand on hip, while giving the middle finger. The cameras went wild. Eden let them take their pictures then said, 'That'll have to do, boys. I've got to get going now. So many models to see, so little time.' And she headed over to where Eddie was waiting in the blacked-out Merc to take her to the studio. But of course giving the paps what they wanted only made them greedier for more, and Eden was forced to battle her way through them to reach the car.

'Fucking hell!' she exclaimed as she got inside the car, slamming the door behind her. 'They really are like animals, aren't they? I've given them their shots, why can't they piss off!'

'Low-life and scum,' Eddie agreed as he pulled away, narrowly missing a pap who was still trying to get another picture. Eden was only surprised that there wasn't a pap clinging to the windscreen.

Chapter Five

By the time Eden arrived at the studio her kick-ass mood had deserted her and she was full of apprehension about seeing Jack again. She kept her dark glasses on as she swept into reception where Sadie was already waiting, sitting in her habitual cross-legged position on one of the electric-blue sofas, sipping a skinny latte and checking through one of her lists.

'Ah, you're here,' her manager exclaimed, standing up and gathering her things together. 'Come on, let's go through and get started. Jack's already in the studio.'

At the mention of his name, Eden's stomach performed a loop-the-loop of nerves.

'So are you okay?' Sadie asked as she picked up her coffee and headed out of reception.

'I'm fine. I'll just be glad when the day's over and the press have moved on to their next victim.'

Sadie reached out and rubbed Eden's shoulder. 'Remember what your mum always said: "Honey, in life it's not what happens to you, but how you react to it that matters. There's no crime in falling down – the shame is in not picking yourself up."' And just as Eden thought that she had finished the lecture, Sadie went on to add, 'I want you to promise me that you won't rush into a relationship with anyone new. This whole Joel thing should be a wake-up call to you. You've got to choose more wisely. Stop being seduced by any pretty face and hot set of abs!'

'I thought I had chosen wisely with Joel. I didn't know he would do the dirty on me like that!' Eden muttered defensively. 'Anyway, no one's going to want me now after reading what he had to say about me.'

Sadie smiled. 'Ah, cupcake, don't be silly. When we've finished re-launching you, you're going to have men queuing up. But until then, focus on the job.'

Focus was the word of the moment, Eden thought. She was only surprised that Sadie didn't get it printed on a tee-shirt. It was another F word entirely that was causing Eden not to focus – like fuck! She was about to come face to face with Jack.

They had reached the door leading into the studio. Through its glass panels Eden could see Jack sitting at the mixing desk, adjusting various faders. He was wearing a black tee-shirt that showed off his muscular arms. Her stomach did another loop, this time of lust as well as nerves. Oh, God! How was she going to be able to sing with him sitting in front of her! For a second she half thought of telling Sadie that she couldn't go through with it. But Sadie was already pushing open the heavy door.

'She's here on time, would you believe? Miracles can happen. So we can get started,' she declared.

Jack immediately stood up and kissed Sadie. Eden was standing behind them, feeling like a shy teenager. Then he moved over to her. 'Hey, Eden, good to see you.' And he lightly kissed her on each cheek. He didn't seem remotely affected by seeing her again, whereas Eden's heart was racing and she couldn't bring herself to look him in the eye. Pathetic! And just the scent of his rich, woody Tom Ford aftershave caused a chain reaction in her La Perla satin G-string. Double pathetic! This was the man who had rejected her.

'Can I get a coffee?' she asked. Her throat felt as dry as sandpaper.

'No vintage pink champagne, arrangement of white orchids, personal masseuse or bowl of M and Ms but only the blue ones?' Jack teased her. 'I know what you divas are like with your demands and riders.'

'Just coffee. Black,' Eden replied, sitting down on the leather sofa as far away as possible from him. She was in no mood for banter.

'Can you see what you're doing in those?' He pointed at her sunglasses.

God! Why wouldn't he leave her alone? 'I've got a bit of a headache, the glasses help,' she muttered. Now she forced herself to meet his gaze. He looked as good as she remembered, but his blue eyes gave absolutely nothing away. She could have been nothing but a distant acquaintance to him. As she looked at him a vivid kaleidoscope of images flashed through Eden's mind. She remembered what it had felt like to be kissing him: his smooth skin with its hint of stubble, the feel of his lips, the warmth of his body against hers. It was insane having to pretend that the kiss had never happened. And back to the question she couldn't get out of her head: why exactly had Jack pushed her away?

A pretty brunette PA wearing a minuscule pair of denim shorts, which would have been very revealing were it not for the black opaque tights she was wearing underneath, sauntered in with coffee. Eden noticed Jack smiling broadly at her. 'Hey, Cherry, how are you?' he asked.

'I'm good, Jack,' she replied. 'Like the hair.'

'Like the shorts!' he bantered back.

They seemed to know each other and Eden wondered if they were anything more than friends.

'Can I get you anything else, Eden?' Cherry asked politely.

'A bottle of water would be great, thanks.'

'Still or sparkling?' Cherry asked, just about managing to drag her eyes away from Jack.

'Still, ideally Evian, at room temperature.' She couldn't resist saying that.

'No problem.' Cherry sauntered out again, showing off her pert derrière. The shorts were *very* tight, and Eden had the bitchy thought that it would serve her right if she got thrush. She realised that she was jealous of Cherry for whatever relationship she had with Jack . . . God, could the day get any worse?

Jack then switched into work mode and played the first track, this time without the vocals, to get Eden into the right frame of mind for recording.

'How are you feeling about it now?' he asked.

'Better.' She wasn't going to tell him how much she loved it.

Then it was time to record the vocals. Eden always found it an incredibly intense experience when it was just her, the microphone and the music coming through her headphones. She had to reach deep inside herself for the feeling and passion. It was a time when she felt very exposed emotionally. There was no place to hide when you sang. She warmed up first, performing a series of singing exercises. Then, reluctantly, she took off her sunglasses as it was indeed too dark.

Jack was sitting directly in front of her behind a glass partition. She could see him talking to Sadie but couldn't hear them. She wondered what they were saying to each other. It was a situation guaranteed to heighten her feeling of insecurity and make her feel even more vulnerable. But then the opening bars of the music came through her headphones, and summoning all her strength, she closed her eyes, took a deep breath and began singing.

The first song, 'Only You', was all about an unrequited love; how she couldn't stop thinking about this man, that he was everywhere she looked, haunting her like a ghost. An ironic song for her to be singing, given what had happened between her and Jack. The song had a slower pace than she was used to, and much more feeling in it. It suited Eden's voice which had a slight catch in it, similar to the singer Adele's, immediately lending the song a richness and extra layer of feeling.

At first she was uncertain while she sang it, too self-conscious, too aware of Jack. When she'd finished, she looked over at Sadie and Jack. Her heart sank when she saw that they didn't seem terribly impressed.

'That was technically good,' Jack told her, 'but it's missing something, I feel as if you're holding back. You've really got to dive into it. No half measures. This isn't one of your disco anthems, Eden, you've got to feel this and the listener has to feel you feeling it.'

Eden wanted to come back with a wisecracking remark, but she knew he was right. 'Okay, I'll do it again. I want it to be perfect.'

They ended up being in the studio for five solid hours, doing take after take of the song. It was a gruelling, intense experience during which Eden felt as if she had been stripped bare emotionally. But by the end of the session she was quietly satisfied with what she had achieved. She felt that she had proved to herself and the others that if she worked hard at something she could succeed in it. She knew she had put her heart and soul into the music and it had been good work, the best she was capable of.

'You both deserve a treat,' Sadie told them as they

walked out together, 'I'm going to take you out for supper.'

'Oh, Sadie, I'm too knackered . . .' Eden started to make her excuses, but Sadie was having none of it. She hugged Eden as she said, 'You were so brilliant today! I'm proud of you, honey, especially after everything that's happened with Joel and the press.'

And so Eden found herself in a black cab heading towards Soho. She sat next to Sadie and Jack sat opposite, his long legs nearly brushing against hers. Eden looked out of the window at the London streets rushing by, to avoid those blue eyes of his. As they walked into a cosy Italian restaurant on Dean Street, Sadie playfully slapped Eden on the bum. 'Rufus's work-outs have definitely been hitting the spot, haven't they? You look in great shape, Eden. I'm so pleased you're seeing him.'

'Yeah, it's been going well,' she replied.

The waiter showed them to an intimate corner table, and Sadie went off to the Ladies.

'So who's this Rufus you're seeing?' Jack asked, as he sat down opposite her. Damn! Was she never going to get away from his gaze? 'I thought you'd only just finished with Joel. You're a quick worker.' He had clearly only caught the latter part of Sadie's comment.

His tone was casual though Eden was sure there was a slight edge to it. But like he was bothered who she saw! She had been trying so hard to play it cool during the day. Now tiredness and vulnerability made her emotions rise to the surface.

'What the fuck do you care?' she replied, more passionately than she had intended. 'You couldn't push me away fast enough after that party. You really know how to make a girl feel good about herself.' Great, now he was going to think that she was still interested in him. Bad move, Eden. She picked up her fork and began drawing circles in the thick cream tablecloth. When she glanced back at him, Jack looked awkward. 'Sorry, Eden, I didn't want to complicate things between us because we're working together. And you'd just come out of that relationship with Joel. I guess I got carried away. You're a very beautiful woman, hard to resist . . . I'm sure that's how Rufus feels too.'

There it was again, that edge to his voice. Their eyes met, each of them daring the other to speak. Eden was the first to lower her gaze. Seeing him again was so bitter-sweet that even though she was furious with him for what had happened, she longed to kiss him too.

'Let's not fall out,' Jack said, and actually stretched out his hand to touch hers. Eden wanted to slap him round the face! She was too angry to reflect that she herself had planned to have sex with him and then move on. She'd had no idea that Jack would have this effect on her.

Somehow she managed to rein in her emotions. Formally she shook hands with him. 'Deal,' she muttered.

'Great. I thought for a minute that you were going to stab me with that fork,' Jack joked. Eden didn't smile back.

Fortunately, Sadie returned from the bathroom, and everyone turned their attention to the menu and ordering. And from then on Sadie and Jack mainly chatted about people they knew in the industry, while Eden sipped her Pinot Grigio, put in the odd word every now and then when her silence became too obvious, and tried to avoid looking at Jack.

At the end of the meal Sadie had to dash off to meet her latest boyfriend whose band were playing at some club in Hoxton. Eden had to admire her manager's energy. She herself was exhausted, and a bath and crashing out in bed seemed the only option.

'So what are you doing now? Seeing Rufus?' Jack asked as they stood outside the restaurant. It was still warm and Soho was packed with people milling around outside pubs, standing drinking on the pavement, wanting to make the most of the spring night.

Eden considered telling him the truth, then thought better of it. Let him think that she had a new boyfriend. 'Not tonight.' And she wanted to ask what he was going to do now. Was he going to hook up with Cherry, the sexy PA? Or someone else? And why was she wasting her time thinking about him? It was a dead end, that was for sure.

A taxi was coming along Dean Street; Jack stepped out into the road and hailed it. As he opened the door for her he said, 'It was a good day, Eden. You worked hard. I've got a great feeling about this album. Take care of yourself and I'll see you soon.' And he closed the door.

He was so in control, so sure of himself, Eden felt like an emotional wreck by comparison. She sat back as the taxi pulled away, and stared moodily out of the window. Why had she complicated her life yet again by rushing into something? If only she hadn't kissed Jack! It was going to make everything about recording the album so much harder. Right now her life seemed littered with regrets. She had to get a grip, sort herself out. She was sick of feeling like this. She wanted to be in control again.

Music was the key. She would throw herself into making this work. Yes, it would be tough spending time with Jack, but with each new encounter it would get easier, she told herself. Just because the kiss had been so amazing, it didn't mean that there was anything else to Jack. She was obviously nothing to him and she had somehow to get herself into a place in her head where he was nothing to her.

Chapter Six

For the next two weeks Eden kept a low profile. 'One and Only' – the track they had recorded – was being mixed. There would be a play-back session before they recorded any more tracks, which would give everyone the chance to see where they were at style-wise and would ensure that they all felt they were going in the right direction. Sadie was frantically busy as Crystal had an album coming out and Eden heard nothing from Jack. The longer she didn't see him, the easier it should be to forget him, shouldn't it? And after all, it was just a kiss . . .

It was easy to say all these things over and over; unfortunately it wasn't so easy to believe them. Eden found herself thinking about him far more often than was healthy. And even though he could not have been clearer about how he felt about her, she would find herself fantasising that he had changed his mind; that he pursued her, confessed that it was all an act and that he wanted to be with her.

'It's good for you to be single!' Tanya told her when she came round for a girls' night in. Jez had popped round too in his capacity as her New Gay BF.

'Tanya's right, you need to work out what you really

want.' That was from him. The pair then high-fived each other for being on message.

'God, you two sound like a self-help DVD! Have you been rehearsing your speeches?' Eden exclaimed as they shared a pizza and a bottle of champagne. She had decided she was allowed pizza every now and then, having been so good the rest of the time. She had sworn Jez to secrecy, not wanting it to get back to Rufus as he would only make her pay for it big time at the gym. Pizza didn't figure in his supremely fit world. 'It's okay for you two, you're in happy relationships. You've forgotten what it's like being out there and single. It's brutal!'

Tanya took a slice of pepperoni pizza, daintily placed it on a napkin and said, 'Eden, you've been single for three or is it four weeks? I don't exactly call that being out there. When it's been six months, then I'll have some sympathy.'

'Any word from Jack?' Jez asked. He was on a strict no carbs diet and had brought round his own salade niçoise sans dressing, but the pizza was proving too tempting and he'd been unable to resist having a slice.

Eden shook her head. 'He's most likely shagging Miss Bum Cheeks.' Tanya and Jez looked confused. 'Cherry, the PA at the studio,' Eden elaborated. 'I think they might be seeing each other. They've probably been having non-stop sex for the last two weeks. But why do I even care what he does?' she exclaimed, getting up from the sofa and pacing round the room. 'It's pathetic! I'm never usually like this.'

Tanya and Jez exchanged glances; they had bonded very speedily.

'We've got a theory,' Tanya said.

'Oh, yeah?' Eden spun round and faced her friends, curious to find out what they had come up with.

'Yes, we think it's because you didn't get your own

way with Jack,' Jez explained. 'We think it's because you can't have him and you're used to getting what you want. And as a result you can't stop thinking about him.'

'So you think I'm some kind of spoilt brat? This from my friends? Thanks a bunch.' Eden knew she sounded petulant but couldn't help it. Were they right? Was her inability to stop thinking about Jack simply down to the fact that she hadn't got her own way with him? She wasn't so sure. He had got under her skin like no other man before.

'Well, I'm sure you would admit to being a little bit spoilt, wouldn't you?' Tanya said, chancing her luck.

'Well, if you're referring to my top-of-the-range BMW convertible, my diamond-studded Chanel watch, my Crème de la Mer skin cream and my Versace bed linen . . . then, yes, I am. And so I bloody well should be, I'm a fucking star!' Eden was joking now. She flopped back on the sofa. 'And pour me some more champagne, you minion – see, I'm such a star I can't even remember your name!' She held out her glass.

'Yes, m'lady,' Jez said, topping up her glass. 'Can I look at you while I do it? Or do I have to avoid eye contact at all costs?' he joked.

'You may look at me, just this once,' Eden conceded as if she was granting him a huge favour.

'Of course, the other reason that we came up with was that you had fallen in love with Jack.' This from Tanya. There was a pause while Eden almost choked on her champagne. 'But it couldn't be that, could it?' Tanya continued. 'Because you don't even find him attractive.'

Eden was gobsmacked, but then again . . . could she rule that out?

'No way! I just wanted to see his big, hard—'

Tanya interrupted, 'Personality?' and everyone giggled.

'Yeah, and his dick!'

'Bad girl!' Jez exclaimed. 'I like it!'

Spending a night laughing with her friends was like receiving a shot of pure happiness. But when they left Eden felt so alone once more. She stayed up late listening to the music for her album, immersing herself in it. Jack's lyrics were so heartfelt and his melodies so beautiful they made the hairs on the back of her neck stand up. But she couldn't work out Jack the man at all. He was an enigma. Maybe that was a big part of her attraction to him; she had been able to read each of her ex-boyfriends like a book . . . and an easy-to-read book at that.

The following morning, after yet another intensive session with Rufus at the gym, which must surely have worked off the pizza and champagne, Eden discovered a series of messages from Sadie on her mobile, all asking her to call urgently. Instantly she thought the worst. *Oh, shit! What had she done wrong this time and who was selling a story on her now?* The endorphin rush after the hard workout fizzled away. She felt she couldn't handle any more bad news and was sorely tempted not to return the call. Then, reluctantly, she selected Sadie's number.

'At last you ring!' she exclaimed.

'I've been in the gym all morning – you know, the place you practically ordered me to go to,' Eden replied, thinking that Sadie didn't sound cross, which was a good sign.

'I have got some amazing news! Amazing!' Now Sadie was practically shouting with excitement.

'Has Marc White offered me a new deal?' Eden asked hopefully. It would be so good if she knew she had her record deal in the bag; it would give her the security and stability that she badly needed.

'Not yet, but I am hopeful he will . . . especially after this! I've been in talks with Dallas. I didn't want to tell you until I knew for sure what was going to happen.'

Dallas – no one ever used his second name – was a music mogul, with his own record label and his own reality TV music series. It was called *Band Ambition* and was a highly successful *X Factor* rip-off, where groups competed to get a music deal with Dallas's label.

'And he wants you to be one of the judges on the show! Charlie,' Sadie named one of the judging panel, 'has had to pull out because of complications with her pregnancy. They're already halfway through the audition stages . . . and Dallas wants to replace her with you!'

Wow, someone actually wanted *her* – that made a change, Eden thought.

'What do you reckon? It's a brilliant opportunity. Look at what the *X Factor* did for Cheryl Cole's career. This couldn't have come at a better time. And it's a great deal financially – I can go through the contract when I see you. Dallas is a ruthless negotiator but I give as good as I get, and we've got great bargaining power because he *really* wants you. And you'll be starting filming next week.'

It really did seem too good to be true. And on top of the boost it was bound to give her career, Eden would be working so much she would have no time to think about anything else, no time to brood about Jack or about her sister who still hadn't replied to any of her emails.

'I say yes!' Eden told her. 'Yes, yes, yes!'

'Oh, Eden, you're on the rise again, baby! And there's also the great news that you'll still be able to work with Jack on your album as he's going to be working on the show too. I told Dallas how well you two worked together and he's agreed to take Jack on. I couldn't have wished for a more perfect situation.'

Fuck! 'He's not one of the judges, is he?' That really would be too much.

'No, no, he'll be working with the acts on their performances, helping with music selection, that kind of thing, but you'll get to see a lot of him.' Sadie said this as if it was a good thing. She might not have said it like that had she known what had happened between them. In fact, Eden was pretty sure that her manager would have been furious if she had known the truth.

'Dallas wants to meet you both ASAP and I've suggested we all go over to his office this afternoon. He's not a man to hang around once he's made up his mind.'

It seemed too cruel to Eden that the thrilling news of her new TV role should be overshadowed by Jack's presence. But maybe when she saw him again she would realise that she was completely over him. That he meant nothing to her at all.

Or not . . . as when she walked into Dallas's impressive top-floor, ultra-modern office with its stunning views across London, and saw Jack sitting on the sofa, Eden's heart did the racing, out-of-control thing. He'd been back to LA and was tanned from his trip, which made his blue eyes look even bluer. She tried to ignore her pounding heart and concentrate on charming Dallas, who was notoriously hard to please. It seemed to be working as he smiled at her when usually he put on the most inscrutable poker face which he had shamelessly modelled on Simon Cowell's.

'Eden, I'm so glad you're on board.' He stood up and greeted her with a kiss. He was casually dressed in a blue-and-white striped shirt and jeans, but the clothes looked designer. He smelt of expensive aftershave, the large rose-gold Rolex on his wrist probably cost the same amount as a one-bedroomed flat and his nails were in better shape than Eden's. Dallas took his personal grooming very seriously. He was bound to have a drawer in his office full of freshly laundered shirts.

'And, of course, you know Jack Steele.' Dallas gestured over at Jack, who raised his hand and said casually, 'Hey, Eden, how are you?'

So she didn't even get a kiss from him! 'Good, thanks, Jack. And you?' Two could play at that too-cool-for-school game.

'Never better.'

Sadie sat down in the leather armchair, leaving Eden no choice but to sit on the sofa with Jack. However, she made sure she sat as far away from him as possible, putting her pink Birkin bag between them like an expensive designer barrier. Dallas presided over all of them from behind his vast sleek black desk. He was a man who seemed to relish status and power. He was an American, a New Yorker, in his early-thirties, though he always seemed older because he was so driven and ruthlessly ambitious.

'We've been looking at the ratings of the show, and it has suffered a slight dip. There are so many other reality shows out there and we've got to raise our game. So we've decided to bring in some changes. For this series it's going to be as much about what happens behind the scenes as what happens in the studio. We're going to film the contestants in the houses they're staying in and we want to film the judges going about their own lives, so we'll have a much more complete picture of all the people involved. We want to give the audience a chance to really get to know everyone. If they invest more time in the show, they will really commit. And I want everyone involved to use social media, so judges and contestants will be expected to post tweets and to set up a Facebook page.'

Shit! Did this mean Eden would have to allow the cameras into her house? She wasn't at all sure she wanted that level of attention.

As if sensing Eden's unease, Sadie looked over at her. 'They will only be filming you when you're backstage or working on your album with Jack. It's not like they'll be in your house or anything. It's perfect timing for your new album, Eden. It's going to generate great publicity.'

Eden still wasn't sure; she couldn't help feeling wary about exposing so much of her life to the cameras. She'd had such a rough ride in the press these last two years, her instinct was to protect her privacy as much as she could.

'And it's a chance for the public to get to know the real you, Eden. We all know that so much crap has been written about you lately, wouldn't it be good to set the record straight?' This from Dallas, who, naturally, was a very persuasive talker. 'We only want to show you in a good light, I promise. And if you're not happy with Marc White's album deal, I'd be only too happy to sign you up. You're a big star, Eden. It's your time to shine again.' He smiled as if sealing the deal, showing off his perfect American teeth.

Still Eden hesitated, but then she gave in. The truth was she didn't have any other options, and this could well turn out to be a boost to her profile and win her the new album deal that she so longed for.

'Okay, I'm up for it.' She sounded way more confident than she felt.

'Great!' Sadie declared and was backed up by Dallas. Eden couldn't help noticing that Jack had been silent during this exchange. Maybe he had reservations about being filmed with her?

*

Sadie and Dallas went on to talk about the show and about the third judge. In the past Sadie had been one of the judges herself. This series the line-up was Eden, Dallas, Ricky Vincent, who had managed two very successful boy bands, and Amber Gardiner, who had been in a girl band in the early-noughties. Eden groaned inside when they mentioned her name. She knew that Amber was no fan of hers. And so did Sadie – she had been careful to avoid mentioning that fact when she sold the project to Eden. She must have known that Eden would not be happy about working alongside Amber.

After Terri had died and Eden had gone off the rails so spectacularly, Amber had slammed her in the press and been quoted as saying how totally irresponsible she thought Eden was; how it was wrong to set such a bad example to her many young fans, that Eden needed to take control of her life and stop wasting her talent. Eden had not appreciated her comments and, instead of staying silent as Sadie had urged, had retaliated by calling Amber a washed-up old has-been, who looked like she needed to eat something once in a while. Amber had hit back by saying that Eden could do with losing weight . . .

No doubt the media-savvy Dallas was relishing the prospect of his two female judges not getting on, as nothing upped the ratings like a good old bitch fest. And hadn't there been rumours that he and Amber had had an affair? He was bound to take her side. What had Eden let herself in for?

Dallas looked over at her. 'Oh, and Amber says hi by the way. She's really looking forward to working with you. I know you guys had a bit of a fall out, but that's all water under the bridge now, isn't it?'

Eden shrugged. 'I guess.' Suddenly she felt the need to assert some kind of control – at the moment it felt as if Dallas and Sadie held all the cards and simply expected her to roll over, say yes sir, no sir, three bags full sir, and be grateful. 'There's just one thing . . . I need to have my own team around me – I want my own hairdresser and make-up artist.'

Dallas began to say that the idea was that she would share make-up artist and hairstylist with Amber, but Eden held up her hand.

'It's non-negotiable, Dallas, I have to have my team. And I don't want them doing anyone else's hair or make-up.'

Yes! She was channelling her inner diva and loving it! Out of the corner of her eye she noticed Jack raise his eyebrow as if to say he had known all along what she was like.

Reluctantly Dallas agreed to her demand. Eden was only surprised he didn't try and deduct the cost from her fee.

'And of course it goes without saying, Eden, that you have to keep your side of the deal by not getting into any, what we might call, "scrapes".' Dallas had to have the last word. No doubt he was referring to the nightclub incident. 'Sadie assures me you have your drinking under control. And there is a clause in the contract that if anything should go wrong . . .' He left a meaningful pause. 'Well, I don't have to say any more, do I? *Band Ambition* is above all a family show.'

Eden rolled her eyes. 'Dallas, I don't have a problem with drink. I admit, I went off the rails a couple of years ago, but that was then and this is now.'

After the meeting, Sadie hung back to talk to Dallas, no doubt to tussle over the fine detail of the contract, leaving Eden and Jack to exit the office together. He didn't say a word until they both got into the lift.

'Are you sure about signing up for this, Eden? You

seemed a little uncertain in the meeting.' Jack didn't beat around the bush with small talk, did he?

'I was until Dallas mentioned Amber – she really hates me. It's bollocks Dallas saying that she can't wait to meet me. She'll be dying to stick the knife in.' Eden paused and looked over at him, leaning against the tinted mirrored wall. As always he seemed so self-assured and confident. How she envied him that. She wondered if anything ever got to him. She fiddled with her white-gold Tiffany bangles. 'Still, I'm used to people not being that nice to me. And I give as good as I get.' Again she put on her self-confident act.

She was totally wrong-footed by his next move. He reached out a hand and lightly touched her forehead. 'The bruise has gone, I see. You look well, Eden.' They both gazed at each other and Eden felt the butterfly rush to her stomach intensified by the lift's descent. She actually felt quite giddy. 'You shouldn't do anything you don't want to,' he said. 'I reckon you will still get the album deal and your album will be a big success even if you don't do the show. I've heard "One and Only" and it sounds fantastic. Even better than I could have hoped.'

Wow, a compliment from Jack Steele! 'Thanks,' Eden said quietly, thrilled by the comment. She was pretty certain Jack didn't go around saying things he didn't mean. Who knows what he might have said next, but at that moment the lift doors opened on to the lobby and as the pair of them stepped out Eden noticed a pretty woman who seemed familiar hovering by the reception desk. As soon as she saw Jack she rushed over, the heels of her high red sandals click-clacking loudly on the marble floor.

'How did it go, Jack? Are you going to do it?' she asked breathlessly as soon as she reached him.

Eden couldn't help staring as she recognised Cherry

from the studio session, this time in a cute red mini-dress. So Jack *was* seeing her! What did Miss Bum Cheeks have that Eden didn't? Apart from a particularly pert rear!

'See you, Jack,' said Eden coolly and started walking swiftly towards the door, anxious now to get away from him. Putting distance between them seemed like the only way for her to stay calm. She was damned if she was going to hang around and be a spectator on their loved-up reunion.

'Yeah, see you, Eden. And remember what I said,' Jack called after her.

But Eden had already pushed open the heavy glass door, thinking bitterly that he was the very last person whose advice she would act on.

Chapter Seven

'Hiya, Eden! So good to see you!' Amber Gardiner breezed into Eden's dressing room just as she was getting ready for the first recording. It was also the first time the two women had come face to face, and it was an encounter that Eden had not been looking forward to. She stood up and braced herself for the air-kissing ritual, which Amber duly performed.

'Good to see you,' Eden somehow managed to get out, though in reality as soon as she saw Amber she remembered all the many reasons why she couldn't stand the silly cow – her simpering smile, her teeny tiny size zero body, the fact that she was so two-faced!

'You look fantastic, Eden!' Amber carried on gushing. 'Have you lost weight?'

Amber knew perfectly well that Eden had because as soon as the press got wind of the fact that she was going to be a judge on the show they had reported on her recent transformation. Sadie and Dallas had put out a press release detailing how Eden was getting her life back on track, how she was working hard on her album, looking forward to being a judge and nurturing new talent; how she had overhauled her body, was working out, and had cut out the booze; how she saw *Band Ambition* as a chance to show the British public the *real* Eden, blah blah blah. It frankly made her want to puke when she read it. But that was show business . . .

'Yep, I have. And you look gorgeous, Amber. Then again, you always do. But you're lucky, it's my wild artistic streak that makes me drink and do bad things. But you don't have that, do you?'

Eden said it so sweetly that Amber couldn't be sure if she was taking the piss. The simpering smile faded briefly as she replied in all seriousness, 'I am very artistic. And I have battled demons of my own.'

Eden just smiled and shook back her hair. She was tempted to reply, 'Oh, yeah, what demons exactly? Whether to have a third rice cake or a carrot? Or whether to watch *X Factor* or *Strictly Come Dancing*? Instead she went for, 'Amber, I need some space now to prepare myself for the show, if that's okay? I have to centre myself and clear my head of all distractions. I want to give this recording a hundred and twenty percent.'

Again Amber looked unsure whether Eden was joking or not, but as Eden managed to keep a straight face, Amber smiled uncertainly and said, 'Okay then, see you later.'

Eden waited until Amber had sashayed her teeny tiny bum out of the room before she turned to Jez, who had paused mid-hair straightening, and they burst out laughing. Jez held up his hand and Eden high-fived him.

'The bitch is back!' she declared. 'The game is on.'

'Eden, you are so going to have that girl for breakfast!' Jez said. 'When you told me she was annoying, I thought you might be exaggerating. But she is off-the-scale annoying!'

'Do you swear never to do her hair?' Eden joked.

'I do solemnly swear, on these my top-of-the-range GHDs, that I will never do Amber Gardiner's hair, so help me God!' Jez bantered back in a very bad American accent.

'Don't you just want to take one of her skinny little wrists and give her a Chinese burn? Or kidnap her Chihuahua or whatever cutesie dog she has and make her cry? Or force-feed her Krispy Kreme doughnuts so she puts on an ounce.'

'Physical violence and threats to animals are never a good idea, Miss Haywood. We could, however, work on the doughnut routine,' Jez deadpanned. 'But, hey, Eden, you mustn't say those naughty wicked things when you're on TV or the audience won't like you. You must be good Eden. The caring, sharing, tell me your problems, I'm your friend, I understand where you're coming from Eden. If you must, channel Cheryl "are you alreet, pet" Cole.'

'Screw that!' Eden came back. 'I know for sure that Dallas wants me to play the baddie. I'm the Wicked Witch and Amber is Snow White. You can see that in the way we're dressed and styled.'

Sure enough Eden was in a tightly fitted purple satin mini-dress, which flaunted her curves, while Amber was in a sweet cream-coloured floaty number, which made her look as if she was off to a prom.

'Oh, babe, you are the fairest one in the mirror! I swear.'

Eden pointed at him, and cackled, 'Are you sure, my pretty?'

'Don't cackle either, it's ageing and *so* Sharon Osbourne.'

Eden sighed and snapped out of the banter. 'Actually, Jez, I'm really nervous. What if the audience hate me? I don't want to be hated.'

'They'll love you! Come on, you'll be brilliant!'

And then there was no more time for reassurance as Eden was called to the auditorium, where she took her place next to Dallas, who sat at the centre of the table, in front of the audience, like the King presiding over his subjects. He was in his show persona which meant he barely said a word; Ricky was smarmy and had a good old leer at Eden; Amber gave one of her simpering smiles. That smile was *really* going to get on Eden's nerves.

Eden had set out wanting to be positive about the acts, but after the first group – a boy band from Wolver-hampton – had murdered one of her favourite songs, the Beatles' 'Let it Be', she realised straight talking was the only way she would come out of this with her sanity intact. She just didn't have it in her to pretend that the boys were any good. The four lads looked about fifteen, but that in Eden's opinion was no excuse. She had been performing from the age of ten; if you couldn't take the heat then you got out of the kitchen. And you certainly did not stand up in front of millions and inflict your tone-deaf vocals on the world!

Amber gushed about how brave they were for choosing that number. Cheers from the audience, a sizeable proportion of which seemed to be made up of members of the boys' families; Ricky said he thought they needed to work a little harder on their harmonies – there were some boos in the cheers that followed. And then it was Eden.

'Boys, I'm going to tell it like it is so you don't waste any more time. That was possibly one of the worst performances I've ever heard. Get back to school and get on with your GCSEs because your journey is going to end right here.'

Deafening boos erupted. The lads looked as if they might actually cry. Amber smiled slyly, clearly hoping to capitalise on Eden's unpopularity.

Dallas struggled to make himself heard as he put up

his hand. Eventually he managed to get the audience to calm down. 'Okay, decision time. Yes or no. Amber?'

'I think the boys were really brave,' she started to say again, but Dallas cut across her. 'Yes or no is all I require.'

Amber shifted awkwardly in her seat. 'I'm so sorry, boys, I think it might have to be no.' Amber looked as if *she* might blub when boos broke out again.

'Sorry, lads,' from Ricky.

And Eden simply gave the thumbs down. Less is more, she decided. It took fifteen minutes to calm the audience after that. Some members who were related to the band had to be escorted out by security. All of which, Eden thought, would be good for ratings, and so wouldn't bother Dallas one little bit.

After that came three more bands, all equally as dire as the first. Eden continued to be the most straight talking, Amber tried to please everyone, and Ricky tried to be cool. By the end of the recording Eden had a splitting headache and doubts about whether she ever should have signed up. At this rate she was going to finish up as a hate figure. She would probably have to hire a bodyguard to protect her from all the angry rejects who would be after her blood, for shattering their dreams and ending their 'journey'. But to her surprise when she had escaped to the dressing room and kicked off the purple satin court shoes that were killing her, Dallas knocked on the door and came in.

'Eden, that was perfect,' he told her. 'Just keep doing what you're doing. You're like a breath of fresh air . . . I love it!' And he actually went so far as to give her a kiss.

'Teacher's pet!' Jez exclaimed once Dallas had swept out again in a cloud of citrus-scented aftershave.

'Yeah,' Eden said grimly, peeling off a false eyelash. 'Dallas is the only one who does like me, though. I think

I should be worried – he's got ice water running through his veins. And I'm not sure if he's got a heart at all. He probably only puts it in for special occasions.'

Jez was about to reply when there was another knock on the door and Jack strode in. Immediately Eden felt self-conscious. She hadn't even realised that he was at the recording.

'I just wanted to check you are okay for tomorrow,' he said, somehow seeming to fill the room with his presence and make the tiny dressing room appear even smaller. She and Jack were supposed to be in the studio then, recording another of the tracks for the album, and Eden was also going to be interviewed for the TV series.

'I'm good to go,' she lied. In fact she had butterflies just thinking about the combination of spending time with Jack *and* being filmed while she sang. Sure, she was used to making music videos and being interviewed when she was promoting an album, but this felt altogether more personal and she would be revealing more of herself, which had clearly been Dallas's intention.

'Cool. Well, I'll see you there.' He was about to go when he added, 'I agree that it's wrong to raise people's hopes when they have no talent, but did you have to be quite so brutal, Eden? Those contestants were so young; you could have broken the news to them more gently. They were devastated by your comments.'

Like she needed this criticism! Insecurity always made her seem blasé so she just shrugged. 'I tell it like it is, Jack. Sometimes you need to be cruel to be kind. And the quicker those boys stop wasting their time and everyone else's, the better.'

He seemed disappointed by her tough reply and muttered, 'Okay, I'll bear that in mind when we're recording tomorrow. See you, Eden.' And he was gone.

Eden instantly turned and looked at Jez, needing reassurance that she had done the right thing in being so direct. He smiled at her and said, 'You were great, really. It had to be said. Amber sounded so insincere. People will respect you more for being honest. But you just might want to take off the other false eyelashes. It's not such a great look for you, honey.'

Eden took an appalled look at herself in the mirror. FFS! Jack had seen her looking like a complete idiot. There was only one way to deal with the day she'd had. Forget about her resolution not to drink. She needed alcohol. Right now. She invited Jez and Rufus to the house along with Tanya and Tyler. Half a bottle of wine later, and with no supper, Eden was thinking all might be well with her world again. She ignored Rufus's disapproving looks and remark that he would be working her extra hard next time they were in the gym. A further glass and the spinny head feeling said that this had not been a good idea. Tanya ended up putting her to bed, with a large glass of water and two Ibuprofen.

And so it was that a hungover Eden rolled up for the studio session an hour and a half late, causing huge stress to the production team. The budget for the series was very tight and practically every second of their time was accounted for. Eden's late arrival would have repercussions for the rest of their day.

Jack barely looked at her when she walked in. He was clearly furious, though he was going to stay cool for the cameras. Eden just hated that. She couldn't bear it when people were quiet and moody with her, she would much rather they shouted and that everything was out in the open.

She responded by being the Eden she had been at the recording the day before; she was offhand with Jack, she didn't take his direction, she was playing the diva. Cherry came in with drinks at one point, which did nothing to improve Eden's mood. The silly cow just wants to get her face on TV . . . or her arse, she thought, as Cherry handed out cups of coffee to the crew during a break. Cherry chatted and smiled away to everyone, generally being the polar opposite to Eden who sat on the leather sofa, staring moodily at her emails.

'Can we get on now?' she cut across the chatter. 'And can everyone else except crew leave the room.' She added a reluctant, 'Please.' The sight of Jack's girlfriend cosying up to everyone was infuriating her. She herself got up and made to return to the recording booth, but Jack had other ideas. He took her arm.

'Eden, I need to talk to you for a minute. Can we go outside?'

She was about to retort that he could say whatever he wanted to say there, but the determined look in his eye made her change her mind and she followed him to the small patio at the back of the building, which everyone used for sneaky fag breaks but which was empty now.

Jack closed the back door and faced her. 'Why the hell are you being like this?'

'Like what?' she shot back, knowing perfectly well what he meant.

'So defensive and hard to direct.' He shook his head. 'This is not what I signed up for, Eden. We're supposed to be a team, working on your album. I'm not some fucking lackey you can disregard, ignore and generally treat like shit! I don't care if that's how you treat other people. That is not how you are going to treat *me*.'

Eden wanted to come back with a scathing reply, but she felt hurt and put on the spot. She wasn't good at dealing with this kind of situation. She could feel tears spring into her eyes. If only Jack knew how vulnerable and insecure she felt. How he had made her feel so rejected after their kiss. How it was taking every ounce of her strength to stand here, acting so defiant, as if she couldn't care less.

She hung her head so he wouldn't see the tears. 'I'm sorry, Jack, I'm really hungover – please don't tell Sadie. I found yesterday so stressful, I guess I lost it a bit last night.'

He frowned. 'I won't tell Sadie, on condition you come back to the studio now and give it your all.' He shook his head. 'And I'm still not sure about how you're being on the show. You're not a mean person, but the public will think you are. And you know how hard it is to change people's perceptions once they've made up their minds.'

Just like you thought I was only worth one kiss? Eden thought bitterly. 'I'm fine, Jack, there's no need to worry about me. Come on, we'd better get back. I don't want to keep the crew waiting any longer.'

And with that she marched back into the studio and sang her heart out for the next two hours until finally Jack was happy with what she had done.

The rest of the week was taken up with filming more of the auditions. By Friday Eden had only voted to put one group through to the next round. Her reputation as the straight talker was signed and sealed, and Dallas was going to exploit it for everything he had to get attention-grabbing TV. He was already planning trailers for the series that had Eden dressed up in a black leather jacket and leather pencil skirt while Amber was in a white evening dress. His symbolism could not be any more obvious, Eden thought. She didn't know why he didn't just go the whole hog and give her devil's horns, a forked tail and a whip! Oh, well, she thought, as the final group of the day took their places on stage, may as well live up to my reputation.

She put her head on one side and adopted a bored expression as they sorted themselves out. Yet another boy band, she thought, big yawn. What song were they going to massacre? But then her attention was taken by the lead singer, who came to the front of the stage to address the judges. He was absolutely gorgeous and blessed with the kind of looks that Eden adored. He was boyishly handsome, with spiky dark-blond hair, deep brown eyes, a devilishly cheeky smile, and a kind of cocky swagger about him that she found irresistible.

'So who are you?' Dallas said coolly.

'I'm Stevie and we're Rapture. And I reckon you're going to love us.' He had a South London accent that just added to his bad-boy charm. As he said it he looked straight over at Eden and flashed her a very cheeky smile. Eden found herself smiling back, until she remembered that she was supposed to be the über-bitch and switched back to looking bored.

'And how old are you?' Dallas asked.

'We're all twenty-two,' Stevie replied.

And then the music started and Eden found herself listening intently and watching Stevie. While the other two members of the group were okay – hell, they could even sing in tune – Stevie was outstanding. He had the natural charisma of a born lead singer, arrogant, sexy, in control, plus he was a brilliant dancer. Eden liked his style very much. As did the audience. Rapture were easily the best band they had heard and seen.

Amber was first to give her comments, and didn't hold back in her gushing compliments to the boys on their performance; she was followed by Ricky who matched her enthusiasm. And then it was Eden. Stevie and the boys were gazing imploringly at her; Stevie actually clasped his hands together as if praying. He really was *very* cute.

'I can't believe what I've just heard,' Eden started off, sounding as if she was underwhelmed. She had to play with them a little, her role of über-bitch demanded it. There was an audible intake of breath from the

105

audience who had heard her savaging the three previous bands; surely she wasn't going to dole out the same treatment to Rapture?

Stevie bit his lip, and shoved his hands in his jeans pockets. The cocky expression had gone and he looked anxious. The air of vulnerability only made him more gorgeous.

Eden left as long a pause as she dared before continuing, 'I'm impressed for the first time all week, boys. It's a yes from me!'

The audience erupted into cheers and wolf whistles. The boys from Rapture jumped around hugging each other. Stevie blew a kiss directly at Eden, which made the audience cheer even louder. And for the first time since she'd started on the show, Eden found that she had actually enjoyed herself.

She was still smiling as she made her way to her dressing room once they had finished recording. She nearly bumped into Jack who was coming the other way. 'He's not as good as he thinks he is,' he said.

'Who?' Eden replied.

'That pretty-boy singer you just put through. He was flat in at least three places.'

'Well, it's nothing that I can't work on with him when I get to look after the group.' Eden was determined that she would be Rapture's mentor. 'I think he's got so much potential.'

'Good luck. I reckon you'll need it. He doesn't look like the type to take direction well. Too busy thinking he's the real deal, when the truth is he's just a slightly above average singer with good looks.'

She didn't know why Jack was being so moody. 'Whatever. At least he's easy on the eye.' And Eden swept into her dressing room.

Chapter Eight

It was her sister's birthday on Saturday. Eden had been dreading the day all week, knowing what painful emotions it would arouse in her. She had sent Savannah a present and a card, and fully expected to have them sent back to her. Still, that hadn't stopped her taking ages choosing Savannah's gift – a Tiffany dove pendant, in rose gold and diamonds – and she was hoping that her sister would see the dove as a peace offering and a chance of reconciliation.

For the last two years Eden had handled Savannah's birthday by going out and getting spectacularly drunk, but this year she wanted things to be different so she arranged to have a training session with Rufus in the morning and then spent the afternoon with Tanya, who was on a detox so there was no danger of any alcohol. The evening was going to be difficult, though, because Sadie was throwing a massive party at her house in Primrose Hill to celebrate twenty-five years in the music industry. There was no way that Eden could be a no show at such a significant event for her manager.

As luck would have it the first person she saw when she walked through Sadie's front door was Jack. Sometimes Eden felt that there was someone sitting up there, pulling the strings like a sadistic puppet master, determined to make her life as difficult as possible. Jack walked over to her and kissed her in greeting, and as a waiter went by he reached for a glass of champagne and was about to hand it to her when Eden stopped him.

'Actually I'm not drinking tonight.' Instead she picked up a glass of mineral water.

'That's restrained of you,' Jack commented, taking a glass of champagne himself, 'I would have thought you would want to kick back after this week. It's been full on.'

'Yep. Dallas is definitely getting his money's worth from me,' Eden replied, thinking how very good Jack looked in his black shirt and black jeans. No, she must not think this. Absolutely must not. 'Any idea where Sadie is? I should say hi.' She needed to make a quick getaway, knowing only too well the impact talking to Jack had on her self-esteem. Any second now she would be remembering that kiss and the mortifying moment when he'd pulled away . . .

'She's in the living room, hugging everyone and telling them how much she loves them, *darling*.' Jack imitated the way Sadie said darling to a T.

'Sounds like Sadie,' Eden said dryly.

'She adores you, doesn't she? I think she sees herself as your surrogate mum,' came the unexpected reply. He looked straight at her, but Eden couldn't meet his eye.

'Well, I guess after my mum died Sadie took it on herself to look after me. She's certainly as straight talking as Mum was, and she never lets me get away with anything.'

'And what about your dad?'

God! Why was Jack asking all these questions? She almost preferred it when he was criticising her.

'I never knew him; he died when I was six months

108

old. He had some heart problem no one knew about and one day in the office he had a heart attack and died. He was only forty.'

Jack looked at her sympathetically. 'Tough for you.'

Eden shrugged. 'Tougher for my mum, who had two kids under five to bring up on her own. As for me, I don't think you miss what you've never had.' She didn't mean that at all, it was one of the greatest regrets in her life that she had never known her father, but she was longing to get away now. She didn't handle personal questions like this at all well.

'So are you close to your brother or sister?'

Was he never going to stop! 'I don't see as much of my sister Savannah as I'd like to. She lives in the States.' Eden had to change the subject and fast. 'So where's your girlfriend? It's Cherry, isn't it?' She resisted saying 'Miss Bum Cheeks'.

It was Jack's turn to look put on the spot. 'She's coming in a little while. And I wouldn't say that she was my girlfriend exactly, we're more good friends.'

'Ah – you're so easy come, easy go, Jack,' Eden said, slightly sarcastically. She was pretty sure that Cherry saw herself as his girlfriend.

He stared at her, looking rattled. 'A bit like you then, Eden. First Joel, then Rufus, I wonder who will be next? You sure get through them.'

'I do, don't I? But to set the record straight, Rufus is my gay personal trainer, so I'm not as bad as you think I am,' Eden bantered back, wondering why Jack sounded so hostile. 'Anyway, I'm going to see the party girl.'

Thankfully Eden spent the next couple of hours with people who didn't want to give her a hard time about her personal life, and she had a giggle with Jez and Rufus, and Travis, Sadie's twenty-two-year-old boy-friend. But all the time she was aware of Jack's presence, like a beat she couldn't get out of her head. She observed Cherry's arrival, saw her throw her arms delightedly round Jack and then cling to his arm, as if she couldn't bear to let go of him. Cherry certainly didn't seem to see him as purely a friend; she had 'girlfriend' written all over her. Eden almost felt sorry for her. Almost. She couldn't resist looking over at Jack, and several times he caught her gaze and each time Eden vowed she wouldn't do it again, but then she would find herself sneaking another glance.

'I think he likes you,' Jez whispered after he had twigged what had been going on. 'He's giving you *the look*. The one that says, "I want you in spite of myself, Goddamit!"'

'No way!' Eden replied. 'He's probably just finding something else to disapprove of.' But she felt a flicker of excitement at Jez's comment. A flicker which was rapidly extinguished when Jack and Cherry left the party hand in hand.

On Monday morning Eden was woken first thing by a Special Delivery – Savannah had sent back the unopened birthday present. Had ever Return to Sender felt as sad as this? Eden shoved the parcel into the back of one of her wardrobes, along with all the other returned presents. She probably should have taken it back to Tiffany's but the prospect made her feel even more depressed.

It was a relief to go to the studio and get ready for another round of auditions. For once Eden was glad Dallas was such a slave driver and wanted the auditions to be filmed and edited as soon as possible; it meant she didn't have time to think, and that was exactly what she needed. Jack was busy working on material for the groups and she didn't see him, which was fine by her.

Eden continued to attract press attention with her role as judge. The papers tried to drag up the falling out between her and Amber and predicted that it wouldn't be long before the girls fell out again. And it seemed that Joel still felt he hadn't got quite enough mileage out of their relationship as he sold yet another story, this time revealing that he had found love again with Bliss. There was a photograph of the pair of them, holding hands as they strolled around St James's Park, which raised a bitter smile from Eden when she realised that the Dolce & Gabbana jacket Joel was wearing had been a gift from her, along with the diamond Theo Fennell skull pendant round his neck.

Joel talked about how much he and Bliss loved and trusted each other. How it was early days but they felt this was right; how she had made him feel that he could fall in love again; how gentle and loving she was. How he had thought he would never be able to open up again in a relationship after the difficult time he'd had with Eden; how she had made him feel so insecure, but Bliss had healed him. Still, he wished Eden well and hoped that she found happiness.

She was reading the article as Jez attempted to straighten her hair – 'attempted' being the word as by then Eden was almost jumping out of her seat in fury.

'Eden, you have got to sit still, sweetie! Or I am going to inflict some serious damage on your hair or your face,' Jez exclaimed, waving the straighteners around to get her attention.

'I wish you could inflict some damage on Joel! Permanently. What a shit! I thought he'd sunk to the lowest of the low with his last story, but it seems there's plenty more where that came from.'

There was a knock on the door and Amber walked in. She certainly knew how to pick her moments.

'Hiya, Eden, I just wanted to see if you were okay. I

read Joel's story. It must be *so* tough for you. But that's life in the public eye, isn't it?'

Amber did not look in the least concerned for Eden's well-being; rather there was an eager glint in her own eyes. The little witch was relishing Eden's discomfort!

'I'm fine, thanks, Amber. I've always believed that there's only one thing worse than being talked about, and that's not being talked about. I'm a survivor and I'm not going to let a little shit like Joel or anyone else bring me down.'

'Good for you, Eden,' Amber replied insincerely. 'Well, I'll see you out there.'

After she had gone, Eden exploded, 'Do you think I could get the silly cow banned from my dressing room! She totally gets on my tits! She's a stick insect who can't even sing very well! I bet she's only here because she had a fling with Dallas.'

'Forget about her, Eden, she's not worth bothering about. You're A-list, she's way down there on the food chain, probably only G slash H,' Jez attempted to soothe her.

But it wasn't easy; she felt too wound up by the morning's events. She was just about to head off to the studio when there was another knock on her door. 'What now?' she exclaimed.

A young woman Eden recognised as one of the make-up artists who worked with the contestants popped her head round the door. 'Hi, Eden, sorry to bother you, but I was asked to deliver this to you.' She handed over an envelope.

Eden thanked her and then tentatively opened it – knowing that with her luck it would be a death threat. Its contents took her by surprise.

Eden, I just wanted to say that meeting you has been one of the highlights of my life. I know how corny that sounds but it's true! I really hope that you get to mentor our group. I respect you so much.

Steviex

P.S. and you are even more beautiful in real life . . . XX

P.P.S. I know I shouldn't be sending this to you, but I just had to let you know how I felt.

'What do you think of this?' Eden asked Jez as she passed him the note.

He quickly scanned it, and said, 'Saucy boy! He's got a hell of a nerve. But I can't fault his taste.'

'Well, at least it wasn't someone dissing me, which makes a change,' Eden replied casually, feeling secretly flattered. Stevie was so good-looking it gave her a real confidence boost to know that he had singled her out for praise. But then she exclaimed, 'Oh my God! Do you think he sent a note like that to Amber as well?'

Jez shrugged. 'I'm not underestimating your considerable charms, but it's entirely possible. He's in it to win it.'

Eden immediately scrunched the letter up and threw it in the bin. 'I've a good mind to report him to Dallas,' she joked, though she had no intention of doing so. Stevie was one of the few people who made the competition bearable.

Another week of auditions went by. Eden continued to be the most honest of the judges and the press continued to play her off against Amber, especially since Amber had recently got engaged to Piers, her long-term boyfriend. So it was all bad-girl, single Eden pitted against blushing bride-to-be Amber. The week was so full on that it was hard getting time to work on her album with Jack. Instead of having one entire day devoted to the studio session, which Dallas had promised them, they ended up with one night after Eden had finished recording the auditions.

Jack was not happy when she turned up at eight o'clock, clearly exhausted. 'Sadie shouldn't have agreed for you to sign up for the show. It's vital we get this album right. The show is just a distraction from that,' he grumbled.

'Sadie is a realist. I need all the publicity I can get,' Eden replied. She slumped on to the sofa. She was worn out and felt as if she was coming down with a sore throat. In fact, she was so tired that she didn't have the usual attack of the butterflies at being around Jack.

'Your music should be what people know about you, not being a judge on a reality show. There's more to you than that. It's too much like a pantomime, Eden, and you're an artist.'

'Yeah, well, thanks, Jack. But I don't think beggars can be choosers. Shall we get started?'

In the recording booth Eden rehearsed one of the slowest numbers on the album, 'Want', a ballad about an all-consuming love. It was strange, she thought once again, that Jack was able to write such exquisite love songs and yet seemed to be so personally detached from love. Did he write from experience? Had someone broken his heart? Or was he just a brilliant writer?

Then she forced herself to stop thinking, to lose herself in the music. And now, late in the evening, when she was tired, when her defences were down, she delivered the most heartfelt performance she had so far on the album. When she had finished, she looked over at Jack, who was smiling.

'I'm going to make all those *Band Ambition* wannabes listen to that, whenever they're struggling to put feeling into their music. That was perfect, Eden.'

'It's easy with such a great song,' she said quietly, and the moment seemed suddenly charged as if the emotion from the song had spilled out into the room. For a second they held each other's gaze. Eden was the first to look away. She stumbled slightly as she reached for her bag.

'You okay?' Jack asked, sounding concerned.

'Just tired, I'd better get home. I'm in studio again at half-nine tomorrow.'

'Why don't we go out for something to eat? There's a great Thai place round the corner and I bet you don't have anything in at home.'

Eden hesitated; she knew that it was never a good idea for her to spend too much time with Jack out of work, but then again, wouldn't it be good if they could be friends?

'Come on, Eden, you need to eat something,' Jack persisted. And Eden gave in; it was only dinner, right?

Ten minutes later they were installed at a tiny table in a dimly lit, crowded Thai restaurant and Eden was realising that she was never going to feel truly relaxed in Jack's company. The table was so tiny that their knees were touching, causing each of them to keep apologising. It seemed ironic that they were so formal with each other after the passionate kiss they had shared. They talked work for a while and then Jack's conversation took a more personal turn.

'So you're not seeing anyone at the moment then?'

Eden shook her head. 'Nope, I'm single. It's probably good for me right now, it's been a bit of an emotional rollercoaster with Joel and—'

She was about to say 'you' but managed to stop herself.

'And?'

'And the show. Like you said, it is full on. Anyway, I'm not sure Rufus would let me, he's very strict about my exercise programme, I have to give it my all . . . no time for romance. He'd probably go mad if he knew I was eating this. Give me extra sit ups.' She held up a spring roll as evidence.

'It's paid off, hasn't it? But don't lose any more weight, I think you look great as you are.'

Eden received the full force of Jack's blue gaze then and instantly received a jolt of adrenaline. She was about to mutter something along the lines that she was working on it when Jack looked over at the entrance to the restaurant and said quietly, 'What's she doing here?'

Eden turned round and saw Cherry making her way over to their table, a big grin on her face.

'Hey! I guessed you'd be here.' She leant down and kissed Jack. She was aiming for his lips but he turned his head and instead she got his cheek. 'I'm starving!' she exclaimed, and, picking up one of the spring rolls, dipped it into the sauce and took a huge bite out of it.

Jack did not seem especially pleased to see Cherry, but that didn't stop her asking a waiter to pull up an extra chair round the tiny table. She was clearly besotted with Jack, head over heels in lust with him, Eden thought, observing how Cherry could barely keep her hands off his arm, his knee, his neck. Jack didn't touch her at all. And he was quiet now, leaving most of the talking to Cherry. She was much prettier than Eden had realised, with striking blue eyes, cupid's bow lips and a cute dimple in her right cheek. She had a fifties-style look with her bright red lipstick and swoops of black eye liner accentuating those eyes.

'It's nice to meet you properly, Eden,' Cherry said. 'I've been listening to the tracks you've recorded with Jack and they sound absolutely amazing.'

'Thanks,' she replied. 'Jack has written some great songs.'

'They are awesome!' Cherry gushed. 'But then he's

so talented, isn't he?' She planted another kiss on Jack's cheek and then rubbed off the lipstick mark. Jack stared moodily at his bottle of Tiger beer. He seemed awkward and ill at ease; Eden had never seen him like this before.

'He is very talented,' she admitted. 'But I wouldn't want to tell him that all the time in case it goes to his head.'

She was joking but Cherry took her seriously. 'Oh my God, Eden! You know what artists are like . . . they need reassurance and love. Creating something is so lonely. You must feel that yourself?'

Clearly a dippy hippy, Eden thought, but there was something appealing about Cherry's enthusiasm. Perhaps Eden had got her wrong when she had put her down as someone who just wanted attention; the girl seemed warm and genuine.

'I do get what you mean. But when my singing is going well it's the most brilliant feeling in the world . . . it's when I feel most connected to everything. I don't think about being lonely, I'm in that song.' God! *She* was turning into a dippy hippy now! She was aware of Jack looking questioningly at her; briefly Eden met his gaze then looked away.

'Well, I'm in awe of both of you for being so artistic. I know that I am more of a planner and enabler. I would love to be artistic like you but I'm not.' Cherry smiled at Jack again, clearly looking for some kind of reassurance herself.

Finally he spoke. 'So, talking of planning, how is the wedding going?'

Cherry looked over at Eden as she explained, 'My sister Daisy is getting married at the end of the month and I'm the wedding planner. They haven't got much money so I said I would help them plan it, suss out the best options for their budget. It's fun but knackering.

I've managed to book the reception at this gorgeous little hotel in Lewes because they had a last-minute cancellation and so it's half-price.

'Oh, Jack, I can't wait for you to see it – it's got a beautiful garden, and I'm going to have candles lining the path, and decorate the trees with white ribbons and fairy lights, and one of my friends is going to play the flute. It's going to be so wonderful and I know that Daisy is going to totally love it.'

Cherry's eyes were shining with enthusiasm and happiness. Eden felt a sudden pang as she thought of her sister's wedding, five years ago, where she had been a bridesmaid; remembered what a magical day it had been, how close she and Savannah were back then, how they had talked about how Savannah would be a bridesmaid at Eden's wedding one day . . .

Jack cleared his throat and then said quietly, 'Cherry, I really don't know if I will be able to go. I did tell you how hectic the series schedule is. I might well be filming that day.'

Cherry looked utterly crestfallen. 'No way, Jack! You have to come. Daisy would be so upset . . . *I* would be so upset. Surely you can get out of filming for one day?' She appealed to Eden. 'What do you think?'

Eden didn't want to be dragged into their lovers' tiff, but she had to say something. 'Yeah, I'm sure he could. He just needs to speak to Dallas who's not totally unreasonable. I reckon even he might make an exception for a wedding.'

Cherry seemed to cheer up at this comment. 'It's just I want Daisy's wedding to be perfect and it would mean so much if you could come, Jack.'

He simply nodded and took another sip of beer. To fill the awkward silence, Cherry ploughed on, 'Have you got any brothers or sisters, Eden?'

Her heart sank as she thought about how to reply.

'Yes, I've got an elder sister – Savannah. I was her bridesmaid in fact. We always said that she would be mine, but with my track record it doesn't seem likely that I'll ever need her services!'

She tried to sound light-hearted, but realised she had failed when Cherry said, 'Oh, Eden, of course you'll find the right man one day! You're so lovely.' And she actually got out of her seat to give Eden a quick hug, before nipping off to the bathroom.

Eden waited until she was out of earshot before commenting, 'She's sweet.'

Jack ignored the remark. 'It's none of your business if I go to her sister's wedding or not. I don't appreciate you getting involved.' He sounded very pissed off. Eden was taken aback. Where did this hostility come from?

'I'm not getting involved, I couldn't care less if you go to the wedding or not, but what else could I say when Cherry asked me about the filming schedule?'

'You didn't have to say anything,' he persisted.

Eden didn't need this. 'Whatever, Jack. What you get up to in your private life is no concern of mine, believe me. We're work colleagues, that's it. And when this album is finished we will never have to see each other again, which I am sure will be as fine by you as it is by me.' She reached for her wallet and pulled out a couple of twenties which she slung on the table. 'Say 'bye to Cherry. She's far too nice for you, by the way. I'm sure you know that.' And she stood up and pulled on her jacket.

'Why are you going? You haven't finished your meal.'

'I've had enough. See you, Jack.'

Chapter Nine

When it came to dividing up the acts between the judges, after the auditions had ended, Eden was pleasantly surprised to discover that she had been given Rapture. Stevie had also caught Amber's eye and she had a mini hissy fit when she found out that Eden had the group. But Dallas was always going to come out top in any disagreement, so Amber ended up with a girl band from Romford. Eden didn't rate their chances; it was always harder for the girl bands to get on as it was women who tended to vote and they voted for the boys. Stevie had 'star quality, written all over his pretty face and deliciously toned body. Teenage girls and their mums and most likely grans were all going to be rooting for him.

Eden was looking at him now as Dallas assembled all the acts in the palatial dining room of his Oxfordshire mansion, to let them know who they were going to be working with. Stevie caught her looking and winked. Eden quickly looked away. Jez was dead right; Stevie was a cheeky boy. She was his boss, though, and Stevie had better get that into his pretty-boy head!

There was an air of anticipation in the room as the acts sat down and looked expectantly at Dallas. They all seemed desperate to prove themselves. Eden glanced across the room and noticed Jack leaning against the doorframe. She hadn't seen him since the night in the restaurant, but from today she would be working with him a lot because he was the songwriter/artistic director Dallas had assigned to work with her and her acts. Eden had been tempted to throw a mini hissy fit of her own when she found that out, but she knew Dallas wouldn't consider changing his plans once he had made up his mind. She would have to grin and bear it. Still, Eden reflected, her gaze once more falling on Stevie and registering again how gorgeous he looked, there were definite compensations.

Dallas raised his hand and immediately the room fell silent. Eden almost wanted to giggle because he had such a pompous expression on his face as he told the contestants how they now had to prepare for the next stage in the competition, how he expected the highest levels of commitment, that their entire focus had to be on their music.

'I'm not interested in people who aren't prepared to put in the effort, who are just here because they want their faces in the celeb mags. No, I'm only interested in talent. And for anyone who doesn't want to put in the effort – the door's right over there.'

Now that was a lie, if ever Eden had heard one! All Dallas wanted was for his contestants to be in the celeb mags and tabloids, as without their support the public wouldn't get behind the show. But she knew that he liked to put the fear of God into the contestants, to add to the atmosphere of tension and drama. He was a showman through and through.

'Also you should know that I will not tolerate any relationships between any of you that are not strictly professional. You're here to work on your music; this isn't a dating opportunity.'

It was funny, Eden reflected, that Dallas's love ban in

the competition did not extend to himself, as it was well known that he'd had flings in the past, with Charlie, who had left the show, and with Amber. It was definitely a case of one rule for him and another for everyone else. She looked at the contestants who were gazing anxiously at Dallas, all except Stevie who still had a cocky smile on his face and was staring at her. Eden knew she shouldn't but she couldn't stop herself from smiling back.

And then Dallas revealed which judge was mentoring which act. Cheeky Stevie actually held up his hand with the fingers crossed as Dallas spoke. Once Stevie heard that his group was with Eden, again he blew her a kiss. Eden arched an eyebrow. Someone needed putting in his place, and she was really going to enjoy doing it. Then, along with the other judges, she left the room and they made their separate ways to the rooms where they were going to meet their acts.

Eden had been assigned the living room. She was well used to luxury but Dallas's taste was for museum quality furniture. It was like walking into a room straight out of the eighteenth century, with silk-covered sofas and chairs, luxuriously thick rugs, oil paintings of the English countryside, ornate cabinets – one full of exquisite pieces of jade, another of Dallas's collection of porcelain teapots. There was a baby grand piano by the window, its highly polished wood gleaming in the sunlight. And looking totally out of place, as he lounged on one of the elegant sofas, there was Jack.

He hadn't shaved for a while, and was dressed down in faded blue jeans, a checked shirt and white tee-shirt. There was also a film crew hovering in the background, getting ready to record the meeting between Eden and her acts.

'Hey, Eden.' Jack didn't bother to get up.

'Hi,' she replied, and sat down on the opposite sofa.

It was the first time they had seen each other since the Thai meal. Eden wondered if he was going to apologise for being so abrupt with her then.

'So how do you want to play this?' Jack asked. Apparently there would be no apology.

'I think we just introduce ourselves and give them the details of what song they're going to be performing this week, and that's pretty much it.' Eden consulted her production notes. 'The girls are first.' She looked over at Gavin, one of the assistant directors, who gave her the thumbs up and told her they were going to start filming.

Then there was a knock at the door and the three incredibly nervous young girls who made up Venus Rising walked in. 'Hiya,' they exclaimed in unison, and then looked uncertain about what to do next.

Eden stood up. 'Hiya, girls, come and sit down.' She kissed each of them in turn, trying desperately to remember their names – Alana, Kasey and Kim. Then she introduced them to Jack and they spent a few minutes talking about themselves. They were all eighteen and had known each other since secondary school. Alana was a hairdresser, Kasey was a shop assistant at Superdrug and Kim worked as a nursery nurse. Eden had found it very easy to be straight talking and honest when it had been the audition stage, but having the girls right there in front of her was something entirely different. They all wanted this success so badly, it was almost painful to watch.

Girls, you've got no idea! she wanted to say. Fame isn't everything. It doesn't last, it won't make you feel better about yourselves, it won't take away loneliness and pain.

'This is our last chance to make it,' Alana said solemnly. She was a very pretty mixed-race girl with shoulder-length black hair, streaked with red. As she spoke she nervously pulled at the sleeves of her pink velour hoodie.

'We are going to work so hard, Eden, I swear.' That was from Kasey, who had long blonde hair extensions and a pretty face, though the layers of make-up she was wearing made her look older than she was. 'There's no way I can go back to my job after having a taste of this . . . I couldn't stand doing the same boring thing, day in, day out.' She gestured round the room as if it was within her grasp to live in such a mansion now she was on the show.

Eden glanced across at Jack, thinking, *Reality check needed!* Finally he spoke.

'Kasey, not everyone in the music business lives like Dallas. He's a multi-millionaire! And the choice isn't between winning this competition or going back to work at Superdrug. You're only eighteen, you've got your whole life ahead of you. You could go back to college, take a year off, travel round the world . . . so many things.'

What Jack had said was entirely reasonable, but as Eden looked at the girls' reaction, she knew that they were not taking on board a word of it. They were locked into their dream and nothing else mattered to them.

'Anyway,' Eden spoke now, 'Jack and I have chosen a song for you. We're going for "Call the Shots" by Girls Aloud. We think it will really showcase your voices. What do you think?'

All three girls nodded. 'We can't wait to get started,' Kim put in. 'We're going to put in everything we've got, we promise, Eden. We won't let you down.' She was channelling a more edgy look than her friends, with short spiky blonde hair and a diamante nose stud.

After the girls had filed out of the room, Eden looked at Jack. 'What do you think?'

He shrugged. 'They're good but I worry about their

attitude. They seem too desperate almost . . . they need to relax more.'

'They're eighteen years old and they're in the biggest competition of their lives, they're not going to relax! They want this so much.'

'Too much,' he replied.

Next up were the boys and the contrast with Venus Rising could not have been greater. All three of them swaggered into the room as if they owned it. And the one who swaggered most of all was Stevie. Whereas Justin and Taylor, the two other lads in the group, shook Eden's hand when she offered it to them, Stevie went ahead and kissed her on each cheek.

'Careful, I'm the star!' Eden joked.

'And if things go our way, we'll be stars too,' he bantered back.

'So no problem with nerves then, boys?' Eden asked. She could sense the disapproval radiating from Jack.

'We're in it to win it.' Stevie again. He flashed his cheeky smile at her, the one she was certain was bound to melt the hearts and knickers of every female in the audience.

'Boys, this is Jack Steele who is also going to be working with you,' Eden put in.

The boys shook Jack's hand in turn. 'So what do you do, mate?' Stevie asked.

'Jack's a very successful songwriter. He's written around ten top ten hits.' Eden thought she had better say something or else there would be a macho stand off between the two men. 'He's also working with me on my album.'

'Wicked! I can't wait to hear it,' Stevie replied, gazing at Eden.

Talk then turned to finding out a little more about the group, or rather Stevie talked, Justin and Taylor just added the odd 'yeah' and 'that's right'. A fact which didn't escape Jack.

'Do you guys *ever* get to talk?' he asked some ten minutes later.

'Oh, yeah, I let them sometimes,' Stevie deadpanned. There was a pause during which Eden thought 'Tosser', and was pretty certain Jack felt the same, and then Stevie added, 'I'm just kidding. I know I'm a big mouth and I need to rein it in. It's probably because I'm feeling nervous.' Now the cheeky grin was gone, to be replaced by a soulful look directed at Eden. And as she noticed his deep brown eyes Eden's immediate reaction was overridden by another along the lines of, *Whooh! He's fit!*

She was still thinking this as Jack told the boys what song they would be working on – Take That's 'The Flood' – and they filed out of the room. As well as having a gorgeous face, Stevie had the body to match, he must work out, she mused, admiring the smooth curve of his biceps, his tight bum . . . and she'd just bet his abs were ripped too.

'Earth to Eden, is there anyone there?' Jack had clocked that she was distracted. 'What did you think? I reckon Stevie is going to need a lot of work. There's a thin line between over-confidence and arrogance, and he's crossed it. He could really put people off.'

'Oh, he's just young and cocky. It's nothing I can't handle.'

Eden smiled dreamily; yes, she was definitely going to enjoy working with Stevie.

The final group were another boy band called Extrema. They were in their late-twenties, three lads from Norwich who had been performing together for ten years in various clubs. They were all pleasant enough, but Eden remembered them from the audition and had a feeling that they were not going to go very far. The oldies never did, not unless they possessed the one-off awesome talent of someone like Susan Boyle. But she couldn't tell them that, so instead she looked sympathetic when Harrison, Phil and Jamie all said how much they wanted to win, that they were going to work so hard, that they knew it was their last chance.

'Pity their girlfriends or their boyfriends,' Eden commented when they had left the room and Gavin had stopped filming.

'Why do you say that?'

'Having to put up with them wanting to make it for the last ten years . . . can you imagine?'

'You're lucky, Eden, you had it all, and you're going to have it all again,' Jack told her. 'But I'm sure you could also tell them that it comes at a price.'

She shook back her hair dismissively. 'Why ruin their dreams? Besides, I absolutely love my life just the way it is.'

Even as she lied, she thought of how lonely she felt at times. But, no, she was not going to let Jack Steele in on that secret. Much better that he continued to think she was shallow.

Back in London Eden got her first taste of working with her acts. They had two weeks to get ready for the first live performance, when the public would at last have the chance to vote for their favourite. Time was going to be really tight. Jack was right about the girls: they were too desperate. They rehearsed so intensively, Eden was worried that there was no room for spontaneity or joy in their performance. She tried telling the girls to relax more and enjoy it, but she could tell the message wasn't getting through. Extrema were easier to work with, and their performance was incredibly polished. But again Eden felt her gut instinct on first hearing them had been spot on. They weren't going to be able to grow as performers, they were pretty much as good as they could get. In contrast, Rapture were raw and edgy, they sometimes got it wrong, but they had such energy and passion, you could feel it coming off them when they performed. And as soon as they started singing, Eden yet again found she could not keep her eyes off Stevie. But she knew she had to be professional and so ended up being tougher on them than either of her other acts.

The boys looked at her expectantly, slightly out of breath as they finished singing. Eden wanted to tell them that they were fantastic and that she loved them. Instead she underplayed it.

'Okay, not bad, but you still need to work on your vocals. Stevie, you were flat in the second verse. You've got to get it right. There are no second chances here.'

Three disappointed faces confronted her then Stevie scowled. He didn't like criticism. '"Not bad". Is that the best you can come up with? We were good, Eden. Okay, I may have been flat, but this is only the second time we've sung that song. Give us a break!'

He actually walked towards her and stood over her, where she was sitting, as if trying to make her back down. She got the feeling that he was used to having things his way, but she was definitely not going to back down. Stevie had to know that she was the one in charge.

'Yeah, and next Saturday you will only get one chance to sing it! There won't be any second chances, so it won't matter how nice I've been to you if you get voted off. You can't afford to make any mistakes.'

Stevie was still scowling at her and Eden knew she had to defuse the situation. 'I bet Cheryl Cole doesn't get this attitude from her acts!' she joked.

'Yeah, well, maybe she's not so hard on them,' Stevie muttered, looking sulky but still utterly gorgeous.

'Why don't we take a short break and then we'll do it

again?' Eden suggested, figuring a cooling off might help. She left the rehearsal room deciding to grab a coffee. She was halfway down the corridor when Stevie caught up with her.

'Eden . . .' he reached out and touched her shoulder. 'I'm sorry about giving you that attitude back there. I was out of order. I know everything you said was true. It's me; I'm in the wrong. I just so want to do well . . . I want to make you proud of me.'

She stopped and leant against the wall. Stevie stood in front of her, clenching his fists together. He looked serious, his dark brown eyes back to looking soulful, not sulky, and she noticed that they had lighter golden flecks in them. How adorable!

'I understand, but you have to be able to take direction. I've been in the business for eight years, I do know what I'm talking about.' She made herself sound stern, even though the soulful brown eyes and general proximity of Stevie were making her feel anything but.

He lowered his voice, making the moment feel intimate. 'I know you do, and that's why I wanted you to be our mentor. You're the best.'

'Sure about that? Sure you wouldn't rather have Amber and her lovely smile and upbeat attitude, saying how wonderful you are all the time?' Eden bantered back.

'I'm here, aren't I?' His voice was low and husky. Eden had to make a real effort to drag her eyes away from his.

At that moment Jack walked along the corridor, heading for the rehearsal room. He stopped when he saw Eden and Stevie. 'Everything okay, Eden?' he asked, barely acknowledging Stevie.

'Everything's fine,' she replied, smiling at Stevie. 'We're just having a short break, so you're in time to hear the boys perform.'

After the break their performance was considerably improved. Stevie's vocals were spot on, the boys sang it like they meant it, and their dance moves were pretty slick as well.

'So much better!' Eden exclaimed, clapping her hands in delight. 'Jack, what did you think?' Surely even he wouldn't be able to find fault with the song?

'Yep, it was good. Justin and Taylor, I can really see that you've been working hard.' He pointed at Stevie. 'But you need to remember you're in a group. You're not a solo artist.'

Eye roll from Stevie. 'Yeah, mate, I do know that.' He shot Eden one of his trademark cheeky smiles as if to say, 'You know where I'm coming from even if he doesn't.'

After the rehearsal Eden had to dash off as she was meeting Tanya for supper. The filming schedule had been so frantic that she had hardly seen her friend lately and felt in need of a good catch up. They met up at Nobu in Mayfair, one of their favourite haunts. Tanya was already there when Eden arrived, attracting a number of admiring glances from the male diners in her figure-hugging white Roland Mouret dress, which made her curves look even more sensational.

'Really, babe, you should have made an effort!' Eden teased her friend as she sat down.

'Oh, this old thing!' Tanya gestured dismissively at the dress. 'It's from this afternoon's shoot, they told me I could keep it. And as I didn't want to be late when I met up with you, I kept it on.'

Yes, Eden was late yet again. 'I'm sorry, hon. We overran with rehearsals. You haven't been here long, have you?'

Tanya looked at her watch. 'You're only twenty minutes late . . . for you that's nothing.' She poured

Eden a generous glass of white wine. 'So come on, what's the gossip? Who's going to win?'

'The public will decide, of course!' Eden replied. 'But my money's on Rapture. The lead singer has got everything. Total star quality.' She smiled as she thought of Stevie. 'That he is absolutely gorgeous as well doesn't hurt.'

'But you're being completely professional, I imagine,' Tanya teased her. 'And not letting on how gorgeous you find him.'

Eden pulled an expression of mock outrage. 'Me! I'm totally professional, as always. I would never be swayed by a pretty face, a gorgeous pair of brown eyes, perfect pecs, ripped abs and a cute bum you just want to grab!'

They both giggled. 'And of course Dallas would go mentalist if he knew that I fancied Stevie, even though I can guarantee that's what he wants every single woman and gay man who watches the show to feel,' Eden added.

'But I bet it's fun, having a bit of eye candy and knowing that he is in your power. Very mistress and servant.'

'Hah, Tanya! Acting out one of your own fantasies again?' Eden teased.

'It's not a fantasy, it's true life. Tyler is totally in my power!'

'So how are the wedding plans going? Have you decided on a date yet?' Eden suddenly realised that it had been a while since her friend had mentioned the wedding and usually she could expect a regular update from Tanya.

Her friend shrugged. 'We haven't yet got a date. To be honest, Tyler's been so busy at work we haven't had a chance to discuss it.'

That didn't sound like Tanya. 'Is everything okay?' Eden asked.

'Everything's fine, thanks. Now come on, give me more gossip. What about Dallas, has he tried it on with you?'

'No way! Tan, I don't see him like that at all.'

'And Jack?'

'Impossible to say. I really don't know what he thinks except that half the time I reckon he disapproves of me.'

'He's probably fighting off the longing he feels for you.'

'Oh, *please!* I think he did that already, Tan. No, Jack and I can only ever be work colleagues. Possibly friends, but I wouldn't like to push it.'

'That's not what you thought after the party!'

The girls giggled and gossiped the night away and it was exactly what Eden had needed. She had been enjoying her new role as judge on the show, but sometimes she needed to kick back, not worry about anything else. And that's what being with Tanya gave her. She was in a taxi on her way home when she received a text from an unknown number. She read the first line and saw it was from Stevie. How had he got her number? she wondered as she accessed the full text.

Hey, Eden, Stevie here, just wanted to say sorry about how I was today. I was an arrogant little s***I know, but it's only cos I want to do well and I'm nervous ☹. Call me if you can, I'd really like to talk to youxxxx ☺

He had some nerve; there was no way she was going to call him back! Who did he think he was? She slung the phone back in her bag, determined to forget all about it. But as she had a bath, and then climbed into bed, the message acted like a beacon in her head, flashing away at her. Was he lying in bed now, waiting for her to call him? Did he simply want to apologise for his behaviour, or was there something more he wanted to say to her?

Oh, for God's sake! she told herself sternly. No more of this obsessing! Let Stevie wonder why she hadn't called him back. It would no doubt make a change from the response he usually received from women.

Chapter Ten

The following day at rehearsal Eden was determined to be as cool and professional as possible around Stevie. It would not do to give him the idea that she fancied him, even though she had spent a fair part of the night thinking about him. She threw herself into working with Venus Rising and then later Extrema, but couldn't deny that she missed the adrenaline buzz of being around Stevie.

In the afternoon a stylist came to see each group to work on their look for that week's performance. All the groups were keen for Eden's input. She had fun with the girls, deciding what image they should go for. They wanted to go for a military look with tight khaki combats and leather military-style jackets. Extrema wanted a more sophisticated image and went for a Rat Pack look with sharp black suits. Eden then walked straight into the boys' rehearsal studio without knocking and got more than she'd bargained for as she found all three boys from Rapture stripped to their boxers.

'Sorry!' she exclaimed, and turned on her heel to make a sharp exit. Ordinarily she would have made a cheeky joke, as she was used to being surrounded by half-naked male dancers for her stage shows and music videos, but because it was Stevie she felt too self-conscious and even a little shy. Even so she couldn't help registering that he looked just as good as she'd imagined he would. His skin was a beautiful golden-brown, he had bold black tribal tattoos inked on his shoulders that she found so sexy, his abs were just as ripped as she'd thought they would be . . . and as for the rest! She felt as if the temperature in the room had just risen by ten degrees.

'Stay! We need you to help us decide what to wear,' Stevie called after her. He was entirely unself-conscious about parading about in his underwear; he must have known how good he looked. It's a tough job, but someone's got to do it! Eden told herself, while keeping her expression neutral. She was the Ice Queen, in control, untouchable. She walked over to where everyone was gathered round the rails of clothes and flicked through the garments before delivering her verdict.

'You've got to be casual. You can flash some flesh, but not too much. It is a family show.'

'Ah, that's a pity. We were thinking of going like this!' Stevie stood in front of her and flexed his muscles. He was totally shameless and totally fit! The Ice Queen was thawing.

Eden tried to make sure her gaze stayed firmly on his face and didn't stray, tempting as it was. She pushed him playfully on the shoulder, on his very lovely firm shoulder, but enough of that. 'I thought you saw yourself as a singer, not some stripper in front of a hen night? You need to put some clothes on! Jeans, tee-shirt, maybe a shirt. If you're very lucky, I might let you show off a bit of chest and the top of your Armanis. But only if you're very good.'

'Aren't I always good for you?' Stevie teased. And Eden felt like the room had just got even hotter . . .

At that moment Jack walked in. If he was surprised to

135

see the three boys stripped down to their pants, he didn't show it. 'Eden, have you got a minute?' He sounded serious.

'Sure.' She followed him outside the studio.

'I've just found out that I need to go to the States to work on an album. I thought it was in the bag but the exec producer and the act aren't happy.' He sighed, and rubbed his eyes. He looked exhausted. 'I'm sorry to mess you around, Eden, but I'm not going to be here for a week or so. It's going to put us behind with your album, and you'll be working with the acts on your own. I'm really sorry to land you in it.'

Eden shrugged. 'It's fine, Jack. My album's coming together and I'll be okay with the acts. Don't worry.' She smiled. 'You look like you could do with some sleep.' Now she was so caught up in her role as judge and had met Stevie, she felt more relaxed around Jack.

'Yeah, well, I'll grab some on the plane. And you're really okay with everything?'

'Absolutely. Everything's cool.' She was distracted by Stevie emerging from the studio and turned her attention to him. 'You put some clothes on then?'

'Thought I'd better, I didn't want Taylor and Justin to feel any more insecure than they already do.' He was probably only half joking, Eden thought. She caught sight of Jack looking scornfully at him. The clash of male egos.

'So I'll catch up with you in a week or so, Eden,' Jack cut across Stevie. 'And you know you can email or text me any time, if you've got any problems.'

'Thanks, Jack.' Eden just about managed to drag her gaze away from Stevie to say goodbye. He waited until Jack was out of earshot before he said quietly, 'Did you get my text?'

She had been wondering when he would bring it up,

but she put on a deliberately vague expression and said casually, 'Oh, yeah. What did you want to talk to me about?'

Stevie was prevented from replying by Dallas's sudden appearance, summoning Eden to a meeting to discuss how the acts were progressing, and by the time she had finished filling him in, Stevie and the boys were being filmed for the show.

But Stevie wasn't going to give up so easily. Later that night he sent Eden another text asking her to call him. Once again she decided to ignore it, telling herself that if Stevie had something to say to her, it could wait until the morning. But it played on her mind as she got ready for bed and she couldn't help smiling as she recalled him parading around in his boxers – he was so naughty! And maybe there was nothing wrong in her calling him back . . . wasn't she just being a good mentor? He was most likely concerned about the show on Saturday and wanted reassurance from her. Her hand hovered over her mobile. It was just a phone call after all. She selected his number, intending to have a short, professional chat.

'Hey, you called,' a sleepy-sounding Stevie answered.

'How did you get my number?' Eden asked. Back to being Ice Queen cool.

'It was written on the contact sheet,' Stevie told her. 'No big secret. I'm not some weirdo stalker, I promise. So, did you have a good night?'

Eden had forced herself to go to the gym, hated every minute of it, and had come back to an empty house that depressed her, but she wasn't going to let Stevie know that. 'Great, thanks. So what did you want to talk to me about?'

He ignored the question and said, 'I'm so jealous of you – going out! I've been in for the last four nights with the lads, and it's doing my head in. All they do is talk about the show and play Call of Duty on the X Box. I'm going stir crazy, Eden!'

'Too right! You should be staying in and getting plenty of early nights. I thought you said that you wanted to win the competition? You won't do that by going out every night and getting shit-faced.' Eden thought she was doing well and sounding exactly like a mentor should.

'But it's lonely being in bed all on my own.' Stevie lowered his voice. 'Don't you ever get lonely, Eden?'

She forced a laugh. 'I'm very happy being single right now; I've had enough of men for a while. And I like having the bed all to myself. I can stretch out and not worry about anyone else.'

'No way, Eden, you just haven't been with the right man.' Stevie's tone was very suggestive. He was such an outrageous flirt.

The trouble was, Eden liked it, and was enjoying their flirtation, though she tried not to let on. 'Yeah, right. I'd better go – I've got an early start. I'll see you in the morning.'

'Don't go yet, Eden, please. I've been looking forward to talking to you all night. Just us, no one else.'

His voice sounded so full of longing that she was sorely tempted to give in, especially as she was imagining him lying in bed as they spoke.

'Stevie, I'll see you tomorrow, we can talk then.' And before he could say anything else, she hung up. See how in control she was? The perfect mentor. And the fact that she spent the next half an hour looking at Stevie's publicity shots on the show website and watching the videos he had recorded was all entirely work-related. Nothing to do with the way he made her heart beat a little bit faster . . .

*

Stevie called her the following night too, and the night after that, and both times she took the calls, and both times, however much she wanted to carry on talking to him, she cut the conversation short. But by the third night her will-power was wavering. She had been looking forward to speaking to him all day. At first they spoke about how the rehearsals had gone, but then Stevie steered the conversation away from work.

'I love talking to you, Eden. It's the highlight of my day.'

Eden laughed, but inside she knew that she felt the same.

'As soon as I met you I knew I could talk to you. I know you're a star and everything but I just feel that we connect.'

It was irresistible hearing him tell her this. Instead of making an excuse and ending the call, Eden found herself talking to Stevie for the next hour. He told her about his family, how he was the youngest of three boys and had always wanted to be a singer from the age of five; how everyone had told him how talented he was but what a struggle it had been to get anywhere. He had very nearly given up. It was Justin and Taylor who had persuaded him to audition with them. He told her how much he admired her talent, how beautiful she was. He was charming, down to earth, and very, very flirtatious. Eden found herself opening up to him, enjoying their conversation and his attention.

It was only very reluctantly at one a.m. that she finally said, 'I really am going to have to go now.'

A groan from Stevie. 'I'll never be able to sleep now, I'll be thinking of you. I wish—' He paused. 'I shouldn't say it.'

'What?' Eden asked, but she instinctively knew what he was going to say and felt a rush of butterflies and a fizz of lust . . .

'I wish you were here with me. Say you're not angry with me for saying that?'

Eden was so tempted to reply that she felt the same, but managed to say, 'I'm not angry, Stevie, but I am going to go. Goodnight.' And she hung up before he could say anything else to her. But she found it hard to sleep after the phone call as images of Stevie chased through her mind. She couldn't help wondering what would happen if she were to find herself lying next to him . . .

The following day it felt as if something had shifted in her relationship with Stevie. They kept exchanging glances when they thought no one was looking, and those glances felt charged with significance. Eden knew that she had to be careful; that it could spectacularly blow up in her face if she was seen to favour one of her acts over another, but it was hard not to think about Stevie. He was so charismatic and so incredibly sexy. And just to replay the things he had said to her last night in her head gave her a rush of happiness after the rejection by first Joel, then Jack. Suddenly she forgot about playing it cool. She wanted Stevie to want her, because she wanted him . . .

'Tell me what you're doing right now?' It was Stevie on the phone again. Midnight.

'I'm in bed, of course! I'm knackered. All you acts have taken it out of me, and I'm an artiste, I need my rest,' Eden teased back. She was very far from being knackered; the adrenaline of talking to Stevie had kicked in. She felt hyper-alert, every one of her senses tuned to the conversation, tuned to him.

'I give wicked massages.' He paused. 'I could come over to your place.'

She had to give him full marks for trying.

'Yeah, and have the paps get a picture of you coming through my front door! They'd think it was all their Christmases and birthdays come at once.' Not that Eden wasn't *very* tempted. The Ice Queen had gone. She seemed incapable of resisting this flirtation. She was completely smitten. Quite simply, Stevie was the best thing that had happened to her in ages.

'Well, if you're going to be so strict . . . there is another way. I could give you a massage over the phone. It wouldn't be quite as good as the real thing, but I'm sure it could satisfy you.' He paused and the rational Eden probably should have stopped him right there, but somehow, instead of wanting to joke that Stevie was planning to have phone sex with her and that he couldn't afford her high rates, she let him carry on. She was intrigued . . .

'So why don't you lie back, Eden, and close your eyes? I'm going to make you feel *so* good.'

Eden did as he asked. She shut her eyes and allowed his words to wash over her, as if he was there, caressing her.

'I'd start with your lips . . . I'd have to kiss them, they're so perfect . . . then your neck, and we would kiss for a long time . . . then I'd slip the straps of your camisole off your shoulders because you know that I have to touch your breasts. But first I would have to look at you lying naked on the bed, your beautiful body laid out before me, and you would be looking into my eyes, knowing how much I wanted you, burned for you. And I'd know how much you wanted me. And your nipples would be hard, and I'd caress them and kiss them . . . And then I'd slide my hands over your body and you know where I want to go now and you are dying for my touch, I can feel how you want me, and then I find you, and you are silky and wet and I want to plunge into you . . . I caress you with my hands and my tongue . . .'

141

It was quite possibly the most erotic and frustrating moment of Eden's life. She was so aroused it was almost unbearable, and the man who was turning her on so much was halfway across London and there was no way she could see him. She let out a sigh of longing.

'I could come over, Eden.'

'No, you can't,' she said breathlessly.

'Eden, what are you doing to me! I've got to see you. I can't think about anything else. *Baby*, please, I want you so much.'

Somehow, even though she knew it was wrong, she found herself saying, 'Tomorrow night, we could meet up. I'll book a room at a hotel. I'll text you the details. But you must promise not to say anything to anyone. *Promise*.'

'I promise.'

The whole of the next day went by in a kind of blur. Eden had fittings for the dress she was going to wear for Saturday's live show and a series of interviews with the celeb mags and tabloids. Dallas had booked her in to do fifteen back to back, from a hotel suite in Claridge's. And all she could think about was that she was going to be in another hotel room that night, with Stevie . . . She felt drunk with desire. It was amazing to her that no one could see that all she was thinking about was him. But somehow she dragged her thoughts away from him and on to the perky, blonde, female journalist from *heat* who was sitting on the sofa opposite and looking at her expectantly. This was her final interview of the day.

'So you've talked about your work life, Eden, and how it's all going brilliantly. Is your love life going as smoothly?'

The journalist was chancing her luck. Eden had already told Dallas that she didn't want to answer personal questions. She weighed things up – she could tell the journalist to piss off and so cement her bad-girl reputation, or she could play the game.

'I'm just happy being single at the moment, thanks. I want to concentrate on my career. As you know, I've kissed an awful lot of frogs, and no prince as yet. But I'm hopeful. Even after everything that's happened, I still believe in love.'

'Even after Joel Wilkes?' Wow, the journalist *really* was chancing her luck! Fortunately Eden felt too loved up with Stevie to rise to the bait.

'Joel who?' she shot back, then laughed. 'Just kidding. There are no hard feelings and I hope he finds what he's looking for.' And she couldn't resist adding, 'But I do hope his new girlfriend's got plenty of cash to splash. Joel's a boy who likes the nice things in life.'

The journalist grinned, clearly loving the fact that Eden had been so indiscreet. Eden looked pointedly at her watch; the journalist's ten minutes were up. Finally Eden was free to race home, and get ready for her date with Stevie.

She had ten voice-mail messages from various friends, including Tanya and Sadie, but she ignored them all as she showered and changed. In fact she had been ignoring her friends for the last week. Stevie was all she could think about. She was well and truly love-struck. She couldn't remember ever falling for someone this hard. She felt consumed with longing for him. She just had to have him; she was incapable of thinking straight, incapable of reflecting that she was engaging in high-risk behaviour which could end up jeopardising her career comeback.

Eden had already texted Stevie to tell him which hotel to come to. She had checked in under a different name. It was a technique she'd employed many times in the past when she wanted to lie low, and the hotel was always very discreet. She was first to arrive at the suite.

143

She opened a bottle of champagne, set out two glasses. She felt charged with excitement and desire, more alive than she had in ages. Somewhere a thought nagged away that she really shouldn't be doing this. But she couldn't stop. Her desire had a momentum all of its own. She checked her phone. There were still more texts from Tanya, asking her if she was okay. Eden didn't reply. She turned off her phone; then switched it back on in case Stevie needed to get hold of her. She checked her appearance in the mirror for the twentieth time, sprayed on yet more perfume, flicked through a copy of *Elle* without taking in a single word. And finally some twenty minutes later Stevie arrived.

Now Eden felt unsure as she opened the door to him. 'No one knows you're here, do they?' she asked anxiously.

'Shush! No one knows,' Stevie put his finger to her lips. 'Don't talk about anything, let's go back to where we were last night.' He held up an Agent Provocateur box. 'I've just blown all my money on this for you. Will you wear it?'

She had imagined them tumbling straight into bed, unable to keep their hands off each other a second longer, but it seemed as if Stevie had mapped out exactly how he wanted the night to unfold. She wasn't entirely sure if she liked that, but she couldn't deny that it was exciting. She took the package from him.

'I'll change in the bathroom. And while I'm doing that you can take off your clothes.' If he could hand out orders then so could she . . .

She opened the box and unwrapped a basque, thong and suspenders in black and pink lace. She had to admit they were very sexy . . . and just the kind of thing she would have chosen for herself. She quickly slipped off her clothes and put on the lingerie, fumbling with the clasp on the basque. She took another look at herself in the mirror. There was no going back now, was there? She opened the door and walked into the bedroom where Stevie was lying on the bed, stripped to his white boxer shorts, ready and waiting . . .

'Do you believe in love at first sight?' he murmured some time afterwards as they lay on the bed, limbs entwined, the sheet twisted around them.

'I think I believe in lust at first sight,' Eden replied, trailing her fingers over his chest. He really was gorgeous. The sex had been good, though it had maybe felt a little too planned and she had the feeling that Stevie was almost acting out the fantasies that he'd had in his head, rather than losing himself in the moment. And Eden was definitely more of a losing herself in the moment kind of woman.

'That too,' he said, kissing her. 'But seriously, Eden, and I don't want you to freak out, I think I'm falling in love with you. I felt it from the moment I saw you.' He gazed at her as if imploring her to believe him.

Wow! Eden had never before met a man who was so open about his emotions! It was very seductive.

'Say something then!' he exclaimed. 'I've just laid my feelings out on the line, don't crush me.'

He was so adorable that Eden found herself replying, 'I do believe in love at first sight.' She paused. 'And, yes, I think I'm falling in love with you too.'

Stevie smiled as if he had won the biggest prize ever, and then hugged her, shouting, 'Eden Haywood loves me! And I love her!'

Eden laughed and tried to cover his mouth. 'Shush! You're being too noisy!' And then she turned serious. 'No one can find out about us until after the competition. Stevie, you have to promise. It could ruin everything for you and for me. You can't even tell Justin or Taylor.'

He calmed down. 'Eden, I would never do anything to hurt you. I swear I won't tell anyone until after the show. But then I'm going to tell the world! Oh my God, Eden, I can't believe that I'm here with you! It's like a dream come true.' He reached for his phone, and before she could stop him he took a picture of her.

'That's a really bad idea!' Eden exclaimed. 'You'll have to delete it. Say someone found it . . .'

'Relax,' Stevie told her, 'I'm not going to put it on Facebook! I just want a picture of you. I've got a password on my phone, no one but me is ever going to see this, I swear. Please, Eden, I'll miss you so much when I go, this will make me feel more connected to you.' He kissed her again, this time more deeply, and Eden's worries melted away.

They made love again and Stevie left the hotel around four in the morning. Eden hated lying in bed afterwards without him next to her; it made her feel vulnerable and lonely. She was exhausted but couldn't sleep. She ended up getting up at six a.m. and checking out. The concierge let her leave through the staff door and arranged for a car to take her home. Eden gave him a very generous tip.

The first live show was just a day away and all of her attention should have been on that, but she couldn't think of anything other than when she would see Stevie again. He had already texted her, telling her he couldn't stop thinking about their night together, that it had been the best night of his life. It was intoxicating knowing that he felt like that about her. After being rejected by Joel and then Jack, Stevie's declarations of love were all the sweeter to Eden. She texted him back that she loved him, and then finally fell asleep for two hours.

*

Jez arrived at ten to highlight her hair. Eden was still in her silk PJs. While Jez was his usual upbeat self, Eden was distracted and kept obsessively checking her phone, something that Jez was quick to pick up on.

'So Tanya says she hasn't seen you for ages and that you haven't returned any of her calls. What's going on, Missy Haywood?' he bantered, when she finally looked up from her phone.

'Oh, I've just been so busy with the show. It's full on, Jez.' Eden just hated lying.

'And how's it going with Jack? Is he still being the lean mean moody machine? Or has he thawed and realised his mistake in being so cruel to you?'

'Jack?' Eden had pushed all thoughts of him out of her head, swept up in her feelings for Stevie. 'Oh, he's in the States, everything's cool between us now,' she said casually.

Jez frowned. 'So what changed things? Only a couple of weeks ago you were obsessing about him.'

She might have known that Jez would find this change-about surprising. Eden shrugged, trying to play it cool. 'I don't know, I just moved on.'

'Really? Well, good for you, Eden, but I reckon he'll come to his senses and realise what a fool he's been over you. I don't think you've seen the last of Mr Steele.'

'I'm happy for us just to be friends,' Eden replied, looking at her nails to avoid Jez's gaze in the mirror. And then, because she hated lying so much, and because she was so desperate to confide in someone about Stevie, she blurted out, 'Actually, Jez, I'm seeing someone. Do you promise not to tell anyone?'

He rolled his eyes. 'Eden, whatever you say to me stays between us, I promise. It's the Hairdresser's Code.'

She took a deep breath. 'It's Stevie Moore.'

'Oh my sweet Jesus!' Jez exclaimed, putting down his comb and whipping round so he was face to face with her. 'When did this start?'

And Eden found herself telling Jez all about her passionate affair with Stevie.

'He's so open about how he feels about me . . . he even told me he loved me! Jez, it is so exciting. I feel so alive!' she ended up saying.

'Hmm.' Jez didn't seem to share her enthusiasm. 'There's nothing like forbidden slash secret love to add a frisson. But you've got to be careful, Eden. If the press gets hold of this, it will be open season. And can you imagine what Dallas and Sadie will say?'

'I know all these things, Jez, but I just have to see him. He's the best thing that's happened to me in such a long time . . . maybe the best thing that's *ever* happened to me.' Just talking about Stevie brought a smile to Eden's face. 'We get on so well, it's not just about sex, although that is amazing . . . I feel so close to him, so connected, like I can be myself.'

'Okay.' Jez clearly realised that there was no reasoning with her. 'But how about you wait until after the competition before taking things further? It's only eight weeks. And then you can be completely open and not worry about anyone finding out.'

'Only eight weeks! There's no way I can wait that long! It would be torture! We'll be careful. I've got an apartment we can use. No one knows I own it. We'll arrive and leave separately. It will work out. It *has* to work out!' She paused. 'You might think this sounds crazy but I think I'm in love with him, Jez.'

She looked so passionate, so convinced of her love for Stevie, that Jez smiled at last. 'It sounds wonderful, Eden, and you so deserve to be happy in love. I don't want you to get hurt is all. You have been through it these past months and you have only just met Stevie.

You don't know him properly yet – just be careful. Don't give your heart away so soon.'

Eden shook her head. 'I know you don't mean that, Jez. You're like me when it comes to relationships, an all-or-nothing person. And I just know that this feels right.'

Jez continued highlighting her hair after that and they chatted about more trivial things, such as what Eden was going to wear on Saturday night, and how unbearable Amber had been, but Eden sensed that her friend was worried about her. After he'd gone she called Tanya and arranged to meet her that night for dinner. She knew she had to tell her best friend the truth now.

She spent the afternoon at the rehearsal studio with the groups. Extrema were as polished as ever. The girls were so nervous that Eden ended up spending a long time with them, something that Stevie pointed out when she finally got round to hearing their song.

'At last!' he exclaimed when she walked into their rehearsal room. 'I hope you're going to spend as much time with us as you did with the girls?' He was back to being cheeky and cocky, but Eden thought it was probably because he was feeling nervous himself.

'Of course. I treat all my bands equally,' she replied, but she avoided looking at him. Just being in the same room as him and not being able to touch him was an exquisite torture. All she wanted to do was put her arms around him and kiss him, to hear him say that he wanted her, that he loved her. 'Let's get on with it, shall we?'

The boys' performance blew her away. It was all she could have hoped for and more – the melodies were spot on, they worked together well, anticipating what each other was doing. And Stevie was brilliant.

'Boys, that was gorgeous!' Eden jumped out of her seat and hugged and kissed each of them in turn, ending up with Stevie. Oh, how she longed to stay in his embrace, but she managed to pull out of it. 'You've got to promise me that you'll perform it just like that on Saturday?'

'You liked it then?' Stevie asked, smiling at her.

'I loved it!' She reached for her bag. 'I don't want you to rehearse any more now, go and have a break. I want you to be fresh for Saturday.'

'Why don't you come out for dinner with us?' Stevie suggested. Eden frowned slightly. It was hard enough keeping up the pretence that there was nothing going on between them when they were in a work situation. Dinner would be pushing it.

'Oh, thanks, but I've got plans.' She possibly sounded more offhand than she had intended.

Now it was Stevie's turn to look unhappy. 'What, with one of your showbiz friends? How very lovely for you.' His tone was far too familiar. She could see Justin and Taylor were slightly taken aback.

'With my best friend. I've been neglecting her lately.' She hoped that Stevie would get the hint. 'Anyway, I'll see you back in rehearsal tomorrow.' And she blew kisses to all of them then left, hoping that Justin and Taylor wouldn't think anything more of Stevie's comment.

Chapter Eleven

'You are joking, aren't you?' Tanya's hazel brown eyes were wide with surprise. She looked stunned by Eden's revelation.

Eden shook her head. 'I know what I'm doing, Tanya. I've fallen in love with him, and that's all that matters.'

'What! Your career doesn't matter? Your reputation? If the press find out you will be in so much shit!' Tanya looked anxiously around the Italian restaurant to make sure no one could overhear them before she carried on, 'You'll never work with Dallas again, that's for sure. It could have an impact on your record deal as well.'

Eden couldn't ever recall seeing her friend quite so wound up. She was expecting Tanya to be surprised by her news, but not so negative. Instead of having a heart to heart over dinner, it felt like she was under attack.

'Tan, I'm not stupid. We're both being really careful, no one is going to find out.' Eden remembered the picture Stevie had taken. Best not to think of that now.

'You seriously think that he won't tell anyone? Eden, you are a huge star, there is no way that lad won't tell one of his friends. He'll want the kudos of having slept with a celebrity. And he'll swear that friend to secrecy, and that friend will promise, and mean it, but won't be able to stop him from telling one of his friends, and meanwhile Stevie won't be able to resist telling someone else, and so on until it gets leaked to the press. Come off it, babe, *you* had to tell me and Jez. Of course Stevie is going to tell someone!'

Eden felt distinctly uncomfortable at Tanya's outburst. Was her friend right? Had Stevie already told somebody? She tried to think about whether Taylor and Justin had been treating her any differently. Surely they hadn't? 'He promised me he wouldn't, Tanya, and I believe him. We're going to wait until after the competition ends before we tell anyone.'

'And remind me how long you've known Stevie? A month? You can't possibly trust him, Eden. You're mad to think you can.'

Eden could really do without Tanya being so outspoken. She had wanted to confide in her friend, tell her how exciting it was seeing Stevie. Instead she was being given a whole heap of grief. She pushed her seafood linguine moodily round her plate; she had no appetite now.

'I thought you'd be pleased for me! After the shit time I had with Joel and then Jack. If it was the other way round, I'd be happy for you.'

'I think you'd feel just the same as me, Eden. You'd be worried that I would end up getting hurt.' Tanya paused. 'And how do you know that Stevie isn't just using you to make himself famous?'

Eden had been so caught up in her feelings for him that the thought had never even crossed her mind. Surely Stevie wasn't another Joel? Insecurity made her bite back, 'Fucking hell, Tanya! I can't believe you're saying all these things! Why do you always have to think the worst of people? I've finally found a man who has made me feel good about myself . . . who loves me! What's so wrong about that?'

Tanya rolled her eyes and let rip. 'Why can't you feel good about yourself *without* a man! You have got to stop relying on men to make you feel better about yourself. Every time a relationship goes wrong you spiral out of control . . . you drink too much, you have one-night stands . . . You need to have more respect for yourself.'

This was too much for Eden. She felt as if Tanya was being really unfair and hard on her. She couldn't see that her friend was only being protective, was anxious about her rushing into a destructive relationship. 'I don't *need* a man, but Stevie loves me and I love him. You can't reason with that kind of passion; not everything is black and white, Tanya. Just because *you* have your whole life and Tyler's mapped out.'

'Oh, what! So you're saying I'm boring and stuck in a rut? Thanks a lot, Eden!' Both women were getting wound up now. The young waiter wandered by. 'Everything okay with your meal, ladies?'

'Fine, thanks,' Eden snapped. 'And you can take my plate away.' Her linguine remained half eaten.

'So now you're going to make me feel bad because I've eaten all my food!' Tanya exclaimed. The waiter looked awkward as he cleared the plates away. 'Do you want to see the dessert menu?' he asked tentatively.

'No!' the two women said at once.

'I'll just have another glass of wine,' Tanya said.

'Me too,' Eden added. They looked at each other as if realising how ridiculous it was that they were on the verge of falling out.

'Large glasses?' the waiter ventured.

'Yes!' from the two women.

Tanya waited until he was out of earshot. 'I'm sorry, Eden, I don't want to sound like a total bitch, I'm just worried about you is all. You're my best friend and I never want us to fall out.' She paused. 'Sometimes I feel that you rush into relationships because of what happened with your mum. But you're not alone, Eden, you've got so many good friends who love you.'

Tanya clearly meant well, but Eden hated her bringing up Terri's death. That was something she could not discuss. She fought against the feeling of panic that was rising in her. It was coming up to the two-year anniversary of her mum's death and she had been trying to block it out. She managed to say, 'And you're *my* best friend, and I do understand how my relationship with Stevie must look to you, but it feels so good, Tanya. I can't wait for you to meet him and then you'll see for yourself that he's perfect for me.'

The waiter returned with their wine. Tanya raised her glass and clinked it against Eden's. 'To meeting Stevie. But *please* be careful.'

Eden had hoped to have a few minutes alone with Stevie at rehearsals the following day, even if it was only to say 'hi', but in the event she didn't get the chance. It was a completely manic day. The girls were a mass of hysterical nerves, as predicted, and needed a lot of reassurance from her. Extrema were consummate professionals, and Stevie, Taylor and Justin were hyped up. She and Stevie could only exchange meaningful looks when they thought no one was looking. They had been sending texts, but that didn't seem like nearly enough. She wanted to hold him, to wish him luck for the following night. Not that she thought he would need it. Rapture were by far and away the best contestants.

'All your acts are coming along impressively, Eden,' Dallas told her, as they walked out of the studio together later that day. The acts had been whisked back to their houses to be filmed and to get an early night. 'I predict great things for Stevie Moore, if not as part of a band, then as a solo artist. The girls and boys love him.'

Eden felt uneasy as Dallas mentioned Stevie's name.

She looked at him, trying to gauge his expression. Did he know something?

But Dallas was wearing his usual poker face and there was no way of reading it.

Back home, Jez and Rufus came over for supper. Eden was grateful for their company. She felt nervous about the show tomorrow night, both for herself and for her acts. She and Jez sat at the kitchen table while Rufus cooked. Eden had offered but Rufus had insisted, and when she saw how good he was at it, she was relieved that he had. There was no way her cooking was in his league. Well, actually, she had intended to heat up three M&S ready meals, but Rufus was doing the real thing, following a Nigella recipe for prawn and mango curry that smelt delicious.

'So how's everything been today?' Jez asked. He had avoided mentioning Stevie so far. But Eden was desperate to talk about him, even though Rufus was there. She couldn't quite believe that Jez wouldn't have told him.

'Okay, I guess, but I'm worried about my girls. They still seem to lack confidence. I don't know why, they're all really good singers.'

'Not like those confident boys then?'

'No, if anything the boys are too confident.' She paused and lowered her voice. 'Does Rufus know about Stevie?'

Jez shook his head. 'Nope, like I told you before, Code of Hairdressers – he doesn't know.'

Rufus was the model of discretion and carried on with his stir-fry.

'Rufus,' Eden said, 'I'm seeing Stevie Moore, but it has to stay secret.'

He didn't look surprised, simply nodded and said, 'Of course, Eden. It won't go any further, I promise.'

155

So now three people knew, she realised.

Her phone vibrated with a text message. Instantly she reached for it, hoping it was from Stevie.

It was from Jack. *Hope everything's going OK. Good luck for tomorrow. I'm sure that you'll be brilliant. Jx*

'It's from Jack,' Eden explained. 'He actually sent me a kiss. I just bet he's the kind of man who, when he can't have something, wants it more.'

Jez and Rufus exchanged a brief smile. 'What!' Eden exclaimed.

'Oh, nothing,' Jez shrugged. 'Just that it sounds a little like someone else we know.'

Eden stuck her tongue out at him. 'Cheeky bastard! That is nothing like me!'

After supper the three friends watched an Angelina Jolie thriller on DVD. By now Eden was feeling extremely nervous and needed something to distract her. She drove Jez mad by fidgeting throughout the film. She was desperate to speak to Stevie. She kept checking her phone to see if he had texted, but he hadn't. Somehow they had got into a pattern where he was always the one who made contact first. As soon as Jez and Rufus left, Eden broke one of her own rules and phoned Stevie. If anyone else picked up his phone or saw her number, she could pretend that she was just being a good mentor, checking up that everything was okay. But Stevie didn't answer, so all she could do was leave the blandest possible message, asking him to call her when he could. She looked at her watch. It was half-eleven. Surely by now he should be tucked up in bed, with his phone next to him?

But Stevie didn't call her back and as a result Eden spent a restless night, waking several times to check her phone. She just couldn't imagine why he hadn't called her . . . Instead of being rational, and thinking that he was most likely asleep, she thought of a whole host of other reasons – that he had already tired of her, that she shouldn't have slept with him so soon. It was just a small step to her feeling worthless and insecure again . . .

Eden didn't hear anything from Stevie the following morning either. She was due at the studio at two for a final rehearsal. As soon as she arrived she headed straight for the green room, where she knew the acts would be hanging out. She was desperate to see Stevie.

As she walked in she was struck by the feeling of tension and anticipation that filled the room. The acts were huddled together in groups, sitting on sofas and chairs looking anxious. She looked around for Stevie and saw him deep in conversation with Alana at the far side of the room. The two of them were sitting close together, seemingly oblivious to anyone else around them. Eden experienced a sickening rush of jealousy. Was there something going on between them? Alana was so pretty, and had a to-die-for figure. She was both younger and slimmer than Eden.

'Hey, Eden!' It was Kasey. Eden managed to drag her eyes away from the couple to look at Kasey who was rocking the combats and leather jacket and looked as if she had stepped off a magazine shoot. Her once scraggy blonde hair extensions had been taken out, and now she had a sleek blonde bob. Her make-up was flawless.

'Hiya, Kasey, I just wanted to see how you were all doing.'

'Oh, you know, we're nervous but we're not going to let you down, Eden.'

Kasey looked so serious, that Eden gave her a quick hug to reassure her. 'You're going to be great.' And then as Kim was next to her, Eden hugged her too.

'Is this the group hug, boss?' Stevie had wandered over. "Cos if you're handing out hugs, I need one bad, Eden.'

She wanted to say that he didn't fucking deserve a hug after not returning her calls, but this was hardly the time or the place, so instead she said, 'Yep, hugs are on me.' And she put her arms round Stevie and gave him a friendly pat on the back.

'I'm sorry I didn't call you,' he whispered. 'I'll explain later.'

Only slightly pacified, Eden pulled out of the hug and quickly turned to Alana. She hung around for a little while longer, chatting to her acts, and then headed to her dressing room. She had to start getting ready for the show. Jez and Darcy were already waiting for her.

'Here she is!' Jez declared as she walked in. 'How are you feeling, sweetie?'

'Nervous for my acts,' Eden said. She quickly went behind the screen and stripped down to her underwear then put on a fluffy white robe and sat down in front of the mirror. 'It's funny, I thought I would be more detached, but I think I'm even more nervous for them than they are. They've all worked so hard. I'm really proud of them.' And indeed she was surprised to discover just how much she did care.

'Ta-da!' Jez waved his hairbrush as if it were a magic wand. 'I now declare that you, Eden Haywood, have transformed into the mould of the nation's sweetheart, Cheryl Cole! Now you've just got to perfect your Geordie accent and start saying, "because you're worth it". . .'

'Screw that! I'm still going to be ruthlessly honest if anyone's crap – except to my acts, of course. I can't wait to comment on Amber's girl band, Precious. They are atrocious! They can't sing and they're dressed like lap dancers for tonight's show.'

'Ah, the lady voters aren't going to like that, are they? They don't like a tart,' Jez said wisely.

'No, they'll all be looking at Stevie,' Darcy put in. 'Have you seen today's *Sun*?' She held up the paper so Eden could see and there was a picture of Stevie. He was stripped to the waist, and looking moody and very sexy.

'Where are Justin and Taylor?' Eden asked. 'He's supposed to be part of a group!' She felt annoyed that no one had told her about the shoot, more specifically that Stevie hadn't told her.

'Stevie's a very ambitious young man,' Jez said quietly. 'He's also far better looking and more talented than Justin and Taylor, and he knows that.'

Eden grimaced at her reflection in the mirror as Darcy got to work. A few minutes later there was a knock at the door. Knowing her luck it would be Amber, on a wind-up mission. But it was Stevie, even though acts were not supposed to come to their mentor's dressing room.

'I wondered if I could have a quick word, Eden,' he asked. And looking at Jez and Darcy, added, 'In private.'

'Have you come to tell me why you're in the *Sun* without Taylor and Justin?' Eden stood up to make herself seem more assertive. But without her heels, Stevie was much taller than she was.

He at least had the good grace to look slightly awkward. 'Oh, that. Dallas called me up last week and asked me if I wanted to do it. I wasn't going to say no to him, was I?'

'It would have been nice if you could have told me. It could really cause bad feeling between you boys, and you need to be working together. This is no time for any tension or falling out.' Eden felt like making him suffer just a bit before she gave in to his request.

Stevie hung his head. 'I'm really sorry, Eden.' He sounded so sincere that she softened. She turned to Jez and Darcy, 'Do you guys want to grab a coffee while Stevie and I have a chat?'

'Sure,' Jez replied, reaching for his jacket. 'We'll see you in ten.'

Stevie waited until they were out of the room, then he moved closer to Eden. 'Look, I'm sorry I didn't call you back. I was feeling stressed and took a sleeping pill so I didn't see your message.'

'What about this morning?' Eden glared at him, folding her arms defensively.

'It's been manic. I literally haven't had a minute to myself, and you're the one who said we had to be careful.'

'You could have found the time . . . it was horrible not knowing why you didn't call me back.'

It was Stevie's turn to glare. 'Eden, this is a massive day for me. I thought you of all people would know that? Don't be like this.' And when she didn't seem ready to give an inch, he shook his head and said, 'I really don't need this now. I only came to say that I was sorry.' He turned to go.

Oh, God! Eden couldn't let him leave like this! She reached out and touched his arm. 'No, I'm sorry, Stevie. It just made me feel insecure. You know, this isn't easy for me either.'

He swung back and reached for her, and they were in each other's arms. Before Eden could reason that this was too dangerous, his lips were on hers and they were kissing. She wound her arms round his neck while he ran his hands over her body, untied her robe, caressed her breasts. He pressed his body against hers and as they kissed . . . deep, hard kisses . . . she didn't think she had ever wanted anyone this much. He slid his hands into her silk briefs and caressed her, turning

160

her on so much that she was ready to fuck him then and there and to hell with the consequences. But then Jez was knocking at the door and calling out, 'Eden, we're back. And Amber's here as well.' Eden sprang away from Stevie as if she had been scalded and frantically smoothed back her hair and refastened her robe. That was too close to call.

Stevie quickly opened the door and called back to Eden, 'Thanks for the pep talk. I feel much better now. I'll see you later.'

Eden could hardly look at Jez when he walked in, closely followed by Darcy and then Amber.

'Were you doing some last-minute mentoring, Eden?' Amber asked innocently enough, though Eden was certain that she was surprised to discover Stevie in the dressing room. Amber was already in her evening dress, a gold sequined number which Eden thought made her look like the Little Mermaid. She wished she would swim off!

'Yes, that's right. I'm running a bit late, so I haven't got long to chat.' She put her hand over her mouth, paranoid that her lips looked swollen after kissing Stevie.

'Oh, I just wanted to say good luck.'

It was most unlikely that Amber meant it sincerely, but Eden had to play the game. 'Thanks, Amber, and good luck to you too.'

She was halfway out of the door when she turned back and said, 'By the way, gorgeous pics of Stevie in the *Sun*. He and Alana make such a stunning couple, don't they? Perhaps we'll all be going along to a *Band Ambition* wedding . . . wouldn't that be fab? I love a romance!' And with that she exited in a swish of sequins, leaving Eden reeling.

She turned to Jez. 'What the fuck is she talking about?' She should have been more cautious as Darcy was also in the room, but Eden was too stunned to be discreet.

Jez looked awkward. 'I have heard something along those lines, but I'm sure it's just a rumour. There are rumours about all the contestants. Forget about it.' He gave her a meaningful look as if to say, *Watch yourself*, and it took all of Eden's self-control to pull herself together. But even as she chatted to Jez and Darcy and tried to pretend that everything was fine, she couldn't help wondering if Alana had been the reason why Stevie didn't call her back last night.

Then it was time for the pre-show rehearsal. Venus Rising suffered a complete meltdown during the performance after Alana came in late with the vocals, which completely threw the other girls. Eden dreaded to think how they were going to perform live. When she went to the green room to give them a pep talk, she once again discovered Stevie with Alana. This time he had his arm round her and was trying to comfort her. Eden should have felt sympathetic towards her as the girls seemed to be on the point of blowing everything. Instead, once again, there was that sickening jolt of jealousy.

'What's going on, Alana?' she asked. As soon as Stevie saw her he withdrew his arm.

'Oh, Eden, I don't know. I just felt so nervous.' Alana gazed anxiously at Eden with her big brown eyes, but Eden didn't feel remotely sympathetic.

'Everyone's nervous, Alana, but you've got to deal with it.' Then Eden realised that she sounded too sharp and tried to tone it down. She managed to soften her voice. 'You're going to be brilliant, you've just got to believe in yourself.' Alana still looked angst-ridden, and Eden forced herself to say something nicer. 'I believe in you.' *So long as you stay away from Stevie*, she wanted to add.

Alana looked gratefully at her, 'Thanks, Eden. I swear I'll get it right next time.'

You'd better, Eden thought, or there won't be a next time. Then she made a point of going up to all her acts to wish them luck.

'Good luck as well, Eden,' Stevie said as she came over to him. 'Will you come to the house afterwards? I thought we could have a drink and discuss our performance.' He sounded very flirtatious as he said 'performance', as if alluding to the night they had spent together. Bad boy indeed!

All Eden wanted was for Stevie to come back to her place and for them to be alone, but she knew that wouldn't be possible. 'Actually, Stevie, it's Dallas's birthday and we're going out for dinner to Le Caprice.'

'Lucky you,' he replied, slightly sarcastically. 'Think of us eating our KFC when you're eating your caviar and drinking champagne.'

'Ah, Stevie,' she teased, 'don't sound so hard done by.'

He glanced round him. When he was sure no one was within earshot he whispered, 'After the competition, I'll take you to Le Caprice – and afterwards I'll fuck you all night.'

'Promises, promises,' Eden whispered back, as she felt a shiver of anticipation. Then she smiled and said, 'Good luck, Stevie, I know you're going to be great,' sounding like the perfect professional mentor.

Chapter Twelve

As Rapture came to the end of their performance the audience went wild. The boys stood on the stage, arms round each other, looks of complete exhilaration on their faces. Tess, the perky red-haired presenter, surveyed the audience and shrugged, knowing it was hopeless to try and speak over them. They needed to make their appreciation heard and they had plenty of appreciation for the boys.

Dallas turned to Eden and flashed her his perfect white smile. Eden felt a mix of emotions: pride that her band had done so outstandingly well, and adoration and longing for Stevie. Rapture had been the final act of the night, and it was quite a finale. They blew everyone else off the stage.

Amber was the first judge to gush about the boys' performance. 'Boys, that was sensational! If that single was released now, I guarantee it would go to number one!'

Stevie, Taylor and Justin all beamed away at her and mouthed, 'Thank you.' Ricky was next and he heaped yet more praise on the boys. And then it was Eden's turn. 'What can I say, guys, that hasn't been said already? You have just delivered a fantastic performance. The audience love you, and I love you!'

All three boys blew her kisses. Then it was time for Dallas to deliver his verdict. 'You are what this competition is all about – finding star quality. You've got it all: the looks, the talent, the charisma. I just know I am looking at the next big boy band to hit the charts. I predict great things for you if you keep delivering that quality of performance.'

The audience went wilder still, whistling, shouting out the boys' names, cheering delightedly. Tess, mindful of the time and knowing she had to wrap things up, appealed to the audience to be quiet. The cheers subsided.

She stood next to Stevie and put her arm round him, provoking a stream of whistles. 'So what's your reaction to what the judges had to say, boys?'

'We're overwhelmed,' Stevie said. 'We couldn't have hoped for better comments. And I want to thank Eden. She has been so inspiring and worked so hard with us.' He looked straight at her, 'Thank you so much, Eden.' Then he addressed the audience. 'And thank *you* for your support. It means the world to us.' He blew kisses to the crowd, whipping them into a further frenzy. He oozed confidence. While Taylor and Justin seemed slightly overawed about being in the spotlight, Stevie looked totally at ease, as if he was born to be on stage. In fact, he seemed more relaxed than Tess who had been presenting for years.

And then she was wrapping up the show and once more giving out all the phone numbers as the huge screens displayed a montage of the acts. Venus Rising had done better than Eden could have hoped for. Alana had overcome her nerves and delivered a fantastic performance; Extrema had been just as professional as she knew they would be. All in all, Eden was thrilled with how well her acts had done.

As she walked into the green room the atmosphere

was one of relief tinged with apprehension. She went up to all her acts and congratulated them, warning them not to stay up too late tonight as the following day the two acts who had received the lowest number of votes would be in a sing off. She didn't for a second think Rapture would feature among them.

'How did we do, Eden?' Stevie asked her. He was still keyed up from his performance, and could hardly stand still. His eyes were glittery with excitement and his cheeks were flushed. Eden knew exactly how he felt as it always took her a while to come down from the high that live performing gave her.

'You heard what I said. I thought you were brilliant. I can't fault you. Try and relax tonight. Tomorrow is going to be a tough day.'

Stevie lowered his voice. 'There is no way I am going out of this competition yet, Eden. We both know that. I'll try and call you later.'

He was breathtakingly arrogant, and Eden should have come back with an instant putdown. But she couldn't. She entirely agreed with him.

After the excitement of the live show, the last thing Eden felt like doing was going out for a formal dinner, though fortunately Dallas had invited Sadie and her boyfriend Travis, along with Dallas's ravishing model girlfriend Brooke, so Eden hoped she would be spared having to sit next to Amber and make small talk with her. She was determined to leave as soon as she possibly could. But there was a surprise waiting for her when they were shown to their table in the form of Jack Steele, dressed in a black leather jacket and jeans, looking tired but as handsome as ever.

'Jack,' Dallas exclaimed. 'So pleased that you could make it after all.'

'Happy Birthday, Dallas,' he replied, standing up

and shaking hands. And as everyone took their places Eden found herself sitting next to Jack. At least she wasn't next to the poisonous Amber, but all the same, she wouldn't have chosen to sit next to him. As hard as she tried to tell herself that she was immune to him, and that what had happened between them was ancient history, there was still something about Jack that got to her. He made her feel self-conscious, and she found herself smoothing down her hair and fidgeting, unable to relax. As usual Jack didn't seem to share her awkwardness at all. She would love to know his secret.

'Congratulations, Eden,' he said, pouring her a glass of champagne. 'All your acts were great. The girls have come on tremendously. Extrema were so polished.' He paused. 'Possibly too polished, but there's not much we can do about that. If they haven't got an edge, we can't give them one. It's the kind of thing that you either have as a performer or you don't.'

'True.' Eden wondered when he was going to talk about Rapture's performance, which for her had been the standout of the night. She was pretty sure it had been for everyone else too. She picked up her glass and took a sip of champagne, aware without looking at him that Jack was staring at her. She still found his gaze hard to hold.

'And Rapture were, of course, everything I thought they would be. They're a typical boy band who tick all the boxes. Teenage girls love them, it hardly matters how they perform.'

He sounded so down on them that Eden was quick to jump to their defence. 'Jack, they were brilliant! Yes, they're good-looking lads, but don't underestimate their talent because of that.'

'If it wasn't for Stevie they wouldn't have any kind of impact. He totally dominates them, and the group stand and fall by his performance. I find his arrogance off-putting. There's just something about him I don't warm to.'

Now Eden did look him in the eye. She was stunned by his analysis and wasn't going to sit back and let him get away with it. 'Ha! You're just jealous because Stevie is so young and good-looking and all the girls love him. I thought you would be more mature about such things, Jack,' Eden teased him. 'I mean, you're so much older than Stevie . . . doesn't age bring wisdom?"

Jack didn't rise to the bait. He simply shook his head and said, 'Nope, not jealous at all. I think he's over-rated, and I also think there's something quite devious and knowing about him. He's so ruthlessly ambitious, I reckon he would sell his own granny to get on.'

That wiped the smile off Eden's face and she frowned as she said, possibly more passionately than she had intended, 'You're completely wrong, Jack. I've spent more time with Stevie than you have and he's not like that at all. Yes, he is ambitious, but what's wrong with that? He's also confident, but that's a good quality as well in my book. The girls have been such hard work by comparison.'

'I see he's won you over,' Jack said dryly. 'Just be careful, Eden. I know some things about him and he's not the loveable guy he would have everyone believe.'

'Like what?' God! Jack was really winding her up now. The man was infuriating. First he totally humili-ated her and now he was doing his best to finish Stevie with this character assassination. The two of them were locked into their argument and oblivious to what was going on around them.

'Like he dumped his girlfriend as soon as he found out that he'd won a place on the competition. Cherry knows someone who knows the girlfriend, before you ask. And they were supposed to be getting engaged.'

Eden stared at him in disbelief. 'So what, Jack? That

doesn't make Stevie a bad person. Are you so perfect when it comes to ending relationships? Oops, sorry, just remembered you don't do relationships . . . you just "hang out". Is Cherry still happy with that?'

'It's got nothing to do with me or Cherry.' It was Jack's turn to glare at her now. 'Stevie dumped his girlfriend by text when she was pregnant.'

That had got Eden's attention. 'Well, maybe he didn't know she was pregnant? Maybe she had got pregnant deliberately?' She couldn't believe she was trying to excuse Stevie's behaviour like this, but she felt compelled to. It had to be his ex-girlfriend's fault. It couldn't be his.

Jack looked shocked by the comment and Eden felt a pang of shame at being so down on another woman. By now both of them were so thoroughly wound up that Sadie had noticed. She leant over and whispered, 'Guys, it is Dallas's birthday, remember? Be nice to each other. I don't think an argument about Stevie's private life is high on Dallas's birthday wish list. Time to order.'

Eden pouted; she had plenty more things to say to Jack Steele. She stared sulkily at the menu and then ordered shrimp and chicken salad, followed by sea bream. She suddenly realised that she was starving as she'd only had one piece of toast and a Cup-a-Soup all day. After the waiter moved on, Eden muttered to Sadie, 'He started it,' then caught Jack's eye and had to laugh at the absurdity of coming out with such a childish comment. 'Sorry,' she conceded, 'I guess I just feel protective of all my acts. I know how incredibly hard they've been working. It's been such a tough week.'

The serious expression left Jack's face as he smiled at her. 'I knew this would happen. You started off being so hard, but underneath you're a big softie. You should try showing that side more often, Eden.'

'Oh, so first you lay into Stevie's character and now it's my turn for psychoanalysis!' Eden joked, but the reply was to disguise how uneasy she felt about Jack turning his attention on her. She had buried her feelings for him very deep, but still cared what he thought of her.

'I wouldn't dream of psychoanalysing you, Eden. You're far too complex and complicated a woman for that,' he replied.

'Hah! I expect by that you mean that I'm a high-maintenance bitch, but I can live with that.'

'At least you know yourself!' Sadie put in.

'That from my own manager!' Eden laughed. It successfully broke the tension between them and Eden ended up having a good time, chatting to Jack and Sadie and Travis. Jack was very knowledgeable about music, and while she didn't agree with his views on Stevie, Eden valued his opinion on everything else. But all the time she was sitting in the exclusive restaurant, she felt as if a part of her was elsewhere as she wondered what Stevie was doing now. Was he with Alana? Would Eden herself get to talk to him tonight? And when would they get to be alone again?

After the main course Eden excused herself from the table and headed off to the Ladies. She was longing to check her phone to see if there were any messages from Stevie, and was disappointed when she found there was nothing. She broke one of her own rules again and texted him. *I'm so proud of you, Stevie, you were fantastic. Can't wait to see you. Call me if you can, I won't be able to sleep unless I speak to you. x* She hung around for a few minutes in the Ladies, hoping that Stevie might reply, but then Amber walked in and so Eden hastily slipped her phone into her clutch bag and pretended she was touching up her make-up.

'This has been such a great night, hasn't it?' Amber

170

declared, slightly slurring her words. 'I think Dallas is pleased with how it went, not that you can ever tell with him. And you must be thrilled by Rapture's performance. They really were awesome. Lucky you for having them as one of your acts.'

'I thought all my acts were awesome,' Eden corrected her.

'Oh, yeah, we have to pretend that we don't have favourites, don't we? But of course we have favourites. We're only human!'

Was Amber drunk? Eden wondered. She was being unusually indiscreet.

'Actually, Amber, I really don't have favourites,' Eden replied. 'I genuinely want all my acts to do well.'

'Yeah, right!' Amber giggled. 'How could you not like Rapture over everyone else! Especially Stevie . . . that boy is so hot! I'd have him any day of the week.'

That sealed it. Amber Gardiner *was* drunk; there was no way she would have come out with a remark like that were she sober. The silly cow had probably had too much champagne and it had gone straight to her head, especially since she had barely touched her food.

'I'd keep that thought to yourself, if I were you. I don't think your fiancé would appreciate it, would he?' Eden said quietly, and made to push open the door.

'Oh, don't give me that bollocks, Eden! You know exactly what I mean. I've seen the way you look at Stevie, and he's right up your street, isn't he? Just like all the other pretty boys you've gone out with.'

'I don't know what you're talking about, Amber.' Eden quickly made her way back to the table, anxious to get away from the bitchy remarks. A few minutes later Amber tottered back, looking very unsteady on her feet.

'Everything okay, Amber?' Dallas asked pointedly as she sat down and nearly pulled the tablecloth with her.

He hated people losing control. His first wife had been an alcoholic, and Dallas now had a zero-tolerance policy where drink and drugs were concerned.

'I'm fine, Dallas. I'm having a great time.' Her cheeks were flushed and her eyes appeared slightly unfocused. She held up her empty glass and waved it. 'Is there any more champagne?'

'I think maybe you've had enough, Amber. You want to be fresh for tomorrow night, don't you?' Dallas said quietly.

Amber looked sulky. 'We're not together any more, Dallas. You don't get to tell me what to do.' She attempted to reach for the bottle and succeeded only in knocking over her glass.

Dallas said something quietly to Piers, Amber's fiancé, and the young man quickly got up and helped her to her feet.

'But I want to stay!' Amber wailed. 'We should go clubbing after dinner, make a night of it.' She looked over at Jack. 'I bet you'd be up for that, Jack, wouldn't you? And Eden? Though you have to promise not to get into any fights otherwise Dallas will get cross.'

She giggled and swayed. Fortunately for her, Piers had a firm grip on her arm. Eden was staring in appalled fascination as the goodie-two-shoes act Amber had been carefully cultivating unravelled before her eyes. The woman was a wreck! Piers took her arm and practically frogmarched her out of the restaurant.

Eden waited until they were well out of earshot before whispering to Sadie, 'Well, it makes a change me not being the one to disgrace herself, doesn't it?'

Sadie simply raised her eyebrows.

After Amber's undignified exit the atmosphere round the table became slightly more subdued and Eden sensed that everyone was keen for the evening to end. Dallas seemed calm enough but Eden knew he had a ferocious temper and didn't want to see it in operation tonight. She stifled a yawn.

'Long day?' Jack asked.

'Long month,' Eden replied. 'I need to head off home soon.'

'So I can't tempt you to have another drink? I know a great little club around the corner. They play really good music.'

Eden remembered only too well what Jack's drinks invitations could turn into. 'Thanks, Jack, but I need to get home.'

'Another time maybe?'

'Sure,' she replied, while thinking, *No way!* She could just about handle Jack in a group or if they were working on her music. But having a drink . . . late at night? She was not going to go there again.

Back home she still hadn't heard from Stevie and once again was unable to resist calling him. This time he picked up.

'Hey, how are you?' she asked, 'Can you talk?' It sounded as if Stevie was in a room full of people and music was playing in the background.

'I'll go outside and call you back,' he told her. It was a full fifteen minutes before he did, by which time Eden had wound herself up into a complete state. How long did it take to walk outside! Was Stevie playing her and deliberately keeping her waiting?

'What took you so fucking long?' she demanded.

'I couldn't find anywhere private. Everyone's buzzing after the show. It's mad here at the moment.'

Eden softened; of course it had been hard for him to make the call. 'No, I'm sorry. I didn't mean to snap at you. It's just I *so* want to see you.'

A sigh from Stevie. 'I know, I want to see you too. More than see you.' He paused. 'You looked so hot tonight, Eden. I wish I could rip that dress off you and lick you until you scream. You turn me on so much . . . You're the sexiest woman I've ever met. I can't stop thinking about you. Even when I was on stage tonight, you were all I could think about.'

Eden felt herself melt with desire. 'Can you come to the apartment on Monday, late-afternoon? You could pretend to be going shopping or something? Say you need some time for yourself?'

'I doubt I can wait that long.'

Eden was so fired up with lust and anticipation she didn't even think to ask him about his ex-girlfriend. She was about to tell him exactly what she wanted to do to him when he said, 'Look, I'm going to have to go, someone's come out here for a cigarette.' And with that he hung up, leaving a very frustrated Eden wondering how *she* could wait until Monday afternoon . . .

'Which is the act you would like to put through, Eden?' Dallas asked. The two acts with the lowest number of votes had just performed again. Both of them were standing on stage looking absolutely petrified. Ricky's boy band was pitted against Amber's girl band.

Eden bit her lip. This was so much harder than she'd thought it would be. She hated knowing that she held the future of all these young people in her hands. She didn't want to be the one to dash their dreams.

'Come on, Eden, I must have your answer now,' Dallas urged her.

'This is so difficult,' she tried to justify her decision, 'but I'm going to have to go with the boys. They had the edge on you, girls. I'm so, so sorry.'

The four girls tried to hold it together, but they couldn't stop themselves from crying. Eden could hardly bring herself to look at them. She had dismissed them only the day before, but the reality of sending them packing was biting into her. All of a sudden she was having flashbacks to the night Terri had died . . . to Savannah telling her what a bad person she was . . .

Amber turned to her and hissed, 'Thanks a lot, Eden! How typical of you to go for the boys.'

Eden ignored her; she didn't want to get dragged into a public slanging match. It was a real effort to hold her head up high and smile as Tess wrapped up the show. As soon as she possibly could Eden hurried back to the privacy of her dressing room. Having the deciding vote on the two groups had affected her more than she had anticipated and she was full of self-doubt. Had she done the right thing, saving the boys over the girls?

Thankfully Jez was in her dressing room. As soon as she walked in he gave her the thumbs up. 'Great show, Eden! And isn't it brilliant that none of your acts was in danger?' He clearly expected her to be over the moon, but she couldn't share his enthusiasm. She hated knowing that the girls were sobbing their eyes out somewhere nearby, no doubt blaming her. She slumped on to the chair in front of the mirror.

'Oh, Jez, I feel so bad that the girls got knocked out. I didn't expect to feel like this. But seeing them all on stage as they found out they weren't going through was just too painful.'

'Honey! That's so sweet of you!' he declared. 'But you've got to get over it. They all knew what they were letting themselves in for, and I'm sure that the girls will be milking their fifteen minutes for all it's worth. Really, there is no need to feel bad.' He continued brusquely, 'They weren't good enough and the boys were better. That's show business.'

But Jez's words made no difference, Eden still felt terrible. She didn't even feel like going to see Stevie and her other acts.

She was wearily gathering her things together when there was a knock at the door and Jack walked in. 'I came to see how you were doing. You had a tough call to make tonight.' He looked at her sympathetically and Eden could actually feel the tears spring into her eyes.

She waved her hands in front of them as if to make the tears go away. 'Don't say anything nice to me, Jack, or I'll burst into tears and I don't do crying. I'm supposed to be the tough, unemotional one, remember?'

Jack smiled. 'I won't say I told you so, but – I told you so.' He actually walked over to her and rubbed her shoulder.

Eden tried to ignore how good his touch felt. 'I'm sure Dallas has got it written into my contract that I have to be the über-bitch. He'll most likely sue me if I say anything nice.'

'Look, forget about it. It's gone, let it go. You made the right call. The girls weren't good enough when it came down to it, it would have been the wrong decision to put them through. Now you've got a couple of days to focus on your album. I've got the studio booked for us tomorrow evening from seven. Is that okay for you?'

'Sure,' Eden replied, thinking it didn't exactly allow her much time alone with Stevie. 'I'll be there.'

The three of them ended up walking out of the dressing room together. Eden was hoping for a chance to see Stevie and was about to go into the green room when Jack said, 'They've all gone. Dallas packed them off in a mini-bus. He's booked them into an American diner in Soho.' He smiled again. 'So we get Le Caprice and they get burgers and fries.'

'Didn't he want us to go?' Eden asked, sorry that she had missed Stevie. A smile from him might have chased away her blues. She was still feeling tense and on edge.

'Nope, I think he thought it would be good for them to have some time away from their mentors. It's been

176

an intense experience for them as well. Though I'm guessing that some of them will handle it better than others.' He paused. 'I'm sure Stevie is loving the attention. He seems born to it.'

'I'm sure he is,' Eden said smoothly. She didn't want another discussion about him with Jack.

Chapter Thirteen

Stevie was forty minutes late. Eden paced around her Thames-side apartment like a caged animal, wondering what the hell was keeping him. All day, or rather all week, she had been waiting for this moment, longing for him, and now he was keeping her waiting and she wasn't happy.

She checked her appearance yet again in the mirror – she'd dressed to thrill in a black mini-dress, so short that the tops of her stockings were visible, and naughty temptress Eden had left her underwear off. Not that Stevie deserved any of this effort, she thought bitterly. She reached for her phone, all set to call him, and then changed her mind and flung it on the sofa. Where was he? She poured herself another glass of wine and took a long sip; paced some more, looking out at the river where a tourist boat was going past. This was so frustrating! And then, thankfully, the doorbell sounded. At last he was here!

Eden raced over to buzz him in. As soon as she saw him any anger she'd felt vanished. Stevie looked absolutely gorgeous. He was dressed in a white tee-shirt and black jeans. His skin was lightly tanned, he'd obviously been spending time in the sun, and he'd had his hair cut even shorter, which gave him more of a sexy edge. He also smelt delicious, of Bleu de Chanel and himself.

She didn't even speak to him but wrapped her arms around him, fastened her lips on his and kissed him deeply. Now at last she would feel okay.

'That is the best thing that's happened to me all day,' Stevie murmured when they broke off for air. He slid his hands under Eden's dress, encountering her bare skin. 'And it's just got even better.' He continued his exploration, turning Eden on, sending shivers of white-hot lust running through her. 'Did you miss me then?' he asked.

'You can't imagine how much,' Eden murmured back, melting at his touch . . . And then Stevie was steering her over to the bed, pushing her back, and they were caught up in their passion and a desperate, urgent need to have each other. Eden unfastened his belt, fumbled with the buttons on his jeans, then pulled them down, releasing his hard cock. She took him in her mouth, teasing him for a few minutes, until Stevie pulled her up to him on the bed, and slid inside her.

It was what Eden had been longing for. She dug her nails into his back, wanting to possess him. As they fucked, she could feel the waves of an orgasm building up inside her. Then Stevie came. Grunting, 'Oh, God, Eden,' he collapsed on top of her for a few seconds, and then, with a kiss to her neck, rolled off. It was over far too quickly for Eden's liking. She was still fired up with desire.

'God, I needed that!' Stevie declared, out of breath. He kissed her. 'I want to do that every day with you. I can't be without you, Eden.'

She laughed and kissed him back. 'Just wait until the competition's over. We'll go away and spend a week in bed. Wouldn't that be fantastic? Just us, no one else.'

She gazed adoringly at him, loving being close to him. She felt intoxicated with desire.

Stevie had folded his arms under his head and was looking up at the ceiling 'Well, I'll probably be promoting my . . . I mean, our . . . single, but it will be a hell of a lot easier to spend time with each other when everything's out in the open, that's for sure.'

Eden was slightly taken aback by Stevie putting his music ahead of spending time with her. But then she tried to reason with herself – of course he was focused on his career. She understood that, it was a massive deal for him.

'You've got to win first!' she teased him, expecting him to banter back. But the look he gave her was serious. 'Of course we're going to win, losing isn't an option. We're the best. You know that, Eden. God, everyone knows that!'

She was silent for a minute, recalling Jack's warning about how arrogant Stevie was. She was wondering whether she should raise it with him when Stevie said, as if reading her mind, 'I didn't mean to sound so arrogant. It's just that this competition means everything to me. Along with you, of course,' he added, and lightly kissed her lips. 'How about we order some food in? I'm starving.'

But Eden sat up. 'Shit! I'm supposed to be in the studio with Jack, working on my album!' she exclaimed. She scrabbled for her mobile on the bedside table to check the time and was appalled to see it was already seven. She was going to be late yet again.

'But I don't have to go yet,' Stevie said. 'Call Jack, cancel, make an excuse. I need to be with you.'

'I can't, I've got to go! We're really behind schedule because of the show.'

But Stevie had other ideas. He pulled her down on the bed next to him and moved on top of her, showering kisses on her neck, her breasts, and then moving down her body so that he ended up between her legs, where he paused. 'We could spend the whole evening in bed. I haven't finished with you yet, Eden.'

She groaned. How could she leave now? She selected Jack's number while Stevie continued to tease her with his tongue . . .

'Where are you?' Jack demanded. 'We should have started by now.' He sounded extremely pissed off.

'I'm sorry, I'm not going to be able to make it tonight, something's come up.' Eden bit her lip to stop herself gasping with pleasure as Stevie circled her clit with his tongue, causing waves of pure pleasure to build up deep inside her.

'Are you okay? You sound a bit strange.'

'I'm fine.' It took all Eden's powers of self-control to speak; Stevie was driving her wild! 'Can I call you in the morning to re-schedule?'

'You'll see me, we're starting work on the next songs for the show. But get your priorities right, Eden, your album is way more important.'

'Um . . .' Eden was fast losing the power of speech as Stevie's caresses became ever more persistent and probing. Really, the things that boy could do with his tongue . . . 'I'll see you tomorrow.'

She let her phone slip out of her hand as she surrendered to Stevie entirely and he brought her to the most delicious orgasm. Just as she didn't think things could get any better, he slid inside her and fucked her hard, which more than made up for earlier.

It was only when she was going home in a taxi around eleven that guilt about letting Jack down set in. It had been inexcusably rude of her. He might well say that he didn't want to work with her again. Surprisingly Eden found that she would mind that happening. She couldn't imagine recording the album without his input; she trusted and respected him. And so she once more selected Jack's number, this time opting to send him a text, apologising for messing him around. She didn't expect to hear back from him but a reply came within minutes. *Understand and I didn't mean to sound pissed off, it's just I know how good this album can be if you work at it. Jx*

It was a relief that he wasn't going to give her a hard time about it, a relief that he still wanted to work with her. Jack Steele – she still didn't know what to make of him. Maybe, after all, they could be friends. She had to admit that Sadie was right. He was one of the good guys; someone you wanted on your side.

'I'll take all of them, thanks.' Eden pointed to the delicate pink, white, orange and yellow freesias that filled two vases in the florist's. If the young girl serving her was surprised that Eden was buying up her entire supply she didn't show it, but carefully plucked the flowers from the vases and wrapped them up.

As soon as she was outside the store Eden buried her face in the bouquet, drinking in the delicate fragrance of Terri's favourite flowers. Today was the second anniversary of her mother's death. Eden walked slowly back to the house. She had woken up early with a numb feeling of grief that made everything about the day seem grey, devoid of colour and happiness. She had half thought of driving over to the crematorium in Golders Green, the resting place of her mum's ashes, but there had seemed little point.

Eden wasn't sure if she believed in God, but she believed in something other than herself, something out there, a spiritual side – not that she would have admitted it, preferring to joke that when you were gone, you were gone, end of, final curtain. Actually she believed that the essence of people lived on somehow.

Back at the house she put the flowers in water and placed them by the photograph of her mum, on the glass Art Deco table, and lit a candle. She sat down and gazed at the photograph. Terri had been a beautiful woman. Eden had inherited her striking looks: her green eyes and blonde hair, her sculpted cheekbones. She had been only fifty-five when she died. Too young. Eden had always felt loved unconditionally by her mum. Even when she was dying, Terri had tried to protect her and her sister from how much pain she was in. She had always put them first in her life, above any other relationship. But three years before she became ill, she had met and fallen in love with Al and had been planning to marry him. Al had wanted to go ahead with the wedding anyway, despite her illness, but Terri had refused, telling him that she knew he loved her and that was enough.

After her death, a heartbroken Al had moved to LA. Eden had always got on well with him, but as she reflected on the past she realised that she hadn't been in touch with him for several months. He had emailed her but she had never got round to replying. Now she felt the sudden need to talk to someone who had known her mum. There was no point in calling Savannah. She reached for her phone as she tried to work out the time difference between London and LA, and then thought to hell with it. If she didn't call him now, another six months would go by.

'Well, hi, stranger!' Al answered his phone after several rings. His voice had already acquired an LA edge. 'Lucky for you I'm a night owl and still wide awake. You know it's one-thirty in the morning out here!'

'I'm sorry, Al. You remember what day it is?'

A sigh. 'How could I forget? We should have been

celebrating our third wedding anniversary, and instead . . . '

He didn't need to finish the sentence.

'So how are things with you, Eden? I've been catching up with everything you've been up to online and it all looks good. Terri would have been thrilled that you were on the show, with a fifth album coming out.'

'You think?' Eden asked, uncertain of everything at the moment.

'I know, kid.'

They chatted about what Al was up to. He was still working as a property developer, along with his son, and doing okay in spite of the downturn. He had always been a canny businessman. 'If you ever want a place out in LA, let me know and I'll find you the best,' he told her, and Eden knew he meant it. He had never tried to be a replacement father to her and her sister, but had instead always been a great friend and support.

'So have you heard from Savannah?' The question that Eden had been dreading.

'No.' She paused, wondering how to make this sound better, and realised there was no spin she could put on it. 'I email her, I send her birthday presents, but she never replies and always returns the presents. I guess I just have to accept that she doesn't want to see me.'

'It's harsh, kiddo, but she obviously isn't ready. She's got the same stubborn streak as your mum, you both have, but I think you're more willing to move on than Savannah.'

'How is she?' Eden asked, longing for news of her sister. She didn't know anything about her any more. Was her hair still blonde, as it was the last time they'd met, or had she gone brunette or auburn? Savannah was forever changing the colour of her hair. And how was she getting on with her husband Carl?

'I spoke to her just last week and everything sounds good with her. The company's still doing well.' Savannah ran her own PR company. She was the can-do girl, the practical girl, the one who had always kept her feet firmly on the ground. She had never given any interviews, had always shied away from the press and the spotlight.

'And she has some big news . . .' Here Al hesitated.

'Go on.' Eden was desperate for knowledge of what her sister was doing.

'She's pregnant. Five months. I'm sorry I'm the one to tell you. Perhaps when she's had the baby, she'll have mellowed.'

Eden was too choked up to speak. The thought of her sister having a baby, going through such a major event in her life and not even telling her, was heartbreaking.

'I did say to her again how Terri would have hated to see a rift develop between you two girls, but she wasn't having any of it. And I worry that if I push her on it, she'll stop wanting to speak to me. And I know Terri would want me to be looking out for you girls.'

Tears blurred Eden's eyes. 'But it's all my fault, Al, everything. Savannah's right, I should have been there for Mum. I was so selfish going off on tour.' She was overcome with grief, sadness and regret about the past.

'Eden Haywood! Will you stop talking like this? It is complete rubbish. Terri wanted you to tour, I know how much she pressured you to do it, and that's because she wanted you to have a successful career. Never forget that she loved you, Eden, and was very proud of you. And she would be very proud of you now.'

Eden wondered if her mum would have been proud had she known about the affair with Stevie. Al's next question completely threw her. 'So I read that you finished with your boyfriend. Are you seeing anyone?'

'Umm, yes, I am, but it's very early days, Al.'

185

'But you're happy and it's going well?'

'Really well, thanks, Al.'

Though Eden cringed inside at not being able to tell him the truth. But at least talking to him had helped to put the day back in perspective. It was so lovely talking about Terri, and swapping memories of her. She'd had tiny size three feet and was forever complaining that she could never find any shoes that fitted properly; she always felt the cold, and had the heating turned up fully even though everyone else was roasting. She looked so slender and fragile but in fact was like a steel magnolia. She had a formidable temper and could swear like a trooper. She also had such presence, and was so charming that she could always get men to do things for her.

Eden ended the call by promising to stay in touch with Al and talked about maybe even flying out in the autumn for a visit. And then she emailed Savannah, offering to help in any way she could. It felt unbelievably sad to be emailing her congratulations about the baby . . .

Eden was still feeling vulnerable and low when she made her way to the studio for the next recording of the show and her eyes were still red-rimmed from crying. She planned to go directly to her dressing room to try and compose herself before she started work. However, as she was walking along the back-stage corridor she saw Jack coming towards her. She felt too emotional to speak to him. Instinctively she lowered her head, so he wouldn't see that there was anything wrong. She was so close to her dressing room, if only she could escape into it then she would be okay, but Jack stopped and spoke to her.

Alana's got a sore throat, the doctor's with her now. You may want to go and see her.'

'Sure, I'll go in a minute.' She waited for Jack to leave, but he didn't.

'Is everything okay? You look terrible.'

Eden bit her lip, and her eyes filled with tears again. She didn't want to tell him, but then again nor did she want to make an empty excuse. 'Today's the anniversary of my mum's death.' She couldn't say any more as the tears streamed down her cheeks.

'I'm so sorry, Eden, I had no idea.'

She attempted to brush away the tears, and sniffed. 'It's been two years and I miss her as much as I ever did.' She made to walk past Jack but he put his arms round her and hugged her close, gently stroking her back to soothe her.

'Hey, it's okay to be upset, Eden.'

She buried her face against his shoulder. Suddenly being with Jack felt like exactly the right place to be. And even in the midst of her sadness she inhaled his aftershave, triggering memories of an entirely different kind. Just as she stepped back, she noticed Stevie walking towards them. He looked shocked to see her in Jack's arms. Shocked and jealous. Great, that was all she needed. She pulled away from Jack. 'I'd better get ready.'

'Sure, just try and take it easy.'

As well as building up the idea of a feud between Eden and Amber, the press and celeb mags had inevitably tried to stoke it up by constant comparisons as to who was the most stylish. Eden didn't care about fashion in the way Amber did, who always made a point of following the latest trend. Eden had her own look and followed her own style. She had gained a reputation for her revealing, body-con dresses, showing off her gym-fit body, but tonight she did not feel like wearing the slinky gold number the stylist had picked out for her.

Instead she put on a black lace dress with long sheer black sleeves, which was still sexy but in an understated way.

'Very elegant!' Jez commented. 'I like it! And how am I doing my lady's hair?'

'I think I'll have it tied back.'

He stood behind her and lifted up her hair. 'Messy pony tail or French pleat?'

'I'll go for French pleat.' Eden smiled at her reflection as Jez got to work. Her mum had always wanted her to be more of a lady, and by looking like this tonight she hoped to honour that wish. Though she could just imagine her mum looking at her and saying, 'Lovely, darling, but not so much eye make-up!'

'So why this change of style?' Jez asked. 'It's not like you to want to be ladylike. Amber will be spitting feathers. I think she's used to winning the style wars and you are *so* going to upstage her tonight.'

Eden had thought she could get away with not telling anyone else about the day's significance but now she found that she wanted to talk about it. Why should she hide away such an important part of herself? She wanted to honour her mum's memory.

'Actually, Jez, it's the anniversary of my mum's death and I wanted to wear this dress for her. I know she always wanted me to look a bit more ladylike.'

'Oh, sweetheart!' he exclaimed, and immediately stopped what he was doing to give her a hug. 'Why didn't you say before! I've been waffling on as usual.' His eyes filled with tears of sympathy. 'You're such a trouper and always put on a brave face, but you can let other people in, you know.'

'I thought I didn't want to make a big thing of it, but it *is* still such a big thing in my life.' She opened up to Jez about her mum and even found herself confiding in him about her estrangement from Savannah. They

188

were so deep in conversation that they didn't even hear the knock at the door and only noticed Stevie when he had entered the room.

Eden was about to ask him what the hell he was doing there when Stevie burst out with, 'I know I shouldn't be here but I have to know if there is anything going on between you and Jack Steele. It's doing my head in, Eden.' He made no attempt in front of Jez to disguise how upset he was.

Eden realised that simply telling him to calm down and go away was not going to cut it. 'I swear there's nothing going on between me and Jack. He was just comforting me because today is the anniversary of my mum's death.'

Instantly Stevie walked over to her. Before she could stop him, he put his arms round her and said quietly, 'It should have been me who held you. I'm sorry.'

Eden rested her head on his shoulder for a minute, needing to be close to him, and then gently pushed him away. Stevie took her hands in his and kissed them. 'I'll be singing for you tonight, Eden,' he told her. 'And I promise that, from now on, I'll behave myself. No scenes.' He lowered his voice. 'But know that I am thinking about you all the time and cannot wait for us to be together.' He glanced over at Jez. 'By the way, this never happened, did it, mate?'

Jez put his finger over his lips and nodded.

Chapter Fourteen

Eden slammed her hand on the table in frustration as once again she came in late to the music. She and Jack had been working for the last two hours, and in stark contrast to their previous studio sessions things were not going at all well. Eden felt as if she wasn't connecting to the music at all.

'Okay, why don't you take a short break and get a different perspective?' Jack suggested on talk-back.

Eden shook her head and said determinedly, 'I've got to get this right, Jack. It's got to be perfect or I can kiss goodbye to my album deal.'

'Eden, sometimes you need to stand back. You can't force it.'

'Jack, if I was performing like this on the show, you would give me short shrift. We both know that I've got limited time and I've got to be on the money.'

'Would it be the worst thing in the world if you didn't get the album? You could do something else. Seems to me like you've been on a career treadmill since the age of seventeen.'

Eden looked at him as if he had gone completely mad. 'I have to sing, that's all I've ever known!'

She broke off as her phone vibrated with a text message. She really shouldn't interrupt the session to check it but she couldn't resist opening it up, in case it was from Stevie.

Hi, beautiful, can't stop thinking about you. Want you want you want you. xxx

She smiled as she read it and felt some of the tension leave her. She shook back her hair and faced Jack. 'Okay, I'm ready to do another take.'

This time round Eden delivered a flawless performance.

'Perhaps your friend should text you more often during studio sessions,' Jack commented dryly, afterwards.

What! Jack had noticed the effect the text had had on her? She really must watch herself. But Eden had always found it hard to hide her feelings.

'Oh, that was just Tanya!' she said breezily. 'And you don't have to worry about me and my singing career. I'm a big girl, I can take care of myself.' She picked up her bag to avoid making eye contact with him.

'Umm, I know that's the image you like to project, but I'm not sure it's the whole story. That's what makes you interesting.' Clearly Jack wasn't going to drop this conversation.

'Are you done with the analysis yet?' Eden demanded, trying to lighten the tone. 'Because I've got to meet Sadie and then spend the afternoon with my acts.'

Jack grinned. 'I'm done for now. See you later, Eden.'

Eden had an extremely positive meeting with Sadie, who had the great news that Marc White wanted to sign her up for another album. He loved the tracks she'd recorded so far, loved the higher profile that she was getting from *Band Ambition*. The news couldn't have been better. 'So all you have to do, Eden, is carry on doing exactly what you're doing and we're on course

191

for great things!' Sadie told her, giving her a big hug at the end of their meeting.

It had been a long while since Sadie had been so happy with her and Eden had a sneaking, insidious feeling of guilt, as she knew how upset her manager would be if she knew Eden was seeing Stevie. As she was driven over to the studio she almost wondered if she should suggest to him that they shouldn't meet up until the show was over. Such good intentions. As soon as she saw Stevie, that idea went out of the window. How could she not see him? He had such a hold over her.

She watched Rapture performing and was so entranced by Stevie's performance she hardly noticed Justin and Taylor. Nor had she noticed Jack come into the studio, and while she was watching Stevie, Jack was watching her. He frowned as he registered that Eden had eyes for no one else but Stevie.

'Gorgeous, gorgeous, gorgeous!' she called out, leaping out of her seat when the boys had finished, clapping her hands. 'I can't believe you've only just started rehearsing, it sounds fantastic!'

'Glad you liked it, Eden,' Stevie said, a broad grin on his face. He turned to Jack then, a challenging look in his eye. 'So what did you think, Jack?'

'It was very good, but I still think it's The Stevie Show and you have got to be more of a team player.'

Stevie gave him a cocky grin and put his arms round Taylor and Justin. 'I don't know what you're on about, Jack. Me and the boys are a team, aren't we?'

'Sure,' Taylor and Justin mumbled, but they didn't look as pleased with themselves as Stevie.

Eden sighed; the last thing she needed was any bad feeling amongst her acts. 'Jack, the boys are doing well, don't give them a hard time,' she put in.

'I'm not, Eden. I just want them to work together as a group. That is the idea of this competition – it's called *Band Ambition*, not *Solo Ambition*.'

Eden was about to reply when her mobile rang. It was Sadie. 'I'm going to take this outside,' she called out to the group. More good news. *Glamour* magazine wanted to do an interview with her and were promising to put her on the cover. It was a far cry from a year ago when she couldn't get any good press. Eden had just ended the call when Stevie walked up to her.

'You look very pleased with yourself. I haven't seen you smile like that since I was fucking you the other night.'

He spoke quietly, but not quietly enough for Eden, who put her hand over his mouth to silence him. 'Shush!'

But Stevie laughed and started leading her along the corridor towards an empty studio. Once they were inside he shut the door and immediately began kissing her passionately.

'Stop!' Eden implored him. 'Someone might see us.' She was too high on lust to reflect that Stevie had not asked her why she looked so pleased or indeed asked her how *her* album was going.

'No one will see us, and I don't believe you want me to stop doing this.' He kissed her again and slid his hand under her silk dress and inside her lace briefs, and Eden found that she did not want him to stop at all. And then she was unfastening his jeans, feverish in her desire to feel him inside her . . . And he had slipped off her briefs, was pushing inside her, slamming her against the wall, and she ignored the warning sounds going off in her head, that this was potentially career suicide. How could she stop . . . how could something so sweet, so intense, so passionate, be wrong . . . this surely was what love was all about . . . it was bold, all-consuming, intense . . . it made her feel so alive, so wanted . . .

'You go back to the studio before me,' she told him afterwards. They were both sweaty and flushed and she was sure they smelt of sex. 'I need to sort myself out.' She reached for her underwear but Stevie got there first. 'Don't wear any knickers,' he told her. 'It would be such a turn on for me.'

'Don't be mad! This is a really short dress.' She went to grab them from Stevie but he shoved them in his jeans pocket and laughingly left the room as he blew her a kiss. Eden didn't want to draw attention to herself by running after him, so was forced to let him go. She caught sight of her reflection in the large mirror on the far studio wall. Jesus Christ! Her dress was unbuttoned, her hair wild and tousled. She quickly fastened her dress, brushed her hair and scrabbled in her bag, where she found a spare lace thong. She slipped it on. Then she reapplied her lip gloss and sprayed on a liberal amount of perfume. She pushed open the door, ready to return to the boys, and bumped straight into Jack.

He looked surprised to see her there. 'I've got to head off now, is everything okay?'

'Absolutely fine,' Eden replied, praying that he didn't detect anything suspicious in her appearance.

'I'll see you tomorrow. Sadie told me about the album deal. It's fantastic news but only what I expected. You should celebrate.'

'Yeah, well, perhaps I'll have a party when the show's over – there isn't really any time at the moment.'

Jack looked at her consideringly. 'I suppose you're right. There's your work as a judge and your album. You're one busy girl, Eden. I hope you're not spreading yourself too thin.'

'Oh, no, Jack, I'm across everything, thanks,' Eden lied. When she walked back into the studio, Stevie winked at her and Eden reflected that she was not across everything at all . . .

That night, along with the other judges and all the contestants, Eden had to attend a magazine awards ceremony for *Glamour* magazine's Woman of the Year. Knowing that she wouldn't be able to spend much time with Stevie for fear of attracting attention, Eden had managed to swing it so Jez came along as her plus one. While she could take or leave awards events, after being to so many in the past, Jez adored them and was only too happy to accompany her.

He called round at her house to do her hair first. Mindful of all the other women who would be vying for Stevie's attention, Eden had pulled out the stops in the glamour stakes and was wearing a sexy LBD, which was super-short and fitted to show off her impressive curves. For contrast she wore a gorgeous pair of Alexander McQueen red suede pumps, embellished with gold skulls. She wore her hair down in her trademark tousled, bed-head look, and went for smoky dark eyes and sheer red lip gloss.

Finally she stood before Jez and asked, 'Do I look okay?'

'You look divine! And look at your legs! So toned and slim.'

'I've got your husband to thank for these,' Eden told him, turning to consider her appearance in the mirror. She loved her new slimmer figure. She hadn't realised how unhappy it had made her when she was carrying extra weight. And cutting down the drink had definitely made her feel so much more together.

'And how do I look?' Jez asked. 'Am I good enough to be your plus one?' He gave a little twirl, showing off his newly highlighted blond hair and extremely dashing grey pinstripe Paul Smith suit.

'Darling, I wouldn't have anyone but you as my plus one!' she told him, giving him a hug.

As Eden got out of the limo she greeted the paps with a beaming smile. For once she was going to enjoy having her picture taken. She and Jez walked arm in arm into the hotel. She was damned if he was going to walk behind her. He was her friend and she was going to show him off to the world. Once inside the luxurious hotel, they were directed to the ballroom where champagne cocktails were being served before the awards started. Eden scanned the packed room for her acts, but didn't see any of them. Instead she had the most unwelcome surprise when her gaze fell on Joel and Bliss. They looked as beautiful, shiny and glossy as ever.

'Bollocks! I had no idea that *they* would be here!' she exclaimed.

'Who?' Jez asked, and then he caught sight of the couple. 'Oh, them. Don't worry your pretty little head about them. I mean, *hello*. Who's heard of Joel since you split up? They're just bland nobodies who've only ever tasted fame by leeching off people like you.'

Eden knew Jez was right but seeing the couple aroused strong feelings inside her. She remembered all the vicious, hurtful things Joel had said about her. She felt herself being dragged into the dark place, the place where she felt vulnerable and alone. She wished Stevie was with her to make her feel loved and wanted. But unfortunately Joel had seen Eden and, to her complete astonishment, gave a wave of acknowledgement and began walking over to her.

'What a fucking liberty!' Jez whispered as he saw what Joel intended to do. 'Remember, he's just seeking out the oxygen of your publicity. Be cool, Eden.'

She barely had time to gather herself before Joel stood in front of her. 'Hey, Eden, how's it going?' For a minute it looked as if he might actually try and kiss her. She took a step backwards to ensure that he couldn't.

'Everything's fantastic, Joel, I've never been so happy.' The nerve of the little shit, coming over to her! She bet Joel was hoping that a photographer would capture their meeting and that he could do yet another story about her. He would probably try and spin some old crap about how she was still in love with him, when nothing could be further from the truth; she loathed him now.

'That's great, I'm so pleased for you. I've been watching the show, of course, and you're a natural at being a judge.'

Eden couldn't even be bothered to reply to his lick-arse comments. How had she ever fancied Joel? He may be pretty but he was shallow and gutless. She was certain he was wearing make-up – foundation and eyeliner. She despised him for being so vain. She knew that he would have spent the previous day getting ready for the event, having a spray tan and a manicure, and then he would have spent hours agonising over what to wear, endlessly asking Bliss's advice.

'Actually, I meant to be in touch before,' he carried on, filling in the silence. 'Bliss and I are getting engaged and we wanted to ask you to our engagement party, to show there's no hard feelings. It should be fun. It's going to be at the May Fair and *OK!* are covering it.'

Jez grabbed Eden's hand and squeezed it as if to say, *Stay cool*, but Eden felt bubbles of hysterical laughter building up in her at the sheer nerve of Joel! It was incredible that he thought, after all the terrible things he had said about her, that she would trot along to his party and have her picture taken next to him and his smug bride-to-be. Hell, *OK!* were probably paying more because he had told them that she would go!

197

She'd been part of the celebrity world long enough to know how these things worked.

But she managed to contain herself, was icily cool when she replied, 'I really don't think it would be appropriate for me to go.'

'Really?' Eden couldn't believe that Joel looked genuinely surprised. She knew that he had never been the sharpest tool in the box, but even so! And it seemed as if he still wasn't ready to give up. 'I know that we've had our differences, Eden, but I would love us to be friends. And it would do both our profiles good, and help to draw a line under what happened with Bliss.'

That did it! Eden had had quite enough of playing it cool. She had to get away from Joel right now before she said or did something she regretted. 'Like I said, Joel, it wouldn't be appropriate.'

And, still holding Jez's hand, she quickly moved away. 'Fuckity, fuck, fuck, fuck!' she exclaimed to him as they wove through the guests, keen to get away from Joel. 'Can you believe that?'

'Eden, if your life was a film I wouldn't believe it!' Jez told her, and reached for a glass of champagne from a hovering waiter. 'There you go, get that down you.' As he chatted away to her, giving her a running commentary on which star he could see, wearing what, and with whom, Eden tried to calm down, but seeing Joel had shaken her. It was an unwelcome reminder of all the many bad choices she had made in the past. Then she caught sight of Stevie weaving his way towards her. Now *that* was something to make her feel better.

'Hey, sexy,' he said quietly, but probably not quietly enough as Jez raised an eyebrow. To Eden Stevie had never looked more handsome than he did in black tie, and it took all her will-power for her not to throw her arms around him. Instead the three of them made small talk about how the competition was going, and

Jez told Stevie what a huge fan of his he was and how all his clients were rooting for Rapture. But all the while Eden was aware that Stevie's attention didn't seem to be fully on what was being said. He kept looking around him, as if worried that there was a more exciting conversation going on somewhere else and he didn't want to miss it. It was his first awards night. Eden tried to see it from his perspective but it wasn't easy. She wanted to be the centre of his attention, as he was of hers.

Alana, Kasey and Kim then joined them. The girls were all dressed up and looked so pretty, especially Kasey who really was stunning in a short silver sequined dress. She seemed to be blossoming before Eden's eyes. She looked sleek and sophisticated with no resemblance at all to the awkward girl with dodgy hair extensions and too much make-up who had stood before her in Dallas's living room a few months ago.

'Isn't this great?' Alana said excitedly. 'And we get to take home goodie bags at the end! It's so exciting. As we came in we had to sign loads of autographs.' She looked at Eden. 'Oh, I know that you must have been to so many of these things, it must seem really boring to you.'

Eden smiled. 'Not at all. It's lovely seeing all of you out and having a good time. I know how hard you've been working.'

She wished she could spend more time with Stevie but by then they were being summoned to their tables. The awards ceremony was about to begin. She was disappointed to discover that she wasn't on the same table as her acts. Instead she and Jez were on a table that included Amber and Piers, Ricky and his wife, and the showbiz editor of a celeb magazine. As Jez chatted happily away to everyone, Eden couldn't stop herself from looking over at Stevie's table. Again she experienced an unpleasant pang of jealousy when she saw that Alana and he were sitting next to each other and seemed to be spending a great deal of time locked in a private conversation.

'Alana looks stunning, doesn't she?' Amber commented to Eden, with her unerring ability to twist the knife.

'She does, doesn't she?' Eden forced herself to reply.

Amber lowered her voice. 'Have you said anything to Stevie and her about being careful? You know Dallas made it clear that he didn't want any shenanigans between the acts. Mind you, I expect it only makes what they've got going on more exciting. The sense of danger . . . And who knows what they get up to in that shared house, once the cameras are turned off!'

Eden took a deep breath. 'Amber, I'm pretty sure that there's nothing going on. And anyway it's not my job to tell my acts how to live their lives. I'm strictly the singing and performing side.'

Amber ignored that comment and continued with her speculation. 'Still, if I was Dallas I would be all for a romance, especially between those two. They're so photogenic! The celeb mags love them.'

The conversation had caught the attention of the showbiz editor, an Australian called Fiona, who leant over and said, 'You must be talking about Alana and Stevie. They're adorable, aren't they?' The woman was so eager for gossip it put a downer on Eden's mood, but Fiona and Amber proceeded to speculate about whether Alana and Stevie were an item.

'But surely you must know, Eden?' Fiona said. 'Come on, give us a hint. I wouldn't say it had come from you.'

She shrugged. 'I don't know. And even if I did, no offence, but I wouldn't tell you.'

Fortunately the host of the awards ceremony came on stage then to kick off the proceedings and conversation had to come to an end, which was just as well as Eden felt she was running low on charm. She was beginning to regret coming along at all. While Alana and Co. were going home with goodie bags, all Eden was going to leave with was a massive dent in her self-esteem, and filled with anxiety about the nature of Stevie's relationship with Alana. And she still hadn't been able to ask him about his ex-girlfriend.

She had hoped that when the ceremony was over she could at least have a few precious minutes alone with him, but Dallas had decreed that the acts had to leave by midnight and Eden could only wave at Stevie, along with the others, as they all dutifully left at the allotted hour.

Chapter Fifteen

Eden checked her phone for about the tenth time. There was still nothing from Stevie. She was at the apartment in the hope that he would be able to get away from whatever he was supposed to be doing. He had promised that he would do all he could to be with her. She hadn't been able to see him alone for over a week. He'd been busy rehearsing, or doing interviews and photo-shoots, or she had been in studio or doing interviews herself for the TV show. It was so frustrating! And what made it even harder, today of all days, was that it was her birthday and she had pinned all her hopes on seeing Stevie, to the extent that she had cancelled the meal out at Scott's in Mayfair that Tanya had arranged for her. Tanya hadn't said anything, she hadn't needed to; Eden could sense how upset she was. But why couldn't any of her friends get it? She was in love with Stevie, and she had to see him.

The apartment felt like a luxurious prison as she paced around it. She had bought a bottle of champagne that she was saving for when Stevie finally turned up. But after an hour of waiting, and no word from him, she ended up opening it by herself.

'Happy Birthday to me,' she said bitterly, raising her glass to her reflection in the mirror. Twenty-four years old today and here she was, all alone, toasting herself. It seemed horribly unfair. Finally she could bear it no longer and called Stevie's number. He answered on the first ring.

'Where are you?' she demanded. 'I've been waiting over two hours.'

He sighed and said quietly, 'I can't talk; we're in the middle of a shoot. It doesn't look like I'm going to be able to make it. Sorry.' He didn't sound sorry, he sounded hassled.

'But it's my birthday!' Eden couldn't stop herself from exclaiming. 'I cancelled everything to be with you!' She was on the verge of tears.

'And I warned you it might not be possible. I swear I'll make it up to you, but for now my focus has got to be on my music.'

'What, like a hundred and ten percent?' Eden said sarcastically, hurt that she was coming a poor second best.

'Yeah, more like a hundred and fifty. I don't see why you don't get that. This is my time,' Stevie replied, sounding pissed off. 'I'll call you tomorrow.' He hung up without an 'I love you' or 'I miss you' or even 'Happy Birthday'! This could *not* be happening. It was too cruel. Eden quickly drained her glass of champagne, grabbed her things and left the apartment. She couldn't bear to spend another moment feeling alone and abandoned on her birthday. She was feeling very, very sorry for herself.

Back home, her mood was no better. As soon as she stepped through her front door she breathed in the heady fragrance from the many bouquets of flowers she had been sent by friends, newspapers and celebrity magazines, and boutique owners. She looked through the accompanying cards but there were no flowers from Stevie. Eden couldn't even face the task of arranging them in vases. She'd leave it for the cleaners to do in the morning.

She felt she could hardly call Tanya and admit that she had been blown out by Stevie. Instead she moodily grabbed the stack of birthday cards from the hall table that she hadn't got round to opening that morning and quickly flicked through them. Again there was nothing from Stevie, and nothing from Savannah. But then, she hadn't expected to find anything from her sister. But surely he could have sent something?

She curled up on the sofa in the living room and channel surfed, then when she tired of that she put on her favourite Alicia Keys album. But every song was a reminder that she was alone. She was only twenty-four, she had the promise of a new album, she had a gorgeous boyfriend, she should have felt as if she had the world at her feet. Instead she felt utterly depressed. She broke all her own rules about not drinking alone and opened a bottle of wine. She quickly drank half of it, something that did nothing to improve her mood, especially as she hadn't eaten. Drunk and depressed – the worst possible combination. In a minute she would try drunk-dialling Stevie . . .

She was just about to crash out in bed – it was only nine o'clock but the day could not end soon enough for her – when the doorbell rang. Maybe Stevie had been able to get away after all? She raced to answer it and found Jack standing on the doorstep, holding a bouquet of pale pink roses. 'I was going to leave these outside but then I saw your light was on.' He handed her the bouquet. 'Happy Birthday, Eden.'

She could have cried with frustration that it wasn't Stevie! But somehow she managed to thank him without sounding like a spoilt brat.

'Anyway, I'll leave you to your evening.' Jack turned to go.

Eden couldn't bear the prospect of being alone again. 'Actually, Jack, you would be doing me a massive favour if you'd have a drink with me. My plans all went wrong and I'm feeling sorry for myself.' She bit her lip, realising what a complete loser she sounded. 'Oh my God! Epic fail! I sound such a saddo, you don't have to stay.'

Jack smiled. 'How could I not, after you've told me what a tough birthday you're having? Of course I'll have a drink with you, Eden. Have you eaten yet?'

She shook her head. She had bought a birthday feast for her and Stevie from Fortnum and Mason and had imagined them feeding each other in bed, after a passionate love-making session. But she had abandoned the food at the apartment in her desperation to get out of there.

She let Jack in and they went through to the kitchen where Eden poured him a glass of white wine, opting to pour herself a glass of water.

'You've got a lovely house, Eden,' he commented, looking round at her designer kitchen and the garden beyond it, which was subtly lit up.

'I know. I'm a lucky girl, aren't I?' She didn't feel at all lucky. Rejected, yes. Lonely, yes. She ticked those boxes all right. Thinking about how miserable she felt, she was afraid she might cry. God! She had to get a grip.

'So, it's your birthday, what would you like to do? We could go out and eat. We could order in. Or I could cook something. It's entirely up to you.'

Jack opened Eden's pink fifties-style fridge. Along with the half-empty bottle of Sauvignon it contained just a pot of houmous, half a pint of semi-skimmed milk, and a jar of olives. Jack gave a wry smile. 'I can see that I'm not going to be able to make anything with what you've got here. So what's your favourite restaurant?'

Eden shrugged. 'I guess it's Scott's, but we won't get a table now.'

'Don't be so pessimistic. Why don't you go and get changed and I'll see what I can do?'

Twenty minutes later the pair of them were in a taxi on their way to the Mayfair restaurant. Eden had taken a couple of painkillers and drunk a pint of water and felt slightly less upset. If only she could find a way of dealing with her feelings for Stevie. She was such an all-or-nothing woman, she found it hard keeping her feelings under wraps. It was taking all her will-power not to send him yet another text, saying that she was sorry for snapping at him.

She walked into Scott's expecting to be shown to a table for two, but instead the maître d' led them to a table where, to her surprise, Tanya, Tyler, Jez and Rufus were already seated. Eden turned back to Jack. 'How come they're here?'

'When you were getting ready, I called and asked them if they were up for celebrating your birthday with you, and they all were.'

'Happy Birthday!' everyone chorused, and Eden found herself being hugged and kissed by her friends. She hugged Tanya tightly and whispered, 'Thank you for being my best friend and putting up with me whatever I do. I don't deserve you, I know that.'

'Don't be silly, I'm just glad you could make it now.' Tanya smiled at her and Eden felt hugely relieved that her friend was so forgiving.

As Eden sat down and her friends showered presents and attention on her, she felt as if she had stepped out of the darkness and into the light. She would get through this blip with Stevie. She just had to learn to detach herself more, not get so wound up. And perhaps not want him so much. It was understandable that he was caught up with the show.

At one point Jack went to take a phone call outside and Eden knew that her friends would ask her about Stevie. Sure enough Jack was barely out of earshot when Tanya said, 'So what happened to Stevie and your romantic birthday celebrations?'

Eden fiddled with the stem of her wine glass and avoided eye contact with Tanya as she muttered, 'He couldn't get away from the shoot they were doing, and then he was going to rehearse the dance moves with the boys. He's under such pressure at the moment. But it's okay, I'm cool about it.' She managed to look over at Tanya, and saw that her friend seemed highly sceptical. Great, Tanya giving her grief was the last thing she needed.

'Well, so long as he's going to make it up to you,' she said.

No doubt there were many other things she wanted to add but Jez cut in. 'Wasn't it great of Jack to fix this for you? He's really going up in my estimation. He's good-looking, sexy, talented *and* kind.' He glanced over at Rufus. 'But not in your league, of course.' Rufus simply rolled his eyes, no doubt used to Jez and his ways.

'Yeah,' Eden admitted. 'It was really lovely of him. If he hadn't come round when he did it was going to be me, a bottle of wine and a possible attack of drunk-dialling. I might even have ordered in a pizza and a tub of Häagen-Dazs pralines and cream, just to max out on the misery.'

'Oh, no, it would be Bailey's ice cream for me every time!' Tanya put in. 'I once ate an entire tub and a packet of Oreos after a row with Tyler.'

He shrugged, 'She made me pay for that, believe me.'

'I believe you.' Eden smiled; she could just imagine her friend giving Tyler a hard time. Rufus was looking most disapproving at this talk of calorific comfort eating. 'Eden, you would have regretted that, I would have had you on very tough measures at the gym.'

'Rufus, you always have me on tough measures at the gym!' she exclaimed.

'It's for your own good,' he continued. 'Do you know how many calories a tub of Häagen-Dazs ice cream has?'

'Oh, Rufus, you're so tough and so perfect, do you never eat or drink too much?' Eden teased. 'What's his weakness, Jez? Let me guess . . . he's a gambler, a shopaholic?'

Jez shook his head. 'I can honestly say he doesn't have one! Except he's a bit of a neat freak in the flat. And as for whenever he feels he's over-indulged, he just goes for an extra-long run. In fact, that's probably his only weakness. He pushes himself too hard and he's too driven.'

Rufus held up his hand. 'Hello! I am here!' he joked, then added, 'Actually Jez is right, I probably do push myself too hard. I guess I should lighten up a bit.'

'You see – we're yin and yang. He's always punishing himself and I'm always letting myself off the hook,' Jez said, pausing to plant a kiss on Rufus's cheek. 'A perfect match.'

Eden looked across the restaurant and watched Jack returning to their table. He attracted the admiring glances of several women as he walked across the room. She smiled as she remembered how she had dismissed him on their first meeting. He was such a handsome man. He had barely taken his seat before Jez was on his case.

'So, Jack, we've been talking about people's weaknesses – Tanya can't resist Bailey's ice cream, I've got a bit of a pash for Alexander McQueen accessories.' And he held up his hand to showcase his latest purchase, a silver skull and butterfly ring. 'What's yours?'

It was typical of Jez to want to push it, to find out

more about Jack. Everyone was expecting a light-hearted answer along the lines of the Häagen-Dazs obsession. Instead he replied, 'Um, I probably find it hard to show my true feelings.' He was looking straight at Eden as he spoke. 'But I am trying to change that.'

She wondered whether he was talking about his feelings for Cherry. And yet, there was something in his gaze that made her feel as if he was talking about her. But he couldn't be, could he?

'Really!' Jez exclaimed, puncturing the fleeting moment of intimacy. 'And there were we thinking you were going to talk about how you can't resist an Aero and like to eat them while lying in the bath listening to JLS!'

Jack smiled. 'No, no, you've got that wrong. It would be a Snickers bar, and my guilty pleasure would be Kylie.'

Jez flapped his hands in front of his face. 'My, my, I'm getting quite hot at the thought. Would you have bubbles in the bath preserving your modesty, or would the water perhaps be crystal clear, affording a clear glimpse of your naked—'

Eden punched him lightly on the arm. 'Jez! You are a terror. Stop right now!'

'No!' Tanya joked. 'I need to know the answer to that too!' It was a most un-Tanya-like comment and Eden guessed it was Jack's particular masculine appeal which made her friend so flirtatious. He did have a way of making all the women in the room suddenly very aware of their sexuality.

Jack grinned. 'I had no idea your friends were so direct, Eden. But in answer to your question . . . probably clear water. I'd save the bubbles for when I was in company.'

Now why did that suddenly cause Eden to have a

delicious image of Jack naked? And of what it would be like to be sharing that bath full of bubbles with him . . . She vividly recalled the feel of his body against hers . . .

'Eden—' Jez shattered the moment. 'Do you want dessert? We could ask if they could bring you that tub of Häagen-Dazs? I'll tell Rufus to go easy on you. Everyone is allowed at least one naughty moment on their birthday.'

But then the lights were discreetly lowered and a waiter arrived at the table carrying a plate with an elegant white chocolate cake in the shape of a heart, a single candle in its centre.

'We were going to have it made in the shape of a cock but it's way too posh here for that kind of malarkey,' Jez whispered. 'And we can't sing "Happy Birthday" but you can still make a wish, Eden.'

She blew out the candle, wishing that Stevie could be with her.

Jack insisted on paying for dinner, in spite of Eden's protests, and then the friends were saying goodnight. Jez and Rufus took a taxi back to North London, Tanya and Tyler headed to West London, while Eden and Jack lingered on the pavement; she wanted to thank him again. She really appreciated what he'd done for her.

'So do you feel better about your birthday now?' he asked her.

Eden looked at her watch. It was just after midnight. 'My birthday's over now, and thank you, Jack. You saved me from the wine/pizza/Häagen-Dazs fate. And now you know from Rufus how much pain that would have cost me at the gym!'

'Any time, kiddo.' Jack smiled. He ducked down and lightly kissed her on each cheek at the exact moment that a lurking paparazzo caught them with his camera.

Eden groaned. 'I might have guessed they'd be around. See you tomorrow, Jack.' And ducking her head to avoid the flashes going off, she quickly got into a waiting taxi.

She was so proud that she had been able to resist checking her phone while she was with her friends, but as soon as Eden sat back in the taxi she fished it out of her bag, desperate to see if there was anything from Stevie. There were five missed calls from him, and he'd left two voice-mail messages. She accessed the first one and was stunned by his angry tone.

'Where the fuck are you, Eden? I'm round at the apartment. Call me.' *He* was the one who had cancelled! What did he have to be pissed off about? The next message was even more worrying. 'I'm near your house. Where are you?' Shit! That was too dangerous. She didn't want to risk phoning him back in case the taxi driver overheard, so she texted, *Back in 5 mins, don't go near the house if you think there are paps around. x*

She felt a rush of nerves. What if someone saw him? How would they explain his presence?

As the taxi drew up outside her house and Eden paid, she glanced along the street but there was no sign of Stevie. She walked up the stone stairs to her front door and looked behind her. Still nothing. It was only when she was fumbling to get her key in the lock that she heard Stevie's voice: 'Leave the door on the latch and I'll come in when I think it's safe.'

He was crouched down in the shadows by the side of the staircase, a black hoodie pulled over his head. Without betraying his presence, Eden did as he had said and then waited by the front door. She made sure that she turned off the security lights, which usually went on when anyone approached the entrance, and so with any luck Stevie could slip in unobserved. A few minutes later, when her anxiety levels were rocketing, he gently opened the front door and then clicked it shut behind him.

There were so many things Eden wanted to say to him, like why had he blown her out earlier, and why did his messages sound so aggressive, and why was he playing such a dangerous game by coming round to the house? But Stevie had pulled her close to him, was kissing her hard, urgently, passionately, and then he was pulling up her dress, ripping down her lace briefs, making her melt with his delicious, persistent caresses.

'Come upstairs,' Eden murmured, but Stevie led her into the living room, steered her towards the sofa, pushed her over the back of it, so her arse was offered to him, and while his fingers still caressed and teased her clit, making her moan with pleasure, he entered her from behind, fucking her hard. 'Happy Birthday, Eden,' he groaned as he thrust into her. And even while the delicious waves of her orgasm rippled through her, she thought he possibly had been a bit too rough with her.

But then they were lying on the sofa together, and he was gently kissing her. 'I love you, Eden, so fucking much,' he told her. 'I'm sorry about coming over, but the moment I knew that there was a chance I could see you, I had to take it. Say you forgive me?'

'I forgive you,' she murmured.

'I haven't had a chance to get you a birthday present, but I will, I promise. Something really special for my girl.' He flashed her his best cheeky flirtatious grin. But again there was something slightly wrong about this picture, Eden thought. He could at least have bought her a card. But she didn't say anything. Now he was here beside her, she didn't want to do anything to drive him away. She snuggled against him, loving the feel of his warm skin. She laid her head on his chest and could hear his heart beating. At last she felt a sense of content-ment. He wanted her.

'Can you get me a drink, babe? I'll have a beer if you've got one,' Stevie asked. 'And have you got anything to eat? I'm starving.'

That killed the moment. Reluctantly she got up, slipped on her dress and went to the kitchen. She returned with a bottle of Beck's and a leaflet from her local pizza delivery. 'Here, you'll have to phone up for a pizza, I've got nothing in the house.'

Stevie sat up, stretched and yawned, scanned the leaflet and declared, 'I'll have an American hot.' He lay back down, clearly expecting Eden to order the pizza for him. She raised an eyebrow as she looked at him. 'What?' he asked. 'You'd better phone in case someone recognises my voice, and it is okay if you pay, babe, isn't it? I haven't got any money on me.'

It was, she supposed, perfectly reasonable, but there was something about the way Stevie had asked her. It was lacking in charm, as if he already took her for granted. Still, maybe she was being over-sensitive because of him not being able to see her earlier and because it was her birthday. Any girl wanted to be treated like a princess on her birthday, didn't she?

Half an hour later, she had watched Stevie chomp his way through an entire thick-crust pizza and drink three beers, while listening to him agonise about how Rapture were doing. 'I just don't think Taylor is pulling his weight. Sometimes I feel when we're singing that he's getting left behind. I don't know, it's like he's labouring the point. Holding me back.'

It was after one a.m. by now. Eden was scratchy-eyed with exhaustion and she had an early start the following morning, when she was being interviewed and photo-graphed for *Glamour* magazine. At this rate every part of her would have to be Photoshopped to stop her looking like a haggard old bag.

'Stevie, I think Taylor is doing the best he can and he's good. Don't be so hard on him otherwise you will end up denting his confidence, which will be totally counter-productive.'

'Can't you say something to him, as our mentor? He'll listen to you.'

'I'll think about it. I want to see how he's performing before I do.' She stifled a yawn. 'I've got to go to bed. How are we going to do this? Do you want to set the alarm and leave really early, or do you think you should go now?'

Stevie pulled her to him and kissed her. He tasted of pepperoni and beer, but he was still a fantastic kisser. 'I don't ever want to go,' he murmured. 'But I guess it would be better if I went now.' He paused. 'But first there's something I need to tell you.'

Eden's stomach lurched. Was this the moment when he revealed that he had feelings for Alana? She gazed at him but he avoided eye contact as he said, 'There's a story coming out in the next few days about me – I don't know when exactly. My ex-girlfriend has sold one. I asked her not to, but she wouldn't listen. I suppose the money was too tempting.'

Another lurch of Eden's stomach. This was not going to be good news.

'We split up just before I got a place on the competition, but I know she's going to come out with some crap about how I dumped her when I found out I had a place. It's going to put me in such a bad light. But I swear we split up before I knew. It's all lies but you know the kind of thing, Eden, don't you? It's happened to you enough times, hasn't it?'

Only too well . . . Eden waited for him to tell her about his ex-girlfriend being pregnant. 'It'll be okay

214

though, won't it? It shouldn't affect my popularity?' Clearly Stevie was not going to tell her the whole story.

Should she push him? She didn't know if she could face doing that right now. Instead she said, 'I'm sure you'll survive it, but you had better deliver a heartfelt performance on Saturday, something that makes people want to cry.' He put his arms round her then and hugged her tight. 'I can do that, no problem. I'll have them crying in bucket loads and creaming their knickers.'

She didn't like the way it sounded so manipulative, and pulled out of his embrace, 'You have such a way with words, Stevie. I wonder if your fans have any idea what you're really like.'

He looked at her. All the cocky arrogance had returned. 'It's true though, isn't it? They all want a piece of me. Their hot little pussies are burning for me.'

He slid his hands over her body, finishing up between her thighs. Eden was simultaneously repelled by his arrogance and incredibly turned on, as his fingers expertly teased and aroused her. 'But there's only one woman I want, and that's you.' And to prove it he slipped off his jeans and pushed his already-hard cock inside her. Eden was feeling sore from earlier but she didn't want him to stop. She wanted him again, fiercely, as much as he seemed to want her.

Chapter Sixteen

Somehow Eden managed to get to the photo-shoot on time the following morning, but she was absolutely exhausted and the face looking back at her from the mirror showed it. There were dark circles under her eyes, her lips were cracked from passionate kissing, and there was a hickey on her neck which she was going to explain away as chafing from one of her necklaces. She had, of course, reckoned without the beady eye of Jez who, when Darcy had left the room, pointed a finger at her neck and said, 'So someone got lucky last night.' A beat. 'The question is, with whom?'

'Oh, God!' Eden groaned, tilting her neck and peering at the offending mark in the mirror. 'Is it that noticeable?'

'Honey, wear it as a badge of honour! It's so bad girl, it's perfect for your image. But come on, 'fess up, who was the giver?'

She rolled her eyes. 'Stevie, of course, do you really think I'm that fickle?'

'No, no, but I don't know how you could resist sexy, manly Jack Steele. Even his name is hard and masculine and makes me think of big, strong, throbbing—'

Fortunately Darcy returned, sparing Eden from Jez revealing the full extent of his sexual fantasies. And

216

then Lexi, the tall blonde über-skinny stylist, popped in to go through some outfits with Eden – or 'scenarios' as she called them.

'I want to get away from your trademark look and try something different. Are you up for that?' Lexi asked, exuding manic energy while waving around fingers decorated with very fashion-fast-forward khaki nail varnish.

Frankly they could have put her in a bin bag, Eden was too tired to care. And so she went along with Lexi's plan which was to have her in an Audrey Hepburn-esque little black dress, hanging unusually for Eden just below the knee, elegant black suede slingbacks, long satin gloves, and several strings of pearls round her neck. Jez worked his magic with her hair, giving her a sleek glamorous French pleat. Her make-up was subtle, with pale pink lips and a swoop of black eyeliner on her lids. She hardly recognised herself by the end.

'Wow! You look like a proper lady!' Jez declared, putting on a cockney accent. 'You should dress like that more often!'

Eden tugged at the dress and fiddled with the gloves; she found the whole get-up too grown-up, and not sexy enough for her. She wasn't going to feel at all comfortable being photographed like this. She had to assert her own style.

'How about I start off just like Audrey and then gradually I relax the look? So, for example, my hair could come down, one strap of the dress could slip off, I could lie back on the bed and ruck my skirt up so you can see the tops of my stockings?'

Lexi was nodding excitedly. 'I love it! It's like you're unravelling, showing us the real you, just as the article is getting under your skin, revealing your essence.'

Yeah, whatever, Eden thought, but smiled politely.

217

'You can take the girl out of Essex but you can't take Essex out of the girl,' Jez commented wryly.

Eden gave him the finger. 'I was born in Hampstead Garden Suburb!'

'Well, it's in the direction of Essex, isn't it?'

Eden shook her head at his appalling sense of geography.

And so instead of being photographed feeling stiff and self-conscious, Eden relaxed in the shoot and had fun. While she might have dismissed as pretentious Lexi's comment about the shots showing the real Eden, in fact they did capture her sensuality, her spirit, and also at times her vulnerability.

After the shoot she happily swapped the dress for her skinny jeans, heels and her favourite top of the moment: a long-sleeved white tee-shirt with a bright red sequined love heart on the front of it. And then it was time to be interviewed by Imogen, the sleek, achingly on-trend journalist, dressed in a tailored jacket and pencil skirt in cream, with nude Louboutin pumps.

Ever since her mum's death, when she had gone off the rails, Eden had had something of a love/hate relationship with the press – more often hate than love. Previously she had always been honest and outspoken, not wanting to talk all that bland bullshit so many celebrities did, but she had come to realise that attitude didn't do her any favours. The press were always going to win and she had learnt the hard way that she had to keep something back, otherwise give them an inch and they would take everything, trample over her heart and not care less about the consequences, so long as it made a good story.

The interview started off easily enough – focusing on Eden's style, what she liked, what she didn't – and there was the inevitable question about how she stayed in shape.

'I work my arse off, of course!' Eden replied. 'I go to the gym at least five times a week, and I've got the toughest personal trainer in the world, who doesn't let me get away with anything. And I try and eat healthily, but it isn't always easy. Of course I have those days when I stuff my face and then regret it. Then it's back to the gym.'

'Don't you think women should feel happy in their own skin and not worry too much about their size?' That from Imogen who looked as if she survived on a diet of edamame beans and fresh air.

Eden shrugged, 'Of course, but I know that I feel happier now I'm slimmer. I mean, I love my curves but it's hard work keeping them under control.' This was bearable, thought Eden, but then Imogen turned her attention to *Band Ambition*, asking her how she found being a judge and what she thought of her acts.

'Stevie's the one everyone loves, isn't he?' she commented, smiling. 'Everyone in my office fancies the pants off him.'

Eden tried not to read anything into Imogen's smile, she mustn't feel paranoid; no one knew anything, least of all this journalist.

'Stevie is very attractive,' she admitted, 'but I think all my groups are hugely talented. They're all so different, and my job is to help them shine.' She felt like such a hypocrite saying that as she suddenly had a flashback to the night before and Stevie's cynical comment about all the women lusting after him. She thought about her own behaviour then and how quickly she had forgiven him and not asked any awkward questions.

Imogen's BlackBerry vibrated with a text. She frowned as she read it, then said, 'It's my editor. Would you mind if I call her back? It won't take long.'

'Sure,' Eden replied, relieved to have a break from

the questions. While Imogen went out of the room, Eden took the opportunity to check her own phone where there was a message from Stevie. *I'm hard just thinking about last night. xx* It triggered a flutter of desire in Eden, but she guiltily deleted the message. She switched her phone off and shoved it back in her bag. She couldn't deal with opening any such message in front of Imogen; she wasn't a good enough actress to be able to disguise her feelings.

The journalist returned and smoothed down her pencil skirt as she sat down. 'Um, I hope it is okay to ask you this, but what exactly is your relationship with Jack Steele?'

Eden stared back at her. She hadn't expected this at all! What did the journalist know? 'Well, we're work colleagues and friends. It's as straightforward as that.'

Imogen shifted in her seat; she looked slightly awkward. 'Apparently my editor heard that there is going to be a picture in one of tomorrow's papers of the pair of you kissing. Is that true?'

It was at times like this that Eden wished she had Sadie with her. She was always brilliant at stopping journalists from asking any awkward questions. But she had to be cool here because unless Jack's apartment was bugged, the photograph Imogen was referring to must have been the one the pap took last night outside the restaurant. Eden managed a laugh.

'That was Jack kissing me goodnight – on the cheek. And that's of my face, for all the perverts out there! I'd gone out with a group of friends to celebrate my birthday.'

'Happy Birthday for yesterday.'

'Thanks.' Eden was tiring of the interview now. Just grin and bear it, she told herself.

'So you and Jack are definitely not an item?'

Just drop it! 'Absolutely not. We're friends.'

'Is there someone special in your life right now?'

Eden dug her nails into the palms of her hands as she had an almost irresistible and self-destructive urge to smile! But somehow she managed to say, 'I am one hundred percent focused on work right now, on the show and on my new album. I'm in no rush at all to jump into another relationship.'

'So what would a man have to do to attract your attention?'

'God, I don't know! He'd have to be sexy and strong and not let me walk all over him. I'd have to be able to respect him. And he would have to be kind.' It was strange, but as Eden came up with 'kind' as a quality, she suddenly realised that while Stevie was many things, he was not kind.

'The perfect man, in other words,' Imogen joked back.

'Yes, I want only the best!'

And then thankfully Imogen asked her about her music. At last Eden felt on safer territory, and by the end of the interview sensed that it had gone okay and that she hadn't given anything away that she shouldn't. But she always had the feeling that being interviewed by the press was like swimming in shark-infested waters. You never knew when something was going to bite.

From there it was straight round to the rehearsal studios to see her acts, and as she was being driven there Eden switched her phone back on. Almost instantly Sadie called her in a state of excitement. 'Is there anything I should know about you and Jack? What's this about a late-night encounter? I'm intrigued!'

'Let me guess. One of your journalist contacts has tipped you off that I was photographed kissing Jack.' Eden was feeling frustrated at the way everyone seemed to be focusing on this, but still at least no one had seen Stevie slip into her house. She very much doubted Sadie would have been sounding so cheerful had that been the case.

'From the way he told it, honey, you two needed to get a room! So what's going on? I didn't think Jack was your type.'

Eden sighed. 'He isn't. He was kissing me goodnight, that's all. So could you please put out a statement saying we're just friends?'

'Just good friends?'

'Just friends will do.'

'Okay.' A pause. 'But it's funny . . . the more I think about it, the more it seems like you and Jack would make a great couple. He's no pretty-boy pushover. He's older, wiser, he's seen the world, and he wouldn't take any shit from you or treat you badly. You could do with someone like that, someone who's more of an equal. He's intelligent, talented and very sexy. Though he's not great at commitment after what happened, I'm sure you could change that.'

Eden was so surprised by the first part of Sadie's comment that she didn't really take in anything else. Instead of asking what had happened to Jack, she jumped in with, 'What are you on about, Sadie? We are just friends, nothing more!'

'Okay, okay, have it your way. Oh, and there is one more thing – a biggie but the kiss distracted me – Marc White now wants your album a month after *Band Ambition* finishes, so you and Jack are really going to have to get a move on. How many tracks have you recorded so far?'

'Four.'

'Well, just eight more to go then. You're going to be spending a lot of time with him in the next few weeks, so perhaps it's as well you're just good friends,' Sadie teased her.

'I said just friends!' Eden shot back, but Sadie had already hung up.

It was such a full-on afternoon with her acts that Eden didn't have time to worry about the photos of her and Jack coming out in the press, and he was in meetings all day so she didn't get to see him. And besides, she thought, it was hardly worth mentioning. But this was not a view that Stevie shared when the pictures were published the following day. Eden was woken up at eight by a phone call.

'Hey,' she said sleepily, 'I was just dreaming about you. D'you want to hear about my dream? I think you'll like it.'

'What the fuck do you think you're playing at?' he shouted. 'Is there something going on between you and Steele?'

Eden sat up. 'No, of course not!'

She was about to explain about the goodnight kiss, but Stevie didn't give her the chance. Well, how the fuck do you explain those pictures then?'

'Oh, for God's sake, Stevie! Jack was just kissing me goodnight after my birthday meal and we were papped. We're friends and colleagues, that's all.'

'Well, I don't want you seeing him any more. You're always all over each other, and I've seen the way he looks at you.' He sounded aggressively macho. She'd never heard Stevie speak like this before.

'What!' Eden said in disbelief.

'You're my girl. I don't want you seeing Jack Steele, not without me being there.'

'You're kidding me! I have to see Jack, I'm making my album with him.'

'Sack him and get someone else. If you loved me, you would do that for me. It's the least you can do after those photographs.'

Eden was about to tell him not to be so stupid when he added, 'Don't bother talking to me until you've done it.' And he hung up.

What the fuck? She couldn't believe Stevie was behaving like this. No way was she going to have him tell her what to do! And he had better apologise for behaving like such a dick. Eden hurriedly got ready for her session at the gym. There she was met by Rufus, looking as ready for action as ever in a tight black Lycra tracksuit that showed off his muscular physique. No wonder Jez adored him!

It was as if Rufus had a sixth sense that Eden might need to let off some steam. After an intense cardio session he got her to put on some boxing gloves. 'Right cross followed by left hook,' Rufus ordered, as he nimbly moved around, and Eden tried to keep up with his fancy footwork and land a solid punch on the pads he was holding up.

Wham! That one was for Stevie, for being such an idiot! Wham! And that one was for the bloody paps! Her strength and force even impressed Rufus; it just showed what sheer rage could do to a girl's ability to pack a punch. By the end of the session Eden was feeling more forgiving towards Stevie. Perhaps she had been too quick to condemn him and needed to see it from his point of view. She knew herself well enough to realise how jealously she would have reacted if she had been confronted with pictures of him kissing another girl, and how hard she would have found it to believe that those kisses were innocent. After all, she had been jealous when she had simply seen him talking to Alana! And so after her shower she made the first move and called him. But Stevie had not mellowed in the slightest.

'Have you sacked him yet? Because that's the only way I'll talk to you.'

He still sounded so angry and aggressive that all thoughts of reconciliation went out of Eden's head. 'For fuck's sake, Stevie, grow up! And this time she hung up on him. It was stalemate.

'Sorry about the photographs ending up in the papers,' Jack said to her as she joined him in the studio a couple of hours later.

'I'm used to it,' Eden said dryly, thinking of the grief it had caused her with Stevie. 'I hope Cherry wasn't upset.'

'Um, I'm not seeing her any more. We broke up.'

Was it Eden's imagination or did Jack seem a little awkward, not quite as together as usual?

'Oh, I'm sorry.'

He shrugged. 'No need to be, we wanted different things.' He paused. 'So, we should get started. We've got a lot to do. Nothing like a deadline to focus the mind.'

And Eden went through into the recording booth and took her place at the microphone. Once she started singing all thoughts of Stevie and the stress of the day melted away. She lost herself utterly in the music.

Some four hours later they had another track in the can and Jack was full of praise for her. 'You know, you just get better and better, Eden. I must admit that I was pretty sceptical about taking this album on. Sadie had to work hard to persuade me that it would be worth doing.'

'Why? Did you think I'd be some shallow pop princess who couldn't sing?' she teased him.

They were both sitting in the studio now, relaxing on the sofa, drinking beer and eating peanuts. Eden didn't want to think about what Rufus would have to say about that combination. Or Stevie, for that matter.

'I knew you could sing, but yeah, maybe I did think

225

you'd be shallow and diva-like. And, if I'm honest, a total pain in the arse!'

Eden swiped a punch at his arm. 'Thanks a lot! Big me up, why don't you?'

'Well, at least I can admit that I was wrong. You're anything but shallow. You're not a pain in the arse, but I'm sure you have it in you to be a diva.'

Eden held up her bottle of beer and joked, 'But I'm only supposed to drink vintage pink champagne out of crystal, diamond-encrusted glasses, poured for me by fit young men who minister to my every whim. And where's my basket of fluffy white kittens to soothe my nerves? And while I'm at it I might have to adopt an adorable and photogenic baby from a Third World country . . . provided I have the right team of nannies, cooks and housekeepers to do absolutely everything for me.'

'Be careful,' Jack warned her. 'You're a little too good at that diva routine.' And then all of a sudden he looked serious. 'Actually, I need to talk to you about something.'

For an awful moment Eden was worried that he was going to bring up Stevie and comment on how close she seemed to him.

'I wanted to say sorry.'

Eden looked at him. She hadn't expected this and was surprised to see that once again he seemed ill at ease, which was most unlike him.

'Sorry about what, Jack?'

He picked at the silver foil round the top of his bottle of beer. 'I've been doing a lot of thinking and I realise I was out of order in the way I behaved towards you – the night of that record company party.'

'Oh. *That* night,' Eden said quietly, while thinking WTF was he doing, bringing *that* night up now? *That* night was history. She had moved on, hadn't she?

'I realise that I didn't handle things very well.' He paused as if steeling himself to continue. 'You're right about me and relationships; I do run away from them. But I wanted to tell you that I don't want to do that any more.'

'Oh, so you're going to work things out with Cherry?' Eden enquired, wondering where this conversation was leading.

'Not Cherry.' A beat. He looked at her. And suddenly Eden realised exactly what was coming next and it was all wrong! She couldn't believe how bad his timing was! 'Eden, I haven't been able to stop thinking about you. You must have realised that I have feelings for you?'

Shit! This could not be happening.

'Oh,' she said again, too stunned to know what else to reply.

'I wondered if you would come out for dinner sometime?' He paused. 'On a date.'

Eden was practically squirming on the sofa with embarrassment. 'Jack, I'm cool about what happened between us that night. I admit that I wasn't for a while, but I am now. And I am happy with the way things are between us, as friends. I respect you, Jack, and like you. And . . . this is embarrassing, but I'm seeing someone else. And it's serious.'

Eden spoke in a rush, running her words together in her awkwardness. All those weeks she'd been tormented by longing for him and Jack chose *now* to declare his feelings, when she was head over heels in love with Stevie? How painfully ironic . . .

For a fleeting moment Jack's blue eyes registered shock and hurt, but then he was back to being the cool, un-fazed about anything man that she knew. Fixing his gaze somewhere on the middle distance, as if he couldn't bring himself to make eye contact with her, he said, 'Wow, that was embarrassing. Sure, Eden, I understand.' He stood up to go. 'Thanks for being so honest with me. I promise that this isn't going to affect our professional relationship.'

They then had the supremely awkward situation of walking out of the building together while Eden tried to make sense of what had just happened. Outside she was about to say goodbye to Jack and pray that there was a taxi she could jump into straight away when, to her amazement, she caught sight of Stevie on the other side of the road. He was leaning against the iron railings outside a church, arms folded across his chest, staring fixedly at her. She expected him to stay put until Jack was safely out of sight but he sprinted over the road, nearly getting run over by a taxi, calling out her name once he reached the pavement.

'What's he doing here?' Jack asked. Good question. Eden shrugged and tried to seem casual, but her heart was racing. How was Stevie going to explain his sudden appearance? He stood in front of them, out of breath from running.

'Eden, I've got to talk to you about the group. There's stuff going on you should know about . . .' At least he'd come up with some kind of excuse.

'Couldn't it have waited until tomorrow? Eden's had a long recording session,' Jack put in coolly. He really didn't like Stevie, she thought.

Stevie glared at him, his fists clenched by his sides, and Eden had an awful thought that he might swing a punch at Jack, in some testosterone-fuelled moment of madness. Fortunately he controlled the impulse.

'It's fine, Jack,' she said smoothly. 'I'll go and have a coffee with Stevie. I'll see you tomorrow. And thanks for everything.' She really didn't feel up to dealing with this after Jack's bombshell declaration!

'Okay, if you're sure. See you, Eden.'

For a few seconds she and Stevie stood looking at

each other. They were standing under a streetlight, and in its orange glow it was as if they were in their own personal spotlight on stage. Eden could only hope that no one was watching the show.

'What are you doing here, Stevie?' She was the first to speak.

'What did you mean, "thanks for everything"? And I thought I said I didn't want you working with him any more.' Stevie was back to being aggressive.

God! So he had just tracked her down purely to continue having a go at her; she thought he might at least have come to apologise. This was a stupid argument and she wasn't going to pander to his irrational jealousy any longer.

'For the last time, there is nothing going on between me and Jack. And no one . . . not you, not anyone . . . tells me what to do and how to live my life.' She glared at him, a look of pure fury in her green eyes. 'I've had enough of this.' She began walking swiftly away, almost breaking into a run in her anger. But Stevie pursued her and grabbed her arm, none too gently.

'Ouch!' she exclaimed, trying to get out of his grip.

'Please, Eden, don't go! I'm sorry.' He certainly looked sorry. There was no trace of the usual arrogance in his face, and finally the aggressive tone had gone. He let go of her arm, and Eden made a point of rubbing it to point out how much he had hurt her.

'I know I've behaved like a complete twat but it's because I thought I was losing you. I couldn't bear it, Eden. I love you so much. You are everything to me. The competition doesn't matter . . . nothing matters except you.' He was gazing at her, a serious, heartfelt expression on his face, a note of desperation in his voice. Immediately Eden softened towards him. How could she not in the face of such a declaration?

'You're right, you've been a complete twat!' she

exclaimed, and Stevie hung his head. He was so adorable in his desperation, she wanted to throw her arms around him then and there, but there were things she had to say first.

'Don't ever treat me like this again. And don't ever tell me what to do.'

'I won't, Eden, I swear. Please say you forgive me?'

She held his gaze for a beat, then replied, 'I forgive you. But I should go and you should get back to the house. People will be wondering where you are.'

'Can't we go to the apartment? I want you, Eden. I have to have you.'

She shook her head even though her heart and body were screaming yes.

'Let me just have a kiss then?' And Stevie took her hand and led her into the dimly lit doorway of an office block. And then they were in each other's arms, kissing with a feverish passion and to hell with the world. Finally Eden came to her senses and pulled away.

They emerged from the doorway. Eden was straightening her skirt when she saw something that caused her heart to miss several beats. A familiar figure. Jack was just ahead of them in the street. He didn't need to say anything. The look on his face told them everything. He had seen them kissing. He stood there waiting for Eden and Stevie to catch up with him.

'I just wanted to check that you were okay, Eden. And it seems that you are.' He sounded distant, cold, judgemental. She winced at his tone which made it clear she had forfeited the right to his friendship.

She started to speak, to implore him not to say anything, but Jack prevented her. 'You don't need to explain, your secret is safe with me. But you're both playing a very dangerous game.' And with that he walked away. For a few stunned seconds Eden watched him go. She was appalled by what she had done.

'Don't worry, Eden, you heard what he said.' Stevie didn't sound at all concerned. 'Let's go to the apartment.'

But she shook her head, too shaken up. She needed to be on her own right now. Needed time to think about what the hell she was going to do about this.

Chapter Seventeen

'I tell you, yet again, that if your life was a film or a book I would be sitting here saying I just don't freaking believe this could happen, it's too far-fetched!' Jez declared.

He and Tanya had answered Eden's frantic SOS calls to them and come straight over to the house. Jack's revelation that he had feelings for her, only to go on and find out about her and Stevie, had left Eden reeling.

They were sitting in the living room; Eden had felt so cold, no doubt from the shock she had had, that even though it was early-July she had lit a fire. Its warmth was giving her some comfort, but as she stared bleakly into the orange flames she didn't know how to begin to deal with the situation. How could she and Stevie have been so reckless? It was complete madness. They both ran the risk of losing everything. A few weeks ago, when she had first got together with him, Eden would have believed that a break from seeing Stevie was out of the question. But now she'd had a reality check to end all reality checks.

'You can't see Stevie alone until after the competition, and that's final,' Tanya exclaimed.

'I know,' Eden said quietly. 'I'm going to call him

later and tell him.' She paused. 'And I think I might have to resign from being a judge too. If it gets out that I started seeing him while I was on the panel it would completely blow my credibility. I'd be accused of favouritism.'

Eden was sure that Tanya was dying to say that she had told her so, but it was to her friend's great credit that she did not. Instead she replied, 'I don't think you should rush into doing anything. I'm sure you can trust Jack. And can you imagine Dallas's reaction if you said you wanted to leave? He's already lost one judge and you're mid-series. He would probably sue you for breach of contract!'

Eden hadn't thought of that, but on reflection she realised Dallas was known to be a ruthless businessman and would certainly not take kindly to his show being severely disrupted by her. On the other hand, she really didn't think that she should continue to mentor Rapture. She might suggest to Dallas swapping groups with Amber or Ricky. She could say that there was a personality clash between her and Stevie, and then pray that Dallas took her at her word and didn't probe too deeply.

And then there was the whole added complication of Jack . . . He had opened up to her for the first time ever, and what had she done? Not only had she rejected him but he'd caught her snogging Stevie straight afterwards! She thought about how it must have looked from his point of view and imagined how judgemental she would have been if she had caught him in such a compromising situation with one of the contestants. This whole thing was such a mess, and once again it was a mess that was entirely of her own making. If only she hadn't been so reckless and headstrong, rushing in without giving a thought to the consequences. It was the story of her life. She thought about how much she'd enjoyed working with Jack, how much she valued his friendship; how much she had appreciated him rescuing her birthday; the wonderful songs he had written for her album . . . there were so many good things, and she had blown it all.

'Poor Jack must have been gutted when he saw you and Stevie,' Tanya commented.

Eden put her head in her hands and groaned. 'Don't, Tan, I feel so bad about it.'

'Well, he did reject you the first time,' Jez put in, trying to lighten the mood. 'It's only fair you should get your revenge.'

It backfired. Tanya frowned at him for being flippant and said, 'He must have issues and I'd love to know what they are. He puts up this image of being so cool but underneath there is obviously all this passion going on. It must have taken a lot for him to tell you how he felt.'

'I know, I know!' Jez put in excitedly, trying to get back in Tanya's good books. 'He's an ice man, but with a burning volcano inside him, waiting to get out! He was all set to erupt for you, Eden, and I bet that would be some eruption! Jack Steele is *so* manly. Every time I see him, I come over like a Southern Belle. I want to swoon in his arms and ask him to fetch me a mint julep, whatever that is. It sounds mighty fine.'

Jez actually put on a Southern accent as he brushed one hand languidly across his forehead. Tanya burst out laughing while Eden rolled her eyes.

'Mint julep my arse!' she shot back. 'What would Rufus say if he heard you talking like this? You're a tart, Jez!'

'Oh, we're allowed our fantasies. It's what keeps our marriage so fresh.'

'What are you going to do about Jack?' Tanya asked.

Eden shrugged helplessly. She had absolutely no idea

how to play things with him. After Tanya and Jez had left, she phoned Stevie.

'I knew you'd change your mind about meeting up!' he said as soon as he picked up. 'How soon can you be at the apartment?'

'That's not why I called,' Eden said quietly. She couldn't quite believe that Stevie sounded as if this was no big deal, when as far as she was concerned Jack's seeing them had changed everything.

'I can't see you again until after the competition. And I am going to ask Dallas if one of the other judges can take over mentoring you.'

Now the jokey tone vanished completely from Stevie's voice. 'What are you saying this for? Of course you can! You heard what Jack said – he's not going to say anything. I *need* to see you. And I want you to mentor us – you're the best there is!'

But Eden was adamant. No matter how hard Stevie begged her, she did not cave in. She felt utterly miserable as she ended the call and was almost tempted to phone him back and say she had made a mistake. But she held it together. She had done enough things she had regretted in her life. She did not intend to add to the list.

The next few days were like a nightmare; every time her phone rang Eden jumped thinking it was going to be the press telling her that they knew. She missed Stevie so badly it was like a physical ache. He tried calling and texting her, but she was ruthless about not picking up and deleting all his messages unanswered. Dallas was surprisingly okay about her request to hand Rapture over to another judge. He accepted her explanation that she found Stevie hard to work with, that he was too flirtatious and didn't take direction, and that as a result he was spoiling the group's chances.

Eden didn't need to acquire another group to replace Rapture as both Amber and Ricky had already lost groups. Dallas decided that Ricky was going to be their new mentor. Eden had the feeling that he thought it was not especially important who mentored them as he had already earmarked Stevie for stardom, if not with Rapture then as a solo artist.

He also put out a press release saying that he had decided to take Rapture away from Eden because she had so much on and needed more time to focus on her own album. The press became full of speculation that the real reason was that she and Stevie had fallen out because Eden was so impossible to work with. All of which would have upset her if she hadn't had so many other things to worry about, and top of her list was Jack . . .

The next time she saw him was when they were back in the studio to record another track. The contrast between this meeting and their previous ones could not have been starker. Jack was distant and formal, as if they were strangers. There was no banter, no teasing, no easy conversation. Eden managed to get through rehearsing one of the songs and then she couldn't bear the tension any longer. She had to have it out with him. She took off her headphones and left the cubicle, confronting Jack in the recording suite. He stared straight ahead as she marched in. He must have realised what she was going to say and it didn't look like he was going to make it easy for her.

Her words came out in a rush as she said, 'I want you to know, Jack, that I'm not seeing Stevie until after the show is over, and I have arranged with Dallas that I won't be Rapture's mentor any more.'

She didn't know what she had expected his response to be, but she was disappointed. Jack simply shrugged and said, while still staring straight ahead, 'It's your business, Eden. It's got nothing to do with me. As far as I'm concerned, I never saw you.'

'I'm sorry, Jack. I know I've behaved badly and that it looks like I've gone behind people's backs.'

Another shrug. 'Like I said, it's your business.' He sounded dismissive. Where was the friendly, easygoing man she had come to know?

'We can still be friends, can't we?' Eden found herself saying.

'Sure, we're friends.' His gaze was still fixed on the glass screen in front of him as if it was a source of great fascination. It looked as if this was all she was going to get out of him. She sighed, ready to go back into the cubicle, and then Jack spoke again. This time he looked at her. 'Just be very careful, Eden. Stevie is ruthlessly ambitious. I think he would pretty much do anything to become famous.'

Eden didn't like the insinuation, and instantly flared up. 'What? Like start a relationship with me? You can't fake the kind of feelings we have for each other! He loves me and I love him!' She paused and then said quietly, 'I wouldn't expect you to understand that.' She wasn't going to let him have it all his own way.

Jack shook his head. 'You're wrong, Eden. I do know what it is to love someone. Forget I ever said anything. Now can we get on? We've had enough distractions.'

With a heavy heart Eden returned to the recording booth. Somehow she had to block out all the negative things that were going on around her and focus on the music. She'd done it before. She could do it again.

The next three weeks seemed to be on fast forward as Eden worked flat out recording her album and the show. She felt as if she was being pulled in too many different directions, wanting to give her all to the show as well as putting everything she could into her album.

Extrema had gone out of the show on the previous Saturday, and while Eden was sad to see them go, she knew that she had done everything she possibly could to help the boys.

She ended every day feeling absolutely shattered. She'd grab something to eat, have a bath and collapse into bed. But she was glad of the full-on activity; it meant she didn't have too much time to brood about Stevie during the day. Night-time was a different story. Exhausted as she was, she still longed for him. She missed him desperately. Jack had thawed towards her slightly, which was a relief. True, there wasn't the easy banter between them that there had been before he'd found out about her and Stevie, but he wasn't giving her a hard time and the album was coming together better than Eden could have hoped for.

The final of the competition was just two days away. The finalists were Rapture, Venus Rising and 4Real, a boy band of Ricky's. The one thing that filled Eden with anxiety was the prospect of having to decide between Rapture and the girls. So far that situation hadn't arisen and she couldn't begin to imagine what she would do if it happened. But apart from that everything else seemed to be going well. The end of the competition *and* finishing her album were within view, and she would soon be free to be reunited with Stevie. And then, as if fate was once more saying, 'This is all too good to be true for you, Eden', Stevie's ex-girlfriend's story finally appeared in the press.

Eden walked into the girls' rehearsal studio to find them riveted by the contents of the *Sun*. Thinking it was most likely the same old recycled gossip, she clapped her hands together and said brightly, 'Come on, girls, we've got work to do! We can't have this slacking!'

All three of them turned round and looked at her, and all three of them seemed shocked. Alana was the first to speak. 'Sorry, Eden, we were just reading this story about Stevie.'

For an agonising few seconds Eden thought that the story was about *her* and Stevie. Then Alana carried on, 'His ex-girlfriend has sold a story on him. It's really bad, Eden. But it's probably not true, is it?'

Feeling hugely relieved that the story wasn't about her she walked over and picked up the paper. 'Oh, the press are always making things up. God knows they've done it to me enough times.' But the words died in her throat as she took in the picture of Stevie's ex cradling a newborn baby, with the caption screaming underneath: 'Stevie dumped me even though I was pregnant. He hasn't even seen our beautiful baby boy. What will I tell our son about his daddy?'

'Oh my God!' she couldn't stop herself exclaiming. She quickly scanned the article. Stevie did indeed come across spectacularly badly, as a heartless, selfish bastard. He had dumped Nicci, his girlfriend, by text as soon as he found he had a place in the competition and, according to her, he had known that she was pregnant. They had been going out together for two years, so it was hardly some casual fling. Nicci claimed that all Stevie cared about was being famous. It didn't matter how he did it. The words were an unsettling echo of what Jack had told Eden about Stevie. But that wasn't the worst thing; that was seeing the picture of his son, the child he didn't acknowledge. What kind of man could abandon his own baby?

'I knew his ex was going to do this story because he told us, but he never mentioned the baby,' Kasey said. She seemed as shaken up as Eden. 'I can't believe he could do that. It's such a shit thing to do.' Of all the girls Kasey seemed most shocked by the story, which surprised Eden because usually she was the toughest and very little seemed to upset her.

'We don't know exactly what happened between them,' Eden replied, trying to sound calm when all the time a voice in her head was screaming out, *Why didn't he tell me?* 'The press can twist things round and make people seem like monsters when they're not, trust me.'

'Yeah, I guess,' Kasey muttered. But she didn't sound convinced. 'He's going to have some serious explaining to do.'

'Okay, let's forget about this for now. We must get on.' Eden tried to pull herself together and rally the girls, but she felt as if a shadow had been cast over her day. She kept thinking about the story. She checked her phone and sure enough Stevie had sent her several texts asking her to call him, telling her that the story was all lies; how he didn't even think the baby was his and was going to demand a DNA test. None of which made Eden feel any better about things.

During a break she wandered to the coffee shop, and on the way passed another rehearsal studio. The door was open and she couldn't help overhearing Dallas shouting at someone who was undoubtedly Stevie. She froze, unable to stop herself from listening in. 'Why the hell didn't you tell me before? I could have managed the situation if you had.' Dallas sounded absolutely beside himself with fury. Eden was sure that he had already pinned his hopes on making Stevie a star and was relying on him to bring in the cash. He was such a control freak, he would loathe being wrong-footed like this.

'I'm sorry, Dallas, I didn't know she would sell the story. She promised me that she wouldn't,' a subdued Stevie replied.

'So, is the child yours?' Dallas snapped.

'Um . . . I'm not sure.'

'I want the truth,' came the reply. 'Don't fuck with

me, Stevie, because I will find out, believe me. I want all the facts laid out in front of me. No slippery business, no wriggling out of this. And try and show some class! You're meant to be a mainstream singer, a star in the making, not some tacky contributor to the *Jeremy Kyle Show*.'

A pause. Stevie was clearly weighing up his options and then he said, 'I'm pretty sure he is. Yeah. I'm sorry, I know I haven't handled this well.'

'On that at least you and I agree,' came Dallas's reply.

Eden closed her eyes and leant against the wall. She felt shaken to the core. How could she ever trust Stevie again? He had deliberately not told her he had a son. What else had he kept from her? She tuned back into the conversation. Dallas was outlining his action plan. How Stevie had to give a statement saying that he was deeply sorry for any hurt he had caused and was going to make sure he paid maintenance for his baby son. That he had been a foolish boy but was now going to behave like a man and take full responsibility. Stevie was dutifully saying yes to everything Dallas said, sounding desperate to get back into his good books.

It made Eden feel sick. She was all set to continue to the café, though frankly she needed a stiff drink rather than a coffee, when Dallas and Stevie walked out of the room. Stevie looked stunned to see her there. He must have realised that she had overheard everything.

Dallas fixed her with his cool grey eyes. 'Eden, I trust we can rely on your discretion?'

She hated the way she was being dragged into their sordid web of lies. 'I guess. But however you spin the story, Dallas, it still doesn't look good.' She was looking at Stevie as she spoke and he put his hand up to his head as if to say, 'Don't give me a hard time.'

Dallas turned to him. 'Can you excuse us now, Stevie, and get back to rehearsals? I'll be in touch later. And don't say anything to anyone without clearing it with me first. It's imperative that we contain this story.'

Reluctantly Stevie walked away. His shoulders were hunched, his head bowed. His usual confidence had deserted him.

Dallas looked at Eden questioningly. 'Why are you so concerned? You're not even mentoring Stevie any more. And I thought you, of all people, would be sympathetic to anyone being given a mauling by the press.'

Eden didn't like being lumped into the same category as Stevie. 'I've done many things in my time, Dallas, but so far abandoning a child isn't on that list. I think Stevie's behaviour has been totally out of order. And the fans will hate it as well.'

Dallas shrugged. 'The fans will come round after he apologises. If anything, it will intrigue them. Stevie the bad boy turned Stevie the penitent. We're going to do an interview about it later and then a press conference. I'm hoping we might even be able to do a photo-shoot with the baby. I'm sure the mother will let us if the price is right.'

Could Dallas be any more cynical? Eden was so disgusted by the way he was manipulating the story, she couldn't even bring herself to reply. Thankfully he was already striding purposefully away, calling his assistant and telling her to cancel all his meetings.

Somehow Eden got through the rest of the day but there was no way she could face going home and agonising over Stevie. She knew how judgemental Tanya would be about the whole situation, and couldn't face her friend either. She ended up calling Jez and he invited her over to his Islington flat where he opened the door to her and immediately gave her a big hug.

'Be brave, my darling, you don't need to be dragged down by this,' he told her, leading her into the extremely tidy minimalist living room. There was not a piece of clutter to be seen. It didn't seem very Jez-like. As if knowing what she was thinking, he commented, 'I told you, Rufus is a bit of a neat freak. Luckily I have a spare room which is full of all my stuff.'

Eden flopped down on the black velvet sofa. She felt completely exhausted and drained by the day's revelation. 'Oh, Jez, it's all such a mess! Why couldn't Stevie have told me the truth? I hate it that he lied to me.'

Jez handed her an extra-large glass of wine. She raised an eyebrow just imagining what Rufus would have to say. 'He's at work, you're safe.' He sat down next to her.

'It's understandable that Stevie didn't want to 'fess up, Eden. I mean, it hardly shows him in a good light, and who can blame him for wanting to gloss over what happened? Maybe the relationship was over before he found out she was pregnant and then he felt trapped. He wouldn't be the first man to feel like that. Not that I think what he did was right,' Jez added hastily.

Eden took a large slug of wine. 'Thank God for you, Jez. I don't think Tanya or any of my other friends would be quite so understanding.' At that moment her phone beeped with a text message from Tanya: *Are you OK? Call me if you need to. Any time. Thinking of you. xx* Okay, maybe she was wrong about Tanya, but she still wasn't sure. Stevie had texted her again and left yet another message pleading with her to phone him, but she didn't. She kept thinking of how he'd acted around Dallas, so eager to please and jump to do whatever was suggested. It didn't exactly say independent sexy man to her.

She turned to Jez, her green eyes full of sadness.

243

'What should I do, Jez? In my heart I know that I love him so much, I can't imagine not being with him, but my head keeps telling me that I have to be careful, that what he did was wrong. If he could do that to one woman, what's to stop him doing it to me?' The questions and doubts were swirling round in her head; she felt as if she was in a tortuous sickening maze and couldn't see a way out of it.

'Okay. For now all you can do is focus on the final show. After that you can have it out with Stevie. But there literally is nothing you can do before that. You can't see him, you can't talk to him, so you're just going to have to accept that.'

It was the last thing Eden wanted, but she knew Jez was right; she didn't have any other option. She stayed for another drink, refusing his offer of food – she had entirely lost her appetite – and then she took a taxi home. She checked her messages – yet more texts from Stevie imploring her to call him – she didn't – and a text from Jack asking her if she was okay. She texted back: *I'm as OK as can be expected under the circumstances. Thanks for asking. x* She pressed send, thinking that Jack must have an even lower opinion of Stevie now.

Back home she was too wired to sleep and stayed up late listening to music, endlessly obsessing over what she should do. Should she tell Stevie that it was over? That she couldn't be with a liar? But the prospect of leaving him tore her apart. She loved him so much, was in so deep, she couldn't imagine being without him. And yet, he had lied and that was surely a deal breaker . . . At one a.m. she was startled by the ringing of the doorbell. Imagining it was bound to be teenagers messing around, she was all set to ignore it when it rang again. Tentatively she made her way to the front door and looked through the spy hole. To her amazement she saw Stevie standing on her doorstep.

'Please, Eden,' she heard him say, 'I know you're there. Please let me in.'

She unlocked the front door and opened it, not at all sure that she was doing the right thing. Stevie walked in. He looked exhausted, drained, his fans wouldn't have recognised him as the sexy confident singer who owned the stage every Saturday night. She shut the door and stood in front of him, arms folded. She wasn't going to make this easy for him.

'Eden, I cannot even begin to tell you how sorry I am. I made a mistake, panicked when I found out Nicci was pregnant. I already knew our relationship was over when she told me – not that I'd told her. I didn't handle it well. I ran away. I was a fucking stupid, cowardly idiot! And I know I should have told you about Nicci and the baby right from the start, but I was always so afraid of losing you. I didn't want you to think less of me because of that one mistake. I love you so much, Eden.' As he looked at her she was stunned to see that his eyes were brimming with tears.

'It doesn't matter to me what happens with the competition. I couldn't give a shit about that any more. All I care about is you. Please tell me that I haven't messed everything up? Please tell me that you can forgive me and that we can move on from this?'

Part of Eden longed to run into his arms. Her heart ached to see him standing before her, so obviously struggling to keep his composure, but she still wasn't sure.

'I just don't know, Stevie. So much has happened. I never thought you would lie to me like this. You've hurt me so badly.'

Stevie clenched his fists as he struggled to hold it together. He closed his eyes briefly and said, 'Then tell me what you're going to do. If you want to end it with me, tell me. I can't go on with this uncertainty.'

'I don't know what to do,' Eden repeated. She felt so bleak and lost. Stevie reached out and gently touched her hair.

'Okay, I understand. If you need time to think, I'll give you time.' He turned to go. Eden suddenly couldn't bear the distance between them to last another second. Couldn't bear to watch him leave. She stepped towards him, and at that moment Stevie turned back. Then they were in each other's arms and holding each other tight.

'I love you, Eden,' Stevie whispered, kissing her hair, her face, her neck.

'I love you too,' she replied, meaning it and knowing then and there that she was going to forgive Stevie, that she would put the past behind them. They ended up spending the night together and for the first time didn't make love but simply held each other. It was only in the early morning that Stevie made love to her, with a tenderness that had been missing from all their previous encounters.

'I hope the paps don't get up this early,' he joked as they once more stood together in the hall. It was half-past six. Eden didn't even feel nervous on that score any more. She had the strongest feeling of what would be, would be. She couldn't fight it. A last kiss and then Stevie said, 'As long as I have you, Eden, I can face anything.'

He opened the door and stepped outside. Eden steeled herself for the sound of cameras clicking away, but none came.

Chapter Eighteen

Dallas was true to his word and lined up wall-to-wall coverage in the press. Stevie publicly confessed how sorry he was for his past behaviour. Somehow Dallas had used his extensive powers of persuasion to get the ex-girlfriend on board, and she did indeed allow Stevie to do a photo-shoot cradling his baby son in his arms. There was even a black-and-white shot of a bare-chested Stevie holding his son and gazing adoringly at him, mimicking the iconic eighties Athena poster. It was a strategy that seemed to have paid off – nearly all the tabloids and celeb mags accepted Stevie's about-face and belated acknowledgement of his son; it seemed his popularity was going to be undented by the story and might in fact even increase because of it.

When Eden went into the green room to wish her girls good luck in the final, Stevie was the first person she saw. He smiled at her but she could see from his eyes how tired he was. In spite of the positive coverage he didn't seem back to his usual charismatic self. There was something subdued about him. His confidence had been knocked by the revelations. Eden just hoped he could pull himself together for the show. She hugged Alana, Kim and Kasey, and told them they would be brilliant.

'Whatever happens, we're so grateful to you, Eden,' Alana told her. 'You've been the best.' Kim and Kasey backed her up and Eden was touched by their words. She was all set to go to her dressing room to get ready when Stevie wandered over. 'What about our good luck hugs?' he asked.

'You're my competition!' she bantered back, but then embraced Justin and Taylor and finally Stevie. 'I'll see you later,' he whispered, and dropping his voice still further, added, 'Love you.'

'You too,' Eden whispered back and then left. Jez was waiting for her in the dressing room.

'Feeling okay about tonight?' he asked when she walked in.

'I'll feel better when it's over,' Eden confessed. She had butterflies in her stomach for Venus Rising, to say nothing of Stevie and herself.

'At least the press has been okay about Stevie,' Jez commented, rubbing serum through Eden's hair. 'You have to admire Dallas for turning it round like that. He's definitely someone you would want on your side, isn't he?'

'Hmm.' While Eden was relieved for Stevie on one level, she couldn't help seeing the incident as a master-class in spin. She had avoided reading the articles where Stevie talked about how sorry he was, knowing that he had only said what he had to say, and didn't necessarily mean it.

There was a knock at the door and Jack walked in. Usually he dressed casually for the shows but tonight he was wearing black tie and looked incredibly handsome. Jez could hardly drag his eyes away from him.

'I've come to wish you luck for the last show. Have you thought about what you will do if you have to choose between Rapture and Venus Rising?' Trust Jack to put his finger on what was worrying her most of all!

Eden grimaced. 'I'll just have to go with whoever performs best, won't I?'

'Good plan,' Jack replied. He hesitated and then added, 'And Stevie seems to have turned things around. I only hope for his son's sake that he meant what he said when he was interviewed, that he genuinely wants to have a role in his kid's upbringing, otherwise he's setting up his son to be screwed up for life.'

Great. More character analysis from Jack on the man she loved!

'I'm sure he wouldn't have said it if he didn't mean it. Sometimes you're too cynical, Jack,' Eden said teasingly, wanting to lighten the conversation.

Jack shrugged. 'I guess I've just been around the music industry too long and it's hard not to be cynical.' He looked serious. 'And you're okay? Really?'

'I'm fine, Jack. I'm looking forward to finishing the show and the album.'

He smiled. 'Yeah, then you won't have me on your case any more about being late.' There was a moment when they both looked at each other and Eden wondered if he was thinking what she was – which was that she was really going to miss working with him. Then the moment was gone as Jack said, 'Well, I'll leave you to it. See you at the after party.' And he was gone.

'My, my,' Jez commented when the door had clicked shut. 'That man certainly does scrub up well. He should wear a suit more often. He looks divine in one!'

Eden clicked her fingers. 'Just concentrate on making *me* look divine!' she joked.

'Sorry, your majesty. I'm only human, I can't help being distracted.' But he did indeed get his act together and gave Eden his full, expert attention, leaving her with a sleek, glossy mane of hair. The production runner then came round and told her she had five

249

minutes to get to the stage. The butterflies intensified. She stood up. 'Okay, will I do?'

Darcy and Jez both gave her the thumbs up. Eden took one last anxious look in the mirror. She had gone for a gold silk Alexander McQueen dress, with a plunging neckline, nipped in waist and short skirt, worn with crystal-studded ankle boots.

The audience was hyped up to hysterical levels as the judges walked on to the stage and took their seats. Eden could feel the excitement and anticipation coming at her in waves. Her girls were on first, singing 'Survivor', a Destiny's Child song.

Eden was rigid with nerves for them, but as soon as they started singing she relaxed. They were on top form and delivered what was easily one of their best performances. They were glowing with confidence and looked as if they had been performing all their lives. The audience loved them and all the judges gave the song their seal of approval.

'It's going to be so close tonight,' Dallas declared. 'You girls have come a very long way. But you fully deserve to have your place in the final, and on the basis of that performance you are potential winners.'

Eden had tears in her eyes at hearing those words and it seemed the girls were struggling with their emotions too when Tess approached them with the microphone. 'What do you say to that, girls?' she asked.

Half laughing, half crying, Kasey spoke for them. 'Oh, no, my make-up's going to run! We want to say thank you to all the people who have voted for us, to our families for sticking by us and supporting us all the way, and to Eden who has just been the best mentor ever. She's helped us achieve our dream and we love her!'

And Eden found that she couldn't hold back the tears on hearing that. She felt as if she had been through so much these past months, so many negative things, but also so many good ones.

Dallas turned to her. 'Well done, you must be very proud.' He actually smiled as Eden brushed away the tears and prayed that her mascara was indeed as waterproof as it claimed to be.

4Real followed and while theirs wasn't a bad performance, it simply wasn't in the same league as Venus Rising's. Eden doubted they were in with a chance of winning. The closer it got to Rapture's performance, the more nervous she became. The tension was drawn out by the ad breaks. Then finally it was the turn of Rapture. They were singing Take That's 'Back for Good'.

By now Eden was on the edge of her seat. She was making a conscious effort to remember that she was being filmed, that her every expression would be captured on camera for everyone to see, but it was incredibly difficult staying composed. The music began and Stevie started singing. It quickly became apparent to Eden that this was not going to be his best performance. He was still good but the events of the past week seemed to have taken their toll on him, he simply wasn't singing with his usual energy and Justin and Taylor were never going to make up for that.

Tess came bounding across the stage when they had finished, and as she had done every week made a bee-line for Stevie and put her arm around him. 'Boys, how did you feel that went?'

Stevie gave his trademark sexy smile, but Eden knew him well enough to know that he must have been fully aware he hadn't given his best performance. 'I'm not making excuses, Tess, I know that I wasn't as good as I have been.'

The audience didn't agree. Many called out, 'No way!' and, 'We love you, Stevie!'

Then it was the judges' turn. Ricky was first up. 'You were great, boys, but maybe Stevie was right. Not quite up to his usual high standard. Mind you, that's hardly surprising after the week he's had!' Ricky gave a knowing smile, clearly expecting the audience to back him up, but was roundly booed.

Amber was next and she trod the safest path possible by telling the boys how fantastic they were.

And then it was Eden's turn. She was torn between wanting to acknowledge the truth about their performance and her desire to protect Stevie. The latter won out. 'You have earned your place in this final, boys. You were fantastic.' Cheers greeted her comments, and Dallas backed her up.

'I'm thrilled that we found you guys. You're what makes this competition. You've got it all – the talent, the looks, the charisma. And whatever has been going on outside the show, you've kept it together and been totally professional. You're stars already as far as I'm concerned.'

The audience erupted and Eden gave a silent prayer of thanks for Dallas's ringing endorsement. And now all they could do was wait. The phone lines were open for the public to decide. The show would be back on air in two hours' time for the results.

The acts and judges all had to be interviewed back stage for clips that would start the next half of the show, so that killed some time. In the green room the tension was unbearable. Stevie was sitting on the sofa, head in his hands. Eden's heart ached for him. Once she had congratulated her girls, she had to go over and comfort him.

'Hey,' she said, sitting down next to him. 'It'll be okay.' She put her arm round his shoulders, and before she knew what was happening Stevie had slid his arms round her and was holding her tightly against him.

'I've fucked it up, haven't I?' he muttered, and she could tell that he was holding back the tears.

'You haven't,' she told him, gently trying to push him away. But he held on to her and whispered, 'Tell me you love me, I need to hear it.'

Eden looked around her anxiously. She was aware that everyone was looking at them. Comforting hugs between the singers and their mentors were common but this was in a different league. She couldn't bring herself to reject Stevie when he most needed her so she whispered, 'Love you. It'll be okay.' And still he didn't let her go.

At that moment Dallas walked in with Jack. Both men were riveted by the sight of Eden and Stevie. Only then did Eden manage to extricate herself from Stevie's embrace and stand up. She was aware that she looked flushed.

'Anything I need to know about?' Dallas asked her quietly as she made her way past him. 'I didn't realise you and Stevie were so close, I thought you two weren't getting along.'

'He's just upset and anxious is all, Dallas. Anyway, if you'll excuse me, I'd better get back to the dressing room.'

'If you say so, Eden,' Dallas replied. Then just as she thought she was on the home run he added, 'But remember, I really hate surprises.'

Eden lowered her eyes. 'Of course, Dallas.'

She hurried back to her dressing room where Alana caught up with her. 'Hey, Eden, can I have a word?'

'Sure, come in.' The dressing room was empty.

Eden expected that Alana wanted reassurance and was all set to give her yet another pep talk. Instead she was stunned when the girl said hesitantly, 'I hope you don't mind me saying this, but I couldn't help noticing how close you seemed to Stevie.'

Oh, God! Eden wasn't expecting this, and she didn't know how on earth to reply. She didn't want to lie, but then how the hell could she come out with the truth?

'Um, well, of course I care about him. It's been such an intense time for everyone and I could tell that he was upset.'

Alana looked awkward. 'So it's just that you're concerned about him as a mentor?'

Eden was wondering how to talk her way out of that when Jez and Darcy walked back in. Eden didn't think she had ever been so grateful for an interruption.

'Ready for a touch up?' Darcy asked. 'I think you're on in fifteen.'

'I'll leave you to it,' Alana said, making for the door. She seemed as relieved as Eden about the interruption.

'Okay!' Eden said brightly, and held up her fingers which were crossed. 'Good luck!'

'Yeah, thanks, Eden. You too.'

It was only as Eden was walking along the back-stage corridor towards the stage that she wondered why Alana had been so concerned about her relationship with Stevie. She remembered how she herself had been jealous of the bond which seemed to exist between Stevie and Alana, and how she had wondered if their relationship was more than that of friends. But then Alana hadn't seemed jealous about Eden and Stevie embracing. If anything she had seemed worried about Eden. There was no time for further reflection as she took her place next to the other judges, with just five minutes before they went back on air.

'The phone lines have been busier than ever,' Dallas commented gleefully, no doubt thinking of all the revenue they'd bring in.

'Do you know the result?' Eden asked, certain that he would.

He smiled and tapped his nose conspiratorially. 'Can't tell you, but I will say that it is extremely close.'

Please let there be an outright winner! Eden didn't want to be in the position of casting a deciding vote.

And then the opening titles started, and the acts came on stage with Tess, to be greeted by huge cheers and thunderous applause from the audience. 'Hello and welcome back to *Band Ambition*. It's the moment of truth for all our finalists – 4Real, Rapture and Venus Rising.'

Tess was doing her serious face to camera. 'Come off it!' Eden thought. 'You're not presenting *Newsnight*!'

'So who is the act that you, the public, have decided should win the competition? The phone lines have closed and I can now reveal that in third place is . . .' She left a long pause, a technique used by reality-show presenters the world over to ratchet up the tension. How Eden wished she would just get on with it! The cameras zoomed in on each of the contestants' faces, and their tense expressions were shown on the huge screens behind them. Just as Eden was finding the waiting unbearable, Tess spoke. 'In third place, 4Real!'

There was applause from the audience and the four boys from 4Real put on a brave face and hugged the other contestants, who were no doubt thinking, *Thank God it wasn't us!* Tess asked the band to comment on how they felt. 'Gutted, but grateful for the opportunity' seemed to sum up their feelings.

Eden put what she hoped was a sympathetic smile on her face, but all the time she was dying to know the outcome of the vote. The waiting was agony. And then to compound the tension they went to another ad break! Oh, for a job as one of the judges on the BBC's *Strictly Come Dancing*, with no ads! The fact that she knew nothing about dance was irrelevant.

Eden glanced at Dallas, who seemed to be relishing the drama. 'This is great, isn't it?' he commented. 'I'm loving what Tess is doing. I was thinking that she was too light-weight and frothy to create an atmosphere of anticipation, but she's showing hidden depths. Sorry about 4Real,' he addressed Amber, 'but I think you'll agree that they did well to get this far.'

Amber, who looked as if she didn't agree anything of the sort, simply pouted.

Dallas smiled, and turned back to Eden. 'And now for the denouement. I couldn't have hoped for a better result.' He was in his element. Eden had a sudden image of him as a Roman emperor presiding over gladiatorial combats in the arena. How he would have loved deciding who lived and who died . . . but maybe she was getting a little hysterical here with the waiting.

The ad break finished and they were back on air. Tess was once more on stage with the remaining two acts. 'Welcome back. Now is the moment you've all been waiting for – who is going to be crowned winner of *Band Ambition*?' Again she followed her declaration with a pause and again the cameras zoomed in on the anxious faces of the contestants. Poor Alana had bitten her lip so much she had caused it to bleed. Kasey looked as if she might be sick, and Stevie and the boys could hardly bring themselves to look out at the audience.

'I can now reveal that . . .' Another long pause. Eden was ready to jump out of her seat and demand that Tess put them all out of their misery!

'I can now reveal that we have a draw between Rapture and Venus Rising, and the winner will be decided by the judges after the two acts have performed one last time!'

Eden felt sick with apprehension; this was exactly what she didn't want to happen. She was going to be put in an impossible position. The acts themselves looked shell-shocked.

'So, judges, final words of advice?'

Ricky was first to speak. 'Congratulations! You're both winners. Just enjoy your moment.' His sentiments were echoed by Amber. And then it was Eden's turn and Tess couldn't let the moment pass without reminding her that she used to mentor Rapture – like Eden needed the reminder!

She wanted to say, 'Please don't make me choose between them!' Instead she managed to come out with, 'I know both acts are nervous, but try and forget about everything but the song. You've already achieved so much and reaching the final isn't the end but the start of your careers as singers. You should be proud whatever happens.' She was mainly looking at the girls as she spoke but at the end of her speech her gaze was drawn to Stevie, who still looked incredibly nervous. It was the first time she had ever seen him show any nerves at all.

Dallas had the last word. 'Just do your best. Own the songs. Give them your all. That's all we can ask of you.'

The show's theme tune was played to allow Venus Rising to take their positions on stage and the other act to leave, and then the band began playing the opening notes of 'Survivor' and Eden's girls were on. She knew how nervous they must be feeling but once again they showed inner strength and resolve and delivered a fantastic performance, easily as good as the earlier one. They had set the bar extremely high.

And then it was Rapture's turn to take their places. Eden could hardly bring herself to look at Stevie, she felt so incredibly nervous for him. Her throat felt horribly dry and she couldn't breathe properly. But this time Stevie was back on his brilliant top form. He exuded all the charisma, confidence and charm that had always marked out his performances. The audience went wild as the band finished, cheering and whistling.

While Eden was massively relieved that Rapture had performed so well, now she had an agonising decision to make. There was so little to choose between Rapture and Venus Rising – both acts had been outstanding. And both really deserved to win.

Another ad break followed, raising the tension unbearably. Instead of staying in her seat, Eden had to make a mad dash to the loo. When she returned, out of breath, Amber commented slyly, 'Tension getting to you?'

Eden ignored her. Now the spotlight was on the judges, who held the fate of the two bands in their hands.

Tess welcomed them back and, thankfully, because they were running short of time, got straight to the point,

'Amber – can you now reveal who you think should win the competition?'

At least Eden hadn't been first.

Big simper from Amber. 'Both acts were brilliant, I think we all know that. But the act that had the edge for me was . . .' and now Amber tried the infuriating pregnant pause trick '. . . the boys. It's Rapture for me!'

The boys smiled broadly, while the girls struggled to smile as they held hands.

'Eden, your turn now. Who do you think should win the competition?'

She was genuinely conflicted. A few weeks ago she would have said that it should have been Rapture without a shadow of a doubt, whereas now the girls were their equals. But how could she pick them over the man she loved? Then again, how could she pick

Rapture over the group she had mentored? Talk about between a rock and a hard place . . .

'Um, this is so difficult . . . I'm not surprised there was a draw in the public vote. Like I said before, you are both winners.' She was playing for time, something that Tess picked up on. 'I'm sorry, Eden, I'm going to have to hurry you. We're up against the clock.'

'Okay, then.' Deep breath. 'I choose Venus Rising,' she said quickly. She looked over at the girls, who beamed at her in delight, then at Stevie who looked stunned by her decision. But she couldn't take it back now. And then it was Ricky, and after waffling for a few seconds about how good both acts were, he plumped for Rapture. Now everything hinged on Dallas. Either they were about to have another draw, and Eden had no idea what happened then, or Dallas too would go for the boys.

'I'm going to repeat what all the other judges have said – this is fiendishly hard, you were both sensational. But there can only be one winner and, in my eyes, that has to be Rapture!'

The audience went wild and the boys jumped up and down, hugging each other, before calming down and going over to kiss and commiserate with the girls.

Then Tess was getting Venus Rising's reactions. Only Kasey was together enough to speak. 'Like I said before, we just want to thank everyone who helped us on our way. And, hopefully, this isn't the last you'll see of us.'

More cheers greeted those words and then it was Stevie at the mic. 'The girls were awesome and I feel very lucky indeed that we won. And that's in spite of one judge not voting for us.' Now he was looking straight at Eden, a challenging smile on his face. 'But it's okay, I forgive her. What else can you do with the woman you love?'

Everyone on stage was staring at Stevie in total amazement. Tess seemed to have momentarily forgotten the fact that she was supposed to be the one holding the show together. The audience went quiet and Eden was aware of all the other judges looking at her. What was Stevie playing at?

'Yes, I love Eden Haywood!' he declared. And now Tess leapt into action. Clearly the producer was talking at her in her ear-piece, telling her to take back control of the moment.

'Well, that's taken us all by surprise. I didn't realise I was hosting that kind of talent show! I'll be after Paddy McGuinness's job on *Take Me Out*. Thank you, Stevie, and no doubt we'll be hearing more about your big news, but for now it's a wrap for *Band Ambition*! See you next time!'

The theme tune took over.

'I think we need to talk, Eden,' Dallas said quietly, a dangerous edge to his voice. But in her eyes the show was over; she had fulfilled her contract, she didn't need him to tell her what she should or shouldn't do. She felt a surge of her old confidence and spirit.

She got up from her seat and smoothed down her skirt. 'Sure, Dallas, I'll get Sadie to fix up a meeting.'

'I meant *now*. We need to talk about what Stevie just said and how we're going to manage the situation. Didn't I tell you earlier that I hate surprises?' Behind them the audience were calling out to her, demanding to know if it was true that she was seeing Stevie.

'There is nothing to manage, Dallas, Stevie and I are in love, that's all there is to it. There isn't a spin you can put on that.'

And before he could come out with anything else, Eden swiftly walked back stage. All she wanted to do now was see the man she loved.

Chapter Nineteen

Stevie was waiting in her dressing room. Jez and Darcy tactfully made to leave when Eden walked in. Jez lightly touched her on the arm as he was about to go out. 'Are you okay?'

She nodded and he left.

She and Stevie stood looking at each other. They were on the brink of something momentous, something life-changing, and they knew it. He was the first to speak. 'I meant what I said: I forgive you for not voting for us. And I'm sorry if I sprung that on you. I wasn't going to, but then it just seemed right. Why wait to tell everyone what we know is true?' And now he walked over and hugged her. 'Tell me you're not angry with me?'

'I'm not angry with you,' Eden told him. 'I love you, you know I do.' And suddenly everything – the competition, Dallas's rage, the press – all seemed to fall away as they kissed each other, with deep, hard, passionate kisses.

'God, I want you so much,' Stevie murmured.

'We could just go back to my place,' Eden replied, longing to fall into bed with him and shut out the world.

'Don't tempt me, but you know I've got to be

interviewed. Dallas is probably freaking out about what I've done and I don't want him to lose it with me completely.'

They talked and kissed some more and then, reluctantly, Eden let him go and Stevie went off to do his interviews. She took a look at herself in the mirror. Her hair was dishevelled, her make-up practically rubbed off, and now she had to face the world. She reached for her red lipstick. She was just putting the finishing touches to her mouth when there was a knock at the door and Sadie strutted in, quite a sight to behold in midnight blue sequined leggings, a matching fake fur gilet and outrageously high heels.

'Well, well, well. You're a dark horse, my darling. I had absolutely no idea you were seeing that gorgeous young man.'

At least Sadie didn't sound angry with her, more business-like.

'I'm sorry, Sadie, I really didn't think I should tell anyone until the competition finished, but you can see why I had to stop mentoring Rapture?'

'Sure I understand. Did *anyone* know?'

Eden hesitated. 'I ended up telling Tanya and Jez. And Jack knows.'

Sadie seemed surprised to hear Jack's name and Eden certainly did not want to go into the details of how he had found out. They hardly showed her in a good light.

'I'm not proud of keeping secrets, but I didn't think I had a choice.'

'And you really do love him?'

'I really do, Sadie.' And Eden shook back her hair and looked her manager straight in the eye. 'And, just so you know, it's not one of my pretty-boy infatuations, I swear.'

Sadie smiled. 'Then I'm happy for you, darling.

Though I expect Dallas is rather less so. You know how he likes to control everything, and I'm sure it wasn't part of his plan that his most promising star should declare his love for someone. He would want to keep Stevie single for as long as he possibly could; wouldn't want to alienate all those teenage fans. But there you go, you can't argue with love, can you? And I'm sure Marc White won't object to the extra publicity it will bring your album.'

'Oh, God, Sadie! People aren't going to think that this is a "showmance", are they? That we've both just got together for publicity?' Eden hated the thought that people might put a negative spin on her relationship with Stevie.

Sadie shrugged, she was a realist after all. 'You'll have to be prepared to take some flak. I advise you to put out a statement, through me, about how much in love you are, how it just shows that you can't choose the right moment to fall in love, and how you were powerless to resist your feelings for Stevie.' She paused. 'I think most women will be able to identify with that! You have bagged yourself an absolute hottie. Though the ex-girlfriend story temporarily made him less desirable, all credit to Dallas, he turned it around.'

'Okay, put out the statement,' Eden said quickly.

'I'll do it right now, and then let's go to the after party. There will be some great photo opportunities.'

'Sadie,' Eden said in a warning tone, 'this is not about publicity, *remember*?'

'I know! But it would be good to give the press something positive, to show them that you're happy and in love. And, Eden, promise me one thing. You won't rush into anything, will you? Enjoy your relationship with Stevie, but take it slowly. And before you tell me to mind my own business, I'm saying this as your friend. Think about what your mum would have said.'

'She would have said, "Go, girl!"' Eden replied, secretly not at all sure if Terri would have done. 'And of course I'm going to take things slowly. You don't have to have any worries on that score.'

An hour later Eden and Stevie were facing a barrage of cameras and questions from a room full of journalists at the impromptu press conference Dallas had set up. Eden hadn't been at all keen to do it, but Sadie had persuaded her, saying it was best to put her point of view across in a controlled way. Eden had her doubts; she still held the belief, that had yet to be proved wrong, that you could *never* control the press. Even if you thought you had, it wouldn't be long before they got one up on you . . .

She held on tightly to Stevie's hand throughout the conference, preferring to keep her answers to a minimum. By contrast he was in his absolute element and seemed to love the attention.

And then came the question Eden had been dreading, from a sharp-faced female journalist. 'Eden, do you have any concerns that if you hadn't fallen for Stevie, Venus Rising might have won? I mean, do you think you took your eye off the ball as a mentor?'

'She had her eye on someone's balls!' another journalist put in cheekily, arousing sniggers amongst the group.

Stevie leapt straight to her defence. 'Eden was a brilliant mentor! She gave her all to her acts – you heard the girls say that, and I know Extrema thought it as well. I was gutted when she said she couldn't mentor Rapture, not just because I wanted to see her but because she was such a brilliant mentor.'

'Ahh, bless!' a male journalist called out, somewhat sarcastically.

'I hope I was always professional,' Eden managed to

get a word in, 'and I honestly don't think I could have done any more to help the girls. I never let my feelings for Stevie detract from my work.'

At this point Dallas stood up. 'I think we're going to finish there. I'd like to thank you all for your time. Any further questions, you can contact my office.' And he ushered Eden and Stevie off the stage.

'Christ, Dallas! Can we have a drink now? I haven't even celebrated winning the show!' Stevie declared. In spite of the press conference he still seemed high on the adrenaline of winning. He draped his arm round Eden and she snuggled closer to him, loving the fact that they could finally be open about their feelings for each other. And then they were being marched to the waiting car to be driven off to the party.

Dallas, unfortunately, was with them and Eden could have done without his presence. He sat opposite them in the limo and immediately got down to business.

'I'll be emailing your itinerary after the party, Stevie. You've got tomorrow off, and then on Monday you will be on breakfast TV, *Loose Women*, various radio stations, and we'll be trying to get you on the *Graham Norton Show* later in the week. I assume you will be staying with Eden?'

She hadn't thought about the practicalities and her head told her that it was too soon for Stevie to move in, but they had been apart so much that now all she wanted was to be with him. Besides, by the sound of his schedule it didn't exactly seem as if she would be seeing much of him. Dallas was certainly going to capitalise on his investment for all it was worth.

Stevie planted a kiss on her head. 'I hope so, because I can't be apart from her.'

'Sure,' Eden said quietly.

'And at some stage I need to meet with Sadie so that

we're both certain about what we're saying to the press. I want us to both be on message.'

Eden bristled at the way Dallas spoke about the relationship, as if it was a business arrangement. 'I've said all I need to say for the time being, Dallas. We're in love; we're seeing each other. The press don't need to know any more than that. I'm not having my private life turned into a fucking media circus. I've had it before and it destroyed those relationships.'

He shrugged. 'I was only thinking of a couple of photo-shoots, carefully arranged interviews with selected journalists.'

'Well, don't – focus on Stevie's career and Sadie will focus on mine. The rest is private.'

Stevie was very quiet during this exchange but when Dallas was caught up with making a phone call, he whispered, 'I might have a surprise for you later and everyone is going to want to know about that.'

'What is it?' Eden wondered what could possibly be more surprising than the events of tonight. But Stevie simply kissed her and said, 'Wait and see.' Then he added, as he slid his hand along her thigh, 'God, I wish Dallas wasn't here. Imagine what we could do if he wasn't.' He inched his hand still higher. Eden had goosebumps just thinking about it, but she put her hand over Stevie's to stop any further exploration. He smiled and murmured, 'Later then.'

As soon as Stevie and Eden emerged from the limo they were mobbed by fans clamouring for autographs and a chance to get close to Stevie. Paps thrust forward with their cameras, taking yet more pictures of the couple. Eden felt intimidated by the crowd surging around them and wanted to get inside the club as quickly as possible. Dallas strode through the crowd unmolested as everyone was so fixated on Stevie.

Eden looked around anxiously, hoping for some security to help her out. She had assumed Dallas was arranging the security for the party and so had given her guy the night off. Big mistake.

Stevie was in his element, as he signed autographs, posed for photos and kissed girls. 'We love you, Stevie!' they shrieked, almost hysterical with excitement at the sight of their idol. Once Eden had signed a few autographs she found herself being elbowed and pushed aside as a fresh group of girls swept forward, all hell-bent on getting up close and personal with Stevie.

'Ouch!' she exclaimed as someone trod on her toe.

'Bitch,' one of the girls muttered. And suddenly Eden felt even more on edge about being surrounded by so many people. Waves of panic began building up in her as she tried to push her way through the crowds and into the club. She looked in vain for any security guards to assist her. But the more she tried to escape, the tighter the crowd surged round her. Desperately she turned round, looking for Stevie to help her, but he was taken up with his fans and didn't see how distressed she was getting. As she turned back she tripped, lost her footing and fell. She tried to get up but no one was giving her any space. She felt as if she couldn't breathe. It was terrifying, overwhelming. She had never had a panic attack before but she was certain she could feel one coming on. She was struggling to breathe, felt as if she couldn't get enough oxygen into her lungs, and the more she tried, the shallower her breathing became. Her Chanel bag was ripped from her shoulder but she was powerless to stop the thief. She tried to call out for help and couldn't even summon the breath to do that.

God knows what would have happened but suddenly a strong pair of arms reached for her and helped her to her feet. It was Jack.

'Hey, give us some room here, can't you?' he called out. He forced the crowd to part, his arm protectively around Eden. She felt dizzy and sick. She had cut her knee in the fall and blood was pouring down her leg. Leaning on Jack, she managed to limp into the foyer of the club where burly security guards were waiting to check the people going into the party.

'Couldn't you see what was going on out there?' Jack demanded, disgusted at the way they had stood by.

The guards shrugged. 'Not our responsibility, we're not insured for outside.'

'Oh, for fuck's sake,' Jack muttered under his breath. 'Have you got a First Aid kit?'

He helped Eden over to a chair.

'I'm okay now, Jack,' she said gratefully, though she was still shaken up.

'You're not okay, you had a nasty scare and a fall. Why the hell didn't Dallas have any security with you? He must have known something like this was likely to happen.'

A stocky, shaven-headed security guard handed Jack a green First Aid box and he knelt down in front of Eden to tend to her knee. He was completely matter-of-fact and un-squeamish about mopping up the blood.

She winced as he applied antiseptic cream, even though he did it gently, then tried to joke, 'Is it going to ruin my career as a leg model?'

He looked up at her and smiled. 'They'll be able to airbrush the tiny scar, I'm sure.' Then he frowned. 'I'm going to find Dallas and ask what he thought he was doing, not having security. It could have been really serious.'

Eden reached out and touched his arm. 'Don't, Jack, I don't want to cause any more scenes. There has been enough going on tonight.' Then she remembered that

268

her bag had been stolen. 'Shit! Someone nicked my bag out there.'

'Did you have much in it?'

'Just my phone and some cash.' Thank God she had deleted all the texts Stevie had sent her, and the texts she had sent him. Fortunately she had her front-door key in her pocket, and Eden suddenly very much wanted to go home, she was in no fit state to swan around the after party making small talk. She should have been euphoric after Stevie's public declaration but found she was too shaken up. She got up and grimaced in pain. Her knee hurt and she now had a pounding headache.

At that moment Stevie and Dallas swept into the foyer. Dallas continued walking through the club but Stevie caught sight of Eden and immediately came over. 'What happened? I looked round and I couldn't see you anywhere.' He looked slightly annoyed to see Jack by her side.

Eden was about to explain when Jack spoke. 'She was pushed to the ground by your fans.'

'Baby!' Stevie ignored Jack and put his arms round her. 'Are you okay?'

'Sort of.'

'Come on through to the party, I'll get you a drink – a brandy's good for shock, isn't it?'

He was all set to lead her through when Eden stopped him. 'Actually, Stevie, I'm going to go home. My bag was nicked and I need to call the police and cancel my phone. And I'm not feeling so great. You go and I'll see you later.'

He frowned. 'Eden, you can't leave! This is our big night! I wanted to show us off to the world. I thought you did too? I've had it with hiding away how I feel.' His tone was sulky.

'I know, Stevie, and I want to celebrate with you, but

for now I need to go home. And tonight is about you celebrating with Rapture. Please understand, I'll see you later.'

Stevie rolled his eyes. 'Yeah, okay. I'd better get in there. Dallas is probably wondering where I am.' He ducked his head down and kissed her. 'Love you.' And then he walked into the party.

As she watched him walk away Eden realised that she had no money to pay for a taxi. Thankfully Jack was still in the foyer, now chatting to the girls from Venus Rising. It was the first time she had seen them since the show finished and she had been hoping to have a drink with them. She hobbled over to the group.

'Hiya, Eden,' Alana and Kim chorused. They both looked concerned for her, but Kasey hung back. 'Jack told us what happened,' Alana said. 'Are you okay?'

'Yes, sore and a bit shaken, but okay. But never mind me, how are you doing? I'm so sorry you didn't win.'

Both girls smiled ruefully and Kim replied, 'Well, we did as well as we possibly could and Dallas has said that he is interested in signing us up to do an album, so that would be amazing, wouldn't it?'

'*You're* probably not that sorry though, are you?' Now Kasey spoke and there was a nasty edge to her voice that Eden hadn't heard before. 'You must be really happy for Stevie.'

There was an awkward pause while Eden tried to think how best to reply. 'Actually, Kasey, I was gutted that you didn't win. I know how it must look now everyone knows about me and Stevie, but I really did try and keep my private life and my work separate.'

Kasey curled her lip as she stared at Eden. 'Yeah, I'm sure you did.' Without saying anything else, she stormed off in the direction of the party.

'Sorry about Kasey. She's devastated we didn't win,

270

but we know it has nothing to do with you,' Alana said anxiously.

As far as Eden was concerned that was the final straw. 'Thanks, Alana. I'll call you in the next couple of days and let's go out to celebrate. We'll have dinner somewhere swanky – my treat.' She turned to Jack. 'I'm going to head off home, could you lend me the money for a taxi?'

'I can do better than that, I can drive you,' he replied.

'No way! I don't want to keep you from the party,' Eden exclaimed.

He smiled. 'You'd be doing me a favour, I hate this kind of thing. All about everyone telling each other how great they are, and then stabbing each other in the back.'

Eden didn't have the energy to persuade him not to and, after saying goodbye to the girls, she and Jack left the club.

Apart from Jack asking her if she was okay, they were largely silent on the drive back. He put on a Billie Holiday CD and the music was like a healing balm to Eden. She sat back in her seat and allowed it to wash away all the stress of the night. And whereas with some people it might have felt awkward not saying anything, it seemed perfectly natural to be silent with Jack. It was only when he turned on to her road that Eden wondered if she had done the right thing by leaving. Would Stevie feel abandoned by her? She hoped he would understand.

'Maybe I should have a shower and then get a taxi back to the party,' she commented. It was after eleven but the celebrations would go on into the early hours.

'You're joking, aren't you? You're exhausted and you had a nasty shock. It's bed for you, Eden.'

'If you say so, Dr Steele!' she replied. 'But I guess I'm worried about Stevie. I don't want him to think that I'm not there for him. It's his big moment.' She was too emotionally strung out to reflect that talking to Jack about Stevie was probably not her best move.

'I'm sure he'll be relieved that you're taking care of yourself,' Jack replied. 'And making the most of all the attention,' he added under his breath.

Eden was about to defend Stevie; then reasoned that it was most likely true, and why not? He had earned it.

Jack pulled up outside her house.

'Thanks for the lift.' She leant over and kissed him on the cheek. 'And thanks for being so discreet about Stevie and me. I really appreciate it.'

He turned to face her. 'No problem, Eden, so long as he makes you happy.'

'Very,' she said lightly, not wanting to have a serious conversation with him about Stevie. 'Goodnight, Jack.'

Chapter Twenty

Stevie didn't come back after the party. Around seven a.m. when Eden woke up to discover an empty bed she called him, but his phone went straight to voice mail. Where the hell was he? Could he still be out celebrating? She checked her home answerphone – no new messages. It would have been nice if he had phoned to let her know where he was, and to see if she was okay. But she tried not to get upset – he was probably caught up in the moment. She shouldn't make a big deal of it. She didn't want to get possessive and needy as she had been with Joel. Stevie was her fresh start. She must not obsess. She got back into bed. She still felt exhausted. She'd sleep for a couple more hours then try Stevie again. Or maybe he might even have returned home by then.

But at midday when she woke up again there was still no sign of Stevie or word from him. She thought about calling Dallas and asking him if he knew where Stevie was, and then thought better of it – she didn't want him knowing everything about their relationship. She could just imagine him using any knowledge he had as future leverage. She respected Dallas as a hugely successful businessman, but that didn't mean she trusted him.

She quickly showered and got dressed.

After the past weeks of dressing up for the show, it was a relief to dress down in denim shorts and a white tee-shirt, a pink Alexander McQueen scarf wrapped round her neck. She finished her look with an oversized pair of purple Bulgari sunglasses and a straw trilby. With any luck that should keep the public from guessing who she was, as she had a crucial bit of shopping to do – she absolutely had to replace her phone. She felt as if she had lost her right arm without her trusty mobile! Her phone company had promised to send her a replacement the next day but Eden couldn't even wait that long.

She opened the front door and instantly had to brave the paps who were loitering outside her house. 'Where's Stevie?' one of them called out as they clicked away at their cameras.

Eden ducked her head down and tried to ignore them as she walked swiftly to her car. Two hours later she was the proud owner of a brand new iPhone, but as she sat in her car and once more called Stevie to find her call unanswered, her resolve to stay calm was rapidly deserting her. Where was he? It hardly seemed a good start to their new out-in-the-open relationship. *Oh, yeah, thanks, everything is going great with Stevie, I just don't know where the fuck he is!*

She sat in her car for a few minutes, trying to work out what to do, and then because the inactivity was driving her mad, started the engine and swung out on to the road. She would drive over to Hampstead, to the house all the contestants had shared. With any luck Stevie would be there.

She hoped there weren't any paps lurking outside; getting papped once in a day was quite enough for her. She parked on the street as close to the house as she could and, pulling her scarf round her mouth and tilting her trilby still further over her face, walked briskly up to the front door. So far, so good, there didn't seem to be any paps. But then again, so what if there were? The story about her and Stevie was out there now.

At first no one came to the door when she rang the doorbell. Eden tried again and finally, just as she was about to give up, Kasey opened the door. She was dressed in a hot pink tee-shirt that barely covered her bum and had clearly just got up. Her hair was tousled and her eye make-up from the night before had smudged. She looked sexy in a trashy kind of way and Eden couldn't stop herself from hoping that she hadn't been parading round in front of Stevie like that.

Kasey didn't seem too pleased to see Eden either, and in response to her breezy 'Hiya' simply muttered, 'He's still in bed. It was a very long night.'

And without even waiting around to show Eden where Stevie's bedroom was, she stomped upstairs, flashing a pert bum in a black lace thong. She really had got the hump with Eden.

The hallway was littered with empty beer cans and wine bottles. It looked as if the party had continued here after the club had shut. Remembering that Stevie had said his bedroom was downstairs, Eden opened the first door she came to, only to be greeted with the sight of a naked Justin lying on the double bed, entwined with two women, the air thick with the smell of booze, cigarettes and sex.

He hadn't wasted any time making the most of his celebrity status, Eden thought, hastily shutting the door. She had always thought he was such a nice boy as well! Just showed that you couldn't tell . . . She couldn't imagine Dallas being pleased with that scenario – she'd like to see him putting a positive spin on a threesome to the press! But then the smile was wiped from her face as she had a sudden horrible thought. If this was what nice boy next-door Justin had got up to last night, what about Stevie?

Her pace quickened as she walked along the corridor to the bedroom at the back of the house. She tentatively opened the door, steeling herself for what she might find. To her huge relief she discovered Stevie seemingly fast asleep in bed, one arm flung across the duvet. She tiptoed closer; even when he was asleep he looked absolutely gorgeous. Eden smiled to herself. She'd give him a wake-up call with a difference.

Quickly she stripped to her underwear and slipped into bed next to him. His skin was deliciously sleep-warmed, and she gently kissed his neck, then slid her hands over his shoulders, his chest, his abs and lower still . . . While he might have been asleep, some parts of his body were definitely stirring. She began caressing him with the light feathery strokes that she knew drove him wild.

'Mmm,' Stevie murmured and turned over on his back. 'You came back for more, did you?'

'Of course I did.'

His eyes opened and momentarily he seemed surprised to see her lying there. 'Eden, babe! I thought I was dreaming!'

'Of me, I hope?' she muttered.

''Course!' In one fluid move he rolled on top of her, and began kissing her. He tasted of booze, and Eden, who had a very good sense of smell, was sure she could also smell perfume on him. She put her hand against his chest. 'Stevie, there's nothing I should know about, is there?'

'Like what?'

'I can smell perfume on you.'

He put back his head and laughed. 'Yeah, I bet you

276

can! The number of girls who came up to me last night, wanting a hug and a kiss! My lips are still numb.' He grinned. 'But not so numb that they can't still pleasure you.'

His answer was so plausible that it had to be true, didn't it? She had seen for herself what a babe magnet he was, and those women who had draped their arms around him were bound to have left traces of their perfume.

'Were they so numb that you couldn't call me last night?' Eden was still pissed off on that score.

'I don't have your landline number, remember? I was going to ask Sadie, but she left before I got the chance, and everyone else just had your mobile and I knew it had been nicked, so please, don't give me a hard time. I'm hungover and horny. And I am going to make it up to you.'

Stevie trailed kisses along her neck, slipped off her bra straps and kissed her breasts, causing a chain reaction of lust in Eden that pushed all other thoughts away.

They stayed in bed for the next three hours, making love twice, talking, hugging and kissing, as if they couldn't get enough of each other. It was such a novelty to spend all this time together and not have to rush off to rehearsals and put on a pretence that they weren't in love.

'Did you know what Justin got up to last night?' Eden commented, when they were both finally thinking about getting up.

'No, what?'

'I went into his room by mistake and it looked as if he'd had a threesome.'

'Did he? The lucky – I mean, the dirty dog!' Stevie smirked.

Eden punched him on the arm. 'Don't say that! Why, have you had one then?' She didn't know why she asked. If he said yes, it would only torment her.

Stevie looked serious. 'Eden, can we have a deal that we don't obsess about each other's pasts? I've done things that I'm not proud of, some of which you know about, and I'm sure you've done some things you aren't proud of either. Whatever we've done, it shouldn't matter because we're together now. I love you and that's all that counts, isn't it? The past is the past.'

'Okay, deal,' she agreed, hoping that she could stick to it.

She came face to face with Kasey again as she emerged from the bathroom after taking a quick shower. Eden felt at a disadvantage as she was only wrapped in a tiny towel that barely covered her body and Kasey was dressed up in a leopard print mini-dress that showed off her toned figure.

'We gather you found him then?' she said sarcastically. 'The walls in this house are very thin.'

Why was she being like this? Eden had always thought that they got on okay and that Kasey liked her. She was fast having to revise that opinion in light of her recent behaviour towards her.

'Kasey, have I done something to upset you?' Eden started saying.

'Nope.' She shrugged, and avoided looking Eden in the eye. 'I've gotta go. We've got to pack up and move out today. Dallas has arranged a flat for me and the girls. It's in Hackney. Not quite your part of town, is it, Eden?' She deliberately put on a posh voice as if taking the piss, which was off the mark as if anything Eden had a London accent. And what was it with these barbed comments?

'I like Hackney. Actually my mum's fiancé was from

278

there. Anyway, I'll be in touch to see how you're getting on and we'll go out and celebrate. Take care.'

'You too, Eden,' Kasey replied, looking her up and down as if assessing her body. She didn't sound sincere.

'Happy?' Stevie asked as they sat in a café on Hampstead High Street. They'd both just polished off plates of scrambled eggs and smoked salmon, and Stevie had insisted on ordering a bottle of champagne which they'd very nearly finished.

'Very,' Eden replied, leaning across the table and kissing him. She knew other diners were watching them, but she was too loved up to care. And she knew that this was the calm before the storm and that the months ahead were going to be challenging with them both working on their albums, but for now she wanted to pretend that they were just like any normal couple in love, free to do whatever they wanted, with no one telling them what to do or where to go.

The waiter came over to clear their plates and poured the remaining champagne into their glasses.

Stevie picked up his glass. 'To you, Eden. You have made me the happiest man in the world. I can't tell you how lucky I feel that you're mine.'

'To us,' she replied, clinking her glass against his. 'I'm the lucky one, Stevie. I thought no man would ever want me after the things Joel said about me. I love you.'

'We're so alike . . . we're both ambitious and sometimes ruthless, we're passionate and also a bit insecure,' he replied, gazing into her eyes. 'God, Eden, I love you, and I want to be with you.' He paused. 'I wasn't going to do this yet, but I think it has to be now. I don't think that I can wait any longer. Close your eyes.'

Wondering what he was planning, Eden did as he asked, and then couldn't resist taking a sneaky peek.

'Hey! Don't cheat. Close them or I'll make you wear a blindfold . . . and I was saving that bit for later.'

This time Eden shut her eyes. She heard Stevie's chair scrape back as he got up. 'Okay, you can open them now.'

He was down on one knee beside her chair. 'Eden Haywood, will you marry me?' He actually had tears in his eyes, and Eden found her own eyes welling up as she said, 'Yes! I will!'

With that the other diners, who had been riveted by the scene, cheered, several people got out their camera phones and took pictures, and the waiter brought over yet another bottle of champagne.

Stevie and Eden kissed each other passionately. 'I'm going to get you a Tiffany engagement ring as soon as I can afford it,' he told her. 'I've just got this one for now.' He slipped a pretty but obviously fake diamond ring on to her finger. 'I know everyone is going to say that it's too soon, but I want to be with you, Eden. I don't care what anyone else says. This feels so right.'

'I know, Stevie,' she murmured, kissing him again. 'It's about us, no one else.'

But by the time they left the restaurant, the paps had been alerted and had decided it was about them as well. Eden and Stevie were greeted by a scrum of photographers and journalists, practically falling over themselves to get close to the couple, shouting out their names, wanting them to pose for pictures. After last night, Eden was extremely wary of crowds and clung on to Stevie, who whispered, 'It's all right, babe, I'm here. Let's just give them their shot and we'll go.' And even though Eden's natural impulse was to get the hell out of there, she faced the cameras and smiled.

'Is it true you're engaged?' a journalist called out.

'Yep, we've been engaged for precisely thirty-five minutes,' Stevie bantered back.

'When are you getting married?' came the next question.

'As soon as we can, mate. I can't wait to have Eden Haywood as my wife.'

'What does your ex-girlfriend Nicci think about this?'

How typical of the press to drag the past up and make something beautiful seem sordid. Stevie ignored the question. 'And now we're going home.' And he somehow managed to push his way through the throng, while holding on tightly to Eden.

Both their mobiles started ringing the moment they sat back in the taxi. Stevie looked at his phone, then turned to Eden and rolled his eyes. 'It's Dallas. I guess I'd better take it.'

Eden checked the number on her own phone. Sadie. News certainly travelled fast.

'I thought you said you were going to take things slowly!' Sadie exclaimed, sounding concerned.

'Yeah, well, Stevie proposed and I said yes.'

'I gathered that,' Sadie said dryly.

Eden immediately felt defensive. 'I'm happy, Sadie! And you don't have to be worried about me, I know I'm doing the right thing marrying Stevie.'

He caught her eye at that moment and reached for her hand. Eden ended the call with Sadie after suggesting that they talk the next day. Stevie was still on the phone to Dallas. Eden wondered if he was giving Stevie a hard time.

'It would be better if we could meet tomorrow, Dallas,' Stevie said, raising his eyebrows at Eden. 'Today is just about Eden and me, if that's okay?'

She could just imagine Dallas wanting to have a summit meeting with the pair of them, and was impressed by Stevie standing up to him.

Back at her house the paps had multiplied and there looked to be around fifty of them outside. God they were like cockroaches swarming everywhere! Eden doubted that they would be able to battle their way through and, even if they did, the thought of all those people waiting outside her front door while they were effectively trapped inside was not an appealing one. As soon as they caught sight of the couple in the taxi they surged forward, all desperate to get their shots.

'Shall we go to a hotel?' Eden said impulsively. They could go to the apartment, but she was worried the paps would pursue them there and find out where her bolthole was, and she liked having a place that no one, apart from her friends, knew about. The paps might follow them to the hotel but at least they wouldn't be able to get in.

'Sure,' Stevie replied. 'We're not going to get through that lot.'

An hour later they were lounging in the huge marble bath of their luxurious hotel suite. Eden had booked them into the Presidential Suite overlooking Hyde Park on the top floor of the five-star Mandarin Oriental.

'This certainly beats the Travel Lodge!' Stevie joked, reaching for yet another glass of champagne.

By now Eden felt she'd had enough to drink, and in spite of Stevie's entreaties that she join him, had switched to water. She was due in studio tomorrow with Jack. The deadline for finishing the album was in just two weeks' time.

She smiled. 'I'd still rather be at home, to be honest. I've spent too much time in hotels over the years, although it feels like a treat being here with you. The worst thing of all is being in a hotel room on your own. It can be the loneliest place in the world.'

'Ah, my poor baby!' Stevie exclaimed, and putting down his glass, he leant forward and kissed her, causing a surge of water to cascade over the side of the bath. 'You need never be lonely again, now you're with me.'

He lightly caressed her breasts. 'Now d'you want to have sex in here or shall we test out the king-size bed? Personally, I prefer the bed, though the bath is great for an appetiser.' He slipped his hand between her legs. 'The bed can be the main course.' His fingers gently teased her, and even though they'd already spent the best part of three hours in bed that day, Eden was more than happy to test out Stevie's theory.

Afterwards they wrapped themselves up in the white fluffy hotel robes and ordered room service. Eden didn't want the day to end, knowing that tomorrow would be hectic, full on, and that they would be apart . . . They both overslept the following morning and it was a mad dash to get ready.

'Will you call me later?' she asked as they kissed goodbye.

''Course,' Stevie replied, but his mind already seemed to be on the day ahead as he glanced over her shoulder at his reflection in the mirror behind.

Jack was already in the studio when Eden raced in. He looked pointedly at his watch.

'Sorry, Jack. Yesterday was manic and I overslept.'

'Twenty minutes is nothing for you,' he replied. 'Anyway, congratulations and all that.'

Was it her imagination or was he avoiding eye contact?

'Thanks, Jack. It may seem too soon to everybody else, but it feels right for us.' She knew she sounded slightly awkward, but that was how she felt with Jack since he'd confessed his feelings for her.

'We'd better get this album put to bed. It seems like you're going to be pretty busy organising a wedding. I imagine you've got big plans?'

'Um, I haven't really thought about it yet, but I would rather have something intimate.'

Jack managed a smile. 'Good for you, Eden, I hope you'll be very happy.' It seemed as if he might be about to say something else about the wedding, but instead he suggested they make a start.

Eden was finally back in front of the microphone. But while it was great to be singing again, progress was slow as she struggled to nail the song. If she was judging herself, she would have said that she didn't own it. The trouble was, she'd been so wrapped up in the show and in Stevie that ideally she needed a couple of days, just to play around and get the vibe back. But they didn't have that luxury, she really had to get it together now.

She could see Jack growing frustrated as they did take after take of the song. By mid-afternoon, it still wasn't in the bag. Eden came through into the studio, and suggested they should go out for coffee, then come back and have another go.

Jack ran his fingers through his hair. 'I'm sorry, Eden, I'm going to have to go now. I've got a meeting about the next album I'm doing. I tried to get out of it, but it's the only time they can make.'

'Oh.' She had an unexpected pang of jealousy at the thought of Jack working with someone else, writing wonderful songs for them and giving them his undivided attention. 'Sure. No problem. I'll see you tomorrow.'

Chapter Twenty-One

A die-hard band of paps were still loitering outside her house. 'For fuck's sake!' Eden muttered out loud as the taxi pulled up. As soon as they saw her, the paps advanced. It was so predictable. She opened the door and already they were crowding round, making it hard for her to get past. She put her head down and forced her way through. No doubt she was going to end up in the celeb mags looking like a right moody old cow, but she defied anyone to smile in the face of such intrusion. Once inside she slammed the door shut, but could still hear them shouting out her name. She could only hope that another story would distract them and they would lose interest in her. She could readily understand why some celebrities ended up moving out to the country, into houses with high security fences round them. Anything to get some kind of privacy away from the paps.

Earlier she had texted Tanya and Jez and asked them round that evening. Stevie was finishing his studio session around eight and had promised to come straight over. She was starting to feel anxious about introducing her friends to him. It wasn't like introducing just another boyfriend; this was her fiancé, the man she was going to marry! She looked down at the fake diamond ring and smiled. She thought it was sweet that he'd given her it, but she could imagine Tanya, who was very materialistic, being shocked that he hadn't bought the real thing.

Eden wandered into the kitchen and switched on her MacBook. Even though she had not heard from Savannah after the last email she'd sent, she still wanted to let her sister know her big news. She had already left a message on Al's voice mail and hoped he would approve.

She couldn't help feeling sad as she sent off the email; sad that Savannah was so far out of reach, sad that she wasn't able to tell her mum. What would Terri have made of her relationship with Stevie? Would she have approved? Eden liked to think that she would. She knew that her mum and dad had had a whirlwind romance and married within five months of getting to know each other. And her mum had always told her that she thought you always knew when you had met the right person, the one. And Eden was sure that Stevie was the one for her.

Mindful of the fact that he would no doubt have been surrounded all day by young female fans, all desperate to catch his eye, Eden made an effort and put on a sexy black silk shirt dress, with a leopard-print camisole underneath, and her black patent killer-heeled Louboutins. She took time over her make-up, so the end result was sexy, sophisticated, and hopefully would knock all thoughts of hot teenage fans out of Stevie's head.

She hadn't done any food shopping in ages, so it would have to be a takeaway for tonight. She hoped Rufus would approve of Thai, as she phoned her favourite restaurant and ordered up a selection of dishes. Then she lit candles in the kitchen/diner and living room, made sure there was wine and beer chilling in the fridge, and nervously waited for her friends to arrive. Jez and Rufus were first, bearing a huge bunch of pink lilies and a giant card with two teddies clutching a love heart, emblazoned with 'You're engaged!'

'I couldn't resist it!' Jez declared. 'It's so adorably kitsch. So where is Stevie?' He looked around expectantly.

'He'll be here around eight.'

'Oh, goodie, so we've got time for an in-depth discussion of the proposal and what you've been doing since Saturday night. I expect it's been hot sex, hot sex and more hot sex!' Jez said cheerfully.

Eden and Rufus exchanged eye rolls. 'You don't have to tell us, Eden,' Rufus said.

'She does!' Jez exclaimed. 'We've been married for *like* ages, we need to get our pleasure vicariously.'

'I thought you got it last night!' Rufus bantered back, in what was for him an unusually personal comment, but maybe he was feeling more comfortable around Eden now.

Tanya and Tyler turned up next. Eden barely had a chance to say hello and hug her friends before Tanya declared, 'Let's see the ring then!'

'Ooh, yes!' Jez put in. 'I was so hung up on the sex I forgot to ask about the ring, but come on, girlfriend, show us your rock!'

'Okay, don't make a big deal of this,' Eden said, holding out her left hand for inspection. 'The ring is just temporary until Stevie has enough money to buy me one from Tiffany's.'

Tanya and Jez looked suspiciously at the fake diamond ring. 'So that's not real then?' Tanya commented, as if she was looking at something particularly distasteful to her.

'No, I don't think you get diamond rings from Accessorize for ten quid, do you?'

287

'A fake engagement ring,' Tanya said almost to herself, as though marvelling that such a thing could possibly exist. She instinctively glanced down at her own exquisite diamond ring, as if to reassure herself it was still there.

'Look! I know that Tyler bought you some fuck-off expensive princess-cut diamond and that's cool, but I really am okay with this ring for now.' Great, Stevie hadn't even arrived and there was already tension in the air. Eden was aware of Tyler looking at Tanya as if to say *Shut it*, and tried to lighten the mood by offering champagne to everyone. Fortunately that did the trick and soon they were all sitting on the sofas, chatting away, all mention of fake diamond rings forgotten. Eight o'clock came and went with no sign of Stevie. Eden texted him but there was no reply.

'I expect he's busy in studio,' Jez said reassuringly when he caught sight of Eden's tense expression. 'You know how those sessions overrun, and I bet Dallas has got them lashed to the grindstone.'

'Yeah, I do.' But Eden wished that Stevie could have texted her. At half-eight the food arrived. Rufus suggested they wait for Stevie, but as Eden had no idea what time he would turn up, she said they should eat now. This was not how she had imagined the evening would go. The whole point of it had been to show Stevie off to her friends.

They were halfway through dinner when he arrived. Eden opened the door to him and Stevie pulled her into his arms as the paps' cameras sprung into action.

'Quick, shut the door!' she exclaimed, feeling that the paps had already had more than enough of them.

'You look hot,' Stevie murmured, kissing her deeply. 'How about we go to bed?' He tasted of beer.

'Later. My friends are here now and they're all dying to meet you.'

Stevie frowned. 'Can't you send them away? I've been in studio all day, I'm knackered.'

It was Eden's turn to frown. 'Of course not, Stevie!' She took a deep breath, trying to stay calm. The last thing she wanted was for her friends to overhear their conversation. 'I know you're tired, but *please* come and be nice to them. For me.'

'What's in it for me?' Stevie pulled her back against him and ran his hands over her body. Eden was in no mood for sex, but she was up for the game of keeping Stevie sweet for her friends, so she replied, 'Let me see. How about, after they've gone, you have a nice long shower and I put on that sexy basque you like so much? And the rest we can make up . . .'

'Sounds good to me. Are you sure we can't slip away now?'

'Later. All good things come to boys who wait.' And she led Stevie into the kitchen.

'Hey, everybody, this is Stevie,' she declared to her friends, and then proceeded to go round the table introducing everyone. Stevie kissed Tanya and shook hands with the men. So far, so good, Eden thought. He sat down next to her and she poured him a glass of champagne.

Stevie looked at the Thai food spread out on the table and wrinkled his nose. 'What's that you're eating?'

'Thai green chicken curry,' Jez said brightly. 'Would you like me to serve you some? It's totally delish.'

Stevie shook his head. 'No, thanks, mate, I can't stand Thai food.' He turned to Eden. 'Can you order me a pizza, babe? American hot, thick crust. And garlic bread with cheese, and a big portion of coleslaw.'

It was on the tip of Eden's tongue to tell him to go and order it himself, she really didn't like being told what to do, and there was something charmless about the way Stevie had asked – it was more like he was issuing a demand. But she didn't want to draw attention to it and so grabbed her phone and dutifully placed the order. Meanwhile Jez was commenting on Stevie's choice of food.

'Stevie, you'd better watch it! Do you know how many calories there are in pizza?' He was teasing, and obviously expected Stevie to banter back.

Stevie shrugged. 'I don't have any worries on that score, mate. Look.' And he lifted up his tee-shirt to reveal his rock-hard abs, giving them a slap to hammer home his point. 'Never get any complaints from the ladies.' He gave his trademark cocky grin.

'You mean, you never used to get any complaints,' Tanya put in meaningfully.

Stevie glanced at Eden. 'Oh, yeah, I never used to get any complaints.' He smiled. 'I'm practically a married man.' And then he reached for Eden's hand and kissed it.

'Yes, congratulations!' Jez put in. 'We should have a toast: to Eden and Stevie!' He raised his glass along with Tanya, Tyler and Rufus. Everyone was trying so hard to be nice to Stevie, but it didn't escape Eden's notice that he wasn't making much of an effort with her friends. He had the air of someone who would rather be somewhere else, as if he didn't think this group quite worthy of his attention.

'And congratulations on winning *Band Ambition*!' This from Tanya.

'Yeah, thanks,' Stevie replied. 'Though I still haven't quite forgiven this one for not voting for me.' He put his arm round Eden and pulled her to him. 'She is going to owe me big time. Can you imagine if we had lost because of it? We were so much better than the girls. There was no contest really.'

He wasn't joking. God, he sounded arrogant! Eden

noticed Tanya and Tyler exchanging glances. But there was no way she wanted to get into an argument with Stevie about the competition, which as far as Eden was concerned was over and done with. She looked over at Jez and luckily he twigged that she needed a get out and started a conversation about where he and Rufus planned to go for their summer holiday. But the topic apparently wasn't interesting enough for Stevie who kept checking his phone. When it rang he took the call, even though it clearly wasn't urgent and it would have been more polite to let it go to voice mail and to stay at the table, instead of wandering into the living room, which was what he did.

'You okay, Eden?' Jez asked sympathetically.

'I'm fine.' She wasn't. She felt let down by Stevie's attitude. These were her best friends and he was treating them as if they were of no importance to him whatsoever. It really grated on her. She had never seen this side of him; usually he was charm itself. A voice inside her said that was because he had been trying to impress everyone before he won the competition whereas now he felt he didn't need to. Had that charming Stevie been simply an act? Oh, God! She hoped not.

She was saved from her negative chain of thought by the arrival of the pizza delivery guy. Eden went to open the door to him and pay, once more triggering a flurry of activity from the waiting press outside. *Hold the front page! Eden Haywood orders pizza!* Really, it was ludicrous what they thought was worthy of a photograph.

By now her friends had finished eating and they all went into the living room where Stevie finally came off the phone, declaring as he took the pizza box from Eden, 'Thank God for that! I'm starving!' He flopped down on one of the sofas and proceeded to chomp his way through the garlic bread and pizza.

'So how's the album going?' Tanya asked her friend.

Eden pulled a face. 'Not so great. And we're on such a tight deadline, I'm worried to be honest.'

'It'll be fine,' Stevie said casually. 'Ours is going fantastically. Dallas reckons we'll have it in the bag in two weeks. I'm well impressed by him. He had everything ready, all the songs lined up and arranged. He's a real class act. Maybe you should think about changing managers and have him instead? I'm sure he'd take you on.'

Eden shook her head. 'Absolutely no way! Sadie is a brilliant manager. I'd never want to be managed by anyone else.'

Stevie shrugged. 'Just a thought, as you seem to be struggling a bit. Dallas seems more of a go-getter than Sadie.'

'He's also completely ruthless.'

Another shrug from Stevie. 'So what? So long as it brings results.' It was on the tip of Eden's tongue to say that you didn't always have to be ruthless to get on, and that Sadie was a much more rounded person who had always been there for her, but she didn't want to draw attention to the fact that once again she and Stevie didn't seem to see eye to eye.

'And maybe you shouldn't be working with Jack. The guy seems so up himself.'

God! Did he ever know how to wind Eden up! He was clearly still jealous of Jack.

'He is incredibly talented. I'm lucky that he's working with me! And remember how discreet he was about us? He didn't tell anyone.' Eden stopped talking, aware of how rattled she sounded.

'I'm sure your album will be fabulous,' Jez quickly put in as he noticed Stevie glaring at her.

'So why don't you play it to us, Eden? I still haven't heard any of the tracks,' Stevie commented. 'Or are you worried about how we'll judge you?'

'Oh, no, I can't play it until it's finished,' she replied, not liking his little dig. She had always been super-stitious like that, only wanting her friends and family to hear her albums when they were completed. '*Please*, let's talk about something else. How's your work going, Tyler?' He was a graphic designer, with his own business.

He grimaced. 'There's been a bit of a downturn, but I'm hoping things will pick up.'

'In the meantime, I'm having to cut back on shopping,' Tanya said quietly. 'And we may have to put the wedding plans on hold for a while longer.' Eden knew how much the couple wanted to tie the knot; they had been saving for the last three years. Both of them wanted a big wedding and they were having to pay for everything themselves as their parents weren't able to help them out.

'I had no idea,' she said quietly, appalled that she had been so caught up in her own affairs that she had failed to realise what her friend was going through. She had thought all those texts from Tanya asking her to call had been because she wanted to talk to her about Stevie, but now she reflected they were most likely about Tanya wanting to confide in her about the delayed wedding. What a bad friend she had been lately. 'If I can do anything to help . . . and I mean anything, like help pay for the wedding . . . then please let me know.'

'No way! We couldn't possibly ask you for money,' Tyler said firmly.

Damn! She shouldn't have mentioned it in front of him; his male pride was always going to make accepting any financial help difficult.

'It would be a loan, Tyler.'

But he still shook his head, while Tanya glanced over at Eden as if to say, *Nice try*.

'I could do your hair and the bridesmaids' and your relatives,' Jez commented. 'And I could pull in a favour from a make-up artist friend. We got married two and a half years ago and I know how expensive it can all get.'

'Jez had to scale down his plans,' Rufus said quietly. 'It was either that, or sell the flat.'

'I did let my imagination run away with me,' Jez admitted. 'And in the end we held the wedding at a small boutique hotel in Brighton, and it was perfect. You really don't have to overspend to have the wedding of your dreams.' He paused. 'Ooh, listen to me, I sound like some kind of money advice expert on TV! Perhaps there's a slot for me.'

'Thinking of your recent credit-card statement, I think it's best if you stick to hair,' Rufus said, but he smiled affectionately at Jez.

'It wasn't my fault! That Vivienne Westwood suit in the sale was just asking to be bought. It had my name all over it.'

'Just as well, seeing as how you're going to be spending the next two years paying for it.'

Everyone laughed, but Stevie interrupted with, 'Well, I want the whole big wedding thing with Eden. I want a stately home, a flashy marquee, a band. Everything. I want the world to know how much I love her.'

He had completely missed Jez's point that it really wasn't about how much you spent. Nor had he and Eden even started to discuss what kind of ceremony they wanted. There was no way that she wanted a big wedding. 'We'll have to talk about that,' she said quietly, and to avoid a further comment from Stevie she asked if anyone wanted coffee. But all her friends seemed pretty keen to leave. Eden couldn't help feeling deflated as she showed them out. They all commented on how gorgeous he was as they said goodbye in the hall – Stevie was on his phone in the living room, *again* – but Eden felt as if they were just saying it to be nice.

She half-heartedly loaded the plates and glasses into the dishwasher, then made her way upstairs. Bugger putting on the sexy basque! All she wanted to do was have a bath, go to sleep and hope that in the morning she would have forgotten what a disappointment Stevie had been tonight. That by the morning he would be back to being the Stevie she thought she knew. She took her time in the bath, hoping that the luxurious bath oil and hot water would relax her. When she came out Stevie was lying on the bed, naked except for a towel round his waist. He had lit candles around the room.

'I wondered when you were ever going to come out. I'm all ready for you. So where's the basque?'

Bollocks! He hadn't forgotten about her earlier promise.

'How about you take off that robe, so I can feast my eyes on your hot sexy body . . . while you feast on my cock.'

Eden glared at him and snapped sarcastically, 'With romantic lines like that, I'm surprised you're not planning to be a songwriter. I can just hear those lyrics in your next hit single.'

Stevie sat up. 'What's your fucking problem then?'

'My fucking problem is that you made zero effort with my friends tonight! You acted like you couldn't give a shit what any of them thought. They're my best friends, Stevie!'

She was expecting him to retaliate angrily, but instead he said, 'Did you think that? Sorry, babe, I was still hyped up from being in studio and I'm knackered. I'll make it up to them next time, I swear.'

Eden wondered whether her friends would feel like a next time, but at least Stevie had apologised.

'Now why don't you come to bed and I can give you a massage? You seem tense, babe.'

Eden approached the bed. 'I'm still pissed off with you, don't expect sex tonight.'

He shrugged. 'No problem. Now, if miss would like to take off her robe and make herself comfortable . . .'

'Miss will loosen the robe, but she's not taking it off.'

It would serve Stevie right if she fell straight asleep and he didn't get the hot sex he had demanded. But as soon as he slipped her robe off her shoulders and began expertly massaging first her back, then her feet, her calves, her thighs, and then finally lightly touched her between her legs, Eden found out that hot sex was exactly what she wanted.

'I'm not sure if a masseuse should be doing *that*,' she murmured, as Stevie gently pushed her legs apart so he could increase his caresses. Her anger was melting away. She was feeling deliciously turned on.

'Ah, but, miss, you ordered the special de luxe version and the client is only allowed to leave once they've had at least two orgasms. So why don't you turn over?'

Eden did as she was told, pausing only to rip off the towel and admire Stevie's hard cock, and then she lay back, and found herself writhing in pleasure as he brought her to an exquisite orgasm, with his hands and with his tongue, and while she was still quivering with pleasure, he thrust his cock inside her and fucked her . . . and they came together this time.

'I love you, Eden,' Stevie panted, as he lay down next to her. 'Don't ever forget that.'

'I love you,' she murmured, putting her head on his chest.

'And I promise, I really will make it up to your friends. I know how important they are to you.'

That sealed it. She had to forgive him now.

Chapter Twenty-Two

Stevie had left for the studio by the time Eden woke up, but he had left a sweet note on the bedside table: *Love u more than words can say, my beautiful, sexy Eden. P.S. I'll book a table somewhere fantastic to take your friends. xx*

Eden smiled; last night had simply been a blip. She should put it down to Stevie being strung out and tired, and move on. She reached for her phone and selected Tanya's number. With any luck her friend would be free to meet for coffee before Eden's own studio session started. As luck would have it she was on her way to a modelling job, but had just found out that the session had been put back two hours, so she had a window.

Eden quickly showered and dressed, and grabbed a taxi to Patisserie Valerie on Old Compton Street in Soho. She arrived to find Tanya wearing a vivid orange maxi-dress and matching hairband. She was sipping an iced coffee, her fork poised above a delicious strawberry and cream cake. She looked as if she should have been lounging by the pool in Barbados.

'You look very glam,' Eden commented, giving her friend a quick hug and ordering herself an iced coffee.

'Thanks for supper last night, it was great to see

everyone,' Tanya said cautiously. It seemed to Eden that her friend was skirting round the issue of Stevie, so she herself had better get to the point.

'Stevie apologises for being so crap last night. He was knackered from recording in studio all day. It was my fault, I never should have arranged for you guys to meet him so soon after the competition. It was too much, too soon.'

'No problem.' Tanya avoided eye contact. She had clearly been less than impressed by Stevie.

'Please don't judge him until you've had the chance to meet him properly. I do love him *so* much!'

Tanya smiled. 'You don't have to convince me, Eden. And I'm happy for you.' She paused. 'I just hope he treats you well.'

'He does, Tan, I promise. But I don't want to talk about me any more! I know that it's been me, me, me, non-stop for ages. I want to talk about you and your wedding. I had no idea that money was so tight.'

Tanya stuck her fork into the cake, 'Apparently my agent thinks I've lost too much weight. I must be one of the few models who is told to eat more!'

'Make the most of it,' Eden said, looking enviously at the cake. 'But don't change the subject, I want to know what's been going on.'

Tanya sighed and then began telling her all about their financial situation. Apparently Tyler had been underplaying just how bad it was. He was currently hardly bringing in any money and they were dependent on Tanya's income, which varied wildly from month to month according to her modelling bookings. They'd had to raid their wedding fund to pay the mortgage and it looked as if their dreams of getting married were slipping further and further into the future.

'Please let me help you, Tan – I could loan you the

money and you could say to Tyler that you'd landed a great modelling contract.'

'Thanks, Eden, I know you would lend me the money, but there is no way I could take a loan and not tell him the truth. I don't want to start our marriage on a lie.'

'Oh, I see what you mean.' Eden bit her lip. She so wanted to help her friend. 'But there must be another way? How about if I paid for the venue as my wedding present to you? Surely Tyler couldn't object to that?'

Tanya shook her head. 'I can't see any way round it. He definitely would object to you paying. But I am going to scale down the plans. I can get a dress off the peg, rather than having one made, and who needs an ice sculpture and a chocolate fountain, a five-course meal and a honeymoon in the Bahamas? We can have a recessionista wedding – champagne buffet and then a pay bar. I've heard that anyone who is *anyone* is doing that now.' She was trying to sound light-hearted, but Eden could tell how upset her friend was.

'Oh, Tanya, I'm really sorry. Promise me you'll think about my offer?'

Tanya managed the smallest of smiles. 'Let's not talk about it any more. You said last night you were worried about your album, what's going on?'

'And so we're back to me again! I've been so caught up with Stevie and the show that I keep thinking that it's not all going to come together.'

'I'm sure it will, Eden. You're so talented, and so's Jack.'

'Yeah, I'm not worried about him; he's a genius and I want to do justice to the songs he's written. I'm really lucky that he worked with me.' She paused. 'In spite of what happened between us, I hope we can stay friends.'

Tanya smiled. 'That's very grown up of you, Eden.'

She shrugged. 'I've lost too many people that I care about.'

'You've got so much going on in your life, you've hardly had the time to concentrate on the album.'

'You can say that again,' Eden muttered. She had checked her phone earlier and there had been several messages from Dallas and Sadie, wanting to set up meetings to talk about the wedding. Dallas had even suggested that she and Stevie record a single together. Eden felt as if too many people were demanding too many things from her. It felt pretty overwhelming.

As she and Tanya stepped out of the café and into the bright sunshine, Eden's phone rang. It was Jack, sounding terrible. 'I'm sorry, Eden, I'm not going to be able to make it today. I've got some kind of virus, I feel like shit.'

He sounded so rough that she wasn't even tempted to joke that he had man 'flu.

'Have you got some medicine in? And plenty of things to drink?' she asked sympathetically.

'I'm sure I've got something.' He broke off as he coughed.

'Look, I'm in Soho right now. Why don't I go to the chemist for some cold relief and then drop it round?'

'You don't have to do that,' he protested.

'It's no trouble, Jack. I'm literally round the corner. Just remind me of your address?'

Twenty minutes later he was opening the door to her. His appearance was as rough as he sounded. He looked feverish, his eyes were bloodshot, and he could barely get a word out before he was overcome with a coughing fit.

'Bed!' Eden declared, trying to ignore the memories that were crowding into her mind from her last visit to Jack's flat. How it had felt being in his arms, the passionate, intense kisses followed by his rejection. If she'd thought those memories belonged to the past, it seemed she was mistaken . . .

'Lying in bed depresses me, I'll crash on the sofa.'

The kitchen was small, minimalist and exceptionally tidy. Eden easily found what she needed and returned with a mug of Lemsip to find Jack stretched out on the sofa.

'Here, drink this, it will make you feel better.'

'Thanks,' he croaked. He was wearing a tee-shirt, hoodie and tracksuit bottoms, and even though it was a warm day he was shivering. Eden went off to the bedroom to grab a cover. She paused in the doorway. The bedroom was just as minimalist as the kitchen, simply a double bed and a bedside table. There were no photographs or personal items anywhere. She knew Jack was housesitting, but still she had expected to see something. It was as if he was ready to pack up and leave at any moment. She gathered up the double duvet and returned to the living room, where she carefully arranged it over Jack.

'I make a good nurse, don't you think?' she joked.

'I appreciate this, Eden. I'm sure I'll be okay by tomorrow for our studio session. You can go now.'

She put her hand on his forehead; it felt as if he was burning up. She dreaded to think what his temperature was.

'I'll stay a while, I haven't got anywhere else to be.' She realised that she wanted to be there with Jack, and she wanted to look after him.

'You really don't have to,' he tried to protest, before a coughing spasm took over.

Eden picked up her bag, and pulled out a selection of mags. 'I've got plenty to read. And it will be a relief that no one knows where I am. That there's no scumbag paps lurking outside.'

301

She sat down in the comfortable, grey velvet arm-chair and tucked her legs up. Jack lay back; he looked as if he didn't have the energy to protest. His eyes closed. Eden smiled and reached for a magazine. She had meant what she'd said to him; it was good knowing that there were no paps outside.

Sunlight streamed through the open sash window and the white muslin curtains drifted on the light breeze. Eden felt as if she was having time out. She yawned; the last few weeks had been such an emotional rollercoaster. Everything had happened so quickly with Stevie, their falling in love, his proposal, that she felt as if she'd hardly had a second to reflect. Her own eyelids felt heavy. She would close them for just a minute . . .

She woke up some time later, to find Jack looking at her. 'I thought you were supposed to be looking after me?' He seemed amused by her Sleeping Beauty act.

Eden struggled to sit up. Oh, God! She hoped she hadn't been slumped in the seat, with her mouth open and dribbling! How undignified would that have been?

'Sorry! I hadn't realised how tired I was. How are you feeling?'

'A little better.' He stretched and checked his watch. 'I reckon we've been asleep for three hours. You must have needed it, Eden. It's been a busy time for you, with work and . . .' he hesitated '. . . Stevie.'

Eden really didn't want to talk about him with Jack, so she simply replied, 'Yeah, it has.' She stood up. 'Why don't I make us some lunch? I went to the deli and picked up some salads and fresh bread.' She smoothed down her hair.

'Sure, but don't worry if you need to go. I'm sure I can make it myself.'

'It's no problem. We would still have been in studio if you were okay. I'm not supposed to be anywhere.'

And so Eden made them both lunch and stayed for the rest of the afternoon. They watched *Legally Blonde* on DVD, as Jack made the surprising confession that he had a bit of a thing for Reese Witherspoon.

'Really?' Eden was surprised. This didn't at all fit in with her view of him. 'I would have thought you would have gone for someone mysterious and sexy, like Angelina Jolie.'

'I wouldn't say no to Angelina, what man would? But there's something very, I don't know, life-affirming about Reese, and when I was going through a difficult time, I remember seeing one of her films and it cheering me up.'

Eden was intrigued about what this difficult time had been. Could it have been the time he'd had his heart broken? The more time she spent with Jack, the more she realised how much about him she still didn't know. She tried to push away another thought, which was that the more she was with him, the more he intrigued her . . .

After the film, they talked for a while and Eden opened up about her anxieties about the album.

'You're being too hard on yourself, Eden. It's going to be great.'

'You really think that?' She was in need of reassurance.

In spite of being ill, Jack raised a smile. 'You know I wouldn't say that if I didn't mean it. I've got a suggestion. My sister lives on a farm in the Cotswolds and I've got a recording studio there. We could go together and finish the album. That way you'll have no distractions. I reckon it will only take us a week.'

For a moment Eden was tempted; then she thought about what Stevie's reaction would be to her spending time away with Jack.

'I'm not sure . . . I think I need to be in London

right now. But it's really helped talking to you. It'll be fine.'

But it wasn't fine, and for the rest of the week Eden was frantically busy. Stevie wanted to go out every night, to a restaurant, then on to a club until the early morning, which was the last thing Eden felt like doing after the hours she had spent in studio. Stevie claimed that he wanted to show her off, but actually it felt more like he wanted to be seen out. He loved the attention he got from the public. Teenage girls continued to crowd round him, wanting his autograph, a hug and a kiss, and at the clubs he would be caught up with talking to his many admirers all night. Eden would drag herself to the studio the following day, feeling increasingly exhausted and drained, and that was reflected in her singing, which was not up to her usual standard. She might joke to Jack that he would have to use the Auto-Tune, but inside she felt like crying that she wasn't delivering the performance she was capable of. On top of that she felt as if she and Stevie didn't have any time to themselves. And the following week he started a nationwide tour along with Rapture and the other bands from the show so she would barely get to see him then. By Friday night Eden was desperate to stay in.

'But we've been invited to the premiere of the latest Vince Vaughn film!' Stevie said when she asked him not to go out. 'It'll be the first time we hit the red carpet together.'

'There will be plenty of other opportunities, Stevie, I promise. Tonight, can't we just have a bottle of wine, order a takeaway and chill out? *Please*. We haven't even had a chance to discuss the wedding.'

Stevie looked sulky as he lounged on the sofa. 'I need to be seen out as much as possible, Dallas told me. It's important I keep a high profile. *X Factor* will be kicking off in the autumn and I don't want to be overshadowed by those wannabes.'

'I don't think one night will make a difference to your profile, but it would really make a difference to me.'

A sigh from Stevie, then a reluctant, 'Okay.'

'Thanks.' Eden leant across and kissed him. Then, as always seemed to happen, she organised the drinks, she ordered the pizza and paid for it when it arrived, while Stevie remained glued to his phone.

'Dallas has suggested the name of a great wedding planner,' he said once he had polished off his pizza and downed a couple of beers. 'She's done loads of other celeb weddings and knows all the ins and outs. And he reckons we could get it all paid for and some extra if we do a deal with one of the celeb mags.' He looked at Eden, clearly expecting her to go along with his idea.

'I'm not sure if I want that kind of wedding, Stevie. I'd much rather have something smaller and private. I don't want everyone knowing everything about us.'

Stevie clenched his jaw, and looked annoyed. 'They wouldn't! We would only give them what *we* wanted to. We'd be the ones in control.'

Eden shook her head. 'We wouldn't be. Once you've signed up for something like that, you find it takes over. And I want our wedding to be about us, not about satisfying some magazine deal.'

Stevie slammed his beer bottle on the table in frustration. 'That's easy for you to say, Eden, you've got this house and plenty of money. I'm still skint and waiting for Dallas to give me my share of the album. I've been skint most of my life! You've no idea what that's like, have you? I can't even afford to buy you a proper engagement ring! I saw the look your mate Tanya gave your ring, when she thought I wasn't looking. Like it was a piece of shit!'

Eden felt shaken by his aggressive tone. 'I'm sure she

305

didn't, Stevie. I know you'll get me a proper ring when you can afford it, and I'm happy to wait. I really don't want a ring that's been bought because of a magazine deal.'

Stevie stood up. 'Well, you'll be waiting a long time, because fuck knows when I'll be able to afford it.'

'I would rather wait,' Eden insisted. She couldn't believe how badly tonight was turning out. She had wanted the chance to get closer to Stevie, but it seemed they were further apart than she had realised. He didn't seem to understand her point of view at all.

'Christ, Eden, can't you see how sick I am of not having any money! You've always had everything you want, you're such a spoilt princess.' Unwittingly or maybe deliberately Stevie had used the same words as Joel in his hurtful kiss and tell about her. Eden flinched as if he had struck her.

'You're wrong, Stevie, I just don't want our private life to be made public. I want to protect what we've got.' She looked up at him, her beautiful green eyes glinting with tears. 'All my relationships have gone wrong. I want us to be different; I want us to last.' Eden felt battered by Stevie's outburst. And it seemed as if he realised he had gone too far.

He sat next to her and put his arm round her. 'Eden, baby, of course I want us to last.' And he held her close to him. 'And I'm sorry I've upset you.' He paused. 'But will you at least think about what I've said, for my sake?'

Eden wanted to say that she didn't need to think about it, that she absolutely knew that she did not want a magazine deal, but she couldn't bear Stevie to be angry with her, so she simply nodded.

'Thanks, Eden, I know we can work this out,' he said, planting a kiss on her forehead. 'Come on, let's go to bed.'

*

306

Eden walked in to The Wolseley with smile on her face as she prepared to meet up with the girls from Venus Rising. She was treating them to dinner at the restaurant they had all chosen because, as Alana had said, they had read about so many celebrities eating there and were dying to try it out for themselves. But as the maître d' showed Eden to the table she was surprised to see only Alana and Kim.

'Where's Kasey?' she asked, after she'd greeted the other two.

Alana and Kim looked awkward. 'She's getting over a sickness bug,' Alana said quietly. 'She says she's really sorry but she's not up to coming out.'

'Oh.' Eden was not at all sure she believed the excuse. To her credit, Alana made a very poor liar. 'Well, that's a shame, I hope she gets better soon.'

What was it with Kasey? Why didn't she like Eden? She tried to push away the negative thoughts and concentrate on chatting to the girls. They were still full of excitement about being runners up in the competition, and Dallas was definitely going to give them an album deal – though Eden doubted they would be getting rich on the proceeds of that since Dallas was such a wily businessman. The girls also had interviews with celeb mags lined up, and next week they would be touring with Rapture.

'So have you thought any more about your wedding?' Kim asked. 'We were gobsmacked when we heard that Stevie had asked you. He doesn't hang about, does he?'

Eden laughed. 'No, he doesn't! But I think that's one of the things I love about him. He is so open about his feelings, puts his heart on the line. Most of the men I've been out with have been so bad at showing any emotion, except when we broke up, and then they were very good at pointing all the bad things out about me.'

She said it jokingly, but she sensed Alana and Kim looking at her sympathetically.

'But you're so lovely! I don't understand men at all,' Alana said.

'Yeah, but I guess we wouldn't be without them would we?' And Eden thought that Alana gave Kim a look then as if to say, *Let's change the subject.*

'So has Jack got a girlfriend?' Kim asked.

'I don't think so,' Eden replied, wondering why she was asking. 'He was seeing someone but I think they broke up.'

'He is seriously gorgeous! Do you think I'd have any chance with him at all?' Kim continued, a dreamy expression on her face. 'He's so good-looking and such a gentleman. And, well, sexy of course!'

She was clearly smitten. Eden looked at her consider-ingly. Would Jack be interested in her? She was very pretty with her blonde hair in its new pixie cut and heart-shaped face, and she had a lovely smile. Before Jack's revelation about his thing for Reese Eden would have thought not, but Kim was cute and blonde . . . Eden suddenly realised that she didn't want Jack to go out with Kim for the very good reason that Eden herself was jealous! Now where did that come from?

'I don't know what he's into, to be honest. He's a bit of a closed book, but I suspect that he might be one of those men who can't commit.'

Kim looked slightly crestfallen, then perked up and said, 'Well, I could always just shag him!' She clearly expected Eden to laugh, so Eden forced herself to smile.

'I know he's probably out of my league, but maybe you could seat me near him at your wedding? Weddings are great for getting off with people, in my experience.' Kim winked at Eden, who thought she would make damn sure that Jack and Kim were sitting as far away as possible from each other. It was her turn to change the subject after that, and they talked about the girls' schedule and how they planned to go to Ibiza in August.

Later, Eden felt rather deflated by her evening as she let herself into the house, and unsettled by Kim's comment about Jack. Perhaps she just felt protective of him as a friend, but she found herself thinking that she really didn't think Kim was good enough for him. She hoped Stevie would be in, as it would be their last chance to see each other for a week. He was leaving early the next day.

He was already asleep in bed, or judging by the three-quarter-empty bottle of Jack Daniel's lying on the floor next to it, had passed out. He had strewn his clothes across the room, and it wasn't the first time. Wearily Eden picked up boxer shorts and jeans and slung them on the chair. She would have to say something to him about it. She wasn't the world's tidiest person herself but she drew the line at leaving her clothes everywhere.

'Love you,' she murmured as she snuggled up next to Steve in bed, but he didn't wake up.

Eden couldn't sleep as she continued to brood about Jack. She was glad he wasn't seeing Cherry any more. And then she stopped herself. Why was she so concerned? She was getting married. But when she finally did fall asleep her dream was not of her husband-to-be. Instead she dreamt that she and Jack were walking on a beach holding hands. And in her dream she felt such an intense longing for him. She dreamt they were kissing, then lying on the sand making love, and the blue of Jack's eyes as he gazed into her eyes was the exact blue of the sky above them . . . and she wanted him so much, wanted to possess him, wanted him to possess her . . . When she woke up, she felt incredibly turned on and it was almost a shock to discover that he wasn't lying there next to her.

'Ah, you're awake!' Stevie said. 'Sorry I was so out of it last night.' He ducked down and kissed her shoulder, slipping off the straps of her silk camisole. 'How about a quickie before I go?' His lips grazed her already-hard nipple as he dipped his hand between her legs. He looked at her and gave her his sexy smile. 'You must have been dreaming of me, you're all juicy.'

'Well, why don't you make the most of it?' Eden murmured, and pushing him down on to the bed, she straddled him. This would surely chase the remnants of her dream away. But as she moved rhythmically on him, and he grabbed hold of her hips and thrust into her, she found herself closing her eyes and imagining that it was Jack lying underneath her. But that didn't mean anything, did it? Everyone had fantasies . . .

Eden pulled back her hair into a pony-tail as she walked along Wardour Street. It was far too hot to have her long hair cascading down her back. The country was suddenly in the grip of a mini-heatwave. In London the temperature was nudging 30 and everywhere she looked people were in summer clothes. City types had taken off their jackets, and some were even wearing shorts. Eden was wearing only a red vest, denim shorts and flat gold sandals, but she was still hot, and fantasising about lying on a beach somewhere exotic. Even the roads seemed to be shimmering in the heat. She was on her way to see Sadie. Her manager had asked for an urgent meeting to discuss the album.

'Hiya, Claude,' Eden called out as she walked into the office, and caught a welcome cold blast of air con.

'Good morning, Eden, how are you today? I'll bring

you a coffee through, shall I? Sadie is expecting you.'
Claude was as efficient as ever.

Sadie was, as usual, sitting cross-legged on her zebra-print sofa. She was dressed in black silk shorts and an off-the-shoulder white tee-shirt with a picture of a roaring black panther on it. Eden had to admire her fashion choices. Not many other fifty year olds would have got away with such an outfit, but Sadie did. She got up as soon as Eden walked in and kissed her.

'Don't you adore this heat! I love it. Now come and sit down.'

Eden got the feeling that she wasn't going to like what Sadie had to say. She sat on the sofa and steeled herself for the worst. Typically her manager got straight to the point.

'Five of the songs on the album are fabulous – your best work ever. But the last four that Jack has played me . . .' She shook her head. 'They're just not good enough. Now, before you throw a tantrum, I've talked about it with Jack and we both agree that you've got to get out of London and nail them.'

Eden rolled her eyes. 'Sadie, I can nail them in London.'

She shook her head. 'Eden honey, you've been in London and it's not been working. You've had distraction after distraction and it's reflected in your work. Sure, Marc White is pleased with how the show went, and I don't want to sound cynical but he loved the fact that you and Stevie are together, but the album also has to deliver or it will be the last one you record for him. And I don't have to remind you how tough it is to get a record deal at the moment. Dallas has been on my case about you recording a single with Stevie, but I'll be honest with you, I've got my doubts about that. I want to focus on you, not Stevie. He's getting enough exposure.'

311

A sigh from Eden. 'So what do you want me to do?'

'Jack's told me about his recording studio in the Cotswolds at his sister's house. I want you to spend a week there and get the album in the bag. Stevie is going to be on tour, so it's not as if you would be seeing him. One week is all I ask.'

One week with Jack . . . she tried to block out the memory of that dream.

'Okay,' Eden said reluctantly, 'I'll do it.' It was just a dream after all.

'Good girl. Now go home and pack your bag. Jack's going to pick you up in two hours.'

'What! You want me to go today?' She wouldn't even have a chance to say goodbye to Stevie as he was in Manchester.

'Absolutely. The sooner you're there, the sooner you'll get to work.'

Chapter Twenty-Three

'I hope you're not too angry with me for suggesting we went away,' Jack commented to Eden. They had been driving for the last hour and a half, so far making small talk and listening to the radio.

'Of course not. I want to do whatever it takes to finish the album.' She didn't tell him that Stevie had been absolutely furious when she'd told him she was going away with Jack; that he had ranted and sworn and told her that she shouldn't be doing it when she knew how much he disliked Jack. How he was sure Jack had a thing for her, that he was an arrogant dick, that she was being selfish just thinking about her own album. Nor had they resolved the argument. Stevie had ended up by putting the phone down on her. She really didn't like that jealous side of him, though she couldn't help feeling slightly guilty since her erotic dream about Jack the other night . . .

'Here it is then.' Jack turned into a long drive leading up to a red-brick farmhouse, surrounded by restored outbuildings, one of which, Eden guessed, must house Jack's recording studio. A young woman with long dark-blonde hair opened the door. She was holding an adorable baby girl, who looked to be around six months old, with chubby cheeks and huge blue eyes.

Jack made the introductions. 'Eden, this is my sister Debs and niece Lulu.' Debs had similar colouring to her brother and a lovely warm smile. She led them inside to a cosy kitchen-diner which was full of clutter: baby clothes drying in one corner, piles of newspapers and magazines on the pine dresser, a fat tabby cat asleep on the windowsill, a sink full of washing up.

Jack raised his eyebrows and Eden smiled. Remembering his bare flat, she commented, 'Debs hasn't got your minimalist gene then?'

'God, no!' Debs exclaimed. 'And he's anally retentive more like! So . . . tea, coffee, wine?'

'Actually I'd love a glass of wine,' Eden replied. The row with Stevie had stressed her out.

'Hold Lulu.' Debs handed the baby over to Jack. She sat contentedly on his lap, chewing on a biscuit and dropping most of it on his jeans. Eden gave him top marks for appearing not to mind.

The three of them then went outside to the garden as it was so warm. As they sat round the table, drinking wine and looking out across the fields, Eden felt some of the tension leave her. Jack and his sister were such easy company, she felt she could be completely herself. When Debs's husband Harry turned up, he was just as down-to-earth as his wife.

'How is it working out with my brother?' Debs asked Eden, several glasses of wine later. 'I bet he's a total slave driver perfectionist.'

'Yep,' she replied. 'He works me so hard.'

'I do not!' Jack retorted.

'Do too.'

They could have carried on arguing, albeit light-heartedly, but Harry cut across them. 'I'm starving. Who wants an Indian?'

And while he took the orders, Debs gave Lulu her

bath. It was getting dark now. Jack lit the outdoor candles and set the table.

'You must have made a very good boy scout,' Eden commented.

'Having fantasies about me in uniform?' he teased, and she flushed because she had indeed been having fantasies about him. By the glow of candlelight he looked so handsome. Too handsome for comfort.

'Of course not!' she protested. 'My fantasy life is entirely based around me and Brad Pitt.'

Fortunately Harry rejoined them then and conversation switched to less dangerous territory.

At half-ten Debs gave a huge yawn. 'Well, it's been lovely but I'm off to bed. Lulu's still waking up in the night. I'll see you guys in the morning.' Harry followed her soon after. Eden was all set to suggest she and Jack have another glass of wine but he had different ideas.

'I want to start at nine tomorrow, Eden, so maybe we should both get an early night.' He grinned. 'I know it's not very rock and roll, but we've got a deadline.'

'I guess,' Eden replied, though secretly she would have liked to carry on bantering with him. Upstairs in her guest room she tried calling Stevie but he didn't pick up. Nor did he reply to her texts. Well, if he wanted to be like that, he could go ahead. For once she wasn't going to obsess about it.

For the next four days Eden and Jack worked flat out in the studio and the results were stunning. Eden felt free from all worries for the first time in ages. Stevie had eventually returned her calls and texts, and after a couple of sulky conversations seemed to accept that she needed to be where she was. And his tour was going great, so that made him happy.

In fact, Eden and Jack had worked so hard that by

the end of the fourth day they had finished the album and went to the local pub to celebrate. They sat outside in the beer garden. It was another beautiful summer evening and the garden looked out across fields of ripening corn. It was an idyllic setting. Eden had always seen herself as a city girl but this time away with Jack was making her consider whether she should have a place in the country too. It was so peaceful out here, and so liberating not being hounded by the paps every time she stepped outside her front door, but maybe that would change if she moved out here. She didn't know, but for now it was good to savour her freedom.

She and Jack had been getting on so well that it was a bit of a shock when he brought up the subject of the wedding. But perhaps they had been getting on so well because this was the first time they had talked about Stevie.

'So you're really going to marry him?'

The question sounded like a challenge and Eden found herself replying rather defensively, 'Yes, I love him. Of course I want to marry him.'

Jack picked up his pint. 'Well, here's to you, Eden, may you be very happy. Stevie's a very lucky man, I hope he realises that.'

Eden clinked her wine glass against his pint and laughingly replied, 'No way, Jack. I'm the lucky one. I'm the one who is marrying the man possibly half the female population of this country lusts after!'

Jack shook his head. 'You're a puzzle to me, Eden. At times you can seem like the most confident girl in the world, and then at others I feel there is someone vulnerable inside you, someone who will do anything for love and to be loved.'

His words were painfully, unerringly, spot on. 'Rubbish! I'm like all women.'

'Nope, you're not.'

Eden felt uneasy at this analysis, so she turned the conversation away from herself. 'And what about you, Jack? Do you think you'll ever get married?' She said it in a light enough tone, but the look he gave her unnerved her with its intensity.

'I've wanted to a couple of times in my life. I can't see it happening again.'

Something stopped her from asking him any more questions and suddenly the mood had switched from a celebration to something darker. They finished their drinks and walked back along the country lane to the farmhouse. By now it was dark and there was a beautiful full moon in a night sky studded with stars. Eden stumbled slightly in her heels and Jack reached out for her arm. They stopped walking. They were so close that she got a hit of his deliciously musky aftershave. And suddenly the moment seemed charged with emotion for Eden as all her old feelings for him rose to the surface, her longing for him, her desire for him. She wished she could put her arms around him. What was going on? She had to break the spell.

'You never see the stars in London, do you?' she said, looking up at the sky.

Jack's reply was unexpected. 'Don't do it, Eden. Don't marry Stevie Moore. I think he will break your heart and destroy your life.'

Eden stood and stared at him, shocked by his words. 'Of course he won't, Jack! He loves me, and I love him. For once in my life everything has fallen into place.'

Jack sighed. 'I know you think I'm doing this because I don't like Stevie, but it's not that. I'm saying it because I care about you. He's not good enough for you. And—'

A pause. 'What?' Eden demanded.

'There's a rumour going around the industry that

317

he's just marrying you for the fame. That he set out to seduce you, knowing exactly what it would do for his profile. That he's been seeing someone else.'

'Jack, you are talking complete crap! He loves me – you can't pretend to love someone. He's not that good an actor.'

'He's ruthlessly ambitious. He will do anything to get on. *Anything*.'

Eden couldn't believe that Jack was saying these things to her, slashing away at her happiness. 'You're completely wrong about Stevie. You didn't like him from the start.' She started walking away as quickly as her heels would allow, desperate to get away from Jack and his hurtful comments.

'Phone him up now and ask him where he is,' Jack called after her. 'And who he's with.'

'I don't need to do that. I trust him!' Eden shouted back. But as soon as she was back at the farmhouse and in her bedroom, she reached for her phone.

She told herself that she wanted to call Stevie because she missed him and had to hear his voice. It had nothing to do with wanting to check up on him. But when she only got his voice mail the doubts started crowding in on her. Where was he? Was he with someone? Damn Jack for making her feel so paranoid! She stayed up for the next couple of hours, flicking between TV channels, willing her phone to ring. Finally at two a.m. a text arrived from Stevie: *Babe, you called! Have been out celebrating with my brother, am a bit pissed. Sorry. Love you, want you, miss you. xxx*

See? There had been nothing to worry about. Finally reassured she texted back, (*Love you too! Have a glass of water!*)

She was woken at eight by her mobile ringing. She fumbled for her phone on the bedside table and saw it was Alana calling. Eden didn't expect a call from her so early in the morning.

'Hi, Alana,' she mumbled sleepily. 'Is everything okay?'

'I just wanted to say that I'm so sorry, I should have told you.' Alana sounded as if she had been crying.

'What are you talking about?' She was wide awake now.

'About the story in today's *Sun*.'

Eden felt sick to her stomach. Was this the moment Alana revealed that she was seeing Stevie? Oh, God, had Jack been right all along?

'I haven't seen the paper, Alana, you're going to have to tell me.'

She heard the girl take a deep breath. 'I'm gay. The story's about me and my girlfriend Chrissie.'

'You're gay!' Eden exclaimed. She felt like laughing out loud, she was so relieved. If Alana was gay then that meant there was nothing going on between her and Stevie, and there never had been.

'Yeah. Sorry, Eden, I should have told you, but I've always felt that my sexuality is my own business.'

'And you're absolutely right, Alana. If I sounded shocked it was only that I thought . . .' Eden broke off.

'Thought what?'

'It sounds so stupid now, but I thought there might have been something going on between you and Stevie. You seemed so close. But now I know that was all in my head. I've got nothing to worry about!' She'd like to see Jack's face when she told him.

There was a pause and then Alana said, somewhat hesitantly, 'Stevie knew I was gay. He was just being supportive when I was feeling nervous about the press getting hold of it, that's all, Eden. So you don't mind that I didn't tell you?'

''Course not, Alana! How's Dallas taken the news?'

She sighed. 'He wants me to do some press interviews about it. Went on and on about how photogenic I was.'

Eden laughed. 'He's just thinking of the publicity opportunities! Don't agree to anything that makes you feel uncomfortable.' She ended the call by telling Alana to call her if she was at all worried about anything Dallas wanted her to do, then swiftly got out of bed, showered and went downstairs, all set to tell Jack that he was wrong about Stevie.

But Jack had already left for London, leaving Debs to give his apologies to Eden for not being able to drive her back. She felt slightly hurt that he hadn't told her he'd be leaving so early. They hadn't even had a chance to say goodbye, and to draw a line under their quarrel of the night before. 'Didn't he tell you that he had this meeting?' Debs asked, noticing Eden's downbeat expression.

She shook her head.

'Typical Jack. He never tells anyone anything. But I've got a surprise for him!'

Debs was then distracted as Lulu banged her spoon on her high-chair table, splattering porridge everywhere, including on Eden.

'Don't get porridge on Eden,' Debs told her daughter. 'She's a pop star! We'll never be able to afford to get her a new dress. It's probably Prada!'

Eden brushed off the blob of porridge that had landed on her black maxi-dress. 'It's Lipsy. So what's your surprise for Jack?'

'It's his thirtieth birthday in a month and in true Jack style I know he won't have planned anything. So I'm inviting him here for the weekend and throwing him a surprise party at the pub, with all his friends. Will you come, Eden? And bring Stevie? I know Jack would love to have you there.'

Eden wasn't at all sure that he would love to have

them both there, but she smiled and said, 'That would be lovely, Debs.'

Eden didn't hear from Jack when she returned to London. She supposed that he was busy overseeing the mixing of the album, but it would have been good to talk to him, to know that there were no hard feelings between them. And there was more . . . she couldn't help missing him. Stevie was still away and would be for another week. Eden had suggested travelling up to see him, but he claimed the tour was so busy that he would only feel guilty for neglecting her. So she decided to take advantage of this time to chill out. It still was so hot in London, too hot to do anything much, and on Sunday afternoon she invited Sadie, Tanya and Jez over to the house for a barbecue while their other halves were working.

The four friends were reclining on sun loungers in the garden. The strong sun had caused all of them, even ardent sun worshipper Jez, to retreat under the shade of the large white parasol.

'Who wants more Pimm's?' Eden asked. Everyone held up their glasses for a re-fill. So far no one had had the energy to start up the barbecue.

'God, it's so hot!' Tanya exclaimed for about the tenth time. She looked like a fifties pin-up in a retro blue and white polka-dot bikini, with red-framed Ray-Bans.

'I love it when it's like this!' Sadie exclaimed. 'The hotter the better as far as I'm concerned.' She was wearing a turquoise kaftan, embellished with silver sequins, matching blue D&G sunglasses and a huge white floppy hat, very Joan Collins circa 1976. 'So, Eden, have you had any more thoughts about the wedding? I've had Dallas on the phone all this week going on about it. He's so obsessed with it, I wouldn't be surprised if he asks to give you away!'

Eden sipped her ice-cold Pimm's. 'He can dream on! I was going to ask Al.'

'Good call, Eden,' Sadie replied.

'I'd still prefer a small wedding. And Stevie is still set on having a full-on one. He texted me last night saying that he wanted to get married in mid-September, but that's only six weeks away. To be honest, I'd rather wait until the end of October at least.'

'Even that's pretty soon. You'll have to send out invites next week. I guess you could text people the date and tell them to expect an invite in the post. We could get Claude to help you. So who would you ask?' Sadie reeled off a list of names and then added, 'And of course you'll have to invite Jack.'

Jez looked over at Eden and raised his eyebrows, and she felt put on the spot. 'I'm not sure, Sadie. I wouldn't have thought weddings were his thing, and to be honest Stevie doesn't get on with him.' Eden couldn't imagine marrying Stevie with Jack there. The picture seemed all wrong somehow.

Sadie frowned. 'What's not to get on with? I hope Stevie isn't letting his success go to his head?'

'No, it's not that, Sadie.'

'Well, so long as it doesn't affect your working relationship with Jack. I would love you two guys to work on another album, you make a brilliant team.'

Eden thought of the row she'd just had with him. She very much doubted that Jack would want to work with her again and suddenly she felt terribly sad at the prospect of not having him in her life any more.

Sadie sighed. 'But you're right about Jack and weddings, he hates them, because of course he's never really got over Laura's death and weddings are always a reminder of what he's lost.'

She had everyone's attention with that comment.

'Sorry, who's Laura?' Eden voiced the question that everyone wanted answering.

Now it was Sadie's turn to look surprised. 'I was sure that I told you. Laura was his girlfriend when he was twenty-two, the big love of his life. I think he would have married her. They were in a horrific car accident together. One of Jack's friends was driving; he lost control of the car as he was overtaking and hit another car. Laura died instantly. Jack and his friend were injured but okay.'

Eden's heart went out to Jack. She'd had him down as being some arrogant commitment phobe, a typical man of their times, and now she found out this. She felt as if everything she had believed to be true was unravelling. She thought of how rejected Jack must have felt that time when he had confessed that he did have feelings for her.

'Oh my God Sadie, I had absolutely no idea. That's so tragic. Poor Jack.'

Sadie seemed lost in thought as she continued, 'I suppose such a tragedy can either make you desperate to have a relationship with someone else, or else you run as fast as you can from ever feeling anything for anyone again. And that's what Jack seems to have done.' She paused. 'He's very fond of you. I know that for a fact.'

'And I'm very fond of him,' Eden said quietly.

'Anyway,' Sadie seemed to snap out of it, 'have you and Stevie managed to agree about wedding photographs at least?'

Eden struggled to bring her thoughts to the present. How petty her arguments about the magazine deal with Stevie suddenly seemed. Somehow she couldn't imagine Jack wanting his wedding pictures to be sold off to the highest bidder.

'Not yet, Sadie, but I'm hopeful that Stevie will come

round to my point of view that we will just release a single photograph and that the money raised will go to charity.'

'Good girl, that's much more appropriate. I'm sure Dallas won't agree, but I'll tell him that sometimes it's better to take the long view.' She checked her watch. 'I'd better go. I said I'd watch Travis and his band rehearse for their gig tonight.'

Eden showed Sadie out, promising to call her about the wedding plans, but she felt as if she was going through the motions because all she could think about was Jack. So many things made sense now; the way he seemed to get closer to her one time only to pull away the next. She wished she could see him, tell him that she understood. And then she stopped herself. She was marrying Stevie. Why should she be so concerned about Jack?

Back in the garden Tanya and Jez were clearly eager to discuss Sadie's news, but for once Eden didn't feel like analysing everything, picking over the details with her friends. She wanted to be alone with her thoughts or to see Jack.

As soon as Jez and Tanya had left, the first thing she did was to text him: *So sorry we had that row. I just want to say thanks for everything, Jack, it's been great working with you, and I hope we can work together again. Can't wait to hear the album. Can we meet up next week? E x* She sent it off, and then spent the next two hours obsessing about why he hadn't replied. She didn't even think about calling Stevie.

It was only when she was in bed around midnight that her phone beeped with a message. Instantly she reached for it and felt a spark of happiness when she saw the message was from Jack: *The album sounds brilliant. All good with me. I fly to LA tom for a couple of weeks. Am sorry too about that row. Take care. Jx*

It was a perfectly friendly text, the kind of message you would send to a work colleague, and that's what they were, right? So why did Eden feel disappointed that there had been nothing more?

The text she then received from Stevie didn't make her feel any better: *Dallas says that Leeds Castle would be a gr8 location for the wedding! Think about it. U would be my princess, I would be your prince, fancy a ride on my charger? XXX Sexy dreams XXX.*

Chapter Twenty-Four

Eden was still in a bad mood the following morning as she got ready for her gym session with Rufus. She had spent a sleepless night, obsessing about Jack and then Stevie. She was haunted especially by thoughts of Jack, going over and over in her mind what had happened to him and feeling such sympathy for him. And then she would think of Stevie, pressing her about the wedding, and how he seemed so caught up in the drama of it all that it seemed less about expressing his love for her than putting on a show. Or maybe she was being hard on him because she hadn't seen him. Maybe she should pay him a surprise visit later that day.

She was in the middle of checking train times to Manchester when the doorbell rang. Eden was always suspicious of anyone coming to her door unannounced; more often than not it turned out to be the paps. But the young woman standing on her doorstep with a tiny baby in her arms did not look like a press photographer. In fact, Eden realised with a sudden jolt of recognition, this was Stevie's ex, Nicci, and baby Liam. What was she doing here? Eden opened the door, not knowing quite what to expect, but all ready to give a friendly 'Hi'.

'Is he in then?' Nicci demanded rudely. She had long

bleached blonde hair and a pretty face, but was spoiling her looks with a scowl. She was wearing a tiny black sundress and high gold wedges, wore long false eyelashes, and way too much fake tan.

'He's away on tour. You could call him now, you might catch him between rehearsals.'

Nicci gave a dismissive snort. 'Like he'd fucking pick up the phone to me!'

Eden winced to hear her swearing in front of her son.

Nicci caught the look and said, 'He's just a baby, he doesn't understand so there's no need to look all arsey. I need to see Stevie because, in spite of everything he promised, he hasn't paid me a single penny for Liam.'

It was on the tip of Eden's tongue to reply that perhaps Nicci should not have spent all the money she'd received for the kiss and tell. 'Well, I'll call him and tell him you came round. I know he wants to be a good dad.'

Nicci looked at Eden as if she had 'Stupid' tattooed across her forehead. 'Are we talking about the same person? No, don't answer. I still remember what Stevie's like at the start of a relationship. He's all over you then, telling you how much he loves you. He's on your case the whole time, saying that you're the one, how he can't live without you. And the sex . . . yeah, he was very good at that. Had one of his special massages, have you?'

Nicci's description of Stevie was a little too accurate for comfort. Eden tried to act as if it meant nothing. 'Like I said, I'll call him.'

Nicci stepped forward. '*You* could give me some money while I'm waiting, something to tide me over.' She glanced up at the house, as if assessing its value. 'By the look of it, you're doing all right. It's either that or I could do another story, with some extra juicy details about Stevie. I'm sure there's plenty he hasn't told you.'

Liam's dummy fell out of his mouth on to the floor then and Nicci bent down, picked it up, gave it a quick suck and plugged it back into her son's mouth. Eden had almost been tempted to give her some money, but her hard-faced, calculating attitude was fast destroying any sympathy Eden had felt. She was about to tell her to go when Rufus turned up, ready to take her to the gym.

'Hiya, Eden,' he called out as he got out of his car.

'One of your staff, is he?' Nicci asked in a sneering voice.

Rufus overheard her as he walked up the stone steps. He looked slightly taken aback by her comment. 'Everything okay?'

'Yeah, everything's fine, thank you,' Nicci said, now in a mock-polite voice. 'Eden's about to ask me in so we can sort out a little matter.'

Eden squared her shoulders and looked Nicci straight in the over-made-up eye. 'I'm not actually, Nicci, and if you don't go away, I'll call the police and say that you've been harassing me.'

'You stuck-up bitch!' Nicci exclaimed. 'You think you're better than me! You think he won't cheat on you. I bet he's cheating on you now, having some tart suck his dick. He's not capable of being faithful to anyone. Not even you.'

While Eden was left reeling inside at the vicious comments, Rufus took over, saying quietly but firmly, 'That's enough.' Stepping into the house, he turned round and slammed the door in Nicci's face.

Nicci continued to shout out, 'Bitch!' And so Rufus put his arm round Eden and led her well out of earshot into the kitchen where he shut the door, to make absolutely sure that no sound carried.

'I can't believe that Stevie hasn't given her any money!' Eden exclaimed as she paced up and down the kitchen. Her trainers made an irritating squeaking sound against the polished wooden floor. 'He promised me that he would!' And inside she was wondering what else he hadn't been telling the truth about. Everything between them felt cheapened and sullied by Nicci's poisonous words.

'For all you know he has given her money and she's trying it on to get some more.' Rufus was the voice of calm. 'Why don't you call Stevie and tell him what happened? I bet there's a perfectly reasonable explanation.'

Eden stopped her furious pacing and went over to Rufus and hugged him. 'What would Jez and I do without you? You're right.'

But when she called Stevie, yet again, frustratingly, he didn't pick up. Eden didn't get what was going on with him and her calls – usually he had his iPhone with him all the time. She didn't want to leave a message about what had happened, so asked him to call her urgently.

'I think we'd better give the gym a miss, Eden. Why don't you get changed and I'll run you to Euston? You can be in Manchester before lunch, and that will give you plenty of time to see Stevie before he performs tonight.'

'I would so appreciate that, Rufus,' Eden said gratefully, giving him another quick hug before dashing upstairs to get changed and pack an overnight bag.

She was too wound up to do anything on the train other than flick mindlessly through a bunch of magazines. Every few minutes she would pick up her phone to check if Stevie had called or texted, but he hadn't. Sadie left a message telling her that the album was breathtaking, and she should call back as soon as possible. Alana also texted, saying that she needed to speak to her urgently, but Eden was incapable of talking to anyone right now apart from Stevie. Alana's problems would have to wait.

The closer she got to Manchester, the more she believed Nicci's claim that Stevie had not given her any money. Eden was starting to feel very angry about his behaviour towards his son, and with the way he ignored her messages and did not call her back. She had thought of telling Stevie to expect her. Now she decided that she would surprise him at the hotel and find out just exactly what her fiancé was doing that was so important it meant he could not return any of her calls.

He was staying at a three-star hotel in the centre of Manchester. Canny Dallas wasn't going to spend good money on paying for his new acts to soak up the five-star treatment. Let them earn it first. Eden raced straight up to Reception, where the young male receptionist instantly recognised her and said politely, 'Good afternoon, Miss Haywood. How can I help you?'

Eden lowered her voice, and looked around to check no one could hear. 'My fiancé Stevie Moore is staying here, and I'd like to surprise him. Can you tell me his room number and let me have a room key?' She slid her hand across the counter and then lifted it up to reveal a rolled up £50 note.

The receptionist carefully put his own hand over the money and slid it off the counter and into his pocket. 'He's in room 204 on the third floor.' He handed her the key card. 'The lifts are to your left. Enjoy your day, Miss Haywood.'

Stevie's going to be chilling out in his room, watching TV, updating his Facebook page, that's all, Eden tried to tell herself as she waited for the lift. There was a perfectly reasonable explanation for him not having called her back. Nicci had only said those things about

330

him being incapable of being faithful because she was bitter. All the same, Eden felt shaky with nerves as she walked along the corridor to Stevie's room. There was a strong smell of carpet cleaner that made her feel slightly sick and the corridor seemed claustrophobically narrow. And then she was outside the room.

She took a deep breath and inserted the card into the lock. The green light flashed on and she pushed open the door. And then she felt as if she truly had entered a nightmare when she saw Kasey lying on the double bed, naked except for a red lace thong.

'What are you doing here?' Kasey demanded, folding her arms over her chest. For a moment Eden wondered if she'd stumbled into the wrong room and then the bathroom door swung open and Stevie stepped out. He was fresh from the shower with a towel wrapped round his waist. He looked completely stunned and one hundred percent guilty.

'Eden!' he exclaimed, 'Kasey was just about to use the shower because hers isn't working.'

Any respect that Eden had left for him disappeared with that blatant lie. 'Don't insult my intelligence.' She didn't feel like crying or shouting. Instead she felt icy calm. Maybe it was the shock but she felt detached from this scene. She wanted to hear the truth and then she would go.

'It's not what you think! I love you, Eden.' He gestured over at Kasey. 'This was nothing, it was a mistake. I slipped up once. I'm sorry.'

'Oh, for fuck's sake, be a man, Stevie, and tell her the truth!' Kasey shouted. She had put on a tee-shirt and was now standing up. 'We've been seeing each other since we met at the auditions for the show. We were seeing each other all the time he was seeing you. You were just part of his game plan, Eden. He was going to marry you, then divorce you a year later for unreasonable behaviour. Your reputation would have made it easy – everyone knows you can't keep a man for long – and then we were going to be together.'

Stevie was shaking his head, but his guilty expression betrayed him. He knew he was about to lose everything. 'I swear she's lying! She's a bitter, twisted bitch because she knows that I love you more.'

'Just like Nicci is lying about how you haven't given her any money for your son?'

He tried to speak but Eden wouldn't let him. 'I never want to see you again.' She pulled off her engagement ring and threw it at him. 'There! Have your ring back. It's fake – just like you.'

And before Stevie could say anything else, she turned on her heel and ran.

The two weeks that followed were like a replay of all the other bad times in Eden's life. Stevie wasted no time in selling a series of stories about how she had dumped him, and what a heartless bitch she was, and how she was only using him for publicity for *her* album. He made no mention of the fact that he had been having an affair! Sadie wanted Eden to put the record straight but she felt too upset.

Once more her house was under siege from the press and to escape she went to stay with Sadie in Camden. She had wanted to go to her apartment and be alone, but Sadie wouldn't hear of it. Eden was devastated by what had happened, and Stevie's betrayal wasn't the worst of it. The most painful part for her was knowing that she had brought all this on herself; that she had walked blindly into another relationship that was doomed to fail. She felt as low as it was possible to be, as low as the time her mum had died. She felt a total failure. Worthless. She had deserved Stevie and his lies.

She stayed in Sadie's house all day, either lying in bed or curled up on the sofa. Her manager tried to get her to listen to the album, but Eden couldn't even face doing that. She felt lost. Jack texted her, saying that he was sorry about what had happened and asking her to call him, but Eden couldn't bring herself to reply. He must think so badly of her. But still, she thought bitterly, it probably wasn't as badly as she thought of herself.

By the second weekend Sadie clearly thought enough was enough.

'Honey, we are going out for brunch,' she declared on Saturday morning. 'There's a lovely café near me and we're meeting up with Jez and Tanya.'

Eden shook her head. 'I can't do it, Sadie, please don't make me.' She clutched one of the red velvet cushions to her chest as if it could protect her.

Sadie sat down on the sofa and put her arm round Eden. 'I don't want to make you do anything, I just want you to put all this behind you. I'm doing it because I care about you. Because we all care about you. And I'm doing it because it's what your mum would have wanted.' She had saved her ace until last.

The tears streamed down Eden's face as she thought about Terri. She had always been brave and strong, no matter what.

'And if there is an afterlife, I want to be able to look Terri in the eye and for her to know that I did all I could to watch out for her little girl.' It seemed that Sadie had pulled the ace on herself now as she had tears in *her* eyes.

'Mum would have been so ashamed of me for what happened with Stevie,' Eden sobbed.

'She would not! Your mum was just as bad as you when it came to falling for a pretty face; she was just lucky that your dad turned out to be such a good one.

333

Al too. But she would have wanted you to get over Stevie, because he's not worth a hair on your head.'

The two women hugged each other, and for Eden it was as if talking about her mum freed something in her. She could move on from this, she *had to.*

'Okay, I'll come out with you,' she said. 'Remember what Mum always said. "In life it's not what happens to you, but how you react to it that matters. There's no crime in falling down – the shame is in not picking yourself up."' She sniffed and brushed the tears away, squaring her shoulders. 'And I'm going to pick myself up.'

'That's my girl!' Sadie replied. 'And I'm going to fix my eye make-up, and you'd better get dressed. Jez will have a coronary if he sees you in those grey sweatpants.'

Tanya and Jez were already sitting at a table in the airy brasserie when Eden and Sadie arrived. As soon as they saw their friend they both stood up and hugged her tightly.

'Don't make me cry again!' Eden exclaimed. 'I've cried enough.'

'I could cry seeing the state of your roots!' Jez declared jokingly, but he had tears in his eyes. 'We've been so worried about you.'

'You look way too thin!' Tanya told her. 'I'm ordering you scrambled eggs and smoked salmon. And we're going to have champagne too.'

'What are we celebrating? That I'm free now to go and jump into another crap relationship?' Eden caught sight of the horrified expressions on her friends' faces and said, 'I'm just kidding! That's it now for me; I'm through with those pretty boys. So come on, why the champagne?'

'The champagne is because you are finally out of the

house – and because Tyler and I have set a wedding date for the beginning of December.'

Eden was prevented from asking any more questions when the waiter came over to take their order, but as soon as he went away, she asked, 'So you're going to have a smaller wedding?'

'Hell, no!' Tanya said with a huge grin on her face. 'Tyler has just landed a massive contract and we can have the wedding we always planned. Will you be my maid-of-honour?'

'Do you even need to ask!' Eden was so thrilled for her friend she thought there was a strong possibility she might start crying again.

The friends laughed and gossiped their way through brunch, drinking champagne, toasting Tanya. And Eden thought that she couldn't be such a bad person if she had such good friends.

'Here's to no more pretty boys!' Jez declared as they opened their second bottle of champagne.

'I want romance and I want the kind of man who will be with me forever! And who will be with me because he loves me, and not for what he can get out of me,' Eden said, raising her glass. 'But not yet, because I've got an album to promote!'

'I'm glad to hear you say that because I was starting to think that all the hard work on possibly the best album I have ever made had been completely wasted.' It was Jack. Gorgeous as ever Jack.

Eden was speechless to see him there. She looked over at Sadie, certain that her manager had planned this, and sure enough she didn't look at all surprised by his sudden appearance. She watched Sadie give Jack the key to her house. 'Take her back this minute and play her the album.'

Jack held out his hand to Eden. 'Come on, you. There's work to be done.'

She put her hand in his and stood up. 'I'm ready.'

She was still holding his hand as they walked out of the brasserie; somehow it felt so right that she didn't want to let go. She curled her fingers round his, loving the feel of his warm, strong hand. And he didn't let go either, nor did he release her when someone spotted Eden and took a picture of them with their camera phone. On the short walk back he talked about his trip to LA, and how his sister Debs was, and Eden was grateful that he did not mention Stevie. Once inside the house she offered him a drink, but really it was displacement activity because she was nervous about listening to the album. And she wanted to tell him that she knew about Laura.

'There's so much I want to talk to you about, but for now it's got to be about the music.' He gently put his hands on her shoulders and steered her to the sofa then set up his iPod on Sadie's state-of-the-art speaker system.

'D'you want to listen to it on your own?'

'No, stay with me, please.'

Jack pressed play on the remote control and sat down next to her. Eden closed her eyes and clasped her hands together as the opening strains of the first track started up, but once she heard her voice she opened her eyes again. It was going to be okay. More than okay. It sounded good, really good. She looked over at Jack and he was smiling.

'See, I told you. It's brilliant. You're a star, Eden.' And he leant over and kissed her lightly on the cheek. Then, and Eden wasn't sure who made the first move, their lips brushed together in a gentle, healing kiss. A kiss that Eden wanted to go places.

She put her arms around him, longing to be close to him, but at that moment the front door opened and Sadie walked in. Immediately Jack and Eden sprang apart guiltily, like two teenagers caught snogging on the sofa. Sadie didn't seem at all fazed by the sight of them. Instead she smiled and said, 'Eden, there's someone here to see you.'

And then Eden got her second big surprise of the day when her sister Savannah stepped into the room.

Chapter Twenty Five

Savannah, who usually looked poised and confident, had an anxious expression on her face, and her hands pressed together over her baby bump. She cleared her throat and said nervously, 'Hi, Eden. I came to say sorry. I've been meaning to for ages, and then when Sadie called me and told me about what happened with Stevie, I knew it had to be now. I'm so sorry.'

As if in a trance, Eden got up from the sofa. She forgot about Jack and Sadie as she walked over to her sister and said, 'No! It's me who's sorry. I didn't know how ill Mum was. I would never have gone away on tour if I had.' She stood before Savannah, hardly daring to trust the evidence of her own eyes, that after all this time her sister had come back to her.

'I know, Eden, and I should have told you, but Mum made me promise not to. Then when she died I felt so angry with you for not being there, when it wasn't your fault at all. Can you ever forgive me?'

'There's nothing to forgive, so long as you promise to be part of my life again?'

Savannah nodded and then the two sisters were hugging each other and crying and smiling at the same time. Jack and Sadie quietly slipped out of the room, saying that they would leave the girls to catch up.

'I'll call you later,' Jack said as he reached for his jacket. 'Good to meet you, Savannah.'

Eden and Savannah spent the rest of the afternoon deep in conversation, going over everything that had happened to them in the last two years, swapping memories of Terri, talking about how much they missed her, and pausing only when Eden went to make them more cups of tea.

'I know I've taken too long to say all this,' Savannah told her, 'I know how stupidly stubborn I've been, so tied up in my grief for Mum and in being angry with you. But being pregnant made me realise how much I missed you and how much I want you to be in my life again.'

'I can't believe you're having a baby! D'you know if it's a boy or a girl?'

Savannah smiled. 'Well, you know what a control freak I am and how I like to plan everything?'

'Yep, I do.'

'Well, with this baby, I'm going to wait and see.'

'Wow, pregnancy *has* changed you!' Eden teased her sister. 'I thought you would have decorated the nursery, bought all the clothes, sorted out the name, booked the christening! *And* put their name down for school.'

'I know one thing. If it's a girl, I'd like her middle name to be Eden.'

'Yeah, because I'm such a great role model, aren't I?' Eden hung her head, thinking of Stevie.

'It's a new start for both of us, Eden. I'm going to look out for you. Starting with – was that Jack who you emailed me about? He is gorgeous!'

And Eden filled Savannah in on the story of her relationship with him. She still didn't know what he thought of her. Was he even now regretting their kiss?

'He's totally fallen for you,' Savannah said in her typically forthright way when Eden had finished.

'How can you tell from that brief meeting?'

'I saw the way he looked at you. It was full of longing, and it seemed like he wanted to protect you as well.'

'So it's true that pregnant women's brains turn to mush!' Eden tried to laugh off the comment, when inside all she could think was that she hoped more than anything else in the world that Savannah was right. And then it hit her. She was in love with Jack. She always had been. Stevie had only ever been an infatuation.

She had to see him! As soon as Savannah had left, Eden texted Jack and asked him over to her house then headed home. She had the roof down on her BMW convertible as she drove through London, and sang along to Aretha Franklin's 'I Say A Little Prayer' at the top of her voice. She said a little prayer of her own. A prayer that Jack had feelings for her too . . .

An hour later he arrived. Eden felt self-conscious as they said 'Hi' and she led him through to the living room. Maybe he hadn't meant to kiss her; it had been another mistake and he was here to say that.

But just as the doubts were threatening to take over, Jack moved closer. 'I think we've got some unfinished business, haven't we?' And suddenly they were exchanging passionate kisses. He was steering her over to the sofa and they lay back on it, feverish in their desire for one another, and Eden forgot about everything else. All she knew was that she wanted Jack, wanted him so badly . . .

She reached up and pulled him to her, longing to feel his body against hers, and as they kissed she explored his body, caressing his smooth warm skin, undoing the buttons on his jeans.

'Not yet,' Jack whispered as he started to explore her body, trailing his fingers along her bare legs, caressing her inner thighs in tantalising circles until she thought she would scream if he didn't touch her there . . . where she was burning and melting for him.

And then he slipped off her lace briefs and moved between her legs, caressing her with his tongue so deliciously. 'My God, Eden, you have such a beautiful body,' he murmured as he gazed at her laid out before him like the most perfect treat. Eden surrendered completely to his touch, feeling intense pleasure. And then she wanted him all the more, wanted to feel him inside her.

She pulled the tee-shirt over his head and Jack shucked off his jeans and boxers so she could feast her eyes on his body: his muscular chest, the curve of his biceps. She put her arms round his neck, pulling him close to her, and her fingers brushed against the scar on his back.

For a second she held her breath, expecting him to flinch away as he had before. But he stayed where he was, kissing her. She gasped as he entered her; it felt so good as he thrust in and out of her. She felt the waves of hot pleasure building up inside her, and just as she felt the sweet release, Jack came, holding her tightly and calling out her name . . .

For a few minutes afterwards they were quiet; Eden lay with her head on his chest, tingling, satisfied, happy. It felt as if all the bad things that had happened in the last few weeks had been swept away.

Jack was the first to speak. 'That was amazing. *You're* amazing, Eden.'

'So are you, Jack.' And what she wanted to say was that she loved him. But he hadn't said it, and that stopped her. Maybe she'd got it all wrong again by sleeping with him? Stevie had well and truly under-mined her confidence. It didn't help that Jack then had to leave to go to an awards ceremony.

'I could try and get out of it,' he told her.

'You should go,' she replied, saying the exact opposite of what she felt.

Sunday afternoon saw Eden driving out of London. It was the day of Jack's surprise birthday party and it had taken all her will-power not to let on to him what was happening. In typical Jack style he hadn't even mentioned that today was his birthday, had just phoned her this morning and asked her to come for lunch at his sister's. Luckily he had accepted her excuse that she was seeing Savannah and so they had arranged to meet that night. He didn't mention what had happened between them, and again Eden felt insecure. Maybe he only saw her as an easy lay . . .

At the local pub there must have been nearly a hundred people, sipping champagne and waiting for Jack to arrive. Debs had pulled out all the stops and transformed the rather basic pub garden, with its wooden picnic tables, into a chic party space. A large white canopy covered the entire area, providing shade, and underneath were circular tables, covered in crisp white linen cloths and decorated with arrangements of white flowers. Colourful Japanese lanterns hung from the trees, and waiters patrolled, offering canapés and champagne. Eden took her place at a table alongside Sadie and Travis. Debs had also arranged photographs of Jack through the years on all the tables. The one on Eden's showed Jack aged around three, an angelic-faced toddler with bright blond hair, digging in a sand-pit with great concentration.

'He was even attractive as a baby,' Sadie commented, and then added cheekily, 'That man has great genes.

Just think what good-looking kids you would have together.'

'Sadie! What are you on about?' Eden exclaimed. She glanced around, hoping no one had overheard.

Her manager raised an eyebrow. 'Darling, the sexual tension between you two has been smouldering from the moment you set eyes on each other. Anyone could see it. Why do you think Stevie, sorry to mention his name, was so jealous of Jack?'

Eden could lie and say that there was nothing between them, or she could be brave; she chose the latter. 'You're right, I do have feelings for him. But I don't know what he thinks of me. He hasn't exactly seen me in a good light these past months.'

'The man adores you! Why else do you think he's been so hard on you? You're the first woman I've seen him want to have a serious relationship with since Laura. It's a big deal for both of you.'

At that moment Debs's husband Harry came out to signal that everyone should be quiet, and a few minutes later Debs led a blindfolded Jack out into the garden.

'This better not be a surprise party, Debs,' he could clearly be heard to say in a silence broken only by the sound of the breeze rustling through the trees. Eden looked around at her fellow guests who were all trying desperately not to laugh. Then Debs whipped off the red bandana, exclaiming, 'Happy Birthday, Jack!' and all the guests applauded and called out, 'Happy Birthday!'

For a moment Jack looked completely mortified, then he laughed and hugged his sister.

Eden felt unusually shy as she watched Jack greet his guests, kissing the women, shaking hands with the men. He looked so handsome, and once more she wondered why she had ever been attracted to Stevie.

Sadie gently nudged her. 'Go and see him, what are

you waiting for?' Eden was about to do just that when Jack caught sight of her and made his way over. She stood up and faced him, butterflies multiplying inside her.

'I can't believe you didn't tell me about this!' he exclaimed, but he was smiling. 'I'll forgive you, on one condition.'

'And that is?' she asked, gazing into his blue eyes.

'You give me a birthday kiss.'

Eden went to kiss his cheek but Jack pointed at his mouth, at his beautiful lips. Eden gave him the lightest of kisses but he put his hands gently on her neck and drew her closer. He kissed her deeply, passionately, so sensuously that tendrils of lust unfolded in her as she put her arms around him, felt the strength in his back, felt his arms circling her. They were oblivious to the cheers and wolf whistles of the guests.

'Now *that* was a birthday kiss,' Jack murmured.

'Did everyone see?' Eden whispered, burying her face in his shoulder. How she wished they could be magically transported away. 'I bet they all think, "*Poor Jack, to be mixed up with that slapper.*"'

Jack held her tighter. 'They think, "*Lucky bastard to be with such a beautiful woman.*" And now you're going to come and say hi to everyone with me.' And he took her by the hand. Everyone was so friendly that Eden quickly felt at ease.

When they finally had a second to themselves, she exclaimed, 'Oh my God, I didn't get a chance to buy you a birthday present!' She thought of all the ridiculously expensive gifts she had lavished on men in the past who had meant so little to her, and for Jack she had absolutely nothing!

'You don't have to get me anything, but you can do one thing. You can sing for me.'

Eden looked around the party. 'Here?'

'Here is as good a place as any. One of my friends plays guitar, you could sing an acoustic version of "Want".' He smiled. 'I wrote it for you after all.'

It was Eden's favourite track. 'It is the least I can do for you,' she said, and made her way to the microphone.

It seemed to her that as she sang she was pouring out all her emotions for Jack. All the longing, all the love she felt for him, was contained in the song. And as she sang she realised something so huge, so momentous, so wonderful, that she couldn't stop the smile from spreading across her face. And it was this – if Jack had written the song for her, then he must love her too!

She looked out across the garden to where he was standing and, seeing the look in his eyes, knew that to be true.

After she had finished, while the guests were still cheering and clapping their appreciation, she and Jack slipped away from the party.

'That was the best birthday present ever,' he told her as they sat down under the shade of an oak tree.

'I know about Laura,' Eden blurted out. She hadn't meant to say it so bluntly, but she realised that she had to let Jack know. For a second his blue eyes darkened with pain and he looked away across the fields of corn that were rippling in the breeze. Oh, God, had she got so close to him only to blow it again?

Then he looked back at her.

'I'm glad. I felt that I could never allow myself to feel anything again after she died. But you've made me see that's no way to live my life. I love you, Eden. I want to be with you.' And, moving closer, he kissed her.

He had said it! He loved her. Fireworks of happiness went off in her head. But she had to tell him how she felt. She broke off the delicious kiss to say, 'I love you too, Jack. I have for so long, but I just couldn't see it. I expected you to make all the moves.'

He smiled at her, and the blue of his eyes matched the perfect blue of the August sky above them. 'We've done so many things wrong, I want us to start over. I want to romance you, woo you, and I want to make love to you like you've never been made love to before.'

'I thought you did that yesterday!' Eden teased.

'We should go on a proper date. I should take you out for dinner. I want to make you feel special.'

'Sure,' Eden murmured. 'But actually I'm feeling hungry now, and I don't know if I can wait that long.' And she kissed him again, pressing her body against his.

'Okay,' Jack replied, unbuttoning her dress. 'This once I'm happy to let you get your own way.'

It was some time later that the couple returned to the party.

'You've both got leaves in your hair,' Sadie pointed out quietly as they joined her. She was smiling as she added, 'And I couldn't be happier for you. And Marc White has just texted to say that he's heard the album, loves it, and wants to sign you up for two more!'

Eden stood on tiptoes and pulled a leaf out of Jack's hair. 'How would you feel about working with me again?'

He brushed a stray lock of hair from her face, and smiled. 'They say never mix business with pleasure, but I'll make an exception for my wife.'

Eden looked at him, hardly daring to trust her own ears.

'I'm asking you to marry me, Eden. What do you say?'

There was only one thing to say. 'Oh, yes, Jack! I will marry you!' She flung her arms around him.

'Now that is the best birthday present ever,' Jack whispered. And then, as the guests cottoned on to his proposal and burst into applause and cheers, he kissed her. And Eden knew there was nothing fake about Jack. He was the real thing.